INCORPORATED EVIL

A Business With One Goal . . .
Absolute Power

PETER WIDDOWS

Monkton
Press

INCORPORATED EVIL
A MONKTON PRESS BOOK

ISBN 9780992933814

Published in Great Britain by Monkton Press, 2014

Printed and bound by CPI Group (UK) Ltd, Croydon CR0 4YY

Typeset by Palimpsest Book Production Ltd, Falkirk, Stirlingshire

Monkton Press
Monkton House, Altrincham,
Cheshire. WA14 2HY
United Kingdom
www.monktonpress.com

Prologue

Saturday, 14th February. Bangkok, Thailand

Sean's heart was suddenly beating faster, as he looked for a way through the crowd of drunken sex tourists. Seeing his chance, as a stag party went by and obscured the view from Lilac, he crossed the street and slipped around the corner onto Soi 23, moving in the opposite direction to his hotel.

Out of sight from Soi Cowboy, he picked up his pace to a sprint. Luckily he was still relatively fit, but the humidity of the Bangkok night made him feel as if he was carrying a horse. He pulled the phone from his pocket and tried to search his contacts, while still maintaining his fast pace. All he knew was that he had to get to the hotel before the two men . . . he had to get to Liz.

Fortunately she was his last dialled number. He hit the number displayed on his 'recents' list, still sprinting in the direction of the hotel, choosing to run on the road and dodge the taxi's and tuk-tuks, rather than weave through the mass of people crowding the pavement.

The call went to voicemail. 'Damn!' He shut it off and dialled again, still running as fast as he could. He could see the hotel some 200 metres away, but it seemed like a mile as his progress was hampered by the impossible traffic.

'Shit! Voicemail again!' he shouted. 'Answer the phone, Liz, please!' he pleaded, dialling again as he entered the lower lobby of the hotel at street level.

There was no lift waiting, so Sean pressed the lift button repeatedly until the doors finally opened. Out of breath, he barged into the lift and pressed the button for level fifteen and then 'door close' as quickly as he could, shaking with impatience at the slowness of the operation.

Just as the doors were closing, he caught a brief glimpse of the two men he had seen outside Lilac . . . they were getting out of a white sedan in the hotel driveway.

Chapter 1

Five Days Earlier – Monday, 9th February. London, England

There was barely a spot to stand on the brightly patterned blue carpet of the Lancaster Ballroom, at the Savoy Hotel in London. Sean McManus dodged his way quickly through the crowd to his reserved place in the second row, where an annual return had been placed on the seat for him. Casting his eyes over it briefly, in the vain hope that it might help him with his impending deadline, he made a mental note of a couple of items. Although, as a ten-year veteran of the business desk at the *Financial Daily*, he wasn't really concerned, knowing full well that he could just rehash whatever was said at today's Annual General Meeting.

Sean hadn't worked on the BW Corporation before, so he wasn't intimate with the detailed information about the company. That didn't really matter though, as he knew enough to craft a piece which would satisfy the low standards set by his editor. In fact, almost everybody did: BW Corporation was the most valuable company in the world, boasting a market capitalisation of some £735 billion . . . making it hard to avoid.

The seat next to Sean was occupied by David Watson, from the *Mail*. He made a quick snoring sound, intimating to Watson that he was bored already. The look on Watson's face confirmed that he was feeling the same way. Attending AGMs was a part of life for the hacks on the business desk, but it was considered extremely dull and a complete non-entity as far as anything newsworthy went. In his years of attending such 'bore-fests', Sean had never seen or heard anything that wasn't known to the media at least three weeks earlier.

Slouching into his chair, Sean ruffled his unkempt hair, causing a young looking man in the seat on the other side of him to shift uneasily, then pull at his pinstriped suit and adjust the position of the ready notepad on his lap. Sean smiled politely, but didn't change his posture. *That was me ten years ago*, he thought. *Clean suit, clipped hair, waiting with fervent anticipation for the words of inspiration that would be uttered by the CEO; the business genius that had risen to the very top of the pile.*

Years on and Sean had seen hundreds of self-proclaimed business gurus. They were invariably egotistical, mediocre, middle-aged men, with their snouts so far into the corporate trough that they had lost any empathy with the people who occupied the real world, and earned a normal salary. As for inspirational words, all Sean ever heard was pre-rehearsed spin, cleverly designed to confuse or impress, without actually crossing the line of lying.

Aware that he had become the stereotype of a cynical hack, Sean had been worn down by years of low pay, browbeaten editors, cowardly lawyers, newswire services replacing journalists, and of course, corporate affairs managers; the internal spin doctors hired by companies to pervert, manipulate, embellish or suppress every piece of information that came out of their employers' organisations. Unlike the fresh-faced boy who came into journalism looking for something special, Sean now dressed in a black leather Stranglers' style jacket, jeans, a t-shirt and scruffy brown brogues.

His blonde hair was shoulder-length and didn't see the bristles of a hairbrush very often. More importantly, he made a point of being overtly disinterested, almost to the brink of rudeness. Indeed, if he had worked for any of the companies that he wrote about, he would have been fired for his bad attitude a long time ago. But in the newsroom, this dress standard was the norm and being seen to 'not give a damn' was cool. Being openly keen, on the other hand, was a sure sign of inexperience and at thirty-four years old, Sean was already the senior reporter in his group.

Most journalists sold out long before reaching his tenure. The large salary on offer as an in-house spin doctor, was usually enough to tempt even the most ardent of critics. Opportunities to more than double his paltry journalist's salary had been thrown Sean's way some years ago, but he had stayed true to his principles and rejected the many offers; something which he now regretted intensely. As each day passed, the large corporation he worked for looked more and more like the corporations he reported on, and his self-important stance made him look increasingly foolish, especially as people that he had trained, who had half his talent, had bought nice flats in the Inner West and treated themselves to flashy German cars.

The grubby one-bedroom box in Whitechapel, which Sean called home, was so close to work that he had never seen the need own a car; not that he could afford one anyway. The borderline poverty, driven by his career choice, was something that he had grown used to and he consoled himself with the fact that most of his friends were either fellow hacks, or intellectuals; a group who had even less money to show for their impressive qualifications than he did. And he made a point of avoiding his university friends from the London School of Economics, who now invariably earned more in a month than he did in a year. Most importantly, Sean had learned to live within his means, which was no easy feat in the money sucking British capital.

There was a brief tap on the MC's microphone, indicating that proceedings were about to start. Sean turned on the recoding function on his iPhone, as he tried to make himself as comfortable as possible on the lightly padded seat.

As indifferent as Sean was, he would admit that he was somewhat intrigued by the Founder and CEO of BW Corp. Charles Barker-Willet was reputedly the richest man in the world, but also one of the most private. In the fifteen years since the Initial Public Offering of the company, which bore his name, he had never given a personal interview and his media appearances were strictly limited to corporate information requirements. Even then, he had a reputation for being short and to the point, allowing little room for any personality.

In Sean's experience most CEOs were about as media-shy as a *Big Brother* contestant; in fact, most actively courted the perverse celebrity that came with their position. Why didn't Barker-Willet? Why was he so different?

As the BW Board of Directors duly filed onto the stage and took their places behind a long wooden table, Sean watched Charles Barker-Willet closely. He had seen pictures of him many times, but had never seen him in real life. *For a man in his early forties he looks well*, Sean observed. Barker-Willet had the physique of a professional athlete and the distinguished looks of a Hollywood film star, with smooth facial skin like a man half his age. *Has he had work?* Sean considered.

Barker-Willet was immaculately turned out in a blue Saville Row chalk-stripe suit, which hung perfectly from his trim shoulders. A potential headline for his piece suddenly crossed Sean's mind. 'THE MAN WHO HAS EVERYTHING'. It would make for far more interesting reading than 'BW CORPORATION AGM GOES SMOOTHLY'. But without any personal information about Mr Barker-Willet, which would require an interview, he was stuck with the latter, and the chance of getting an interview was negligible. Barker-Willet had reputedly rejected approaches from just about everybody, including the BBC's *Hard Talk*. Unfortunately, Sean knew he didn't compete in those leagues.

When proceedings finally got underway, to Sean's surprise Sir Giles Penrith, the Non-Executive Chairman of the company, took centre stage. The ageing hereditary peer presented the results, which were remarkable, and fielded most of the questions. When a question was asked directly of Barker-Willet, his answer was short, factual and left no room for debate. *His reputation isn't wrong*, Sean thought.

BW's results were better than any Sean had ever seen, yet Barker-Willet seemed happy to let somebody else take the credit. Why?

For the first time in years, Sean's interest was piqued by a person from the corporate world. He had grown so used to the dull homogeneity of company executives, that he had lost any hope of ever having somebody interesting as the subject of a piece. Could Barker-Willet be that man? Was he really different?

Sean flicked quickly through the financial statements again until he found what he was looking for; the small section headed 'Executive Remuneration'. What he read surprised him even further. In most large corporations the CEO's salary stood out from the other executives, and was often well into the millions. Charles Barker-Willet didn't even feature in the disclosure for the top five earners in BW Corp. In the section headed 'Directors' Remuneration', Barker-Willet was only paid a director's fee of £25,000, and astonishingly, this seemed to be the sum total of his earnings from BW Corp.

Barker-Willet owned forty-one per cent of BW and the company had paid dividends totalling £57 billion during the year, meaning that the CEO would have received a £23 billion dividend. So he obviously didn't need the money, and even the most outrageous of CEO salaries paled into insignificance when compared to those sums. But in Sean's experience, CEOs always separated the benefits they received through ownership of stock – dividends – from their remuneration, ensuring that most not only received huge dividend payments, but also multi-million pound salaries and bonuses.

Why are you so different? Sean wondered, studying the BW CEO.

After the uneventful meeting, Sean decided to do a little background research for his story. *Perhaps I'll make it something more than the usual boring predictable rubbish,* he considered. Despite his overt portrayal of disinterest, Sean still clung on to the diminishing hope that he could escape the drudgery of the business desk and make a career for himself as an investigative journalist; the dream most hacks aspired to. It was the reason he had chosen journalism in first place, above the more lucrative offers made by the financial institutions when he graduated from university.

Once he got back to the dreary Aldgate offices occupied by the Daily News Group, Sean headed straight into the newspaper's research department. Liz Channing, the beautiful, if frosty, head of research was busy scrolling through some screens of data. 'Hi, Liz,' Sean said smiling.

'Sean,' Liz replied, looking up warily from her screen. 'I thought you were at the BW AGM.'

'I was,' he replied.

'And you didn't stay for the free press lunch? Not like you.' She smiled sarcastically.

'What do you know about Barker-Willet?' he asked, ignoring her jibe.

'The company, or the man?' she replied, suddenly taking his presence more seriously.

'Well, both I guess, but mostly the man.'

'I know a fair bit about the company, but Barker-Willet himself is a complete enigma. He makes no public appearances, other than those required by his job. We know that he started the company in Thailand, in 1995, when he bought a tuna-processing facility just outside Bangkok. From there, he rapidly acquired a number of companies across Asia, until he listed on the London Stock exchange in 2000. Since then the growth rate has been astounding, fuelled by one acquisition after another.' Liz smiled, pleased with her summary.

'How do they fund the acquisitions?' Sean asked.

'Same as everybody else: debt,' Liz said.

'But I didn't see a lot of debt on their balance sheet?'

'No, you wouldn't. The difference with BW is that they have been very successful at turning acquisitions around quickly and using the profits to pay down the acquisition debt.'

'What? They're slash and burn merchants? Surely that would catch up with them eventually through slowing growth?' Sean commented on the common practice of buying a company and then ripping costs out and selling assets, in order to reduce the debt burden created by the acquisition. This often looked good for the first few years, until the implications of such deep cost-cutting and asset-stripping started to hurt top-line growth, and by direct implication, profit.

'Apparently not. Of course, I can't say with certainty, but they don't have a reputation for asset-stripping, or cost-cutting for that matter. In fact, the opposite: their reputation is that they tend not to make wholesale redundancies or sell assets following an acquisition.'

'Then how do they get the profits up so quickly?' Sean asked frowning.

'I can only assume the old-fashioned way.' Liz shrugged.

'Which is?' Sean also shrugged, making Liz laugh.

'Good management, sales growth, margin growth, etcetera.'

'Does this bear out in the accounts?'

'Yes, at an overall and segment level. They aren't required to report anything below that, and of course, they're so big it's impossible to see the performance of any individual acquisition.'

Sean was impressed by Liz's grasp of the information that was available to them. 'What about independent data, market share, etc.?' he asked.

'Useless in the markets they are big in: Asia, Africa, Eastern Europe and South America. It's just not reliable, as it's extrapolated from a very small portion of market sales.'

Liz's knowledge again impressed Sean. Since she had taken over as head of research, the department had been far better informed about their subject companies. 'I thought they had European and North-American assets?' he queried.

'Yes they do, banks, casinos and hotels; nothing that we can really track market-share data on accurately.' Liz twisted her mouth cutely.

'So this is the biggest company in the world and we can't get any granular detail on it?' Sean shook his head in disbelief.

'Yes, that's how it works, I'm afraid. However, they are audited and if the numbers as a whole make sense, then the detail behind them can't be too far out. I'm sure some of their acquisitions are less successful than others. But when a company makes sixty-seven acquisitions in one year, then that detail is almost impossible to see, and of course they don't tell us about their failures.' Liz paused and smiled. 'What's wrong? Why do you want all this detail anyway? Your stories are almost always purposely bereft of detail. Do you think they're up to something?'

Sean laughed quietly at Liz's response, not wanting to show that it had shocked him slightly. He knew it was true, but he hadn't realised that everybody else considered his work to be so bland. 'No, nothing of the sort. In fact, the opposite. I'm impressed by BW and intrigued by Barker-Willet himself.'

Liz cocked her head to one side in mock disbelief, but Sean

ignored the gesture. 'I was considering writing a personal interest piece on him. You know, actually do some real journalism for a change. He's such a mystery, it'll take a bit of work to dig up the information,' he said.

Liz burst out laughing. 'Good luck with that! You know this place has been devoid of any real journalism for the last twenty years. But won't you need to get an interview with Barker-Willet to give your piece any credibility?' she smirked.

'Possibly,' Sean retorted.

'You *do* know that he turned down far more credible interviewers than you?' she chuckled.

'Thanks for that,' Sean responded.

'Have you spoken to John about it?' Liz asked somewhat facetiously referring to Sean's editor and their boss; a man known for his complete lack of enthusiasm for anything beyond getting the paper out on time each day.

'Not yet. I suppose I should pass it by him,' Sean said sighing. 'Thanks anyway, Liz,' he said, leaving the room and returning to his desk in the open-plan newsroom, where he opened the screen on his laptop and started to type. The words 'BW AGM GOES SMOOTHLY' appeared on his screen and Sean read them aloud to himself.

Really, is that the best I can do? he thought. *I should at least try.* Then doubts filled his mind again. Why? Why should he try? He wouldn't get paid any more and it was hardly top-level investigative journalism; just a crappy personal interest piece. He began typing again.

BW's record profits make it easy for the company to present to its shareholders. His fingers felt numbed by each keystroke as he typed the sub-heading, and he looked across the open room to John's office, making his decision.

John Hammond, the assistant business editor, had the only office on the floor and didn't like to be disturbed unless it was important. As his senior reporter though, Sean had managed to form a decent relationship with him over the years, to the point where they were almost friends. He still approached John's office cautiously, putting his head around the open door.

'Got a minute?' he asked, raising his eyebrows.

John looked up sharply at the disturbance. 'Sure. How did the BW AGM go? As boring as expected?'

'Yep! At one stage I thought I'd lose the will to live,' Sean admitted.

John glanced at his watch. 'Finished the piece on it yet?'

'No, not yet,' Sean looked at him sheepishly. 'I was thinking about doing a more in-depth piece on Barker-Willet himself. What do you think?'

'Brilliant idea. Has he agreed to be interviewed?' John grinned.

'No, not yet,' Sean replied quietly.

'Then please have your piece about the AGM on my desk before 3:45, as agreed,' John said, still smiling.

'But, John, this is great story . . . you know . . . English businessman taking over the world. Do you know that if you'd invested just £1,000 in the IPO fifteen years ago, that investment would now be worth £1.75 million?'

John sat upright. 'Yes, thanks for reminding me. Unlike you, I did have a small share portfolio fifteen years ago and I did see the BW prospectus. Using my remarkable insight, I passed on it, choosing to invest my hard-earned money in RBS instead, and we all know how that story ended.' He paused. 'What's brought all this on, Sean? It's not like you; you would normally have the piece written, submitted and be having your first pint at the Dog and Duck by now.'

Sean laughed. 'I know, I know, but there's just something about him, Barker-Willet. He intrigues me. You know he doesn't take a salary?'

'He's worth billions, why would he need to?'

'He wouldn't, but most do anyway. It's almost an ego thing, you know: who gets the most. And why is he so media-shy? Why do we know so little about him? We know far more about far less important people.'

John's expression changed to one more sympathetic than before. 'Sean, you know we don't have the budget for any investigative or in-depth work. Newspapers just don't make money anymore. We print yesterday's news for people too cheap to buy an iPad. The only people doing that kind of work now are freelance.'

'Does that mean you'll let me write a freelance piece?' Sean jumped on the point.

John sloped his head to the side in thought. 'Sure, why not . . . as long as you meet all your other deadlines and do it in your own time.'

'Can I use the paper's resources?' Sean asked.

John paused to think again. 'Databases etc., yes; personnel no. I can't afford to have anybody else dragged into this kind of crap.'

'Thanks, John,' Sean said, uncharacteristically eager, and then dropped back to his usual casual demeanour. 'I assume I'll be paid for it if it's used?' he queried.

John laughed. 'Cheeky bastard! Yes, I'm sure we can pay you the normal freelance rate if it's printable. You still owe me the AGM piece for tonight though, so you'd better get going.'

Sean turned to leave, then added, 'Expenses?' as he was walking through the door.

John shot a mock serious look at Sean. 'If you do manage, by some miracle, to get an interview with Barker-Willet, you can rent the fucking Space Shuttle for the day. If not, not even a can of beans for dinner in that crappy Whitechapel dive of yours, *capisce?*'

'*Si.*' Sean left quickly, knowing from experience when not the push a point with John

Kaiping, Guangdong Province, China

Three men dressed in the ill-fitting uniforms of the Chinese People's Liberation Army were standing rigidly in the middle of a disused warehouse. The grubby building was hidden in the cluttered inner city of Kaiping, a small conurbation in the west of Guangdong Province, famed for being 'the world's factory'. Even through the closed wooden doors they could taste the noxious blend of chemicals in the grey fetid air outside. The three soldiers were visibly agitated, the modern comforts afforded to them in the larger city of Guangzhou, which was just three hours' drive away, seemed a lifetime away from the squalid, rat-infested warehouse. But this particular problem required their personal attention.

Three gold stars with a wreath adorned the shoulder epaulettes of one soldier, announcing his rank as a General, while the other two officers displayed three gold stars inside gold lines, indicating that they both held the rank of Colonel. Just three metres in front of them, a civilian, dressed in a torn black leather jacket and scuff-marked jeans, knelt with his head bowed low. His arms were tied tightly behind his waist, the thin plastic cable ties cutting into his wrists, while thick red blood ran from a deep cut to the side of his left eye, and his nose sat lopsided on his face, crushed with blunt force. As he spoke, he sobbed quietly, making the broken Mandarin difficult to hear through his blood-drenched lips. 'Sir, please, I beg you to believe me. It's all there is. It was a very bad month for us in Kaiping. I haven't taken anything . . . please.'

A white plastic shopping bag lay on the floor between the beaten man and the General. 'You ask me to believe that you can only raise 30,000 Yuan, yet last month it was 60,000, and previously, it was over 100,000 Yuan. I know that you have been stealing it. That is not my question. I want to know where it is. Where have you hidden my money?' The General's tone was hostile, but the words were delivered calmly and clearly, emphasising the General's control of the situation, as he pointed a spindle-like finger at the plastic bag.

In contrast, the man on his knees looked straight at the General, pleading his case passionately. 'Please, sir, it's the truth. The takings were very poor. I don't have the money. Look at me! I can't afford good clothes. I live in a filthy slum. My wife doesn't dress well, and my son doesn't eat exotic food,' he spluttered, as blood mixed with saliva spat from his broken lips.

The General nodded his head, almost indiscernibly, to one of the two uniformed soldiers that were standing guard, in front of the wooden, barn-like, doors to the decrepit warehouse. Acknowledging the signal, the soldier opened the door slightly and slipped out without making a sound. Only a few seconds later, he returned dragging a young Chinese woman by her long black hair into the warehouse, her body stooped to the height of the soldier's hand. Despite the obvious pain being inflicted, she made no effort to fight against the violent tugging, choosing instead to screen her naked breasts, which had been exposed through a large rip down the front of her dress. A long deep laceration across her face made it impossible for her to convey any facial expression, as the muscles required to do so had been severed.

The civilian man in the leather jacket twisted his torso painfully to observe what was happening behind him. When he caught sight of the woman being yanked viciously by the hair, pain and hatred filled his eyes. 'No, No!' he screamed. 'She has done nothing to you.'

The young guard forced the half-naked woman onto her knees, next to the man pleading vociferously on her behalf, and returned to his post by the door. She looked ahead, making no attempt to speak, contempt written into her stare.

The taller of the two colonels pulled an army issue pistol from the brown leather holster attached to his belt. Without hesitating, he raised the black metal gun and pulled the trigger. The loud crack from the bullet stopped the beaten man from shouting and the acrid smell of cordite suddenly replaced the pungent stench of pollution. A jet stream of blood spattered backwards from the woman's head, as the bullet exited the rear of her skull. Then her knees buckled, sending her limp corpse crashing down onto the grimy floor.

The shock of the shooting stripped the beaten man of any remaining defiance and he rolled onto his side, convulsing violently as he retched from his mouth onto the shoes of the General. He tried to reach out to his wife using his head, but it was hopeless as his tied hands restricted any ability to move across the floor. 'Why? Why did you do this? You pigs! You leave my son with no mother!' he cried out.

Looking down at the blood mixed with vomit on his clean black shoes, the General contorted his face with disgust, again signalling with a nod, this time to the Colonel who held the smoking pistol in his gloved hand. 'Also, no father,' the General said quietly.

A single bullet from the pistol entered the side of the dishevelled man's head, as he lay prone, still convulsing on the floor. Within seconds his breathing stopped and he convulsed no more. A pool of dark red blood quickly spread around his body, as if a bag of thick red dye had been punctured.

The General again indicated that the guard by the door should do something. The young soldier ran forward and bent on one knee in front of him. Using the cuff of his jacket, he cleaned the blood and vomit from the General's shoes, then scampered silently back to his post.

A short time later, a quiet tap at the door forced the same soldier to slip outside. He reappeared less than twenty seconds later, this time accompanied by a white man in his mid-twenties, who was dressed casually in black jeans, a blue hooded parka covering his short-cropped brown hair. After glancing down at the two dead bodies, the new entrant raised his head, directing his eyes towards the General, his silent stare conveying no emotion.

Still displaying his disgust at the mess around his shoes, the General pointed to the white plastic bag on the floor between himself and the two bodies. In response, the white man nodded and collected the bag from the floor, carefully avoiding the spreading blood pool. He opened the bag and looked inside at the bundles of used Chinese Yuan notes, then closed it again, rolling it tightly to fit inside his parka.

Without speaking, the clean-cut white man left the warehouse through the same wooden door that he had used to enter.

Chapter 2

Sean was pouring a coffee, when Liz Channing entered carrying a copy of the morning paper. 'You drink that shit?' she asked, as she produced a green teabag from her hand.

'Not by choice, Liz. It's free,' Sean answered. 'If I bought coffee from the stand downstairs each time I needed to get away from my desk, I'd be living on bread and water,' he smiled.

'Oh, come on, we're not that badly paid; we get more than nurses,' she said smiling in return.

'True, but how many nurses do you know with a first from the LSE, or Oxford, come to think of it? That is where you went, isn't it?' Sean replied.

'Ah yes, but they don't get the intellectual challenge that we do. Speaking of which, I note that you capitulated and wrote the same boring crap you have for years about BW.' She raised her eyebrows, making the point.

It would be easy to hate her, if she wasn't so bloody gorgeous, Sean thought. 'Actually, I *am* writing the piece on Barker-Willet,'

17

he lied. In truth, he had decided not to bother, after a couple of pints of Guinness and a reality check on how little free time he had to write such an in depth piece.

'Really? John gave you the go-ahead?' Liz's tone changed to that of surprise. 'I'll help you with the research if you like?'

Sean's heart fluttered a little. The thought of working closely with Liz on a project was certainly appealing, but he had been told that he couldn't use internal personnel. 'Thanks. Normally I'd jump at the offer, but I promised John that I wouldn't use any of the department staff. He thinks we're all too busy. He actually only gave me the go-ahead to write it as a freelancer, in my own time.' Sean's face conveyed his obvious disappointment.

'Cool! Then I'll help you in *my* own time. He can't stop me doing that, can he?' She was now intermittently smiling and sipping her tea. 'I've got nothing better to do, Elton John stopped inviting me to his parties years ago,' she giggled.

Sean studied her. She looked strangely vulnerable, when previously she had always looked completely unapproachable. Her jet-black hair fell loosely around her shoulders and her high cheekbones accentuated the beautiful shape of her face. Liz's mother was Korean and her father English; the blend of the two races had given her the most stunning features. Ever since she'd arrived some seven years ago, Sean had secretly admired her, but he had always considered her to be way out of his league. To hide his attraction he had resorted childishly to his usual devil-may-care demeanour. Had he missed an opportunity all this time? Was Liz really a shy vulnerable girl who did nothing outside of work? He studied her perfect features again, questioning his previous ideas. *No, impossible*, he decided.

Liz's offer of help had thrown Sean, and he considered his position quickly. On one hand, he had sensibly decided not to write the piece, because he didn't have enough free time. On the other, his free time was currently taken up by getting drunk in the Dog and Duck, debating the woes of the world with his flea-bitten intellectual friends, and only dreaming that girls like Liz Channing were even remotely interested in him.

'Great, when shall we start?' Sean said, a little too eagerly.

'Tonight?' Liz suggested, casually shrugging her shoulders.

'Perfect,' Sean replied, trying to think of a suitably impressive venue.

'We can use my place. I have a small dining table we can work at, my internet is fast, and well, I've heard your place is . . .' She pulled an ugly face.

Sean blew a metaphorical sigh of relief. If Liz had suggested they used his place, he would have spent the remainder of the day looking for a new flat. 'Sounds good to me,' he said, showing his pleasure at her idea. 'Where do you live?' he asked.

'Near Parsons Green in Fulham. It's not the easiest to find so why don't we just go straight there when we finish work. I can rustle up something to eat,' Liz said.

'Great! Just let me know when you're ready to go,' Sean said, before walking back to his desk.

By the time Liz finally showed up at Sean's desk at 7:30 p.m., Sean had long finished his real work, which consisted of writing a short piece about a coat-hanger manufacturer that was branching out into clothes pegs, after fifty years in business. For four hours, he had been trying to pen some ideas for the piece on BW, but his mind constantly drifted to Liz Channing, forcing him into the realisation that, although he was truly interested in Barker-Willet, he was far more interested in spending the evening with Liz. A few times during his wait, he had thought about going to the research department to query whether she had forgotten their arrangement, but he didn't want to seem too keen and risk scaring her off.

'Sorry. John had me digging out some old transcripts of a legal case against Bell Petroleum. It took me longer than I expected.'

Sean felt embarrassed as he pulled on his tatty, ill-fitting, Barbour jacket over his dated black leather number. *When did I start dressing so badly?* he cursed himself, thinking about the designer outfits Liz wore to the office.

The freezing February air bit into them sharply as they left the building and scurried along the well-lit pavement to Aldgate East Tube station. When they finally arrived, shaking off the rain, Sean saw that Liz's home was nothing like he had anticipated. He had envisaged a girly, cute place, full of clutter and cushions. Instead, it was large, minimalist and adorned with expensive artwork and designer furniture. It was also almost certainly worth way more than she could afford on her paltry newspaper salary.

'My grandfather bought it for me,' she said, interpreting the look on Sean's face.

Sean laughed. 'I'm really glad we didn't go to my place. The Jack the Ripper tour stops outside my building every hour, while the tour guide states that it's the only murder site which hasn't undergone a major renovation.'

Liz laughed loudly. 'What do you eat? Do you like Korean food?' she asked.

'Can't say I've ever tried it, but I like everything, so whatever you have is good. What's your Wi-Fi password? I'll get online,' he said, pretending to be keen to start work.

Liz began to prepare some food, rattling cabinets in the open-plan kitchen, while Sean continued his pretence at work. He'd never imagined that he would be here with Liz Channing, waiting as she prepared dinner, watching her over the top of his laptop screen.

Within half an hour, she filled the table with an array of dishes, some meat, some vegetable, and some rice-based. She thoughtfully gave Sean a fork as well as chopsticks, but seemed impressed when he knew how to handle the thin wooden implements. 'Chinese takeaways,' he smiled.

Liz's food was a fantastic array of flavour and was the best meal he had eaten in . . . well, maybe ever. It wasn't hard to beat his usual diet of pork scratchings, Guinness and doner kebab, but this was really great food and he said so, probably too often during their shared meal. Looking embarrassed, Liz just laughed and said 'thank you' each time.

After they had eaten, the conversation turned to work and the task at hand. 'How do you think we should go about this?' Sean asked.

Liz giggled into her wine glass. 'I don't know. You're the hack. I'm just the researcher, remember? How would you normally go about something like this?'

'I'd request an interview,' Sean said cockily.

'And when you don't get one?' Liz cut him down playfully.

'I'd give up and write about somebody else,' he laughed, telling the truth.

'So, is that what you want to do here, give up?' Liz shrugged.

There was no way he was giving up the gift of personal time with Liz that easily, even if it was the most sensible thing to do in these circumstances. 'No, I think we have to assume that any interview request will be rejected, given his track record to date. So while I think we should still request an interview, we should crack on with as much background research as possible. Hopefully, we can get enough to piece a story together. What do you think?' He breathed out, hopeful that she would agree.

'Okay, where do we start?' Liz said.

'God, I don't know. You're the researcher,' he smiled.

Following some brief deliberation, they decided that Liz would try to piece together Barker-Willet's life prior to the establishment of the BW Corporation in Thailand, and Sean would work on the time thereafter, including the information on the company. This seemed sensible as Liz was an experienced researcher and could cope with the more complex of the two tasks.

So at 9:30 p.m., they each fired up their respective computers in earnest and Liz opened another bottle of wine, noting that they may as well at least enjoy this unpaid work.

When they started, Sean noticed that he worked very differently from Liz. He scribbled hand-written notes on a pad each time he found something of importance. Liz just seemed to key everything, obviously making digital notes. She was hitting keys quicker than Sean could think, and her frequent sound effects, of 'Hmm' and 'oh' were very endearing to Sean.

Two hours passed before either broke off from their research. 'Find anything juicy?' Liz asked, pulling a concerned face. 'You seemed to be making lots of notes.'

Sean shook his head. 'Well, there's plenty of information on the company, starting with the prospectus for the IPO, through to the present-day accounts, but I couldn't get anything before that, and there is no information other than that contained in the financial statements and directors' returns about Barker-Willet himself.'

'And?' Liz asked.

'Well, the company seems to be all it's touted to be. It went from an original IPO value of £42 million, to its current value of £735 billion in just fifteen years. This seems to have been achieved by a catalogue of acquisitions across just about every industry sector imaginable, in over 100 countries.'

'Anything seem odd in the info?' Liz enquired.

'No, not a thing; everything seems to stack up perfectly, but . . .' Sean hesitated.

'But what?'

'Well, the debt thing is bugging me. Over the years, there have been plenty of serial acquirers, none as aggressive as BW, but plenty nonetheless. Invariably they carry a huge debt burden and have very low interest cover ratios, making this strategy for growth extremely risky. BW doesn't: it has hardly any debt, just £7 billion, despite the fact that it made some 67 acquisitions last year, and not small ones, it's total acquisition spending was £122 billion,' Sean shook his head.

'Could they be hiding the debt somewhere off the balance sheet?' Liz asked.

Sean shook his head again. 'If this were the bad old days, pre-Enron, I'd have said yes, almost certainly they could be. But it's not, and auditors take their job seriously today. It's unthinkable that a FTSE100 company could have material off-balance sheet liabilities,' Sean said convincingly.

Liz nodded. 'Agreed. So what's the conclusion?'

Sean shook his head slowly and shrugged. 'That this guy really is the real deal: a business guru. If you rule out off-balance sheet finance, I don't think their debts are suddenly forgiven for some reason. So the only answer is that they have been repaid. That means BW Corp has cracked the code for rapidly improving the profitability of acquisitions, without asset-stripping them. Thus they have taken out the obstacle that impedes all serial acquirers, which is debt capacity. I can't see any other explanation; they can't just magic up the cash,' he said, lifting his shoulders.

'Okay, that makes sense. They are under the scrutiny of the financial authorities in a 100 plus countries and the Stock Exchange here, so I doubt there's anything materially wrong with their accounting,' she added. 'Barker-Willet himself though is a complete ghost.'

'What do you mean?' Sean asked.

'Well, just that. He has no digital footprint at all, just articles about the company, where he's commented. I've been through all the places where you usually find out information on people of his stature: he has no Wikipedia page, despite the fact that he's reputedly the richest man in the world. Even *Coronation Street* actors have Wikipedia pages now. He doesn't have a LinkedIn profile. He has no Facebook profile. I got his date of birth from the Companies House directors' records, but I couldn't find a record of his birth. I couldn't find a record of him at any British University, and so on and so on. The company information on him is useless; there isn't even a detailed bio to be found in any of its public archives.' She raised both of her hands in despair.

This perplexed Sean, Liz was the best researcher he had ever worked with. If she couldn't find anything, it probably wasn't there. 'Wow! So what do we have?' he asked frowning.

'Nothing. The first record of him is in Bangkok, in April 1995, when he bought a tuna-processing factory for £600,000 in cash. Prior to that, nothing.' She opened her palms again to make the point.

'How did you get that info? I couldn't find anything prior to the IPO prospectus?' Sean asked.

'I have access to the Thai Companies Information Centre as part of my job. The records were there: the company was registered on 4 April, 1995. Two weeks later it acquired a 100% interest in a tuna-processing facility just outside Bangkok, for 25 million Thai Baht, and settled in cash. Six months after that, it began acquiring companies across Asia, using debt, which, as you know, it quickly paid down.'

'Isn't that database in Thai?' Sean asked quizzically.

'Yes. I speak Thai and Korean, Japanese, Mandarin, Cantonese, some Vietnamese and Italian,' Liz said, almost shyly.

'Italian?' Sean asked about the odd language out in the list.

'Yes my grandfather has a house in Forte dei Marmi on the Tuscan coast. We used to spend summers there every year.

'Sounds nice,' Sean commented.

'It was, but I can't really remember much about it,' Liz said looking in the air. 'I should go back there. I have a memory of the nicest old ice-cream stand right on the beach. It served the most delicious *gelato* I've ever tasted.' She smiled sadly at the distant memory.

'Wow! And you have a first in economics from Oxford. Shouldn't you be at some hedge fund making millions, planning its Asian strategy?' Sean said, referring back to Liz's impressive language skills.

Liz giggled sweetly at the complement. 'I've never really cared much for money. My parents are rich, so it's always been there and research for a newspaper is much more pure than research for a hedge fund. Plus, I don't have to put up with the ego-maniac dicks that work there. Anyway, didn't you say that you got a first from the LSE?' she asked.

'Yes, but I'm just some intellectual no-hoper peasant. You, on the other hand, are truly talented.'

Smiling at Sean's second compliment, Liz reached out her hand and put it on his, then leant over the table and pecked him on the cheek. 'Thank you, that's very sweet,' she yawned. 'God, it's past midnight, I need to get some sleep. You can stay if you like. I have a spare room and I know the last Tube has gone already.'

'Thanks, that would be great.' He wanted to reach out, take her in his arms and kiss her, but he just couldn't muster up the courage.

Sean's love life, if it could be called that, had not been much to write home about of late. Aside from the odd fling with a couple of the hippy types, that frequented the pub, he hadn't really been in a relationship since he started at the newspaper. He was aware that he wasn't unattractive; he had a lean body, a childishly handsome face and bright blue eyes. Indeed, while at university, he had never been short of female attention. But in the last few years, he had really just let his appearance go. He dressed badly, grew his hair and made no attempt to actually talk to women he found attractive.

Outwardly, Sean blamed his lack of success with women upon the company he kept and the places he chose to hang out. After all, the Dog and Duck wasn't exactly known for its long line of supermodels, queuing at the door to get in. But inwardly, he knew that he had just lost confidence somewhere along the way. His career was going nowhere and he was getting older; he just wasn't the catch that he used to be.

Could this be an opportunity to kill two birds with one stone? He considered the possibility that not only could the Barker-Willet piece set his career back on track if he got it right, but it also might give him the opportunity to be close to a woman that he found incredibly attractive.

This was surely the best chance he would ever get to test the water with Liz. They were alone, in her apartment and she had just been quite affectionate to him. *Was she signalling her interest?* he agonised. Knowing that he should make a move, he just stood in the hallway, blank-faced, as she walked slowly by him, lingering, before she bade him goodnight and went into her room.

Sean slid off quietly into the spare room, climbed into bed and thought about what it would be like to hold her. He cursed himself for being such a wimp. Why couldn't he take the opportunity? It is obvious Liz liked him, wasn't it? Doubts instantly filled his mind again. She was clearly too good for him, wasn't she? Looking at the crumpled pile of clothes on the floor, he felt his unkempt hair. *What would a girl like that see in me?*

Just as he had convinced himself that Liz was only being friendly and was more interested in the project than she was in him, the door to the spare bedroom opened. Through her loose-fitting silk nightgown, he could make out the athletic curves of her body, silhouetted by the light behind her. 'I thought the men were supposed to make the first move,' she said smiling, as she pulled on the silk cord holding her gown together. It dropped from her shoulders to the floor and she walked gracefully around the bed towards him, as naked as the day she was born.

Las Vegas, Nevada, USA

An unmarked Gulfstream 650 private jet pulled up by a secluded hanger, hidden from the scorching runway, but close to the famous Las Vegas Strip. As a black Cadillac limousine pulled alongside it, the plane's door opened to reveal the steps. Just then, three men of oriental origin emerged from the luxurious jet, dressed in smart casual suits, with shirts open at the neck. They climbed into the limousine through the rear door, which was held open by a uniformed chauffeur. Inside, a squat, bespectacled man, attired in a blue business suit, who projected the appearance of an accountant, waited for them patiently.

'Good afternoon, gentlemen. I trust the flight was pleasant?' the squat man asked politely.

One of the three men laughed and spoke in Korean to the other two, causing each to laugh and comment in return. 'They said the last 7,000 miles from Seoul to here were perfect. Thank you for the use of your plane. The first 100 miles from Pyongyang to Seoul, were terrible. I can attest to this also.'

The bespectacled man smiled. 'We'll see what we can do next time. Your suites are ready for you and lines of credit have been arranged at the casino for $10 million each. Enjoy your stay, General Kim.'

The squat man adjusted his glasses carefully and climbed out of the limousine with equal care. The long car then swept away effortlessly in the direction of the bright neon lights of the strip.

Chapter 3

Liz looked stunning as she pulled the toast from the shiny chrome toaster, and Sean had to pinch himself to check that he wasn't dreaming. 'Jam?' she asked, smiling affectionately at him. He nodded and she quickly slapped some raspberry preserve on top of the white toast then came to sit beside him, kissing him on the cheek as she sat down. Sean could easily have stayed in that moment for the rest of his life.

'Did you think any more about the BW piece last night?' Liz asked.

'I didn't really get the chance,' Sean said, joking about the voracity of Liz's sexual appetite, and noting that she hadn't given him much time to sleep.

'Hmm, I wonder why that is? I thought about it all night.' She kissed him again, this time on the lips. 'Why do you think there's no digital footprint of him?'

Before responding, Sean looked at Liz thoughtfully for a while. 'I don't know. Could be a number of reasons I guess. He may have paid somebody to delete the data. He's certainly paranoid about privacy. On the other hand, maybe he's not who he says he is.'

'Hmm, I gave that some thought too. Removing an identity from government databases is not only difficult, it's illegal, so I doubt that's what he's done,' she said, playing with her lower lip.

'You're probably right,' Sean acknowledged. 'CEOs of FTSE100 companies tend not to overtly break the law. So why the black hole in the data?'

Liz tapped her lip in thought. 'Of course, I can't be certain, but I'll bet he's changed his identity for some reason.' She frowned. 'I guess the million-dollar question is why?'

'Yep, and how the hell do we figure that out?'

Liz chuckled. 'You were the one that was craving some real investigative journalism. Well, this is it, I think. My guess is the only way we can prove that somebody isn't who they *say* they are, is to prove who they *really* are. How we go about that is another matter altogether.'

'I think the first approach is to try asking him. I'll call his PR monkey to try to set up an interview,' he said.

'You could use our discovery for leverage to get the interview,' Liz suggested, raising an eyebrow.

'Not really. Julie Benning is the BW PR monkey. She'd just call the paper's lawyers and tell them to back off. Then I'd get my head handed to me by John. No, we're going to need to be more creative than that,' Sean said.

'Shit, really? I hate her. She was such a bolshie bitch when she worked at the *Daily*. I think we have to assume that we'll get a flat rejection to the interview request. So what then?' Liz queried.

For the first time in the conversation, Sean looked more serious. This was the first time he'd been really interested in something to do with work for years, and to be doing it with Liz, just made it feel even better. 'I don't know, but something tells me we need to look into his time in Bangkok. We can be pretty much certain about the time post the IPO: he's been in London, working as the CEO of BW Corp. We can safely assume that if he did anything out of the ordinary in that period, it would've been reported somewhere, which it hasn't. As far as we can tell, before he registered the company in Thailand in 1995, he didn't exist. So we've got five years when we know he was based in Thailand, we know he bought a tuna-processing plant for £600,000, and we know that he grew that business to be worth £42 million at IPO, just five years later. I think that period's the best place to start,' he said.

'Agreed,' Liz said nodding.

'There are some obvious questions that we need to answer: Where did he come from? Why was he in Thailand? And how did a twenty-two-year-old man get £600,000 in cash?' Sean continued.

'I'd also be asking why a twenty-two-year-old man, with £600,000 in cash, spent it on a tuna-processing plant in Bangkok. Most men with cash to spare in Thailand choose to spend it differently.' Liz pulled an ugly face.

'Yes, you're right. There has to be some personal connection to that plant, otherwise it is just doesn't make any sense.' He paused briefly thinking about an approach. 'How do you fancy a holiday? I've heard the beaches are nice in Thailand,' he suggested jokingly.

Liz smiled and lifted her head to kiss him. 'I'm in. I'm due a good holiday, and I'm sick of the weather here.'

Sean lingered on her kiss for a while and then smirked. 'You do know I was joking, right?'

Liz returned the sarcastic smirk. 'Yes, but why not? Why shouldn't we go? This is certainly the most interesting thing I've ever worked on, and I've seen the rubbish you turn out daily.' She poked him in the ribs playfully. 'So why not? We can kill two birds with one stone: a holiday and a story. I know we've only just got together, but I kinda like you and I think that you like me, so it will give us a chance to get to know each other better.'

When Liz said that she liked him, it was just about the best thing Sean had ever been told. She could have asked him to come on a military training exercise in Chechnya, and he would have been packing his camouflage Y-fronts within the hour. But a holiday in an exotic location, with the woman of his dreams, while also furthering his craving to do some real journalism . . . life just couldn't get any better. 'Well, I've got holidays due as well, so why not? I'll call BW today and request the interview. If that gets turned down, I guess we should book something.'

Liz immediately pulled a fake disappointed face.

'What's wrong?' Sean asked.

'I just said I like you and you didn't say anything back,' she said, sulking playfully.

The comment made Sean blush. 'Liz, if I told you how I really feel you'd run a mile.' He pulled her towards him and kissed her softly on the lips. When he finally relaxed his hold, he said. 'Just a question though, what the hell are we going to do when we get there, other than lie on the beach and have lots of sex, of course?'

'Firstly, there are no beaches in Bangkok, it's big, dirty and polluted; secondly, you'll be so knackered after a day wandering around there, that you won't have any energy for sex; and last but not least, my family have some fairly good business connections there. I'm sure they can point us in the right direction.' Liz said, giggling shyly at Sean's suggestion.

'My god, you really are amazing. My family's only connections were at the local chippy, in a small village north of Manchester,' Sean alluded to his less than salubrious upbringing, in the working-class northern suburbs of Manchester. He didn't mention that he no longer had any living relatives.

'Oh, I love fish and chips. I knew you'd come in handy,' she said, before her expression turned to a more serious one. 'Before we do this, you have to promise me one thing though,' she said frowning.

'Go on,' Sean nodded.

'There are a lot of very legitimate reasons why somebody might want to change their identity. I mean, he could be in witness protection or hiding from some kind of psychotic family. If we discover that his reasons are legitimate, I want you to promise me that you won't pursue the story further. I don't want to have the death of an innocent man on my conscience.' Her voice had taken on a more serious tone.

Knowing that she was right, Sean looked into her eyes and agreed that there were probably more legitimate reasons to change your name, than dubious reasons. 'Absolutely. Even if it was just because he didn't like his original name,' he said, pulling her towards him again, feeling the warm wetness of her lips against his.

Later that morning, Sean called Julie Benning at BW Corp. To his surprise she took his call straight away. 'Hi, Sean, I heard you were on the BW Corporation list now. Congratulations. We'll probably be seeing a lot of each other. Sorry I didn't catch up with you at the AGM, but I couldn't find you at the lunch. What can I help you with today?'

Julie Benning had been, without doubt, the most difficult person he had ever worked with. She had a chip on her shoulder about being a woman, another about being fat, and another about the fact that she hadn't been made editor at the age of twenty-seven. Now that it was her job to get Sean to write good things about her employer, she was suddenly Miss Sweetness and Light. It almost made him sick. 'Hi, Julie, thanks for taking my call. I'm thinking about doing a human interest piece on Charles Barker-Willet, and was wondering if he would be amenable to an interview. I was very impressed with him at the AGM and thought it would make a good story.'

There was no hesitation at all on the other end of the line. 'Well, that's nice, Sean, and I'm sure he will be flattered, but

Charles is both a very busy and a very private man. He doesn't do interviews unless they are for the benefit of the company, or for his foundation. If you have any questions about either, please feel free to forward them to me, and I'll do my best to get answers. But, please, don't ask anything of a personal nature about Charles: many have tried and all have been rejected.'

'Okay, thanks, Julie. Perhaps I'll write about Donald Trump instead.' Sean had got the answer he'd expected and hung up the phone, quietly pleased with the result.

When he left his desk to get a drink, John was in the small kitchenette pouring himself a cup of the murky brown liquid, that claimed to have some association with coffee.

'So did you get an interview with Barker-Willet?' John smirked.

'I think you know the answer to that.' Sean laughed.

'Thought not. I assume I shouldn't expect a piece then?' John's tone was saying, 'I told you so,' without actually saying it.

Even though Sean found it irritating, he thought better of telling John what was really happening. 'Probably not, I thought I might take a couple of weeks off. I've got some holiday owing,' he said, informally asking permission to take leave, and lying about the story at the same time.

'Ha, that's funny. I've just had Liz ask me the same thing. You're not going together, are you?' John put on a cheesy grin.

'I wish,' Sean lied.

'Yeah, right. She's way out of your league. No problem, I'm sure we won't go under without you. Gerry and I can cover your list while you're gone.'

'Cheers, John. I'll bring you back a stick of rock,' Sean said, walking out of the tearoom.

That afternoon he and Liz booked their tickets to Bangkok, leaving on Friday night in two days' time. That same evening they made love four times at Liz's flat, and got no work done at all. Sean was secretly hoping that was the way the holiday might go.

Sana'a, Yemen

The decrepit warehouse, constructed from the traditional mud brick of the region, towered above 26 September Street, in the ancient heart of the city of Sana'a. Uniformed paramilitary soldiers pointed AK47 assault rifles through the windowless frames on its second floor, carefully scanning the street below.

In any normal city, this would draw attention to the building, but in the Yemini capital, where children as young as ten carried AK47s in the street, it went unnoticed. The Yemini people had thirty years' experience of not noticing what was going on around them; it was a matter of survival.

The bustling crowds went about their daily business on the busy road in front of the ramshackle building. Women dressed in full burkas glided by like herds of ghosts, carrying their daily shopping, as children played in the roadside gutters, clutching on to their precious rifles, and men squatted in the shade of buildings, chewing *qat*, the amphetamine of choice in Yemen.

The crowds parted as three military trucks pulled up to the gate. Almost instantaneously, the wooden doors opened, without the need for any of the soldiers to dismount, and the three trucks moved inside quickly. None of the people on the street made any attempt to see what was happening through the

open wooden doors, knowing intuitively that posses-
sion of information like that could be dangerous. As
soon as the trucks had passed, the pavement filled
up again and people drifted by, blissfully ignorant
of the goings on behind the large doors.

The trucks circled the small internal driveway and
reversed up to a broken loading dock, dropping their
tailgates automatically onto the concrete platform.
From nowhere, eighteen uniformed paramilitary
soldiers ran from the warehouse and onto the trucks,
then, in teams of six, they began checking the green
boxes on the back of the vehicles. Randomly opening
one box on each pallet, they inspected the military
hardware inside. It was as they expected: Russian-
made assault rifles; rocket-propelled grenade
launchers; landmines; and finally, 300kg of Semtex
H. Enough explosive to arm their suicide warriors
for years to come.

The deadly load confirmed, one of the paramilitary
soldiers walked around the first truck and banged
firmly on the door. Following a brief conversation
with the passenger in the front of the vehicle, the
door swung open, revealing a middle-aged man,
dressed in the combat uniform of an army colonel.
Carefully checking his surroundings, the Colonel
jumped down from the truck and walked around the
vehicle, before he climbed some steps leading into
the warehouse, calling behind him for an army
captain to come from the second vehicle.

Two pallets, piled high with bundles of Yemini
Rial, were lined up just behind the warehouse door.
The note bundles were neatly stacked and held onto
the pallet with cling film wrapping. Taking a knife

from his belt, the Captain cut a hole in the cling film halfway up, then pulled out a bundle of notes, flicking his fingers through it, to ensure that the notes were real.

'One billion Rial?' the Colonel questioned.

'Seems about right. We can't count it,' the Captain replied.

'Okay, get the men,' the Colonel instructed.

Following the instruction, the Captain walked outside and made a signal to one of the drivers. Soon four non-commissioned soldiers joined the Colonel and the Captain in the warehouse. As the soldiers entered the warehouse, the paramilitary soldiers began securing the army trucks, some then jumped on the back while six took up their positions in the front seats. When the vehicles started to move, two of the army soldiers opened the doors to the warehouse and the paramilitaries disappeared out onto 26 September Street, in the three trucks.

Before closing the doors the soldiers signalled to the driver of a white unmarked van, who had been waiting patiently across the street. The van quickly pulled into the warehouse and the doors closed behind it, as the driver backed into the loading dock.

The traditional Yemini dress worn by the two inhabitants of the van looked odd against their pale skin, as they opened the rear doors of the van and pulled out a pallet trolley. Without speaking to any of the six soldiers present, they loaded each of the two pallets of cash onto the van and secured the rear doors. Less than five minutes after they had entered the small compound, they were back out on 26 September Street.

Once the van was out of sight, the Colonel, Captain and the four soldiers, walked out of the warehouse and headed on foot in the direction of their barracks.

Chapter 4

Saturday, 15th February. Bangkok, Thailand

Sean pulled Liz closer to his shoulder, as he looked out of the window of the luxury Mercedes sedan, sent by her uncle to collect them from Suvarnabhumi airport. The cool chill of the air-conditioning was a welcome relief from the oppressive humidity that Sean had experienced, even on the short walk to the car from the terminal. The hectic pace of Bangkok life passed by in the double-glazed window of the car, like a silent movie, offering the car's inhabitants a strange and privileged detachment from the harsh reality of life in the Thai capital.

Liz's uncle had also kindly arranged accommodation for them in the Sheraton Grand Hotel, in the heart of the steamy city. It was midnight when the car finally pulled onto Sukhumvit Road, but the late hour didn't mean that passage down the notoriously busy strip was easy. The scene in front of them was chaotic: tuk-tuks were zipping in and out of side streets, only just avoiding the oncoming cars, and people were crammed onto the raised sidewalks, jostling past each other, eager to get to the next bar, or market stall.

'It's as busy as Piccadilly Circus at midday,' Sean commented.

'Welcome to Asia,' Liz replied, smiling and kissing Sean softly on the lips.

Although Sean had travelled a little in his life, he had always stuck to less adventurous routes, such as Australia and the US, purposely avoiding the places which were now, somewhat politically correctly, called 'developing markets', as opposed to the previous, somewhat derisory tag of 'third-world countries.' His only time in less developed countries was when he took a travel job as a waiter/tender cleaner on a large yacht. They had called into some dodgy places en-route to the more glamorous spots, but they rarely got off the boat. And he only lasted a month before he was fired for taking an unauthorised spin around the harbour in one of the tenders.

The following day, at midday, Sean decided that it was respectable enough to order a beer. His mouth salivated as he watched the waiter coming out from behind the bar with the tall glass of golden liquid, covered in condensation. Just as the young man, dressed in black and white arrived at his lounger, Liz appeared through the glass doors from the hotel.

'No time for drinking. We've got work to do,' she said smiling.

'I'm gagging,' Sean said.

'Well, have a soft drink,' Liz laughed and turned to the waiter, ordering two cokes in Thai. 'When you've drunk that, get some normal clothes on. We've got an appointment.'

'Really, who with?' Sean asked, sitting up.

'The man who sold the tuna factory to Barker-Willet in 1995. He's a friend of my uncle,' Liz said, pecking him on the cheek as she sat.

Two hours later, their borrowed Mercedes sedan pulled up outside the modern, white-rendered façade, of the Bangkok Golf Club. A uniformed doorman opened the rear door of the car immediately. 'Good afternoon, sir,' he said in heavily accented English, as Sean stepped out.

Sean felt instantly out of place, dressed in his cargo shorts and white work shirt, rolled up at the sleeves. Although they had only driven for forty minutes or so, they seemed to be in a different world from the bustling dirty streets of downtown Bangkok. Porters scurried around in their white uniforms, loading electric golf carts for their immaculately groomed members, while small armies of caddies walked behind the carts, carrying umbrellas to shade them from the hot sun.

After Liz said a few words to the doorman in Thai, they were promptly escorted into the opulent club.

Boonsong Wongsawat was a Thai businessman in his early sixties, dressed in checked trousers and a bright yellow Lacoste t-shirt, Sean thought that he would look more at home in Palm Beach than the sweltering Thai capital. It was a great relief to Sean when he started to speak in English.

Khun Wongsawat, as Liz had instructed Sean to address him, turned out to be a charming host, ordering a spread of food fit for a king and some very nice French wine. He was also very open to discussion about the transaction he had made some twenty years ago and the conversation flowed freely, as he seemed completely at ease when asked questions by Liz or Sean.

'So the business lost money before you sold it?' Sean asked, picking up on a comment made by Boonsong.

'Yes. Actually it never turned a profit while I owned it,' Boonsong said casually.

'So why would Barker-Willet pay twenty-five million Baht for it then?' Liz asked.

Boonsong laughed. 'I don't know and I don't care. I inherited the business from my father. I worked twenty-four hours a day and still lost money. I was on my last 10,000 baht, when this guy showed up and offered me twenty-five million out of the blue. Now I play golf, eat good food and enjoy life.'

'How did Barker-Willet make your business profitable then?' Sean asked.

'I have asked myself the same question for twenty years. He didn't change any of the frontline staff, just the finance department. I still know all of the people there; they're my friends and they say that the volume has never increased,' Boonsong shrugged.

'Could he have increased the price or reduced costs?' Liz asked.

'Price no; canned tuna is a commodity unfortunately. Costs possibly . . . slightly; but not to the extent that he could make the place profitable. Sixty-five per cent of the cost of a can of tuna is made up by the price of raw fish, and the sales price varies based on that; because Western companies force Thai co-packers into fixed margin contracts. So if the tuna price went down, we actually made less money.' Boonsong's answer was confident and he seemed knowledgeable to Sean.

Even though it made sense, Barker–Willet *had* increased profits and used the acquisition as the basis for a huge empire, so there must be more to it than that. 'Were you surprised that such a young man had so much money to spend?' he asked.

Boonsong looked confused by the question for the first time. 'Young?' he said shaking his head. 'This man was not so young: mid-fifties I would say.'

It was Sean's turn to look confused. 'But Charles Barker-Willet is only in his forties now. Were you dealing directly with him, or was it his advisor?'

Boonsong nodded. 'I only met him once. The transaction was arranged quickly through his lawyer. But as is tradition in Thailand, we had a signing ceremony upon completion of the deal. He was alone and wasn't a man in his twenties, unless he'd had a very bad life.' He shook the wine bottle, indicating what he meant by a bad life.

A picture of Charles Barker-Willet, with his athletic physique and his youthful, face crossed Sean's mind. *He could pass for thirty-five now,* he thought, *twenty years on.*

Liz went to speak, but instinctively Sean knew she was going to push the point on age, so he squeezed her hand under the table, to indicate that she should leave it.

'Do you know anything about how he lived personally after he bought the company? I think he lived in Bangkok for five years,' Sean asked, changing the subject deliberately.

Boonsong shrugged casually again. 'I don't know. I didn't like him, so I didn't try to stay in touch. I heard that he hung out in the bars on Soi Cowboy, you might want to try there.'

'Soi Cowboy?' Liz exclaimed, screwing up her face, showing her distaste.

Boonsong laughed. 'Yes, not a place for you, young lady. You should go alone,' he intimated to Sean. 'Ask for Nok, the Mama-san, in a bar called Girl House, and say that I sent you. She's been there for years and knows everyone who comes and goes regularly.'

They continued lunch, chatting about the background of the tuna factory and Barker-Willet, but it was clear that Boonsong had already told them everything that he knew. So, after a delightful two-hour lunch, they said their respective goodbyes and left, just as Boonsong ordered another bottle of wine. In the car on the way back to the hotel, Liz and Sean spoke quietly as if sharing some naughty secrets. 'Curiouser and curiouser,' Sean said quoting Lewis Carrol.

'Yes, what do you think it means?'

Sean put his index finger to his lips in thought. 'How about this: the younger Barker-Willet, murdered the elder, and stole his business?' he said speculating.

Liz laughed out loud. 'You're wasted as a hack. You should write novels. How about, the younger Barker-Willet is the son of the elder and was left in charge of the business? The older one is probably just one of those weird guys who gave his son the same name. You'll probably find out the younger one is actually called Charles Barker-Willet III, or something stupid like that.'

'It does sound more feasible,' he said, 'but not such a good story.'

'No, real life rarely is,' Liz smirked.

'God, really,' Sean sighed, 'you think this whole thing could turn out to be nothing more than that?'

'Yep, maybe,' Liz laughed. 'We'll still have a nice holiday.' She kissed Sean on the lips.

Freetown, Sierra Leone, Africa

Two middle-aged white men, dressed in beige chinos and colourful beach shirts, looked as if they were ready to hit a sleazy bar in Miami's South Beach, but they were a long way from the Atlantic coast of Florida. The ramshackle house overlooking Susan's Bay in the centre of Freetown was devoid of anything that made it look homely. There was no furniture other than a small plastic table in the lounge, positioned neatly by a huge windowless hole in the wall, with three plastic chairs pushed underneath it. The stifling heat of the African night poured in through the opening and the two out-of-place white men sweated profusely into their gaudy shirts. They moved to the table nervously and took two adjacent seats. From their position, they could see fishing boats moving in and out of the harbour, their tiny lights seeming to bob on the water, not attached to anything.

The tranquillity of the setting was soon broken as a small convoy of three military vehicles, followed by a black Mercedes limousine, pulled up outside the house. Uniformed soldiers jumped out and began to secure the area. When they were happy the area was safe, the driver of the limousine climbed out of the car and opened the rear door. Moments later, a rotund black man, in the uniform of a general in the official Sierra Leone army, emerged. He walked straight into the house clutching a small leather satchel.

The two white men stood when he entered the room and then returned to their seats, as the General walked slowly over to the table, with the swagger of a man scared of nothing. 'Gentlemen,' he nodded to each in turn. 'The money?' he asked questioningly.

'General,' the elder of the two men spoke nervously in a thick South-African accent, 'the diamonds?'

The General dropped his considerable frame into the last remaining seat. It creaked as if it would break, which brought a grin to the General's face, exposing the gold crowns on his teeth. He placed the small leather satchel in the centre of the table. 'The diamonds,' he said.

Without speaking, the younger of the two men reached under the table and pulled out a scruffy leather briefcase.

The General smiled cynically and reached for the briefcase, emptying its contents onto the table in front of him. As ten large bundles of US$100 bills fell onto the filthy plastic surface, he called out in Krio, the local dialect, to another man outside the room. Almost immediately, a young captain arrived at the door, and following a brief conversation, again in Krio, he began to count the money.

At the same time, the older man pulled a jeweller's loop from his pocket and placed it into his right eye. He emptied the contents of the leather satchel onto the table and began to view the diamonds quickly, using a pocket torch.

The captain finished his counting within fifteen minutes and nodded to the General. It took a further five minutes to finish the inspection of the diamonds. Happy with the contents of the satchel, he nodded to the younger man, placed the diamonds back into the small container and stood, anxious to leave.

'Wait! A drink for celebration,' the General said in English. The Captain hurried away, returning with a bottle of Glenlivet single-malt Scotch whisky.

The two white men returned to their seats, sweat pouring nervously from their heads. The General was not a person that anybody wanted to spend too much time with, especially if he got drunk, when he could become dangerously unpredictable. They drank their respective drinks quickly and again made to leave, but the General quickly refilled the empty glasses. 'Gentlemen, we must finish the bottle once opened. It's a tradition,' he said with a sadistic grin.

'Of course, General. Cheers!' the younger of the two men said, as he skulled his second whisky.

The process was repeated a further four times, until the bottle was empty. 'How much will you get for my diamonds?' the General asked. He was now overtly drunk and grinning broadly.

Neither of the white men spoke.

'I know the real value would be over US$1 million, if the damned interfering politicians hadn't labelled them *blood diamonds.*' He paused. 'Blood diamonds! What do those idiots know about Africa? They say we must look after ourselves, stop relying on aid. Yet here I have US $1 million worth of diamonds and I have to sell them to two South-African thieves for $100,000. Where is the justice in that?' The General's mood swung quickly from jovial to angry.

'Ah, General, we agree, but we don't get anything

like that for them. We too are Africans, and are also ripped off by the damned European do-gooders,' the elder of the two men spoke, wiping sweat from his brow.

Making a pretence of listening to his explanation, the General eyed the older man suspiciously. 'Maybe I should keep my diamonds and your money. I could sell them ten times to greedy South-African white men, like you. Then I would get my price.' He pulled the same sadistic grin as earlier.

'But, General, that wouldn't be fair. We've done everything you asked. We delivered your money, in the denominations you asked for; on time; in full.' The younger man spoke more calmly than the elder. 'We could do business again. People like us, that deliver, are hard to find.' He smiled weakly, reflecting his fear.

'Ha! Greedy white men are hard to find? I don't think so. For this cheek alone I will keep my diamonds and your money,' the General said, laughing loudly.

'But, General,' the younger man protested, then stopped as the General reached for his pistol.

'Go now, white pigs, before I also take your lives,' he said angrily.

This time the elder man put his arm on the other's shoulder and pulled him up. Then they scurried out of the door and onto the street, running in the direction of their seedy Freetown hotel, as fast as their overweight sweating bodies could carry them.

Picking up the satchel of diamonds and walking to the door, the General's demeanour changed quickly, reflecting the fact that he was faking his drunkenness.

Out of the darkness, a motorbike entered the driveway at the front of the house and a clean-cut white man, dressed in shorts and a t-shirt, walked straight into the house without stopping.

'On the table,' the General said, waving his bloated hand in the direction of the pile of cash on the table.

Walking straight past the General, the man took out a pair of surgical gloves and a small black plastic bag. Then he carefully picked up the cash, placing it in the bag. Without so much as a word, he left on his motorcycle, less than one minute after he had arrived.

Chapter 5

Despite their earlier conclusion that they were probably chasing nothing special, Sean and Liz agreed that they should still follow through with their enquiries in Bangkok, on the off chance that it would lead to something that would at least be printable. Sean decided to follow up on Boonsong's lead and visit Nok, the Mama-san, on Soi Cowboy, while Liz remained in the hotel room to get some sleep.

Only two blocks from the hotel, Sean turned left off Sukhumvit Road and onto Soi 21. The street lit up like Times Square on New Year's Eve as a mass of neon signs came into view. Soi Cowboy was a pedestrianized street, which ran parallel to Sukhumvit Road. It had a large neon sign spanning its full width, depicting a cowboy lying down and swinging a lasso. Once on the infamous street, Sean assessed the scene before him. The street itself was about 100 metres long and both sides were crammed with bars and clubs, their respective signs alluding to the varying brand of depravity a person could find inside. Some showed schoolgirls in uniform, others women in sailor suits, and so on. Outside each of the institutions, groups of young women gathered, dressed in the uniforms on the sign, trying to persuade the passers-by to go inside.

Sean had never seen anything like it. He had been to Soho, Amsterdam and even Kings Cross in Sydney, but none of those places had prepared him for the social extremes of Soi Cowboy. As far as he could tell, the visitors to the area fell into three distinct categories: genuine tourists, male and female, gawking at the sights and taking photos to show their friends that they had been there; groups of drunken young men, either post-business meetings, or on stag parties, swaggering from bar to bar, jeering at the girls; and then a far more sinister group, who were mostly alone, mostly middle-aged and mostly white. This third group were trawling the edge of the bars, seeking out their prey. They didn't seem to be having any fun, unlike the other two groups. They weren't taking photos and they didn't look drunk. They simply walked slowly past the bars, leering at the goods on offer, occasionally stopping for what appeared to be a negotiation. Then, they either entered the bar, or moved back to their silent stalking. Sean shivered: this was the famed seedy side of Bangkok, and its customers seemed to fit the stereotype of sex tourists.

Girl House was towards the end of the street on the left. A group of young girls wearing sailor suits with short skirts were standing outside, trying to encourage passers-by to go in. At the entrance, a few Australian men in their early twenties were haggling with the girls over drink prices. Sean took the opportunity to slip in, without having to speak to any of the girls.

Inside, the club was smaller than Sean had imagined and was set up with a short raised catwalk down the middle. Half-naked girls strutted from one end to the other, displaying their wares to a salivating crowd. Their movements could be better described as jiggling, rather than dancing. Two rows of seats faced the catwalk and most spots were filled with the second category of men Sean had observed. They were drunk, loud and mostly obnoxious, spilling beer and shouting obscenities, as they tried to paw the girls. Sean noticed that the first category, the real tourists, didn't enter the bars, they just took their photos out on the street and left quickly.

The third category, the sex tourists, didn't sit in the front two rows by the catwalk. They sat at the back, alone in the shadows, groping at the young girls and negotiating their lewd desires. The sight made Sean sick to the stomach. Men who probably lived perfectly normal lives in their own countries, came to Thailand as sex predators, preying on underage girls. It seemed bizarre that a behaviour, which would condemn them to prison and social isolation in their home countries, was practised so openly here.

Finding a seat in the second row, Sean looked around for somebody that appeared to be in charge. Liz had informed him that 'the Mama-san' was the nickname given to a woman who ran this type of establishment. It didn't take long to find her. She was sitting behind a curtain close to the entrance, on a wooden dining chair, pulled up to a small desk. On top of the desk there was an old till with its drawer open. The Mama-san was counting its contents carefully. She was considerably older than the girls on the floor and was carrying a lot of weight on her short frame. Her facial expression seemed to be one of permanent anger, which was understandable given the detestable nature of her job.

A young waitress offering drinks, and possibly more if he wished, approached Sean. He ordered a beer and smiled politely. As she walked to the bar to get his drink, another girl, who was stripped to the waist, sat in the seat next to him.

'Buy me a drink?' she said in broken English, smiling through her crooked teeth.

Sean shook his head. 'No, that's okay thanks.'

'I'll suck your cock if you buy me a drink,' she said, still smiling.

Sean laughed instinctively; she vocalised the words as if she had offered nothing more than to lend a library book. 'How about I buy you a drink and you don't have to suck my cock?' he said, declining her offer.

'Okay, tequila slammer, please,' she said surprised. She waved her arm at the waitress, who seemed to know what that meant.

Sean studied her. She was quite pretty, with a slight frame, long black hair and a cute smile, but she was very young, possibly sixteen or less. 'Could you tell Nok I would like to speak to her, please?' he asked politely.

The girl perked up quickly, the smile spreading across her young face. 'You pay my bar fine?' she said expectantly.

Sean looked puzzled. 'What?'

The girl giggled cutely. 'You pay bar fine to Mama-san and I go to your hotel.'

Sean laughed, surprised at how openly she discussed the transaction. 'No, sorry, I just need to speak to her.'

'Okay. 500 baht,' the girl said, still holding a cheeky smile.

Sean pointed to the woman behind the curtain. 'That's her, isn't it? I'll just go myself.'

The young Thai girl pulled a fake sulk. 'Yes, but give me 200 baht and I will introduce you properly, as is custom in Thailand.'

Sean doubted there was any such custom, but the bare-faced cheek of the smiling young girl had charmed him. She seemed so happy and yet he couldn't help but feel sorry for her, as he pulled 200 baht from his pocket and gave it to her.

Beaming the same winning smile, she stood up and went behind the curtain to speak to the Mama-san briefly. Sean noticed that she handed over the 200 baht and the Mama-san quickly dropped it into the till, before the rotund brothel keeper then stood and walked over to Sean.

'You want to pay bar fine for her?' she asked Sean aggressively.

'No,' Sean said, holding his hands up. 'I would like to talk to you in private, if possible?'

'Not possible: drink, find girl, pay bar fine is possible, but that's all,' the older woman frowned angrily.

'Boonsong Wongsawat sent me,' Sean said, trying to rescue the situation.

Nok's demeanour changed instantly and a broad smile broke out on her round face. 'Well, why didn't you say? Come through,' she said, her English improving dramatically. She stepped behind the shabby curtain and sat down. 'How is the old devil?'

There was no seat, so Sean stood behind the curtain. 'He's well, playing golf and enjoying life. He sends his regards.'

'Good. We don't see him so often anymore. Tell him to come back,' she said with mock sternness. 'Now, how can I help you?'

'Sorry to intrude like this, but Boonsong said you had been here for years and you might know a man called Charles Barker-Willet?'

The Mama-san's face broke into a broader smile. 'Yes, of course I do: Charlie. He used to come here five times a week. Then he suddenly stopped, just like that,' she clicked her fingers.

'Do you know what happened to him?' Sean asked.

'No. Went back to Australia, I guess,' she said shaking her head.

'He was Australian?' Sean asked in surprise.

'Yes, from Melbourne. He often talked about it to the girls.'

'When did he stop coming?' Sean enquired.

Nok moved her head from side to side and then started to count on her fingers. 'Sometime in the late nineties, I think.'

'What was he like?' Sean asked.

Nok paused. 'Nice; a gentleman, you know; old-school. Not like these idiots that come here now. He always tipped the girls and bought drinks. Most nights he would be too drunk to take any girl home, but he would never be rude or violent. He'd just stagger out and jump in a tuk-tuk. He never wanted the young girls either; he was happy with the older ones.'

'How old was he?' Sean asked.

'I don't know for sure, but fifty-ish would be about right. He had grey hair,' she said, waving at her head.

Sean pulled out his iPhone and showed the Mama-san a picture of the younger Charles Barker-Willet. 'Do you know this man?' he asked.

'No, I don't think so.' she said, studying the photo carefully, shaking her head as she scanned the digital image

Disappointed, Sean replaced the phone in his pocket.

'Wait, let me have another look,' she asked. She studied the photo again deliberating. 'No, I don't know him. I thought it might be someone, but it's not him. Try Po at Lilac bar, six doors down from here. She might know him.'

Having completed everything he could, Sean thanked the portly Mama-san for her help and stepped from behind the curtain.

'Anything for a friend of Boonsong. Tell him not to be such a stranger,' she replied, as he was leaving.

Lilac Bar was in the same strip of seedy go-go bars. Its Mama-san, Po, was almost a carbon copy of Nok. She was overweight, middle-aged and grumpy, but Sean hoped that mentioning Nok's name would change this, as it had with Boonsong's name in Girl House previously. He approached her and introduced himself, stating that Nok had sent him.

'No discount,' she said in broken English.

Explaining that he wasn't looking for discount, Sean showed her the photo. 'Do you know this man?' he asked politely.

'No, don't know,' she said, without even looking.

'Please, at least look,' Sean said appealing to her.

She took the phone out of his hand angrily and scanned the photo. Sean noticed her eyes widen when the image came into focus. She hastily passed the phone back to him. 'No, don't know him,' she said in the same angry tone.

Something wasn't right. He was almost sure he'd seen some recognition on her face, but why would she lie? What did she have to hide? 'Okay, but if you remember anything, please let me know.' He passed her his business card. 'I'm staying at the Sheraton Grand, Sukhumvit,' he said, before walking through the door of the gaudy Lilac saloon and out into the bright neon lights of Soi Cowboy again.

Trying to gather his thoughts, he stumbled across the pedestrian street to a bar opposite Lilac. The bar had stools and small tables outside, and surprisingly, didn't appear to be a seedy go-go bar. Although there still seemed to be a smattering of girls applying their trade, as he ordered a beer and zoned out from the scene in front of him.

Nothing he had found so far was conclusive evidence of anything, but he had to admit that Liz's supposition was still the most likely . . . that Charles Barker-Willet the Younger, was nothing more sinister than the son of Charles Barker-Willet the Elder, and was an Australian, which is why there was no trace of him in the UK Government databases. His publicity shyness was probably just that; shyness. He wouldn't be the first billionaire to avoid contact with the media.

Sipping at his beer, Sean noted that the sweaty heat of the Bangkok night made it taste even better than it usually did. 'Here's to a great holiday with Liz,' he toasted to himself, as he downed the rest of the glass.

Chapter 6

As Sean stood to leave the tacky little bar on Soi Cowboy, contented that he had gleaned as much information as he could from the two mama-sans, he caught sight of two men rounding the corner from Soi 21. His eyes were instantly drawn to them. The two young men stood out from the crowd and didn't fit into any of the categories that Sean had observed earlier. They were young, white, clean-cut, sober and well-dressed. More to the point, they walked with an almost military purpose, instead of the drunken swagger of other men their age on Soi Cowboy. There was something else about them that seemed strange, but Sean couldn't put his finger on it.

He instinctively moved into the shadow projected by a neon sign, observing their movement. As he did, a drop of sweat fell from his forehead onto his shirt. Looking at it briefly, he realised what else was odd about the two men: they were both wearing jackets, in thirty-degree heat and at ninety-five per cent humidity. Why?

Staying in the shadows, Sean didn't know why he was hiding from the two men, but something nagged at him, as he watched them make straight for Lilac, the seedy go-go bar, which he had just vacated. Displaying an air of authority, they pushed their way through a crowd of drunken twenty-somethings that had gathered at the door. Seconds later they emerged through the same door, holding the Mama-san by her upper arm.

One of the two men seemed to be asking Po questions, but Sean couldn't hear what they were saying. She broke free of the man's grasp and waved her arms in the air excitedly. Then Sean saw something that almost made his heart stop. She produced a small white card from her pocket and gave it to one of the men. Even from the twenty or so metres away that Sean was standing, he could see that it was a business card; his business card.

'Shit, Liz!' he said aloud.

Sean's heart was suddenly beating faster, as he looked for a way through the crowd of drunken sex tourists. Seeing his chance, as a stag party went by and obscured the view from Lilac, he crossed the street and slipped around the corner onto Soi 23, moving in the opposite direction to his hotel.

Out of sight from Soi Cowboy, he picked up his pace to a sprint. Luckily he was still relatively fit, but the humidity of the Bangkok night made him feel as if he was carrying a horse. Unsure of why the two men would take his card, he pulled his phone from his pocket and tried to search his contacts, while still maintaining his fast pace. All he knew was that he had to get to the hotel before the two men. He had to get to Liz.

Fortunately she was his last dialled number. He hit the number displayed on his 'recent's' list, still sprinting in the direction of the hotel, choosing to run on the road and dodge the taxi's and tuk-tuks, rather than weave through the mass of people crowding the pavement.

The call went to voicemail. 'Damn!' He shut it off and dialled again, still running as fast as he could. He could see the hotel some 200 metres away, but it seemed like a mile as his progress was hampered by the impossible traffic.

'Shit! Voicemail again!' he shouted. 'Answer the phone, Liz, please!' he pleaded, dialling again as he entered the lower lobby of the hotel at street level.

There was no lift waiting, so Sean pressed the lift button repeatedly until the doors finally opened. Out of breath he barged into the lift and pressed the button for level fifteen and then 'door close' as quickly as he could, shaking with impatience at the slowness of the operation. Just as the doors were closing, he caught a brief glimpse of the two men he had seen outside Lilac, as they were getting out of a white sedan in the hotel driveway. His heart pounded against his chest, as he pleaded for the lift to hurry up.

Finally, the lift started to move upwards, but its journey was cut short when it stopped on the main lobby level. Exasperated by the delay, Sean caught sight of a group of young white men, with Thai girls in tow, making to enter the lift. They were making a lot of noise and were clearly drunk.

As the first of the drunken young men stepped into the lift, shouting back to his friends in German, Sean pushed him out forcefully and shouted, 'Fuck off!' and pressed the door close button. Stunned by the sudden violence, the group of young Germans stepped back, but as the doors were closing the man that Sean had pushed put his leg out to stop the door.

'You fuck off!' he said in English, with a German accent.

Without thinking, Sean instantly reacted by swinging his leg forward and kicking the man firmly in the kneecap, causing the German to shriek with pain and withdraw his leg. As the injured German's friend ran forward to accost Sean, the lift doors closed in front of him.

The wait for the lift to climb fifteen floors was agonising, as Sean knew that the two men would be at the hotel's reception getting his room number and he would have, at best, two minutes to get Liz and get out. When the lift finally reached the fifteenth floor, he almost ripped the doors open to get out, before sprinting around the corner and banging on the door of his room. 'Liz, Liz,' he shouted.

It seemed like ten minutes, but was actually only twenty seconds, when the bolt finally clicked on the door. Allowing Sean to rush in, pushing Liz back as he did.

'Sean, what's up? What's going on?' Liz said, wiping sleep from her eyes.

'Grab what you can – passports, money credit cards and laptops – and let's go.' Sean said, in a panicked tone.

'What? Why? I'm not dressed,' Liz stumbled backwards, protesting as he ran into the room.

Sean grabbed a pair of Liz's jeans and a t-shirt, pulled the two laptops and passports from the safe and stuffed them into a small backpack. 'You can get changed on the stairs,' he said, pulling her out of the door, still dressed in her silk pyjamas.

Waking up quickly, Liz stood her ground. 'Sean, no. I'm not going anywhere until you tell me what's going on.'

'Liz, this isn't a game. Come on, I'll explain later,' he said in a firm tone, glaring into her eyes.

Sean didn't know whether it was the seriousness in his tone, or just blind faith from Liz, but she suddenly took his hand and said. 'Okay. Let's go.'

Thankful that she understood, he guided Liz swiftly across the corridor and into the stairwell. Once they were on the landing, the soft-close door shut slowly and silently. Frustrated by the speed of its action, Sean turned to push it closed, but his efforts were fruitless, the hydraulic piston easily resisting his strength.

Just before it finally closed, the hotel lift chimed its arrival on the fifteenth floor. As Sean squinted through the closing crack between the door and frame, he caught sight of the two young men he had seen on Soi Cowboy earlier, moving quickly out of the lift and striding towards the room he and Liz had just vacated. The last thing he saw, before the door to the stairway slid silently to a close, was one of the men pull a black pistol from a holster, hidden beneath his jacket. Panic surged through his body. *Are they here to kill us?* he thought, terrified by the possibility.

Turning quickly to Liz, he put his finger to his lips, then pointed down the stairs, intimating that they should quietly move down, without mentioning the gun that he had seen.

They took the first flight slowly, trying not to make any noise, then nerves forced Sean to increase the pace, the sight of the young man going to their room with a pistol drawn etched onto his mind. Soon they were moving as quickly as they could, jumping two stairs at a time. Liz didn't seem to mind that she had bare feet and this helped keep the noise level down, but Sean's shoes clattered against the bare concrete, echoing the sound right through the stairwell.

When Sean and Liz had covered five floors, they heard the door swing open above them, frightening them into standing still and trying to conceal the sound of their heavy breathing. But as the footsteps above them hit the landing that they had left earlier, it forced them to run again. This time without care for the noise they made.

The two sets of footsteps above seemed to be gaining ground on them, as they clattered heavily against the concrete steps. Sean visualised the two men: they looked like soldiers; were physically fit and strong. He tried to run faster, but Liz was at full pelt and he wasn't about to leave her behind. As the floors whizzed by quickly, soon they were at the fifth floor and footsteps behind were now only two floors away. Somehow, they had gained three floors and would soon be close enough to see them, *or even shoot at them*, Sean thought macabrely.

Making a quick decision at the third floor, Sean pulled Liz through the exit and into a wide lobby. It was as he remembered from his walk around the hotel in the morning. The third floor was a banqueting floor and it was empty, but there was a huge spiral staircase, which swept down from it, through the second floor restaurant and down to the main lobby.

Having only descended down the first few stairs, Liz and Sean caught a glimpse of the two armed men, bursting onto the banqueting floor landing. Both had pistols drawn and Liz saw them for the first time. Rather than panic, she seemed to speed up, finding extra strength and they made it to the top of the second flight of stairs before the two men reached the top of the first flight.

The two groups were in clear view of each other now, as Sean held his breath and hoped his gamble had worked. Without looking back, he and Liz carried on down the stairs as quickly as they could.

The sight of the two guests sprinting down the stairs, one dressed in pyjamas, both sweating profusely and panting hard, brought two of the staff out from behind the long reception desk. The two reception staff were quickly joined by a security guard and then the hotel concierge. 'What's wrong?' a female receptionist asked in English.

Liz and Sean instinctively turned back towards the stairs, where the two armed men would be if they had followed, but nobody came.

Breathing a sigh of relief, Sean realised that his gamble, that the men would not want to be seen chasing them into a lobby filled with people and security cameras, had paid off. But he knew the respite was temporary; they would be waiting in the shadows for them to step out of the hotel.

'It's nothing; we were just playing a lovers' game,' Liz lied to the receptionist.

The assembled staff laughed nervously. They knew that there was more to this than just some silly game, but if that is what the guest said, then they must go along with it.

'Do you mind if we sit down?' she spoke again in Thai, this time directly to the receptionist.

As they were guided to a chesterfield sofa in the centre of the lobby and given two glasses of water, Liz thanked the receptionist, but made it clear they wanted some privacy to talk.

Sean explained in detail what had happened on his visit to Soi Cowboy and apologised repeatedly for getting Liz into such a dangerous situation. He stared into her dark eyes, hoping that his actions hadn't ruined their budding relationship. Liz listened carefully, nodding and reassuring Sean that it wasn't his fault and noting that it was she who had forced her way into this investigation.

'I think I should call my uncle,' she said quietly, when Sean had finished.

Sean nodded his agreement, before Liz made a call to her uncle, which lasted no longer than two minutes. He had no idea what had been said, as the conversation was in Korean, but Liz assured him that it would be alright, and he trusted her completely.

Exhausted and scared, they held hands tightly on the fake Chesterfield sofa in the lobby of the Grand hotel, until, thirty minutes later, a familiar car pulled up outside and Liz's uncle walked into the lobby, followed quickly by a bulky bodyguard.

Chapter 7

The drive from Bangkok to Hua Hin took approximately two hours. Liz and Sean were huddled together on the back seat of the car, while Liz's Uncle sat in the front passenger seat. The car, driven by the bodyguard, sped quickly through the deserted streets, until they arrived at the beach house belonging to Liz's uncle.

Using the time on the way down to explain what had happened, Liz addressed her uncle affectionately as *Sam-chon*, the informal Korean for uncle, but told Sean to address him as Mr Woo. Sean would have guessed that he was in his mid-to late fifties. He was no more than 5'5" and of very slight build, but he hopped around athletically and seemed to have a lot of energy. As they pulled onto the driveway, Liz told Sean that he was her favourite uncle, because he had always been rebellious and didn't like to conform to the strict Korean cultural norms. 'Which is why he was sent to Thailand to run the family business here,' she said quietly.

True to form, the first time Sean addressed him as Mr Woo, he laughed and said. 'Please, call me Bill; everybody else does.'

Bill's beach house turned out to be a huge Italianate mansion, nestled right on the main beach at Hua Hin, the small village that was home to the summer palace of the King of Thailand. Next door to the house was an international health retreat and on the other side, another large beachfront mansion.

Somehow managing to stay awake for an hour or so, Sean and Liz decided that they were out of their depth and should just focus on enjoying the rest of their holiday. They didn't know what the events of the night meant, and to Sean's surprise, Bill had warned them against going to the Thai police. Agreeing that they would tell John the story upon their return to work and leave it for him to pass on to more suitable journalists, they finally slept, looking forward to their holiday together.

Partly relieved by their decision and partly disappointed, Sean had a strong feeling that there was far more to the story than they had uncovered and if he could dig it up, it could mean a real career boost for him. However, he was unwilling to do anything that would put Liz in danger, and if he was really honest, he had been very scared himself, worried by the experience. He concluded that it was for the best, and felt a growing excitement at the thought of spending two weeks in a tropical paradise with Liz.

Still holding Liz around her slender waist, Sean felt the velvet-soft skin of her back against his chest when he woke in the morning. Over her shoulder, he could see the azure blue water of the gulf of Thailand. When Liz awoke, a few minutes later, they made gentle, intimate love. Although it was far quieter and more considered than their previous sex, it was so intense that Sean couldn't hold back. His eyes were fixed on Liz, while their bodies intertwined, never parting, just the gentle rocking of their torsos confirming that they were actually having sexual intercourse. 'I love you,' he said, so quietly it could have gone unnoticed.

Pulling him in to her even closer, Liz whispered, 'and I love you,' in the faintest whisper.

Following a long intimate shower, Sean picked up Bill's Wi-Fi signal on his phone and scanned his emails. There was the usual pile of spam to filter out before he got to anything of interest. Gerry, the reporter covering his list while he was away, had a few queries and John also had a couple of questions about some work items. He responded to them both briefly, but when he was about to switch his phone off, another email arrived from John, which was odd as it was 2 a.m. in London.

Sean, WTF are you up to? I've just spent 6 hours with our less than happy lawyers, after they had been summarily A** f****d by BW's lawyers. I thought you said you weren't following through on the BW piece? Anyway, you're not now. Back off and I mean it. That goes for Miss Perfect Knickers as well. John

Sean immediately hit the reply button:

John, Sorry to cause you pain. Don't worry. We have well and truly backed off. Long story. We're relaxing on the beach now. Talk when we get back. Sean.

A minute later a reply came.

"We?" I don't know how you pulled that off, you lucky bastard!

Choosing not to respond, he just closed his laptop. He was a lucky bastard, he knew it, but the last thing he was about to do was discuss Liz with his, and her boss.

Making a joke of it, he told Liz that they had officially been told to back off BW, and was surprised by her response. 'Well, I guess that proves that BW was behind last night.'

'I guess it also proves that he has something to hide,' Sean said, nodding his head in agreement.

'Yes,' Liz noted, 'but it's not worth risking either of our lives for. Let's hit the beach and have some fun.'

Hua Hin beach was not as nice as Sean had anticipated: the water was a little murky and there were a lot of large jellyfish in the shallow surf. The sand itself was soft and warm, but again, it wasn't as clean as he had expected it to be. It didn't ruin their morning though and they walked hand in hand along the long beach, to the large golden Buddha on the hill at one end. There they took in the beautiful view and kissed for hours, like errant school children.

Back at the house, they shared a sumptuous lunch with Bill, had a grand siesta and then walked in the other direction along the beach, into the small town, arriving at dusk. The town was busy with shoppers buying food and trinkets at the night market. Most people were tourists, although there seemed to be a good smattering of locals eating at the various stands. The smell and the theatre of the market held Sean mesmerised, as he held onto Liz's petite hand.

Carefully assessing the market, Liz dragged Sean, who was eyeing up the various food offerings, away towards the centre of town. 'I don't want you complaining about stomach cramps for the rest of the trip,' she said smiling. After wandering the streets of the small town for a little while, they came across a seafood restaurant, perched on top a wooden pier above the harbour. 'This should be clean,' she said confidently.

The restaurant stretched right to the end of the long wooden pier, with plastic tablecloths covering plastic tables, and plastic chairs pushed underneath. It was packed to bursting point. 'A good sign,' Liz noted.

They finally found a table halfway up the pier and Liz ordered without even looking at the menu. Only minutes later, two large beers and a feast of seafood and curry arrived at the table. Sean couldn't remember a time when he'd been happier. Last night's horrors were well behind them and they were now enjoying their holiday, just like the other tourists in the restaurant around them. Liz looked stunning, dressed in a powder blue summer dress that she had borrowed from her late aunt's wardrobe. Her thick black hair was pulled back tightly away from her face, accentuating her high cheekbones. 'I really do love you,' Sean blurted out clumsily, after his third large beer. Liz blushed and giggled, then blew him a kiss across the mound of unfinished food.

Following their long lazy dinner, the lovers strolled through the small town holding hands, relaxing in the warm night air and stopping frequently to exchange kisses. Hua Hin, although small, wasn't without its sleazy area. It looked fairly low-key compared to Soi Cowboy, but they made a point of walking around, rather than through its tawdry streets.

After another hour of aimless wandering they decided to head back to Bill's house. It was still quite early and they chose to walk along the beach. When they got onto the sand, they noticed that there were no lights on the beach, making it quite dark. They were able to navigate their way by the streaks of light coming from the beachside hotels and houses, which created bright yellow stripes across the sand to the water.

It took them almost an hour to walk the two kilometres back to Bill's house, mostly due to Sean's insistence on kissing Liz every ten paces. When they approached the grand beachfront villa, the living room light was on and they could see some shadows moving around.

'Bill's still up,' Sean said.

'Good, it would be nice to have a proper chat with him. I didn't get chance last night.' Liz squeezed Sean's hand lovingly.

They took a few more paces towards the back steps, which led up to the house from the beach. Suddenly Sean saw something that made him freeze and he crouched, pulling Liz gently down with him. 'I thought I saw one of the men from last night,' he whispered.

'What? No! *Sam-chon!*' Liz exclaimed, as she stood and started to run towards the house.

Reacting quickly, Sean ran after her, catching her as she reached the steps. 'Liz, don't! If it is them, they have guns and there's nothing you can do.' He stared into her eyes in an attempt to emphasise the seriousness of his point.

Straining against his arm half-heartedly, she conceded, knowing that he was right. They quickly took up a position close to the wall, which gave them a good view into the large living area. From there, they could see one of the young attackers from the previous night: he was strutting up and down in the lounge, seemingly arguing with somebody, but their vantage point didn't allow them to see who it was, so Sean told Liz to stay still and moved quickly across the wall to get a better view.

His heart almost stopped with fear when he saw Bill, on his knees in the middle of the floor, with the other young man from the previous evening holding a pistol to his head. With his head still reeling in shock, he quickly returned to Liz. 'Run!' he said. 'Go to the town and get the police. They're holding your uncle at gunpoint.'

Initially, Liz went to stand and run towards the house, but Sean stopped her forcefully. She looked terrified and shook with fear. 'And what the hell are you going to do? Come with me,' she said, grabbing at his arm.

'I don't know,' Sean shook his head, 'but I have to at least try. Go, please. Get the police.'

Liz pulled out her phone and dialled 191, the emergency number in Thailand. 'I'm going nowhere,' she said.

Scrambling clumsily up the steps and onto the pool deck, Sean had no idea what he was going to do, but he knew that he needed to distract them, just long enough for the police to arrive. The argument inside seemed to be escalating in tempo, making Sean think that whatever he could do, he must to do it soon. Adrenalin surged through his veins like electricity: he had never felt so scared, or so alive. All of his senses were working on overdrive and time seemed to pass in slow motion.

As he got closer to the house, he could see the prone body of Bill's bodyguard, lying motionless on the floor, with a pool of blood building around his head. 'Shit!' Sean said under his breath, every instinct he possessed telling him to run, to get Liz, and to run for their lives. But Liz's favourite uncle was an innocent bystander in this mess and Sean had to try something. But what?

Suddenly an idea crossed Sean's mind. He had seen the familiar red boxes scattered around the house, but in order to get to one of them, he would need to get inside without being seen. He crept around the side of the house and checked the door: it was unlocked, but on a tight latch. With the thugs in the lounge now less than fifteen metres away, any noise would bring them out in seconds. Leaning in hard, he put his shoulder against the door, to take the pressure off the latch and turned the handle gently, gradually easing the pressure from the door, as it came open silently against his shoulder.

Suddenly, Sean could hear the conversation inside. 'Do they have a key, or will they ring the bell?' one of the two assailants asked, his English pronounced with a strong Australian accent.

Bill didn't speak.

'Stay silent if you want, pops, but it won't make any difference. I'm only letting you live now so that you can watch me put a cap in that bitch niece of yours.' The young man spoke in a dispassionate tone. It was clarification to Sean that these men intended to kill them, not just scare them off. Then he heard Bill spit at one of his attackers.

'For that I'll make you watch as I rape her first.' The Australian's tone was aggressive but controlled, his words chilling Sean to the bone, but equally firming up his resolve to act. For the first time in his life, he thought that he could kill another person.

The fire-alarm box was only three metres in front of Sean, attached to a wall in the hallway, but in order to trigger the siren, he needed something to break the glass with. He had seen a broken brick on the ground by the door and he returned to it, lifting it carefully into his hand. He wanted to just charge into the room and smash it into the heads of the two aggressors, negating any chance of their vile threat being carried out, but any attempt would be futile against the armed attackers.

Surprised by his sudden desire for violence, Sean focused on the small red box. The strike needed to be quick and accurate; he couldn't afford to miss the small glass window, as there would be no time for a second attempt. Holding his breath and leaping forward, he crashed the brick into the fire alarm, shattering the glass into small pieces.

Before the alarm sounded, Sean pivoted around athletically and leaped back out of the side door. Then the piercing sound of the alarm filled the night air, accompanied by a multitude of flashing lights on the outside of the building. Sean saw Liz's head bob up over the wall and then disappear quickly.

Only a few seconds later the Australian, who had made the threats about Liz, came crashing through the same door. Sean saw that the attacker wasn't holding a gun, but he wasn't going to take any chances with the muscular young criminal. Picking his moment carefully, he swung the half-brick down and smashed it into the top of the aggressor's skull. The dull crack as it connected would stay with Sean for a long time, then the athletic young Australian fell limp, crumpling to the ground, as if he had been turned off by a switch.

The sickly sound didn't go unnoticed by his accomplice. 'Stevo?' Sean heard the shout above the alarm.

With the second man approaching quickly, Sean prepared to hit him in the same way as the first. As the young gunman reached the door, Sean steadied himself for the attack, knowing that this man would be holding a pistol, knowing that his strike needed to be true and quick, thus giving the assailant no time to take aim and pull the trigger.

When the second thug stepped out of the door, gripping the pistol in his right hand, Sean sprang forward aiming his strike. But as he lunged, two piercing bangs shattered through the air, almost bursting his eardrums. He fell to the ground, having only scuffed the shoulder of the attacker, landing heavily on top of the first assailant, with a chilling thud and waited for the pain from the bullets to bite. Thoughts of Liz immediately filled his head and he cursed himself for letting her down.

Regardless of his wounds, the rape threat to Liz made by the savage attacker filled Sean with a newly found will to fight, and he pushed himself up to carry on. As he did, the second attacker collapsed on top of him and Sean saw that most of the thug's head had been blown away by the shots, and he felt sticky hot blood running down onto his back. Confused, he twisted his body, craning his neck to see what had happened, just as Bill was lowering the smoking pistol to his side.

Chapter 8

Sean, Liz and Bill were hunched over the dead body of Bill's bodyguard. 'He was my closest friend,' Bill said emotionally, looking at the corpse. 'And he had three children,' he added, as Liz put her arm on his shoulder to console him.

'I will find who is responsible for this if it's the last thing I do,' Bill said.

'I think we have some idea,' Sean responded. 'It must be something to do with our investigation into Barker-Willet. Whether he's involved personally, who knows, but there's something they are obviously desperate to hide.'

'Then we need to find what that is and bring these people to justice,' Bill said angrily. 'Otherwise, this is just another murder in Thailand that will be put down to people-trafficking, or drugs.'

The sound of sirens broke the silence. 'You need to go. I'll deal with the Thai police.' Bill said quickly.

'No, you need witnesses,' Liz said.

'In England maybe; in Thailand, I need money. Now go!' Bill's voice was unusually stern, letting Liz know that he meant it.

'Where do we go?' Liz said shrugging.

'For tonight, just jump over the wall and sleep on the sun

73

loungers in the health place next door. At this time, most people will have already gone to bed there and the security guards will just think you are romantic lovers. In the morning take the train to Surat Thani, then take a boat to Koh Samui. From there you can get an international flight out of Thailand. I don't think the Thai police will be looking for you, but best not to take the risk of going through Bangkok.' Bill stood and walked over to a safe that was hidden behind a picture, opened it and took out a large pile of US$ banknotes and handed them to Sean. 'Take this. You may need it. Pay with cash until you are out of Thailand.'

Sean quickly gathered their things and placed them in the same small backpack they had escaped Bangkok with. 'Thank you, Bill,' he said shaking Bill's hand firmly. Before she and Sean ran out of the rear door, Liz hugged her favourite uncle tightly and told him that she loved him.

Scaling the wall was easy and only seconds later they heard the police cars skidding to a halt on the driveway outside Bill's house. Liz explained to Sean that the place was a health retreat where people came to lose weight, exercise or just generally be healthy for a week. As a result, the guests were usually in bed exhausted by ten o'clock. 'So the grounds should be deserted,' she said.

They moved further into the property, tiptoeing carefully past a large Thai pavilion, where the complex then opened up to reveal a huge square swimming pool surrounded by sun loungers. They skirted the pool, choosing not to lie in such an obvious place. The small restaurant on the other side of the pool was long since closed, and they worked their way through the wooden tables and chairs to the other side. Against the far edge of the property, two sun loungers overlooked the sea from a quiet hidden corner of the courtyard.

'Perfect,' Sean said, and jumped down to the small area where the sun loungers were. He pulled the two beds together quietly and they huddled up closely, watching the waves break on the beach. 'Your family don't do things by halves, do they?' he said, as he counted the US$30,000 note bundle handed to him by Bill. During the night, they saw a security guard twice, but as Bill said, he just ignored them, obviously assuming that they were guests.

When dawn broke, the resort came to life, with guests taking group Thai Chi lessons on the beach and staff setting up for breakfast in the small poolside restaurant. Sean squinted at two of the guests bending from side to side on the beach in front of them. 'Is that . . .?' he said pointing.

'Probably,' Liz nodded, acknowledging that she had also seen the two Hollywood film stars. 'This place does attract those types. It's hideously expensive, even by Western standards, but that does mean it's a place that the Thai police would think twice before they came blundering into. We'd better get going.'

White crime scene tents blocked any view of the activities in Bill's place, when they walked back out onto the beach, and the frenetic scene was alive with people. Seeing this, Sean and Liz moved on quickly, making their way towards the train station.

'I feel like I've been here before,' Sean said, following the twenty minute walk to the ornate station building. Its steep red roof and cream panelled walls stood out against the dingy new buildings of Hua Hin.

'I assume you've seen *The Killing Fields* then,' Liz said smiling.

'Yes, but that was Cambodia, wasn't it?' he said frowning.

Liz giggled. 'Well, the story was based in Cambodia, yes, but I think they try not to make films in war zones, so they used Thailand. This train station was actually a Phnom Penh hotel in the film. Beautiful, isn't it?'

The train journey to Surat Thani took five hours and, as they didn't want to stand out from other backpackers on the train, they decided to buy third-class tickets only. Once on the train, however, they realised that backpackers travelled first-class in Thailand and the third-class carriage was basic, to say the least. Wooden benches with vertical backs, like church pews, faced each other, leaving just enough room to fit people in between them. The windows were permanently wedged open, as there was no air-conditioning and all types of flying insects hurtled into the faces of the unwitting passengers. In all, it was a very unpleasant trip, made worse by the constant stops, where local people selling fish on a stick and other indescribable treats, entered the carriage, shouting in Thai to announce their wares. Vowing that he would never criticise British rail operators again, Sean jumped down onto the platform, feeling like he had endured ten rounds with Muhammad Ali. His back was close to seizing and his legs were numb.

Surat Thani was a welcome sight, although the dingy town, once the gateway to the booming tourist island of Koh Samui, had declined rapidly since the airport had opened on the island. There were still a few boats heading over to Samui, bobbing around against their moorings, in a dirty river close to the town centre. Liz and Sean chose to take the 'express boat' and almost immediately regretted it when they were directed to an aging wooden boat that could best be described as a Thames river barge, built in the nineteenth century. As the ill-equipped boat hit open waters, they realised that their initial instinct had been a good one. The short crossing was meant to take only two hours, but that time passed without any sight of land. Then three hours passed, then four. It was only when the crew disappeared and returned wearing life jackets that Sean became really concerned, particularly when he looked for jackets for him and Liz and couldn't find any.

As Liz threw up over the side of the boat, Sean held her tightly against the side rail, comforting her with his arm. Each time the decrepit old barge crossed a swell, it creaked as though it would break in two and Sean winced, mentally holding it together. Eventually, the rough seas broke as Koh Samui came into sight and its land mass blocked the large swells of the Gulf of Thailand. When they finally docked on the wooden jetty in Nathon, the capital of the small island, they were exhausted, ill and annoyed. But at least it was still only early in the evening and they would have plenty of time to get a flight out of Thailand, without needing to stay overnight.

Before taking a cab to the airport, they decided that they should eat, having gone without food all day. Quickly seeking out a nice looking restaurant on the seafront, they took a table on the pavement outside. A free Wi-Fi sign swung loosely from a ceiling fan and Liz pulled out her phone, using the service to scan her email. The first email was from her mother:

Liz, I hope you are okay? Your uncle has been arrested and charged with murder. You must get out of Thailand as soon as possible; the Thai police are looking for you. Apparently, they were tipped off that you were at the house. If you can avoid using your own passports it would be wise, but if not, just use them and get out. If you get into trouble call the British embassy. Failing that the Korean Embassy.

Love you and take care
Mum

Liz typed a quick reply.

Mum, we're fine. Uncle didn't murder anyone. We were there. Liz xx

Almost immediately she received a response.

Liz, I'm so relieved that you are okay. We know your uncle didn't murder anyone, but we will have to work our way through the Thai legal process, which usually means a bribe.

Don't worry about him, we will fix it. Get yourself out of
Thailand now and turn off your phone. Don't contact me again
until you are out of Thailand unless it's an emergency. Mum
x

'The police are looking for us,' Liz said in a matter of fact way.
'Shit!' Sean said. 'What now?'

'We should get to the airport as quickly as possible, unless you
know a way to get fake passports in Koh Samui?' Liz was crying
as she spoke and Sean moved over to comfort her. 'Bill's been
arrested for murder,' she said quietly into his ear. 'What have we
done?'

'Liz, we've done nothing. We're just dealing with some very bad
people,' Sean said, strengthening a little, knowing that Liz needed
him.

Liz sniffed and wiped a tear from here cheek.

'Wait here a second,' he said, as he stood and approached
two tourists that were sitting on a couch sipping water. The
two unsuspecting tourists looked like hippies, but were probably
just backpackers who had gone a little overboard with their
uniform.

After speaking to the two hippies, Sean returned to Liz and
felt inside the backpack for a while, then quickly stuffed some
money into his pocket. Liz went to speak, but he put his finger
to his lips to hush her and winked. Before moving back to the
table where the backpackers were sitting and making a quick
exchange. Seconds later he returned to Liz. 'Let's go,' he said quietly.

On the way to Koh Samui's tiny airport, he explained that he
had bought two British passports from the tourists and they had
agreed not to report them stolen for three days.

'Smart boy,' Liz nodded, 'but we don't look anything like them.
She's white for one,' Liz laughed.

'I know, but it is worth a try. You know, they don't look properly when you leave the country. They only check properly on arrival, and we can use our own passports when we get back to England.'

Liz shrugged. 'I guess. How much did you pay?'

'Two grand,' Sean answered nervously.

'I'd have got them for £500,' Liz said laughing.

The taxi ride to the airport took less than fifteen minutes and they wandered casually into the small terminal. The TV screen that showed departures only listed three flights left for the day: Bangkok, Kuala Lumpur or Melbourne, via Singapore. 'Shit!' Sean said. 'No UK flights today.'

Studying the board carefully, Liz said, 'Let's go to Melbourne. At least it's out of Asia and the police aren't corrupt.'

'Makes sense. I've got friends in Melbourne,' Sean said, looking for the sales desk for Virgin Pacific airways. The flight wasn't full, so they got two seats in economy, and the sales assistant said that they would have the whole row to themselves, so they should be able to get some sleep. Sean paid cash and re-joined Liz with the boarding passes. As they had no luggage, the sales desk had been able to print the boarding passes straight off, avoiding at least one level of passport checks.

'We should go through Customs when the queue is longest; they'll be in a hurry trying to get people through and won't look so hard,' Liz said, studying her new passport. Julie Wiggins, the real owner of the passport, was twenty-eight, and the only similarity to Liz in the photo was that she had dark hair. 'Have you seen *The Bangkok Hilton* with Nicole Kidman?' she asked Sean, shivering with fear.

'Yes, where she gets thrown in a Thai prison after having drugs planted on her.' He laughed. 'I don't know why you're mentioning that though. We're not even in Bangkok.' He winked and pulled her close to him, reassuring her. 'We'll be okay. Just look straight ahead,' he said confidently, belying his true level of anxiety.

The queue for security started to build up about one and a

half hours before the flight was due to leave. 'Okay, let's do it,' Liz said, putting down her drink.

As they stood, four policemen entered the hall, searching around, looking for something. Liz froze. The policemen were carrying pictures of two people, but she couldn't make them out. Noticing the same, Sean tugged Liz forward into the line and turned his back on the policemen, sheltering her behind his body. The queue seemed to be moving very slowly, *which is a bad sign*, Sean thought. *They must be inspecting the documents.* As they moved forward slowly, the four policemen spilt into two groups and were now making their way around the busy hall, getting closer by the second.

There were only two people in front of them now in the queue, but Sean could see that the passports were being inspected carefully. When the two people in front stepped forward, he noticed that they had Chinese passports and his heart sank. In Sean's experience, it usually meant that they would be asked questions and inspected further.

The two Chinese nationals handed over their passports to the immigration official, who took one look at them and called out to a colleague for help. Both of the officers then seemed to be looking through the passports, discussing something, while two of the policemen were now only ten metres from Sean and Liz, scanning the people around them.

In front of them, the Chinese couple were being asked questions in English, which they couldn't understand, and the two Customs officers were getting frustrated by their lack of response. Seeing this, a third officer arrived and started shouting at his fellow officials, pointing at the growing queue.

The angry third immigration officer then moved across to the booth adjacent to Liz and Sean and called them over. Sean's heart was beating fast and he was sweating badly as he handed the two British passports over to the officer, trying not to catch his eye. Without even looking at Sean or Liz, the angry official stamped the two passports and waved them through, to an audible sigh of relief from Sean, as they entered the departure lounge.

'We're not on the plane yet,' Liz said, looking at the two policemen walking through the staff entrance and into the departure hall.

The departure lounge at Koh Samui airport was small, offering little opportunity to hide, and with over forty minutes until boarding, Sean believed that they were certain to be caught. 'We have to split up,' Liz said quickly. 'They're looking for two people together. The Thai police are lazy; they won't look properly.'

'Okay, but stay where I can see you. I'm going to buy a baseball cap to cover my head. You should too,' Sean said.

'That's good. Cover up that blonde mop of yours. I don't need one: half the girls in here look like me,' Liz replied. There were lots of girls of Asian origin, with long straight dark hair and light brown skin tone. Liz was right. Sean nodded his agreement and went into the gift shop, as Liz moved to an empty group of seats and lay down, showing only half of her face.

A couple of minutes later, Sean emerged with an 'I Love Samui' baseball cap pulled low onto his head. He chose a group of seats on the opposite side of the hall to Liz, but ensured she was in sight. When he pulled the new cap over his eyes, he left a big enough gap to see out across the room to Liz and to keep an eye on the policemen.

The two policemen were now only a couple of metres from Liz, looking at people, then at the photo and were steadily making their way around the room. One of them stepped up behind Liz, seemingly looking over her shoulder at a couple on the bench opposite. The short policeman studied the photo in his hand then shook his head and moved on. *He didn't even look at Liz,* Sean thought. The second policeman had already moved across to another row, performing the same ritual: looking at people and then the photo, shaking his head and moving on.

Sean noticed that they were only looking at the photo for reference when they saw a couple. Liz had been right again: they were safer apart. But Sean still stood out; at six feet two, with a mop of long blonde hair. As one of the policemen turned, Sean got a glimpse of the photo that they were using. Even at the twenty or so meters away that the policeman stood, it was clear that the picture was of him and Liz.

Feeling sure that he would get caught, Sean weighed up his position. The problem was that he was just too obvious and if he did get caught, they would know that Liz was here too. That would send them into overdrive and they would go back and search everybody, until they found her. He slipped off the seat and back into the small gift shop, realising that he couldn't cross the hall to where Liz was without making it obvious. The shop assistant's jacket was on the back of the seat, as it had been before, with the security tag attached by a small bulldog clip, while the assistant helped a customer with an 'I love Samui' t-shirt.

Sean made his move and quickly unclipped the security tag, tucking it into his pocket. The staff exit was close to the shop and from what he had seen of the earlier comings and goings, it led directly to the check-in hall. Liz was now sitting up, watching him and looking scared. Seeing her fear, he thought about sitting down again and taking his chances, but knew he couldn't. It was either just him getting caught, or both of them and he had to give her the best chance to get away.

Signalling Liz to call him, Sean immediately slipped around the side of the gift shop, pulled the security tag from his pocket and swiped it through the lock. The gate door opened automatically and he walked quickly through into the check-in hall, somehow unnoticed *Thai security is somewhat less than it should be*, he thought. Without delaying, he walked straight out of the airport, noting that two of the policemen, who had been there earlier, were still checking faces against a picture. On the pavement outside, he saw a tuk-tuk and jumped in.

'Where to, boss?' The driver said in a chirpy tone.

Sean felt dazed. 'I don't know, anywhere,' he said, his mind racing.

'Chaweng,' the driver said and started to move before Sean could respond.

Reaching inside his backpack, Sean turned on his phone. As he did, he felt something in the pack and realised that he had Liz's real passport, her purse and her laptop. The cash from her uncle creased against his hand and a bolt of guilt ran through him, knowing that Liz would have to enter Australia on a false passport, ensuring that she would almost certainly be detained. Better that than charged with murder in Thailand: an offence which he was sure carried the death penalty.

His phone rang almost immediately. 'Liz,' he said.

'What the fuck, Sean?' she said, whispering.

Sean explained that he was certain that he would get caught, and equally that would ensure that she did also. Remaining quiet while he explained, Liz said, 'I'm coming out.'

'No, go. Get out of here. I'm okay. I'll make it,' he said firmly.

There was a long pause on the line, while Liz thought. 'Okay, I love you. I'll call you from Singapore. Stay safe and turn off your phone for three hours, then turn it on until I call you.'

'I love you too,' Sean said, as he hung up.

Chapter 9

Liz decided against telling the Australian immigration officer that her passport had been stolen on the plane, considering that they would almost certainly check with the Thai authorities and as she hadn't cleared immigration there, it could lead to a multitude of problems. Until she cleared Australian immigration, she was at risk of being returned to Thailand, where the police would be waiting for her.

If she was caught trying to enter Australia using the false passport Sean had bought, she thought it likely that she would be detained in Australia. That would mean entering Australian jurisdiction and would make it difficult for the Thai police to get to her. As far as she was aware Australia didn't have an extradition treaty with Thailand. She hoped she was right.

She spoke to Sean for as long as she dared from Singapore. He sounded scared but okay, and she couldn't afford to compromise his location by using his phone any more. It was painful to be so brief, but it was important. He had found a hotel in Chaweng on Koh Samui, and was thinking about the best way to escape

Thailand. For future communication, they had both created new Gmail accounts that would be untraceable, and Sean had agreed to turn off his phone unless it was an emergency, and use only public computer terminals to send messages.

The Australian immigration hall was packed to bursting point as Liz joined the back of the long snaking queue and tried to tame her nerves, knowing that she needed to look completely at ease when she got to the front. The line moved quickly through the twenty or so immigration booths and she was approaching the desk far quicker than she had anticipated, but that was good: it gave her less time to think about the consequences of capture.

The immigration officer looked like he was about thirty years old, as he smiled at people in the line, checking their passports and processing them very quickly. It gave Liz a small confidence boost, as he processed somebody so quickly, he surely couldn't have made any real check.

As Liz stood on the painted line in the floor, which meant it was her turn next, the young immigration officer looked up and made a comment to his colleague. When he called Liz forward she could sense his eyes on her and although she couldn't be sure, she thought he was checking out her body more than her face. She walked forward and presented the false passport, fighting her fraying nerves with every ounce of effort she could muster.

The young immigration officer put the information page face down into his scanner and waited. His eyes were fixed on Liz's cleavage, rather than her face, so she subtly nudged one of her dress straps from her shoulder, exposing a little more of her breast, than she would normally consider decent.

Without lifting his head, the immigration officer stamped her passport and passed it back to her. 'Welcome to Australia,' he said, still eyeing her breasts.

Liz quickly moved on and entered the baggage claim hall. It was even more packed and chaotic than the immigration hall. The queue of people, with their freshly claimed suitcases, stretched around two carousels and must have contained at least 300 travellers. As she didn't check in any luggage, Liz simply joined the back of the long queue.

A Customs officer with a dog was making her way down the line slowly. She stopped to talk to each group of people, asked a few questions, let the dog sniff the luggage and inspected the Customs declaration, writing on it as she did.

When she reached Liz, she spoke politely. 'No luggage, madam?'

Liz shook her head. 'No, my boyfriend is on a later flight. He has it all.'

The uniformed officer laughed. 'Nice boyfriend. Could I see your Customs declaration please?'

Liz passed her the faded orange form quickly, keeping her passport in her hand and the officer scrutinised the form briefly, then said. 'Okay, please go over to the right-hand side and through the door marked "A".'

'Damn!' Liz cursed herself for not thinking. Of course she would look suspicious with no luggage. *I should've bought a bag in Singapore.* She didn't move.

'It's over there,' the customs officer said, pointing to a pair of large sliding doors with the letter A emblazoned on a sign above them.

'Thanks,' Liz said nervously, as she stepped out of the long line.

As if stepping to her death, Liz moved cautiously towards the door, looking for a way to escape. *Perhaps just into the toilet?* No, she would still face the same issue when she came out. The female Customs officer had written something on her declaration, which was clearly in some kind of code and probably meant she was in for a full body examination. But that was the least of her worries: it would also mean that they would almost certainly inspect her passport and it would be a far more thorough check than the previous cursory glance.

It didn't take her long to come to the conclusion that she had no choice: she would be caught if she did something stupid and ran, and she would be caught in Customs when they inspected her.

At least the latter would give her more dignity and she would probably get a better hearing than she would if she were caught trying to run back through immigration . . . the way Sean had in Thailand. Australia wasn't Thailand and she knew that she would be picked up in seconds. *At least I'm on Australian soil and they can't send me back to Thailand*, she thought, hoping again that she was right.

Door A had no queue in front of it and was guarded by a lone male Customs officer. It looked relatively inconspicuous, concealed in the corner of the large hall, well away from the main inspection line. Liz closed her eyes in dread, thinking about what waited for her on the other side.

She approached the Customs officer with a bowed head and handed the declaration to him quickly.

'Straight through, please,' he said, after glancing at the card.

Trembling with nervousness, Liz stepped towards the sliding double doors. They opened in front of her with a swishing sound, only to reveal a bluestone wall and a short corridor to her left, leading to an identical set of doors. She paced slowly towards them, preparing herself for the ordeal to come.

The doors opened with the same swishing noise as the previous set and Liz was instantly hit with a wall of noise: not the noise of a Customs examination hall, but the cacophonic noise made by hundreds of people going about their business. Cups chinked against saucers, cutlery banged against plates and people shouted, laughed and cried.

Liz stepped through the double doors and straight into the arrivals hall of Melbourne's Tullamarine airport. As a sense of relief surged through her body, she started to cry, trembling as she did. 'Safety at last,' she said to herself.

Out of the corner of her eye, she saw a uniformed chauffeur holding up a sign with her name on it and the symbol of the Crown Towers Hotel. 'Thanks, Mum. I thought I'd have to walk,' she said quietly.

The sumptuous room that her mother had arranged at Crown Towers was better than she could have hoped for. After so many years in London, trying to make it on her own, she had almost forgotten the lavish lifestyle she had grown up with. But all the luxury did nothing to diminish the anxiety she felt for Sean and her uncle. It was now 10 a.m. in Melbourne, which meant it was 6 a.m. in Thailand. She wanted to call Sean, but dare not. So she settled for writing him a short email. When she logged in to her new Gmail account using her phone, she was surprised that she had already received a note from Sean, sent the night before:

Liz,

It was so nice to speak to you in Singapore and know that you're safe. I sent your passport by express courier after we spoke. Apparently it will be with you tomorrow. Fast, eh!

I'm heading to bed now. No clue what I'll do in the morning. You got any smart ideas?

All my love.

Sean.

Liz typed her reply:

Sean,

I can't think of anything now, but my family have a lot of contacts throughout Asia and they're pretty resourceful. I'm sure we'll come up with something. I think the best thing to do is to sit tight and stay where you are. I don't think they will expect you to be in a hotel in Samui.

I'm safely in the hotel in Melbourne now. I won't tell you how lovely my room is, but I can't wait for you to get here so we can give this huge bed a workout!

Love you

Liz xxx

The window of her room looked out over the Yarra River and she gazed at its brown water, moving quickly under a low road bridge, which led to the centre of the city. It was the height of summer in Australia and the temperature was set to hit forty-four degrees centigrade later in the day, according to the weather forecast left on the huge bed in Liz's room.

The riverside boulevard below the hotel bustled with people: buskers were setting up for the day, and the long line of cafés were full of people sipping coffee, sheltered from the sun's glare by huge canvas awnings. The hotel was part of an enormous casino and entertainment complex, nestled against the South Bank of the river. Opposite, on other side of the river, large skyscrapers dominated the skyline of the downtown area of Melbourne, their sides blurred by the heat haze from the stifling dry heat of the Australian summer.

Never having been to Melbourne before, Liz decided to go out for a walk. She really needed to buy some clothes, as her borrowed powder blue dress was starting to look somewhat tatty, and her underwear . . . well. A $10,000 cash deposit had been arranged by her mother with the hotel. It was way more than she needed, but very like her family. Taking a few hundred dollars from the small pile of Australian dollar notes, she locked the rest in the room safe.

At the concierge desk, she enquired where the best shopping was to be found and then made her way over a footbridge and under Flinders Street train station, emerging in the city. She soon found some casual clothes to wear that were suitable for the sweltering temperatures and kept on a pair of khaki shorts, white singlet and flip-flops, making her indistinguishable from most of the people on Swanston Street.

The heat was already oppressive, but dry heat didn't make her sweat the same way cooler humid climates could. The warm steady wind made her feel as if she was standing in front of a warm hairdryer. After she had made a few more purchases and had a large juice drink, she drifted through the town centre aimlessly, her mind switching to Sean and her uncle.

At the top end of Swanston Street, a busy street filled with trams, shoppers and students, she noticed a large sandstone building, with a brass plaque announcing it as the Victorian State Library. The fruitless search of the UK Government databases suddenly came back into her head and she bounced up the steps clutching her shopping bags, walking swiftly into the grand marble lobby of the library building.

The signposts indicated that the reference section was at the rear of the building, on the ground floor. The reference room itself was a spectacular circular room, with a high ornate ceiling, carved wooden panels and marble pillars. An abundance of computer terminals were lined up on desks throughout the room and the paper reference section was behind huge glass frameless screens, at the back of the room.

The area was busy but not full, and Liz pulled up a seat at one of the vacant terminals. She quickly found her way around the system, then clicked on 'Births, Deaths and Marriages: Victoria.' She entered Charles Barker-Willet into the search criterion, bringing two entries onto the screen:

Birth: Essenden, 1943
Marriage: Melbourne, 1998

There was no death record. Did that mean that he was still alive? Also, there was no record of another Charles Barker-Willet. What did that mean?

Liz clicked on the first record. It showed the birth of Charles Barker-Willet during the Second World War, to Bernhard Barker and Emily Willet. Bernhard was evidently a lawyer/soldier. Then she clicked on the marriage entry. Charles Barker-Willet married Nam Chattawat, a Thai national, born on 27 May, 1973. The wedding had taken place in the Melbourne Town Hall Registry

Office on 6 June 1998. There was no record of any children.

Switching approach she searched an address site for 'Charles Barker-Willet, Melbourne', but wasn't surprised when nothing came up. Most people concealed their contact details if possible.

The ASIC, Australian Securities and Investments Commission, website was her next hope. As she entered a director's information search for the same name, three proprietary companies appeared, but to obtain the information she needed to pay $18. 'Shit!' she cursed, not having her credit cards with her.

'Can I help?' a male student working on the screen next to her turned around.

Liz blushed at her audible expletive. 'Oh, I forgot my credit card and need to do a company search.' She thought quickly. 'I don't suppose you could do it for me, and I'll pay you 100 bucks?' she said, then added. 'It only costs $18.'

The student thought about it for a while, obviously trying to work out what the catch was.

'It's my job. I need to do it or I'll be fired, and they're waiting for it. I'm such an idiot!' Liz added.

'Okay,' the student said. 'What do I do?'

Liz gave him a $100 bill and took him through the process, turning away while he entered his credit card details. Within seconds he had the details on his screen. 'Could you print that for me?' she asked smiling.

The paper soon came out from the printer and Liz studied its details:

```
Mr Charles Barker-Willet
DOB: 13/04/1943
Address    11 Ballard St
           Albert Park
           Victoria
           3206
```

Chapter 10

Totally exhausted, but unable to sleep, Sean rose early and sent an email to Liz, letting her know that he was okay, then he just lay by the hotel pool, watching the small beachfront resort slowly come to life. How he wished that he could be just like the other tourists, happily welcoming a new day in paradise. The realisation that he was wanted by the police, probably for murder, had hit him hard and left him rueing the day that he had ever set eyes upon Barker-Willet. His woes were compounded by the fact that he had no idea where to start when it came to finding an illicit way to sneak out of Thailand.

At first, he considered going to the British Embassy in Bangkok. Perhaps there he could explain what had happened and they could get him out under a diplomatic protection order? But why would they do that? He wasn't some errant royal, caught with his pants down. If every time a Briton was arrested abroad the British Embassy smuggled them out of the country, Britain would soon lose diplomatic relations around the world. Maybe if he had irrefutable proof of what happened, then he might have a chance with the embassy, but he didn't; he had nothing.

In her email, Liz suggested that he sit tight and wait for her family and that would be his back-up plan, but he wanted to get out of Thailand as soon as possible. Just sitting around, waiting to be captured by the police – or worse still, Barker-Willet's men – wasn't something he was prepared to contemplate.

The way Sean saw it, he had two things: a fake passport that would not be reported stolen for two days, but one that he had used to clear Immigration already, making it a high risk to use; and US$26,000 or so, in cash. With that kind of money he could probably buy a fake ID and with some subtle changes to his look, he may get through immigration. *But where do I start?* he thought, banging his fist on the sun lounger. He knew that there would be people he could pay to arrange his silent exit from Thailand, but he had no idea how to find them.

Surveying the scene in front of him, as middle-class Western families played in the pool and people ordered morning cocktails from the waiters, he came to a quick conclusion. He certainly wouldn't find what he was looking for here.

Since he'd come to Thailand two days before, there was only one person that he had met that he thought might be help him: Nok, from Girl House. In her line of work she would probably come across people who operated outside the law and although the thought of going back to Soi Cowboy sent a shiver down his spine, what other option did he have? But how could he be sure that Nok wouldn't call Barker-Willet's men, or the police, as soon as she saw him? Acknowledging to himself that it was a high-risk strategy, he concluded that it was still his best chance.

Returning to his room, Sean gathered his things and checked out. If he moved quickly, he thought he could be in Bangkok by midnight. On the way out of the hotel he stopped briefly to check his email on the old computer terminal in the lobby. There was nothing more from Liz, so he typed a quick note to her:

Liz,
    Going to Bangkok. Can't think of any other way.
    Love
    Sean xx

The boat trip to Surat Thani was less eventful than the journey in the opposite direction, and it took the designated two hours on calm seas. Sean quickly found a coach that was heading to Bangkok and bought a ticket. The modern coach that he boarded seemed comfortable, so he quickly chose a seat halfway down against the window and settled himself in for the journey. That brief moment of comfort was the last he would feel for the whole nine-hour journey to Bangkok. The driver seemed to think he was in a race and that he was driving a sports car, rather than a fifty-seat passenger vehicle. Sean was amazed that they arrived in Bangkok in one piece, but was relieved when his feet finally hit the tarmac of the Bangkok bus station.

It was late, but Sean found a hotel room in the Westin Hotel, right opposite the Sheraton, on the busy Sukhumvit Road and close to Soi Cowboy. Even at such a late hour, he thought that he might need somewhere to hide, if things went wrong when he visited Nok at Girl House.

As he stepped out of the hotel onto the heaving street, he almost turned in the opposite direction to his planned destination. It would be easy to just bury his head in the sand, get drunk, and hopefully get some sleep in the luxurious hotel. But an inner drive, an urgency which he had never experienced before, drove him on and pushed him in the right direction.

At that moment he would rather have been anywhere but the seedy street where this nightmare had begun, but facing the facts, he plucked up his courage and walked out onto Sukhumit Road. It was close to midnight, the pavements were packed with tourists and the street was crammed full of tuk-tuks and taxis. Sean made his way as quickly as possible along the crowded pavement to Soi 21 and turned left. The bright lights of Soi Cowboy immediately came into view and he stopped, again plagued by second thoughts.

When he eventually found the ability to move again, he did so carefully, trying to blend in. Unable to pass himself off as a young man on a stag party, or as a normal tourist, as he was alone and sober, he swallowed his pride and made like the other category, the sex tourists, who stalked their human prey from the shadows. Moving slowly, he skirted the bars, ogling the girls, his stomach churning with revulsion, as he mimicked the behaviour of the odious beings. Lilac had a swarm of people outside, slowing the traffic and Sean looked in the other direction to avoid being spotted by the angry Mama-san, who had betrayed him to Barker-Willet's men. Further along, outside Girl House, the young girls were gathered as before, dangled like human bait for a particular kind of hunter. Wasting no time, Sean walked straight through the doors, avoiding any conversation with the girls outside.

Once inside, he didn't take a seat, or order a drink as before. Instead, he went straight to the curtain which concealed the old-fashioned till and the portly Mama-san. Looking up angrily at the disturbance, ready with some verbal rebuke, she stopped herself abruptly and changed her demeanour as she recognised Sean. 'You!' she said startled. 'I thought you'd be dead!'

'Why?' Sean asked, taken aback by the remark.

'Po, the Mama-san from Lilac, scolded me for sending you to her,' Nok laughed. 'She said that she'd fed you to the sharks.'

Sean didn't join in the laughter. 'Yes, some people tried to kill me. Do you know who the man in the photograph was, and why they tried to kill me?' Sean asked.

'I don't know. When you showed me the picture, I thought I

recognised him, but he was older and his nose and chin were different. It was his eyes: he has evil eyes and they are hard to forget.' Nok shook her head ruefully.

'Who was the man that you thought it was? I remember you took a second look.'

'He called himself David and he hung around Soi Cowboy in the early nineties, mainly at Lilac, because no other bar wanted him. He was evil to the core and had a reputation for doing unthinkable things to the youngest girls. After abusing them, he often refused to pay, just throwing them out onto the street, where they would then be beaten by their owner for bringing no money in. I had hoped he was dead,' Nok said, shivering in disgust.

Taking the opportunity, Sean showed her the picture of Chares Barker-Willet again on his phone. 'Take a close look. Is that him?'

Nok studied the photo in detail. 'I'm not sure. It could be.'

'Where did he come from?' Sean asked.

'He was British, like you. Wait here one second,' Nok said, as she stood and disappeared around the curtain.

Still trying to control his nerves, Sean waited uncomfortably behind the curtain, which separated the sexual fervour of Girl House from its business affairs. *Is she calling Barker-Willet's men?* he wondered. It was a possibility that he had considered before he came in, but riddled with indecision, he stayed rooted to the spot, like a deer caught in the headlights of a car. The simple fact was that he needed Nok and she was integral to his only plan to evade capture. Plus, something at the back of his mind told him that she could be trusted: he wasn't sure why, but there was something about her.

A few moments later she returned, accompanied by another woman, who looked about thirty years old and walked with a stiff limp. 'This is Ping, my bar manager,' Nok introduced the young woman, then took Sean's iPhone and showed her the photo of Barker-Willet.

The expression on Ping's face changed immediately and she started to hyperventilate, before Nok sat her down at the small table and massaged her shoulders, speaking softly in Thai. Finally, breathing normally again, Ping stood up, straightening her shoulders and in one move, she nodded her head and passed the phone back to Nok. Then, without uttering a word to Sean, she returned to the bar.

Puzzled by the strange episode, Sean aimed a quizzical expression at Nok.

'In 1992, Ping's mother worked as the Mama-san in Lilac, where this man was a regular. Ping was a twelve-year-old girl, who was not part of this filthy business. Her mother saved money and sent her to school, so that she could escape the horrors of this street.' Nok paused choosing her words carefully. 'Ping was sleeping in the office of Lilac one night, when this man saw her. He entered the room and raped her for three hours: in the mouth, in the vagina and in the anus. It was only after he left that her mother found her, bleeding on the floor, nearly dead. As you can see, she still limps from the experience.'

'Is it definitely him?' Sean asked, horrified by Nok's revelation.

'Yes. She will never forget that man,' Nok said, wiping a tear from her eye.

'Didn't the police do anything?' Sean asked.

Nok shrugged. 'Things that happen on Soi Cowboy don't get reported to the police.'

'That's awful,' Sean added.

'Yes, and imagine, from this rape Ping became pregnant and had a baby girl. She had to give up school and became a sex girl like the others here. This pig stole her dreams and she has never been the same since.'

'And the daughter?' Sean asked.

Nok again looked sad, and then cast her eyes towards the catwalk. 'She's there, the third girl from the left.'

Sean looked at the beautiful young girl, shaking her half-naked torso at an elderly man, clad in a bright Bermuda shirt. Then he turned back to Nok. 'He should pay for this,' he said angrily.

'Yes, but he won't; his type never do,' Nok said quietly.

During his time as a business journalist, Sean had listened many times to Western companies boasting about coming to places like Thailand, to exploit its people for cheap labour. On each occasion, the comments had repulsed him. To hear now, that the world's richest man thought that he could get away with the brutal rape of a child, just because she was poor and too afraid to tell anybody, made him boil with anger.

To think that only a few days ago, Sean had thought that Barker-Willet might be somebody to look up to; a different kind of leader, possibly somebody he could believe in. Now he hated the insidious CEO with every bone in his body.

'Well, at least we should try,' Sean said boldly. 'Could you get a lock of hair from each of them, both Ping and her daughter, and a copy of their ID? I need something that shows their date of birth.'

Nok shook her head, confused by Sean's request. 'Yes, but why?'

'I can't guarantee anything, but we may just be able to prove that he raped her, and get him sent to prison in England,' Sean said, still seething with enmity.

'Okay,' she said, nodding her head, suddenly understanding Sean's idea.

'One more thing,' Sean asked. 'I need a fake ID to get out of Thailand. The police are looking for me. Can you help?'

Nok laughed. 'Fake ID to get out of Thailand? There are easier ways. In Bangkok they're very strict at Customs, but our border with Burma is like a sieve. I know a man who can get you to Mawlamyine, in Burma. From there you can get a bus to Rangoon.

Sean was unsure. Burma? Wasn't that out of the frying pan into the fire? 'Do you mean Yangon?' he asked.

'We still like to call it Rangoon, and from there you can get a flight to London using your own ID,' Nok said, picking up on Sean's uncertainty, before she stood up and went over to Ping. The two ladies held a brief conversation, before Ping called her daughter over and the three women went into a room through a rear door in the club. Only a few minutes later, they reappeared. Nok was carrying a sealed white envelope. 'Locks of hair and copies of their ID. Good luck.'

Ping stared at Sean with tears welling in her eyes. 'Thank you,' she said sincerely and touched Sean's hand softly.

'Now, where are you staying?' Nok asked.

Again Sean hesitated. The last time he had let that information out, two men had come to kill him. But there was something about Nok which he found trustworthy. 'The Westin,' he said quietly, making sure that nobody else heard.

'Good. A man will meet you there in one hour. His name is Bank and he'll drive you to Burma. You should cross the border before dawn and be in Mawlamyine by early morning.'

'Thank you,' Sean said, putting his hands onto hers.

Chapter 11

Tuesday, 17th February. Melbourne, Australia

No. 11 Ballard Street stood out from all of the other houses in the upmarket Victorian suburb of Albert Park. It was new, modern and boasted a two-storey copper façade, angled from its corner like a huge sail. It was designed to make a statement, and to Liz it said, 'rich, confident and not afraid to show it'. She knew a little about the astronomical property prices in Melbourne from her research, so she was aware that a place like this would fetch an eye-watering sum, as it was only 100 metres from the beach and just 3 kilometres from the city centre. Clearly *this* Charles Barker-Willet wasn't living on a State pension.

A nagging feeling within her told Liz that she shouldn't be poking around anymore in Barker-Willet's affairs. Indeed, she and Sean had agreed as much, but her natural curiosity and the possibility that she may find something to help her uncle drove her on.

A wooden bench in the small park opposite the copper-fronted house, gave her a good vantage point from which to view the comings and goings. After an hour or so, a woman emerged through the huge copper door. She was of South-East-Asian origin and in her early forties. 'Nam,' Liz said to herself. Shortly after, a man came out of the house behind her, holding a walking stick. Nam turned hastily to help him down the steps from the door to the short path and out of the front gate. He was older. 'Maybe seventies or even eighties,' Liz thought. 'The details fit well, Charles and Nam Barker-Willet.'

The couple shuffled slowly along Ballard Street and past the narrow Victorian terraced bungalows. Once they had travelled a little way in front of her, Liz followed, casually looking at the ornate façades of the small houses. The Barker-Willets turned left at a major junction and onto a wide boulevard with tram tracks running down its centre, then continued walking. Keeping her distance, Liz made sure she didn't lose sight of them.

A short way along the wide street, the road curved to the right and into an area with cafés and shops. As the Barker-Willets rounded the wide curve, Liz sped up in order not to lose them. She didn't need to as they immediately took a table outside a small but busy café, which had a huge bright white awning, announcing it as the Albert Park Deli.

Avoiding the apron-clad waiters that rushed in and out of the doors, Liz managed to find a seat at a table next to the one taken by the Barker-Willets and pretended to study the menu, while eavesdropping on their conversation.

They were discussing what to have for lunch and Liz noticed that customers were required to order at the counter inside, before their food was carried out to them by one of the many waiters. Having made their decision, Nam stood and went inside to make the order, leaving Charles behind. Liz seized upon the opportunity. 'Charles Barker-Willet?' she enquired of the old man on the neighbouring table.

'Yes, that's me. Who's asking?' he replied politely, with a broad Australian twang.

'Julie Wiggins,' Liz stuck out her hand formally. 'I was wondering about your relationship with another Charles Barker-Willet, the CEO of BW Corp in London?'

The old man didn't shake her hand and immediately stopped smiling. 'Ha, as I've told your lot ten times over. I don't have a relationship with Mr Barker-Willet. I wouldn't mind his money though,' he said sarcastically.

'My lot?' Liz asked, in response to the comment.

'Journalists. That's what you are, aren't you?' he said, lifting both eyebrows knowingly.

Of course, if she could get this far so easily, so could others. Liz kicked herself. How far had other journalists gone? Bangkok? 'I've just come from Bangkok. Boonsong sends his regards,' she prodded.

The answer to her thought was instant. Other journalists hadn't gone that far. Barker-Willet suddenly looked less sure of himself and turned to look for his wife. 'I have no idea what you're talking about.' He didn't wait for her to reply, 'Young lady, you clearly have the wrong man.'

'No, you're the Charles Barker-Willet that bought a Thai tuna factory from Boonsong Wongsawat in 1995. I've checked the Thai Records Office.' She paused and looked at him, faking a puzzled face. 'What I want to know is, who is the Charles Barker-Willet that runs the company now?'

The comment agitated the old man. 'Look, yes, I bought the company from Boonsong, but it didn't work out, so I sold it,' he said, turning again to look for his wife.

'Who to?' Liz came back quickly.

'I don't recall,' he said snappily.

'I couldn't find a record of a sale between 1995 and 2000, when the company was listed. Why are you lying?' Liz pushed the point hard.

'Young lady, I suggest you drop this line of enquiry, for your own sake.' He looked up as his wife was on her way back to the table. 'That's very nice. I hope you enjoy your stay,' he said in a sudden happy tone. 'The young lady is over from England, visiting friends, dear.'

'Hi,' Liz smiled, playing along.

'Ah, nice. Better weather than England, I think.' Her Thai accent was strong and her English broken.

Without ordering food or a drink, Liz left the deli and walked up the broad street past a tram stop, until she was out of sight of the deli customers. Then she hastily doubled back, circled around the back of the Albert Park Deli and returned to her vantage point in the small park, opposite the Barker-Willets' house.

During her wait for their return, Liz thought about her brief interchange with Barker-Willet. It was clear that Charles was lying, but why? And why wouldn't he speak in front of his wife? *Maybe she was the weak link? Maybe she will tell me the truth?* Liz considered.

It was obvious to Liz that Barker-Willet was wealthy, but where did he get his money from? Her Internet searches of him had thrown up nothing and the three companies that he owned were nothing more than holding companies for rental properties, which was a common tax-avoidance scheme. *A man with enough money to buy a house like this would turn up in some kind of record. It doesn't make sense,* she thought. In her experience, all rich people left a digital trail and she was good at following it. It had been her job since leaving university and had earned her the prestige position as the head of research for a major newspaper.

After an hour or so of waiting, watching people bring their dogs into the park to chase balls and defecate on the burned grass, the two familiar bodies come around the corner onto Ballard Street. The Barker-Willets were returning home from their lunch and seemed to be in no more of a hurry than they had been on their way. Charles punched a code into the chrome keypad by the copper door and the two of them entered the house. A glimpse of the sparkling swimming pool through a glass side wall of the house shone into Liz's view. 'Very nice, but how do you pay for it, Charles?' she said under her breath.

Shortly after, the door opened again and Nam stepped out with a golden retriever straining against its lead. She walked straight across the road and into the park. Once she was around the brick building at the front of the park and out of sight of the house, Liz caught up with her.

'Oh, hello again. Fancy seeing you here,' Liz said speaking Thai.

Nam spun around sharply, obviously surprised to hear her native language being spoken. 'Oh, hello. I didn't think you were Thai. You look more like Japanese or Korean,' she said, eying Liz carefully.

'I'm Korean,' Liz answered, 'but I speak Thai. Could I talk to you briefly?' she asked.

'What about?' Nam asked suspiciously.

'Did you meet Charles in Thailand?' Liz asked.

'Yes, but we are married here. It is legal. I have papers,' she responded defensively.

'I'm not from the DIBP,' Liz said smiling, referring to the Australian Department for Immigration and Border Protection. 'Did he tell you about his business interests in Thailand?' She carried on with her questioning.

Nam looked puzzled. 'No. Why?'

'Did you know that he owned a tuna factory, for instance?' Liz persisted.

'No, why? What do you want?' Nam said angrily.

Far from being the weak link, Liz thought, Nam was the possibly stronger of the two. Barker-Willet may have lied to her, but he had been polite throughout their brief interchange. Nam's tone was defensive, even angry.

Trying a different approach, Liz pulled out her phone and showed Nam the same photo of Charles Barker-Willet that

Sean had been using. 'Do you know this man?' she asked.

As she saw the picture, Nam's eyes widened just enough for Liz to see that she did recognise him. 'No, never seen him before. Please go away. I call police.'

Realizing that she had made a mistake in thinking that she could get to Charles through Nam, Liz quickly left her alone and exited the park by the side gate, then made a pretence of walking away from the small park, but instead hid behind a car and watched as Nam hurried back to the house.

Charles and Nam argued heatedly by the large window, next to the copper door. Then Charles suddenly came out of the door, carrying his walking stick and moving more quickly now than earlier. He got into a silver BMW 5 series, started the engine and drove along the street towards the place where Liz was hiding. Taking a calculated risk, Liz came out from her hiding place and stared at him provocatively, so that he could see her. Suddenly, he slammed on the brakes and reversed to her side. 'Get in!' he said, as the window came down smoothly.

It wasn't what Liz had expected and she felt her pulse race, while she looked around hoping to see other people. She didn't dare move, or speak.

'Look, you talked to Nam. That was stupid. If you know what's good for you, get in before you get killed!' he said, almost apologetically. He looked and sounded sincere. But could she trust him?

Against her better judgement Liz climbed into the car, driven on by her need to find information to free her uncle.

'We only have a few minutes as I've just nipped out to get a bottle of whisky,' Barker-Willet said. 'Now listen carefully. The people you are asking about are not people who enjoy scrutiny, especially from the press. I would suggest you give up and go home.'

'I won't,' Liz said indignantly.

'Look, young lady, I'm trying to protect you from yourself. They *will* kill you. They've done it before when people got too close.' He said sighing.

'I know. They've already tried. Back to Barker-Willet: can you answer my question or not?' Liz knew that she was taking a risk, and she really had no idea what she was doing, but she pressed on.

The old man looked at Liz like a father would a daughter, bringing back memories of what Sean had said when he told her that Nok had called him an old-school gentleman.

'Please,' she pleaded, 'my uncle is facing a lethal injection because of this man. I need to know why.' Tears ran down her cheeks as she spoke.

Barker-Willet breathed in deeply and closed his eyes, as if to shut out some kind of pain.

'Are you okay?' Liz asked touching his arm gently.

He shook his head. 'If you want to know, I'm dying of bowel cancer.'

Liz bowed her head and pulled on the door lever to get out of the car. 'I'm sorry,' she said. 'I shouldn't have bothered you.'

Barker-Willet reached out and stopped her. 'What the hell, I'm dying anyway. Killing me would be a relief,' he took a deep breath and started. 'The man you know as Charles Barker-Willet approached me in Bangkok, around 1995, and asked me to buy the tuna company for him in my name. He provided the money.'

'Who was he?' Liz asked.

Barker-Willet shook his head. 'You may not believe me, but I honestly don't know. He called himself David Wilson, but that wasn't his real name. I checked later.'

He continued his story. 'I was down on my luck, getting ready to come back to Australia, when he showed up and made me an offer that seemed too good to be true. I know now that it was.'

'What was the offer?' Liz asked.

'That I buy the company in my name, but not get involved in it after that. And also . . .' he paused again, shaking his head, ' also, that I adopt him as my son.'

106

'Wow! You adopted him? Why?' Liz asked.

'I can only speculate, but it allowed him to take my name without any real scrutiny and avoided the need for him to purchase the company from me. He just took over.' Charles said.

'Didn't the adoption records show his real name?' Liz asked.

'No, they said David Wilson. They were fake. As I said, I checked years ago.'

'So you never sold the company to him? Then you own BW Corp?' Liz frowned.

'No, I didn't sell it to him. He just assumed life as me in Thailand. Then he floated in the UK. I don't own BW Corp though. He has a private contract with me to sell any interests I may claim from him, plus any prior income from those interests for a penny, should the need arise. He's no fool. He thought everything through.'

'Yes, clever,' Liz commented. 'What do you get out of it?' she asked,

For my services he pays me $500,000 a year. Every month the money comes without fault, and my only requirement is that I keep quiet.'

'Why are you telling me this?' Liz asked, genuinely concerned for the polite old man.

'Because I don't want to be responsible for anybody else being killed,' he said, a tear running down his cheek. 'I have been a coward all these years, taking my money and hiding away, but I always knew I would tell someone when the time was right. Well, the time is right now,' he said, regaining some strength in his voice.

''Thank you,' Liz said honestly. 'Other people have been killed?' she asked.

'A young journalist from Hong Kong came down here asking the same questions in 2007. Nam murdered him in his hotel room. I know because I followed her there.'

'Nam?' Liz changed tone.

'Yes, she is how he keeps me quiet. I love her, but her loyalty lies with him,' he said, wiping another tear from his eye.

'Do you know what the journalist was called?' Liz asked.

In response to the question, Charles routed around in the centre console of the car briefly, then produced a business card. 'That's his name card.' He handed it to Liz. 'Get him some justice. Please.' He looked at his watch. 'I have to get going. Nam will suspect something if I'm out too long.'

'Why doesn't he kill you?' Liz asked.

The old man shrugged. 'My name. I guess it would draw too much attention to him, so he keeps me silent with Nam. It suited me for a while, but now I wonder what manor of ill deeds have been done in my name.' He looked at his watch again. 'Please go and get far away from Melbourne. They'll be looking for you.'

As Liz climbed out of the car, he immediately sped away towards a strip mall in the distance, where he stopped outside a bottle shop. On the walk back to her hotel, she was careful to ensure that she wasn't being followed, only relaxing once she was inside her room.

There were two emails waiting for her when she logged on, the first from Sean letting her know that he was heading to Bangkok. She replied briefly:

> Sean,
>> Be careful
>> Liz xxx

The second email was from her mother, telling her that the family were all heading to Seoul for a crisis meeting regarding Bill and it would be good if she could get there. She replied quickly:

> Mum,
>> I'll be there. Just waiting for my passport.
>> Liz

Chapter 12

Wednesday, 18th February. Bangkok, Thailand

Sean checked his email in the lobby of the hotel. There was one from Liz telling him to be careful.

> *Liz,*
> *I was careful and survived Soi Cowboy. Found out some interesting stuff, but don't have time to tell you now.*
> *I'm off to Burma. See you in Melbourne.*
> *Love*
> *Sean xx*

Bank, the man Nok had put him in contact with, was waiting for him in a battered old taxi outside, and he climbed quickly into the front passenger seat.

'Burma here we come. Hold tight,' Bank said.

When he said 'hold tight', Sean hadn't realised that he meant it. Once they had cleared the smooth roads of Bangkok, the quality of driving surface deteriorated quickly, until they were driving on nothing more than dirt roads. This didn't seem to matter to Bank, who just put his foot down as far as it would go and steered. At times, Sean thought that the ancient car would fall apart, but it kept going and Bank kept smiling.

After four hours of intense driving, Bank slowed the car down and turned off the lights. Sean turned to him frowning.

'Burma,' Bank said, pointing to a light in the distance as he pulled the car off the road and parked it in an old wooden shed. 'We go now,' he said, getting out of the car.

The sight of the cross-country motorbike in the shed sent a shiver down Sean's spine. He'd always been afraid of motorbikes and had no desire to get on one, especially with an accelerator-happy driver like Bank. Starting the engine, Bank indicated that Sean should get on the back. Hesitantly, he did as he was told and climbed into the pillion position on the back of the tatty motorcycle, expecting Bank to pass him a helmet, but they sped away, neither wearing any kind of protection.

Heading away from the road, on a tiny dirt track into the dark and dense woodland, branches from trees scraped against Sean's arms and legs, but he somehow managed to stay on the bike, clinging to Bank as he manoeuvred through the thick bush. Bank seemed to know exactly where he was going, despite not having lights on and the path being nothing more than two feet wide.

After about twenty minutes of hard riding, they arrived at a high mesh fence, with a barbwire coil on top. The area was deserted and the fence seemingly unguarded. 'Burma,' Bank said again, grinning broadly, showing his yellow teeth. Fifty metres further along the high fence, they came across a gap that had been cut into it. 'Bank door to Burma,' his jolly guide said, as he crossed from Thailand into Burma, through the gap in the fence.

They rode for a further twenty minutes, through what seemed to be even denser bush, before joining a road again. Sean was ready to jump off the bike and walk, but Bank kept going as fast as the bike could take them. Just as it was getting light, they arrived in the Burmese City of Mawlamyine. The streets were already busy with fruit traders setting up their stalls for the day and Sean felt a sense of some relief at being out of Thailand, even though he had never expected to be in Burma. News clips of atrocities committed by the military government flashed across his mind, making him shiver.

Bank dropped him at the main coach station in the city and disappeared briefly, returning with a ticket. 'Yangon,' he said, pointing to a modern green and cream coach.

'Thank you,' Sean said, as he reached into his bag and pulled out ten crisp $100 bills and shook Bank's hand firmly.

'No thank me. Make right for Ping,' he said, climbing back on his dirty motorbike.

Sean scrutinized the ticket carefully. Luckily it was partly in English. The bus didn't depart for an hour or so, so he took the time to wander around the bus station. It looked surprisingly new, with a clean red-tiled roof. It was two stories high and had a row of restaurants on the bottom floor. He walked into one of them and took a seat, exhausted, scared and hungry. The menu was on a printed sheet with photographs, so he pointed to a dish and ordered a Coke to go with it. The food arrived quickly and was as tasty as it looked, Sean almost inhaled it he was so hungry. Then he sat and sipped at his Coke, watching the people of Burma go by. For a country that had been so oppressed for so long, Sean noted that the people seemed incredibly happy as they went about their daily business.

The bus journey to Yangon was uneventful, but the scenery was stunning. Rice paddies lined the sides of the road and the hills opened out to glimpses of the bright blue Indian Ocean. Just three hours later, they started to enter the outer suburbs of Yangon: poverty stricken areas where people sat on the sides of streets that were filled with corrugated tin shacks. As they got closer to the centre, the streets got busier and the buildings bigger, and Sean was surprised to see so many colonial style old buildings, still standing in the city centre. Following the Japanese occupation and the later military rule, he had expected that they would have been destroyed.

The bus station was nothing more than a huge car park, with buildings scattered randomly around it. It was a hive of activity and Sean caught sight of what looked like a line of taxis. Waving his arms, he quickly went to one and said. 'Airport,' expectantly.

The taxi driver indicated that he should get in and they set off at break-neck speed into the chaotic traffic . . . hopefully for the airport. The modern development he saw in Yangon – a city he had considered shut off from the outside world – surprised Sean. The city centre itself was filled with tree-lined streets, which wouldn't have looked out of place in Paris.

It took them just over an hour to get to the airport, where the driver asked for 20,000 Kyat. Sean reached into his bag and pulled out the handful of notes that the café owner had given to him, as change for his US100 bill. He gave the driver 30,000 Kyat, which was about US$30 dollars and thanked him.

Yangon airport was modern and clean, with marble floors, chrome and glass fittings and flat-screen monitors showing departures and arrivals. There were Internet terminals dotted around the building and Sean stopped at one to check his email, immediately opening the note from Liz:

> Hi Sean,
>   I hope you're safe, let me know, I'm worried.
>   My family are all flying in to Seoul for an emergency meeting about Bill to see what we can come up with. I'm going as soon as I get my passport. Meet me there?
>   Hope you're safe?
>   Liz xxx

He replied:

> *Liz,*
> *I'm in Yangon (Rangoon) at the airport. I'll see you in Seoul.*
> *Love*
> *Sean xx*

He clicked onto Safari and looked for flights from Yangon to Seoul. There was only one direct flight, which was due to leave in two hours on Korean Air. The Korean Air desk was nearby and he got the only seat left on the flight, which was in business class. 'Thanks, Bill,' he said, as he handed over $1,500 for the short flight. Clearing immigration was easier than he had anticipated, as they didn't seem remotely concerned that he didn't have an entry-stamp and just stamped him out.

Once on the plane and settled in to his large business class seat, Sean ordered a beer and relaxed properly for the first time in days.

Chapter 13

It was only 8 p.m., but Liz decided to get some sleep, her mind wracked with guilt about her uncle and worry for Sean. She hoped that her passport would arrive soon, making it possible for her to leave in the morning and fly to Seoul, to be with her family. If anybody could sort this mess out, she thought that her powerful and wealthy family could.

Before she started to undress, the phone rang shaking her out of her thoughts. 'Yes?' she answered.

'Ah, Miss Channing there is an urgent parcel for you at reception,' the caller said.

'Brilliant,' Liz said, putting the phone down quickly, before speeding down to the lift and into the enormous black marble foyer of the hotel. The receptionist smiled as Liz signed for the small package, which she opened at the desk. As expected, it was her passport and credit cards. 'Thanks, Sean,' she said to herself, clutching the burgundy passport.

While she was waiting for the lift, she took in the over-the-top black marble lobby of the hotel. It was designed to impress, as many casino hotel lobbies were.

An ornate staircase rose from the middle of the hotel lobby, seemingly going nowhere and Liz wondered who would design such an elaborate structure. Standing by the bottom of the black metal railing, a man caught her eye. He was holding a piece of paper, that looked like it had a photo on it, and looking straight at her. Seemingly having seen enough, he reached into his pocket and pulled out a phone. Fear shot through Liz's body, almost paralysing her, as she realised she had been found.

When the lift arrived, she hit the button for the seventh floor, which was two floors below her own. At the seventh floor, she ran up the stairs and entered her room on the ninth floor, packed the small backpack that she had bought and went straight back out into the hallway.

She decided not to take the lift and went into the stairwell instead. But as she stepped onto the landing, she immediately froze: somebody was coming up quickly in the other direction.

The door to the hallway hadn't closed fully yet, so she stepped back into the long passageway as quietly as possible, scouring the area for a place to hide. Although the dark wood panelling in the doorways was impressive, it didn't make for a lot of places to hide. In the opposite direction from her room, she saw a small porch, which was used to link two rooms for a family and slipped inside, trying not to make a sound, as she crouched down shaking with fear.

The full length of the corridor was reflected in the floor-to-ceiling glass window just a few metres away from her, giving her a clear view when a young man, with short cropped brown hair, came out of the stairwell. He looked up and down the hallway, before the lift made a ping, announcing its arrival on the ninth floor. Another young man, roughly the same build, also with short cropped hair, climbed out of the lift. After confirming that they were alone, the two of them made their way to the door of Liz's room. *How the hell did they get that? Who are they?* Liz thought, as the brown-haired man slid a card into the lock. Then the other intruder produced a gun, sending a terrifying chill through Liz's body.

As soon as they entered the room, Liz sprinted towards the stairwell, but as she ran, she noticed that the lift was still open. Pivoting with agility, she dived in and hit the button for the ground floor, begging for the doors to close quickly. They did, and she was on her way.

When she arrived at the ground floor, she walked casually into the marble lobby that she had left only minutes before, but noticed immediately that the same man was looking at her, smiling, as he pulled out his phone again. No longer pretending to be calm, Liz rounded the bank of gold-plated lifts and sped out of the hotel reception, into the lobby of the Crown Casino. She walked as quickly as she could, without drawing attention to herself, past a tacky indoor water feature and stopped at the bottom of a huge sweeping marble staircase. Without even pretending otherwise, the man from the lobby followed, twenty metres behind her and stopped when she did.

His actions made it obvious to Liz that he obviously didn't want to approach her in such a busy place, so she walked to her right and entered the casino floor. Knowing that it would be filled with security cameras, staff and early evening gamblers, she thought that she would be safe there and it might give her some time to think of a way out.

Just inside the security gate, a round bar overlooked the lobby and Liz took a seat on a bar stool, looking back towards the lobby. Just metres behind, her shadow followed and sat on a stool on the other side of the same bar, grinning at her through his thin lips as he ordered a drink from the barman. The delay as the barman pulled the beer gave Liz an opportunity to make a move and she slipped from the stool, walking deeper into the casino. The bright lights of the slot machines were a blur as she sped by, looking for a way to give her shadow the slip. When she saw a large group of people, gathered around a roulette table, she circled around them, looking back to see whether he had followed. Unfortunately, he had and he just stopped by a slot machine, not even pretending to play it, looking straight at her.

His stare chilled her and knowing that he had called his colleagues, Liz decided that she had to make a move soon. They would be on their way back from her room already, giving her only seconds to make a decision. Out of the corner of her eye, she spotted a large group of young men, standing by a bar that was central to the gaming floor. They were young and athletic, like a sports team, but also drunk and rowdy. Smiling broadly, Liz walked towards them. 'Hi,' she said to the closest one of them.

'Hi,' he said, looking pleased as his friends whistled.

'What are you guys up to?' she asked.

'We're a footy team, just having a boys' night out, and you . . .? Sorry, I didn't get your name?'

'Liz,' she said extending her hand. 'I just had dinner with a friend and was on my way home, but do you see the man, over there, in the brown jacket standing by the craps table?' she said, flirting with her eyes.

'Yeah,' he said frowning, suddenly realising that perhaps his luck wasn't as good as it might otherwise be.

'I think he's a pervert. He's been following me for ages and it's making me really scared,' Liz looked sincerely at the young man.

'Really? We'll see about that.' The young athlete turned immediately to three of his friends. 'Come on, guys, we've got a pervert to dispose of.' He winked at Liz.

Five of the young footballers immediately put their drinks down and walked directly towards the man who was following Liz. She waited until one of the young men grabbed his jacket, then she ran in the opposite direction searching for an exit. But the casino floor was huge and it was a good way before she found herself in another lobby. Finally, through the wall of glass doors, she saw a line of yellow taxis waiting for customers.

When she ran to the bell desk, the first taxi in line pulled forward for her to get in. 'The airport, please,' she said, as she climbed in the rear seat. As the taxi pulled away, she scanned the forecourt of the casino, looking for anybody that might be following her. When she didn't see anybody, she let out a sigh of relief and within no time, they were passing over a large bridge, with the bright lights of Melbourne below them. From there, the journey to the airport only took a further fifteen minutes.

Climbing out of the body odour-infested cab, Liz took in a deep breath of air and entered the check-in hall, quickly surveying the departure board. There were no direct flights to Seoul still to leave this evening, but there was a China Southern flight to Guangzhou, leaving at 11:30 p.m.. Liz knew that there were plenty of flights linking the large capital of Guangdong Province to Seoul, and she could get one when she arrived in China in the morning.

So that nobody would be sat next to her, Liz chose a first-class ticket and paid in cash. She passed through security without any problem, using her own British passport, which gave her confidence as she approached immigration. The man on duty in the blue marked express lane was older, maybe in his fifties and didn't appear to be paying much attention as she handed over her passport and departure card, looking straight at him.

'When did you come to Australia?' he asked.

'Two days ago,' she said confidently.

He frowned and looked through her passport again. 'Why isn't your passport stamped then, Miss Channing?'

'I don't know,' she said, faking a puzzled look.

The officer shook his head. 'Come with me, please,' he said, as climbed out of the glass booth and guided Liz by the arm towards an office, with a two-way mirror on the front of it. Once through the door, she was steered into a small room with the name plate, 'Interview Room 2' attached to the door. Inside, a grey table and four chairs were the only furniture, and a digital security camera observed the events from the corner of the room.

The officer that had taken her there told her to sit down and then left her alone in the spartan interview room. Liz hadn't anticipated this problem and was unsure how to play it. Then a terrible thought crossed her mind: was this them, Barker-Willet's men? Did their reach extend into Australian Immigration? If they had the resources to find her in a Melbourne hotel, anything was possible.

A few short minutes later, another immigration officer arrived. He was younger than the first and had an officer's rank markings on his epaulets. He took a seat opposite Liz and smiled. 'We can't find any record of your arrival. Could you have used a different passport?' His tone was polite and helpful.

Liz shrugged. 'No, I only have this and my Korean passport, which is at home in England.'

The officer considered her answer. 'That's odd, as we have no record of you arriving on this one.'

'It must be a mistake,' Liz said, pretending to be a little annoyed at the inconvenience.

'Maybe, but we don't usually make two mistakes at the same time. For this to be a mistake, we must have not passed your passport through our immigration system and also not stamped it. Do you see my problem?' he raised his eyebrows theatrically.

'Well, I see your point, but there is no other explanation.' Liz bluffed again.

'You only bought your ticket ten minutes ago. Why are you in such a hurry to leave Australia?' he said changing his approach.

'My grandfather is sick in Korea, and I need to get there. I don't want to miss my flight,' she said, even more aggressively.

'Why were you in Melbourne?' he said, ignoring her aggression.

'Visiting friends,' she said, without thinking.

'Oh, do you have a name and address for these friends?' he raised his eyebrows again expectantly.

Shit! I should have seen that coming, Liz thought. 'Nam Barker-Willet, 11 Ballard St, Albert Park,' she said, breathing in.

The officer noted the details, then stood and left the interview room without commenting.

At the end of her tether, Liz started to cry. Only four days ago her life had been normal: she had a new boyfriend and everything was going well. Now she was being treated like a criminal by Australian immigration, some real criminals were trying to kill her, and she was wanted for murder in Thailand. How could all of this happen so quickly? she cried to herself.

The immigration officer suddenly re-entered the room and sat down, seemingly unmoved by Liz's tears. 'Okay, lucky for you that name and address checks out, and because you say your grand-father is sick, we're going to let you leave.'

'Thank you,' Liz said, through her tears.

'For the record, I don't believe you. I think you entered Australia using a false passport. What I don't know is why, and as Interpol have never heard of you, and the Australian police haven't either, I have no legal grounds to keep you here. But we still have an hour before your flight leaves Melbourne and I will be looking for something,' he paused. 'You're free to go . . . for now.'

Choosing not to add anything to the conversation, Liz simply left the room, shuddering with fear as she was escorted through a blank white door and into the departure hall.

The next hour was the longest of her life, as she expected that any second, an immigration officer would come to arrest her. But none came and soon she was happily on board, in her first-class seat. Then when the wheels finally left the ground, she relaxed and ordered a glass of champagne, in the knowledge that in Korea she would be legal and not have to worry all the time. Also, in Korea she knew people, and her family had influence. In Korea, she would be safe.

Chapter 14

Sean held onto Liz's hand tightly as they swept up the long snow-bound driveway, leading to her grandfather's house. They had only been together again for an hour or so, when the black limousine had arrived at the hotel for them. In their short time alone, they had managed to make love, and update each other on their respective adventures. It was hard for Sean to hide his concern that Liz had gone off to investigate the elder Barker-Willet alone, especially following the note from John, telling them in no uncertain terms to back off. But she explained that curiosity had just got the better of her and he melted into her arms again, unable to be angry with her.

The Woo family home was a modern mansion, set in vast ornate grounds, surrounded by high walls and manned security gates. As they climbed out of the car, Liz explained that her family were one of the richest in South Korea and that the family wealth came from their huge trading empire, which had operations across the world. The company had been founded by her grandfather, the family patriarch. 'I'm his favourite granddaughter, so he may be a bit forthright with his questions,' she warned.

When they entered the ornate marble hallway, Liz's grandfather was waiting and greeted her warmly, hugging her closely. After they had exchanged a few affectionate words that Sean didn't understand, he was introduced to the elderly man, who despite his advancing years, seemed to be both very alert and light on his feet.

'So this is the man that got you into all this trouble,' he said in English, without a trace of a Korean accent.

'Yes, Grandad. This is Sean and I'm more than capable of getting myself into trouble. He was just there,' Liz laughed.

The family patriarch didn't laugh at Liz's comment and turned to Sean quickly. Preparing himself for a barrage of rebuke, Sean stretched out his hand optimistically. Then without hesitation, the spritely elderly man grabbed Sean's hand and shook it firmly. 'My son told me that you risked your life for him. That means you will always be welcome in my house, even if my beautiful granddaughter finds somebody else.' He smiled warmly and then led Sean and Liz into a large meeting room, where other members of the family were already in talks with the family's lawyers.

When Liz entered the room, the conversation stopped and all of the family members gathered around her, hugging her and kissing her. It was a while before she got the opportunity to introduce Sean.

There were twelve people in all around the large boardroom table; Liz's parents, her grandfather, two lawyers, a security advisor, Liz's brother and sister and two more of her uncles. Sean didn't think he would remember all of their names, but Liz's grandfather made sure they all knew that he had saved Bill's life in Hua Hin. It was the first time that Sean realised that maybe he had done something that, from an external perspective, could be considered brave. To him, it had been just something he had had to do. The fact that he had been petrified throughout the experience didn't exactly make him feel heroic either.

The proceedings of the meeting were kicked off by Liz's mother: speaking in English for the benefit of Sean, she explained that Bill had been formally charged with one count of murder and two of aiding and abetting. As a consequence, he was being held in a Bangkok prison, where the family lawyers had spoken to him and he had the occasional use of a phone. Most of the people gathered here had been able to speak to him at some time in the days since his arrest and commented on his mood.

The family patriarch then spoke, noting that they had exhausted all 'normal' means of dealing with the Thai police, offering ever-increasing bribes, up to five million US dollars, but their contact had just insisted that it didn't matter. For some reason, an army general was making sure that her uncle wasn't released, and in Thailand, army generals were much more powerful than even the head of the police.

'Will he get a fair trial? We know he didn't do it,' Liz asked.

The family lawyer then spoke. 'In Thailand, with an enemy like that, not a chance and the charge carries the death penalty should he be convicted,' he said in a grave tone.

Liz went to speak, but was silenced by her grandfather. 'Hear him out,' he said quietly to her.

'We have two options. One: we can try to bust him out of jail and then get him out of Thailand. I think we must make plans for this as a contingency. We all need to be aware though, that it's a last resort and would be very dangerous for both Bill and anybody else involved. Two: we can find out who is really responsible for this. If we have solid proof, the Korean Government will get involved and make it a diplomatic issue.'

'Will that make any difference, if this general is behind Bill's situation?' Liz's mother asked.

'The Thai Government will not risk international embarrassment to protect a general. This is the only way we can go over his head,' the lawyer added.

'Can't we get the Korean Government involved now?' Liz asked.

'I have made my case to them, but they cannot get involved until they have evidence that he is innocent,' her grandfather replied.

'We were there. We can give statements,' Sean said.

'Yes, and that will help,' the lawyer jumped in, 'but we need to know who was responsible and why, to create a real case.'

Sean explained in detail what he had learned from Nok on Soi Cowboy, and Liz followed with what she had discovered in Melbourne.

'It seems a bit excessive to hide the rape of a prostitute in Thailand,' the security advisor spoke.

'Not if you're the CEO of a FTSE 100 company,' Sean suggested.

'Yes, but why did he need to hide his identity in the first place? Why this adoption, false names etcetera? There are too many gaps for it to make real sense,' the security advisor added.

Sean nodded his agreement. Deep down, he knew that they had only uncovered the tip of the iceberg on this story.

'We need to find out who the younger Charles Barker-Willet really is, and find out what it is in his past, that he is so desperate to hide,' Liz's grandfather said.

The lawyer held up his hand to bring order back to the conversation. 'I agree that there are still a lot of gaps in the information that we need to fill in, but if we can get Barker-Willet convicted of child rape in England, the fall-out from that may just put enough pressure on our general to accept an alternate bribe,' he said canvassing the idea.

Sean explained that he had lockets of hair as DNA samples and that he had copies of two IDs belonging to Ping and May Chottawat, showing their relative dates of birth. 'That's pretty good evidence in my humble view,' he added.

'We can get them tested in our lab here,' the security advisor said, 'but that will only tell us if they are related to each other and give us a DNA sequence to work with. We really need to get DNA from Barker-Willet to prove a link.'

The gathered clan members around the table all nodded in agreement, making various comments of support.

The meeting continued for another hour and it was decided that Sean and Liz should return to London to meet with the family's UK security advisor. There, they would plan a strategy to get the required DNA evidence from Barker-Willet and bring the evidence to the British police.

The others would continue the family effort from Seoul, including planning the prison breakout, except for Liz's father, who would return to work at his bank in the UK and provide any money Liz and Sean may need to fund their efforts there.

Liz, her father and Sean were booked on an evening flight to London in first-class, so that they could all get some sleep and be ready to work as soon as it landed at Heathrow.

Chapter 15

During the short journey down the A4 from Heathrow to Fulham, Liz checked her emails, clicking on one from the security advisor in Seoul.

> *Dear Ms Channing,*
> *The two women are definitely mother and daughter, their DNA analysis is attached.*
> *Yours sincerely*
> *Dr Han*

Seeing the small picture of a paperclip in the corner of the email, Liz clicked on it. There were two files attached and she opened one, it was Ping's DNA analysis, but the series of graphs didn't mean anything to her, so she closed the file again.

Looking forward to getting home, they climbed the stairs to Liz's apartment, but she immediately noticed that something was wrong when they got to the door. The lock had been tampered with and there were screwdriver marks down the inside of the doorframe. She pushed open the unlocked door.

Inside the scene was one of utter carnage. The apartment had been completely ransacked: drawers were turned out, shelves ripped bare and cushions slashed. Liz broke down and crumpled onto the floor, crying through her clenched hands. 'When will all this end?' she said to Sean.

'When we make sure that bastard is in jail,' Sean said, angrily surveying the mess. 'They were obviously looking for something, any idea what it could be?' he asked.

Liz shook her head. 'No idea. There's nothing here that could help them.'

'We should call the police,' Sean responded.

'No, not until we have what we need. Remember what Dr Han said,' Liz said, disagreeing with him.

Reluctantly, Sean agreed. 'We should get showered and to our meeting then,' he said, consoling her with his hand on her shoulder.

The meeting with the family's London security advisor had been arranged for 11 a.m., in his Mayfair offices. Clive Miller was an ex-Detective Superintendent at the Metropolitan Police, who now hired out his services to corporate and wealthy individuals seeking advice and help with legal matters in the UK.

Clive wasn't like normal private investigators, who invariably spent their time looking for errant husbands as part of divorce claims. His work was more serious, requiring all of the contacts, experience and discipline a person earned as a Detective Superintendent, in one of the world's busiest police forces. Commensurate with his ability, his fees ensured that only the wealthiest and those with the greatest problems used his discreet services.

Liz and Sean arrived at Clive's offices on Dover Street, Mayfair, shortly before 11 a.m. and were escorted to a small, but well-furnished waiting room by an efficient looking receptionist. On the dot of 11 a.m., Clive Miller came out to meet them. He wasn't at all what Sean had expected. Standing at least 6´4" tall and carrying a little excess weight around his middle, he sported a completely bald head, above a pair of designer glasses. A well-tailored grey suit completed the image, which was more city banker than private eye.

Sean soon learned that Mr Miller, as well as being extremely articulate and well-mannered, possessed an intellect that would grace any boardroom in the country. It was hard to imagine him as a policeman. It took a while for Liz to explain the situation in full, and to Sean's surprise, he didn't ask any questions until Liz confirmed she had told him everything.

'So you want me to find a way of extracting some DNA from Charles Barker-Willet?' he asked.

'Yes, I guess so,' Sean agreed.

'Stealing somebody's DNA is illegal, and even if we could do it, it wouldn't be admissible in court. You do know that?' Clive said.

Liz shook her head. 'No, we hadn't thought of that, but it will still tell us whether he committed the rape, won't it?' she asked.

'Quite,' Clive said politely. 'May I suggest a slightly different approach?'

'Yes, of course,' Liz said.

'We should process the DNA from the victims through the Police National Database first, to see if it throws anything out. It might show a link to somebody, and it sounds like Mr Barker-Willet has something to hide. Maybe it's previous form.' Clive frowned.

'You can do that?' Sean asked.

Clive nodded slowly. 'Yes. I'll need to call in a few favours, but it's possible.'

It was obviously a better approach, and Liz and Sean agreed that using the Police National Database was the best place to start.

'Oh, I nearly forgot to tell you. My apartment was broken into and ransacked while I was away.' Liz said.

'Anything taken?'

'No, I don't think so.'

'Okay, you need to be careful, stay away from your apartment. Your grandfather asked that I make sure you're safe as well, So I've employed around-the-clock security for you: three men who work in eight-hour shifts. They're in reception now, waiting for you.' Clive added.

All three of the guards were stocky, military types. Just the sort of people Liz would normally go out of her way to avoid. In the current circumstances, she was glad they were there though and introduced herself to them politely.

'You won't even know we're there,' Colin, the elder and presumably man in charge of the three said.

Liz laughed. 'I'd be happier if I did,' she said.

'We will be, 24/7, but we're more effective if we stay in the shadows, so the bad guys don't know we're there. Just take a good look at the three of us, so that you recognise us, in case we have to get you out of a situation quickly.'

Sean and Liz studied the three men carefully, making mental notes of their appearance before walking back out into the frosty London weather. The meeting with Clive had lasted for just over an hour and with nothing left to do but wait for the DNA results, they decided, against Sean's better judgement, to go to his apartment in Whitechapel, to find out whether it too had been ransacked.

'You may not be able to tell,' he said to Liz, dreading showing her the squalid living conditions he endured.

'I can't wait to see it,' she said, squeezing his hand, giggling.

As they approached Sean's apartment from the dirty communal corridor, it was obvious that it too had been broken into. The lock was virtually smashed through the door. Once inside the tiny one-bedroom flat, the scene was the same, with the contents of drawers tipped on to the floor and cushions split with a knife.

'So this is how you live,' Liz said, taking in the tiny space, which Sean called home.

'We don't all have a rich mummy,' he said smiling.

'Let's go to a hotel,' Liz said. 'I'll feel safer there.' She called her father and told him what was going on. After warning her to be careful and to listen to Clive, he said that he would arrange a hotel. A few minutes later, he called back to say that he had arranged a room at the Connaught, under the name Helen Davidson, and all bills would be charged to him.

'The Connaught? If it had been left to anybody in my family, when they were alive of course, we would be staying in a dodgy motel in Kings Cross that rented rooms by the hour,' Sean exclaimed.

Chapter 16

Following a decadent breakfast in bed, Liz received a text message from Clive Miller telling her that he needed to see them both, this morning if possible. They showered quickly, got dressed and made the short walk to Dover Street.

'Not good news,' Clive said. 'We got a hit on the DNA, it was partial but good enough and it doesn't belong to Barker-Willet.'

'How do you know without getting Barker-Willet's DNA?' Sean asked.

'Because the DNA match that came up is from a man now in his seventies,' Clive said.

'Who?' Liz asked.

Clive paused. 'A man named Franky Findlow, who I doubt is in any way connected to your case.'

'Damn,' Sean said. 'Ping seemed so sure.'

Clive shook his head. 'It's possible that Franky Findlow was there and also raped her. Did she say whether there was more than one attacker?'

'No, she didn't say,' Sean conceded. 'Who is Franky Findlow? Maybe he'll lead us to the person behind Barker-Willet's façade?'

Clive didn't speak, clearly grappling with something. Then when he did finally speak, it was calmly, in an informative tone. 'I can't see how there could be any connection. Franky Findlow is a vicious thug from the East End of London and not a person that you should be asking questions about, or I'll need more than three men to protect you.'

'How would we find him?' Liz asked.

Clive smiled. 'Well, that's easy. He's in Portland Bill prison, serving twenty-five years for murder.'

'Could we see him?' Sean asked.

Clive laughed, letting down his guard briefly. 'And say what? "Good morning, Mr Findlow, we have DNA evidence that you raped a twelve-year-old girl in Thailand. What we'd like to know is, was Charles Barker-Willet with you at the time?" Not a chance. You'd be dead before you reached the prison gates.'

'Could you tell us something about him then? Perhaps we could do some research; maybe find a link between him and Barker-Willet?' Liz asked.

Clive paused for thought again. 'I don't know that much about him, other than that he is a man to avoid at all costs: a notorious gangster, who evaded arrest for a long time, despite having a full task force dedicated to nicking him.'

'We could try the newspaper's archives,' Liz said to Sean.

Clive held up a hand to stop the conversation. 'Okay, before you go charging around like bulls in a china shop and bring half of the worst criminals in London to your door, I'll introduce you to the DCI that locked him up. He'll be able to tell you more, which will hopefully be enough to warn you off.'

'Okay,' Liz agreed, as Clive made a short phone call and arranged for the three of them to meet in the Audley pub on Mount Street, close to their hotel, in an hour's time. Unfortunately,

Clive couldn't make it, but assured Sean and Liz that they could trust the ex-DCI.

Ex-DCI Peter Dawson was a completely different prospect from Clive. He was in his mid-fifties, with a lean, hardened look and spoke with a strong East End accent, which complemented his scruffy jeans and oversize woollen jumper.

'Franky Findlow is a bad lot,' Dawson started, while gulping at a pint of bitter. 'We got him for one murder, but that is only one of over thirty that we suspected him of. It doesn't surprise me that he raped a little girl in Thailand; he's a pig; a vile and vicious pig.'

'What kind of crimes was he involved in?' Liz asked.

'Everything. Franky was the banker to the criminals. He financed their operations when needed, laundered their money and killed anybody that stood in his way,' Dawson spoke the words with a venom that showed the level of his contempt for the East End gangster.

'If I said the name Charles Barker-Willet to you, what would you say?' Sean asked.

The ex-detective smirked. 'I'd say he was the richest man in the world and the CEO of BW Corporation. I may be from the East End, but I can read. Why?' he asked.

'Could he be connected to Franky Findlow in any way?' Sean continued.

Ex-DCI Dawson laughed. 'Not in any way that I could think of. Franky was East End through and through. He grew up there, lived there and did his business there. As far as I know, he never left there. I don't know how he'd meet a toff like Barker-Willet.'

'But he was obviously in Thailand. That's a long way from the East End of London,' Sean said.

'Yes, I did think that was a bit exotic for Franky. If you'd said Marbella with all the other scum, I'd have said sure, but I guess a man like Franky Findlow would go a long way to hide the fact that he's a nonce.' He paused. 'A child molester to you.'

'Is there a place that he hung out, people we could ask?' Liz asked.

Dawson looked worried by the question. 'Jesus, this isn't the Krays that we're talking about. These guys are current-day organised criminals. They don't do bus tours. If you go into the wrong place and ask about Franky, you'll leave in a body bag.'

Sean shrugged, disappointed, but at least better informed. 'Well, okay. Thanks for your time, Mr Dawson. At least we know what we're dealing with.'

Dawson twisted his mouth into a wry grin. 'Anytime, but stay away from Findlow. I don't want to read about you being found face-down in the Thames. Okay?'

Following the brief meeting, Sean and Liz left the pub and walked back down Mount Street to the Connaught. 'Let's get a drink,' Sean said, steering Liz into the wood-panelled bar at the front of the hotel. They found two comfortable wing-backed chairs and Sean ordered a glass of Shiraz for Liz and a pint of Guinness for himself.

'It doesn't make any sense,' Sean said. 'Ping seemed so sure.'

'Maybe they were playing you; sending you on a wild goose chase,' Liz said.

Sean considered her comment briefly. 'Possibly. Do you think that's what this is; a wild goose chase?' he asked.

Liz thought for a moment, then spoke. 'Maybe. It would seem that way at the moment. The only evidence we have of a link between this Findlow character and Barker-Willet is the word of a Thai prostitute, who obviously didn't tell us the full story.'

Feeling deflated, Sean studied Liz. She was right: they had nothing to go on. Even if they could prove a link between Barker-Willet and Findlow, what did that mean? It certainly wasn't proof that Barker-Willet had raped Ping. Without the DNA evidence, they would have to put the two men together, in the bar, on the night that Ping was raped, and then rely on Ping to testify. It was a long shot at best and wouldn't be helped by the twenty-two-year gap between the rape and now. 'God, I just thought. Is there a statute of limitations on rape?' he asked.

'No, I don't think so,' Liz said, after pondering the question. She was playing with her phone, obviously distressed by the situation. Her uncle was still in prison and her family were relying on her to find a break through. At the moment, she was failing them badly.

'What are you looking at?' Sean asked.

'I've just googled our friend Franky Findlow. Would you believe that he has a Wikipedia page, when Charles Barker-Willet doesn't?' she said shaking her head.

'Anything in it?' he enquired.

'No, just some claptrap about him being the king of the East End; typical crap, written by the mindless idiots who idolise these thugs.' Liz pulled a sullen face, then suddenly she frowned. 'Wait a minute. There's an old article here from one of those free newspapers, the *Mile End Gazette*, from 1980.'

'And?' Sean queried.

'There's a picture of Franky Findlow with two children on his knees.' Liz passed the phone to Sean

The picture showed a chubby man, probably in his forties, wearing a double-breasted pinstriped suit and sporting a large handlebar moustache. His dark hair was slicked back to his head and he held two young boys, one on each knee. All three were smiling for the camera and the headline above the photo read: 'HEIRS TO AN EMPIRE'.

'So he has children?' Sean shrugged.

'Don't you see?' Liz said. 'Clive said that DNA link to Franky Findlow was partial: there was no direct match. So if Findlow has children, the match could apply equally to them, as they'd have some of the same DNA as their father.'

'So you're saying that Charles Barker-Willet could be Franky Findlow's son?'

'Yes. It would make sense that he wanted to change his identity before starting a company. Who would do business with the son of a notorious gangster?' she said confidently.

'It does fit,' Sean said tentatively. 'That's a good reason to change his identity, and the rape could be what he is now trying to hide,' Sean smiled. 'You're a genius, Liz Channing.'

'Why didn't Dawson tell us that Findlow had kids? Surely he would know that? After all, it was relevant, as we told him about the DNA,' Liz said, showing a sudden sign of panic, as she looked around the room for Colin. When she caught sight of him standing inconspicuously at the bar, picking at a bowl of nuts, she seemed to relax a little.

'You don't think he's one of them, do you?' Sean queried.

'He wouldn't be the first policemen to be on the payroll of organised criminals,' Liz answered. 'We need to see Clive Miller again,' she added.

Sean paused for a moment. 'Does he know where we're staying?'

'Yes, that's why we arranged to meet in that bar; it's close to the hotel.'

'Then we need to change hotels too.'

Chapter 17

Reluctantly, Sean and Liz left the Connaught behind, after only one night in the sumptuous bed, exchanging it for a boutique property, close to the Theatre Royal. That night, they ate in the hotel restaurant overlooking the Haymarket and tried to relax. The meeting with Clive Miller was arranged for the morning, at his offices.

Following a quick croissant for breakfast, they made their way to Clive's Dover Street offices and explained their theory about Barker-Willet and their concern about Dawson.

'It sounds plausible,' Clive admitted, 'except for the bit about Peter Dawson. I've known him for thirty years and he's not the bent type. Plus, he was the man who put Findlow away.' He paused for a moment. 'Let's get him in and have a chat with him.'

Liz immediately went to protest, as Clive held up his hand. 'It's okay. I'll have Colin's men here. You'll be safe.'

'Just don't tell him where we're staying,' Liz said. 'I really like our new hotel and I don't want to move again.'

Peter Dawson arrived at Clive's offices within the hour. Apparently he worked for Clive occasionally, so tended to be on-call when Clive needed him. The atmosphere was tense when the four of them sat down at the small meeting table in Clive's office, until Clive broke the ice by asking if anyone wanted coffee. All three guests politely declined the offer.

'Peter, did you know that Franky Findlow had two sons?' Clive started the conversation.

Dawson blew out an agitated sigh. 'Yes,' he said, not embellishing upon his answer.

'Well then, you would also know that it is material information to our enquiry. Why didn't you say anything?' Clive continued.

'I didn't think it was relevant,' Dawson said aggressively.

'Bullshit!' Clive said.

Dawson put his head down and then looked up at Clive. 'You're not my Super anymore, Clive. I don't have to take that from you.'

Clive didn't flinch. 'No, I'm not, but I was, and I would never have put you in bed with scum like Findlow.'

Dawson reacted angrily, his face turned red and he stood up. 'Is that what you think? That I'm on the take? I put that bastard away for twenty-five years and it would have been more if the CPS had done their job properly. Fuck you, Clive!'

Clive again didn't flinch. 'What else can I think? Tell me, because that's what it looks like!'

'I'm not protecting Franky Findlow, Clive,' Dawson said, shaking his head.

'Then who are you protecting, Peter?' Clive asked.

Dawson looked at Sean and Liz furtively, then at Clive. 'Okay, but this goes nowhere. Agreed?' He looked at all three again in turn, re-enforcing the threat.

'Agreed,' they all said together.

Dawson started speaking methodically, telling a story. 'When you spend years investigating somebody, you get to know them, and by default, their family. Right, Clive?'

'Yes,' Clive nodded his agreement with the statement.

'Well, I investigated Franky Findlow for twelve years. I never got to know him that well – he would just tell me to fuck off! – but while I was looking for somebody to turn, I did get to know his kids. They weren't like Franky. He had given them all the privileges that money could buy; they went to Eaton for god's sake, and Franky kept them well out of his business dealings. It was probably the only decent thing he ever did.'

'And?' Clive asked.

'I made a deal with one of them not to reveal who his father was. I even acted as a reference for him,' Dawson said, staring at Clive.

'Why?' Clive asked, his tone less threatening than before.

Dawson shrugged. 'Because he was a good kid, who didn't deserve a father like that.'

'What happened to him?' Liz asked.

Dawson smiled for the first time. 'Brigadier Sir Anthony John Findlow has had, and is having, an outstanding military career. He has a beautiful wife and two great sons to boot.'

'Does that exempt him from raping a young girl in Thailand in 1992?' Liz asked.

'No, but being in Bosnia on peace-keeping duty with the UN does. I already asked him about the dates. He said that he can prove it if necessary.'

'You spoke about our enquiries to Findlow's son?' Clive said angrily.

'Yes. I thought he should know that there was trouble brewing. I knew he wouldn't be involved. For the record, he said that his father often went to Thailand on private trips and he wasn't surprised to hear that he may have raped a little girl while there.

What you have to know is that Anthony Findlow hates his father and all that he stood for. He hasn't had any contact with him since he went to Sandhurst at twenty-one.'

'And the other brother?' Clive asked.

'David Findlow wasn't such a good kid. He had his father's genes, but he was very smart. After Eaton, he went to Oxford and studied international finance, graduating with a first in 1991. Then he joined his father's firm and started making noises that he was taking over, standing on a lot of powerful toes. He was our prime suspect in a few murders that year.'

'So why isn't he in the frame?' Clive asked.

'Because, in April 1992, two months before the rape, he was found dead in a burnt-out car in Hamburg. There was a bullet hole through his skull and it had all the marks of a professional hit. Speculation in London was that he had gone over there to expand the family business and ran headlong into a Russian syndicate that didn't like his plans.'

'Are you sure it was him?' Clive asked.

'Yes, both British and German forensics identified him. I'm afraid to say he got what was coming.' Dawson smiled.

Dawson left, apologising for not telling them sooner and reconfirming their promise not to involve Anthony Findlow.

Thanking him for his honesty, Clive showed him to the door.

'Where does that leave us?' Liz asked.

Clive pondered her question briefly.'Well, we know that Franky Findlow is the only person we can link to the rape in Bangkok. So the rape isn't of interest to us now. It's pointless pursuing him, he'll die in Jail anyway.'

'But we're still no closer to finding out who Charles Barker-Willet really is, or why he's trying to kill us,' Sean said.

'Let's see if we can get his DNA then. If we can get it, we can put it through the database to see if it throws anybody out,' Clive said.

Sean nodded. 'Makes sense.'

'How?' Liz asked.

'Let's call it a day for today and reconvene tomorrow with some ideas on that subject,' Clive said.

Chapter 18

The lack of progress frustrated both Liz and Sean immensely. How could it be so hard to find out who somebody was? How could somebody like Barker-Willet hide his real identity in plain view of the public? And why had nobody else picked up on it?

'Bollocks!' Sean said, as they walked down Piccadilly towards their hotel. 'Every time we think we know something, it turns out to be something different.'

'I know,' Liz laughed. 'Were really crap investigative journalists, aren't we?'

'Let's go and get pissed somewhere. Maybe it'll help with the creative juices!' Sean suggested.

'That sounds like a damned fine idea. At the very least, I might stop being terrified for an hour or two,' Liz agreed.

'I didn't know I scared you so much,' Sean laughed.

Liz stopped suddenly and looked at Sean seriously. 'The only thing that scares me about you is how much I like you after such a short time together. I really do love you,' she said, pulling him gently into the Burlington Arcade and kissing him passionately.

'Posh or slums?' Sean asked.

'Posh,' Liz said. 'Why not? We may be dead tomorrow.'

'This way then,' Sean said, as he led her back onto Piccadilly and hailed a cab.

They started the afternoon in the bar at the Mandarin Oriental Hotel in Knightsbridge, where they had cocktails. Then they moved on to an upmarket Japanese restaurant just around the corner, where they ordered champagne and ate at the *robata* grill. Every morsel tasted like a piece of heaven, Sean felt like he was in some kind of paradise, sipping champagne and nibbling on the delightful food, between kisses with Liz. Life couldn't offer better. When they felt like they couldn't eat any more, they moved on to the Dorchester Hotel for more cocktails.

As each cocktail went down, their mood became more euphoric, they knew that it was nothing more than running away from their problems, and that their nightmare would return when they sobered up in the morning, but for tonight, they were just young lovers, celebrating their new relationship and they didn't let go of each other for a second, touching, caressing and kissing all the way through the night.

Sometime around 2 a.m., they were making their way out of a non-descript Soho bar, heading for a much needed coffee. The streets were still buzzing with people, making their way between bars and nightclubs. A police van sped past them and then jerked to a swift halt. It was a common sight in night-time Soho, so Sean didn't pay it any attention. When four uniformed policemen jumped out of the back of police van and onto the pavement, right in front of them, Sean and Liz just ignored them and kept walking, thinking nothing of it.

'Stand still!' one of the policeman called from behind them.

Assuming that he was shouting to somebody else, Sean and Liz just continued walking, holding on to each other for support.

Seconds later, Sean felt a heavy gloved hand on his shoulder, then another hand on the other shoulder, as he was forced hard against the window of a sex shop, squashing his face tightly against the glass. He heard a dull thud as Liz hit the glass next to him.

'That's called resisting arrest where I'm from, sonny,' a policeman yelled in his ear.

'What have we done?' Sean yelled in return.

'This is a stop and search procedure, sir. We have reason to believe that you have illicit drugs about your person.'

'Don't be ridiculous,' Sean shouted. 'I've never taken drugs in my life. Anyway, I thought we were in London not Baghdad.'

'Meaning what?' the policeman said.

'That we are civilised and that the police don't just randomly attack innocent people on the street,' Sean added.

'Keep quiet!' the policeman said, as Sean's legs were spread out and a policeman began patting him down. Within seconds, a small bag of white powder was produced from his jacket pocket.

'Is this yours, sir?' the policeman said, holding up the package.

Sean looked at the small zip-lock bag. 'No, I've never seen it before.'

'Then why was it in your pocket?' the policeman asked.

'I would hazard a guess to say, because you just put it there,' Sean said cockily, buoyed on by the alcohol.

A female officer was now searching Liz in the same way and again, within seconds, she produced an identical bag of white powder, before she showed it to Liz and asked the same question.

'Is this a joke?' Liz said.

The policewoman didn't answer. Instead, she began to read Liz her rights. At the same time, Sean also heard his rights, before they were both pushed into the back of the police van. Out of the corner of his eye, Sean saw Phil, one of the bodyguards. He was speaking into his phone. 'Shit, he's in on it?' he said to Liz loudly.

Before the doors were slammed shut, Liz turned to see Phil, watching from about twenty yards away and making no attempt to help them. Liz began to weep uncontrollably. 'We can't trust anybody, Sean. We're going to prison, in fucking England. I don't believe it! We'd have been better off taking our chances with the Thai's. At least they *know* they have a corruption problem.'

Sean was seated opposite Liz in a metal cage built into the van and two policemen were in the van with them, but outside the cage. The restraints that held him to the side of the cage, stopped him from consoling Liz as she wept, further fuelling his outrage.

'How does it feel being on the payroll of one of the most dangerous criminals in England. Do you sleep at night?' Sean said to the policemen.

There was no response.

'That's it, stay silent, you fucking cowards!' Sean said. 'We know you're just scum that work for Franky Findlow. Well, I'm a journalist and I'll make sure everybody in the country knows who you are. The dirtiest cops in London,' Sean said with venom.

The sudden outburst stopped Liz from crying and she was looking at Sean, either concerned or entertained, he couldn't tell.

'I wouldn't go making allegations like that, you junkie scum,' one of the policemen said.

'Why not?' Sean seethed. 'The last time I checked, fair comment was the best defence against slander.'

'Save it for the magistrate in the morning,' the other policeman said, trying to calm the situation.

Sean wasn't interested. 'Oh, so you do actually speak then. For a few minutes I thought you were too stupid to master the art of dialogue. But then again, I suppose you do need to speak, in order to negotiate your filthy deals with scum like Findlow.'

'Watch your mouth, son,' the second policeman said, pulling a contorted expression.

'Why? What are you going to do? Arrest me?' Sean waved his cuffed hands. 'Oops, you already have! Maybe you'll charge me with assassinating Kennedy, or murdering Sandra Rivett, but I suppose that's too imaginative for morons like you. So you just plant drugs on people. Fuck! You were even too stupid to make the two bags look different,' Sean shouted.

Liz was now shaking her head, trying to get him to stop, scared by what might happen to him if he continued.

But there was no stopping Sean now. He knew the policemen were at breaking point and could see them clenching their fists in an attempt to control their temper. Suddenly the van came to jerky stop and the two policemen quickly clambered out of the side doors. Within seconds, they were at the back of the van, pulling open the doors fiercely, then unlocking the cage. Everything seemed like a blur, as the first of the two grabbed Sean roughly by the handcuffs and dragged him out of the van, crashing his body into the ground. A searing pain shot through him as his shoulder hit the tarmac with a thud.

'I wouldn't do that if I were you, constable,' a voice came from behind the two policemen.

'Who the fuck are you?' the first policeman replied, turning around sharply.

Twisting his body to look up, Sean winced with pain, as Clive Miller's bald head came into focus. He was dressed in scruffy jeans and looked unkempt, like he had just climbed out of bed, but that didn't detract from his confident posture, asserting that he was in control. 'I'm the person that will have the IPCC crawling up your arse before you can spell your own name, if you actually can. Now go and get the Custody Sergeant.' Clive pointed to the police station building that they had pulled up outside.

'Sir, you are interfering with a police arrest. If you don't move back I will be forced to arrest you,' the second policeman spoke angrily.

Clive turned around. 'Phil, are you videoing this?' he shouted.

'Yes, clear as a whistle,' the reply came.

Unsure of what to do, the hapless policemen just stood

motionless, moving their eyes between Sean, Clive and Phil. Completely unfazed by the situation and having stopped the immediate threat, Clive pulled out a mobile phone from his pocket and dialled a number. 'Charlie, it's Clive Miller here. Sorry to get you out of bed, mate, but I'm at your nick and two of your PCs are about to do something they'll regret for the rest of their lives.' Clive paused. 'Will do. Say hi to Maureen. Cheers.'

'Your Superintendent would like a word,' he said, holding out the phone to the first policeman, who hesitated at first and then took it.

The muffled shouting through the earpiece was loud enough for Sean to hear from where he lay. 'PC Hibbert, sir,' the policeman said, in response to the first barrage of abuse. Following another series of muffled expletives down the phone, the PC passed the phone back to Clive.

'Okay. Thanks, Charlie. See you soon.' Clive placed the phone back in his pocket.

'Superintendent Atkinson said that we were to do as you ask, sir,' the policeman said apologetically.

'Good. Now that little misunderstanding is cleared up. I already told you what to do. Go and get your Custody Sergeant,' Clive said smiling, at the dazed policeman.

After saluting Clive, the constable ran into the police station and returned a few moments later with a uniformed police sergeant, who approached the van warily and looked at Clive. 'Mr Miller, how nice to see you. Coming out of retirement? I wish you would. We could do with a proper Detective Super around here.'

'Thanks, John. Nice to know I'm still wanted,' Clive smiled and shook the Custody Sergeant's hand, as the two errant police constables looked on nervously.

'Now, John, your constables have arrested these two young people.'

'Yes,' the Custody Sergeant shrugged.

'Well, they're clients of mine and I just wanted to make sure they made it into the cells safely,' Clive smiled.

'Of course,' the Sergeant eyed the two constables suspiciously.

'Superintendent Atkinson is on his way. I'll wait for him inside if you don't mind,' Clive said.

'No problem,' the Sergeant said as he turned to the two constables. 'Get these two inside and take those cuffs off them,' he said angrily. 'I'll deal with you later.'

Following the Sergeant's orders, the two policemen picked Sean carefully from the tarmac, causing him to wince with pain from his shoulder, but he stood and was glad to be rid of the uncomfortable handcuffs.

'If there is so much as a scratch on either of them, you'd better clean out a cell for yourselves,' Clive said to the two PCs.

Sean had been in the small cell for less than an hour when the door opened and Clive entered, accompanied by a senior police officer. 'This is Superintendent Atkinson,' Clive said, introducing his companion, as the second man stepped inside the cell and closed the door behind him.

'Tell me what happened,' the Superintendent said in a calm voice.

After apologising for being so abusive in the van, Sean explained the events of the night to the Superintendent.

'Are you prepared to go on record and make a formal complaint?' Atkinson asked.

Unsure of what to say, Sean looked at Clive for guidance. Clive nodded without speaking.

'Yes, okay,' Sean said.

Atkinson smiled. 'Good. Thank you. You're free to go home now. There won't be any charges. Somebody from the Independent Police Complaints Commission will be in touch.'

When Atkinson left the cell, Sean was alone with Clive. 'What happened?' he said. 'How did you do that?'

'Contrary to what you journalists would have people believe, there are still a lot of straight coppers in the Met, and Charlie Atkinson is the straightest.' Clive smiled.

Sean shook his head. 'Thanks, Clive. I don't know how to repay you. How did you find us so quickly?'

'Phil,' Clive answered. 'He couldn't interfere with your arrest, but he called me and followed the van.'

'Liz?' Sean asked.

'She's in reception waiting for us. She's in a bad way though,' Clive said seriously.

'What, did they hurt her?' Sean said, suddenly angry again.

Clive laughed. 'No, she's drunk and was sick in the cell. There was half-digested sashimi everywhere, and last I saw, the two policemen who escorted you here were cleaning it up.' Clive laughed. 'More seriously, I think that was a warning about how powerful the people we're dealing with are. They wanted to send you a signal, and perhaps get something they could use against you later, to discredit you.'

'God, what have we got ourselves into?' Sean asked.

Clive shook his head. 'I don't know, but there's no going back now. I don't think they'll give up. The only way to stop them is to see it through.

Chapter 19

After collecting their things from the hotel, Sean and Liz spent the night at Clive's apartment in Mayfair, which sat on top of his office building. In the morning both were suffering badly from hangovers, but they were extremely grateful to Clive for getting them out of trouble the previous evening.

Over a greasy breakfast of bacon and eggs, Clive announced that he had doubled their guard to two people per shift, given what he called, the 'imminent threat'.

'Now, where do we go from here?' he asked enthusiastically.

'Seems like we have nothing,' Sean commented.

'Yes but obviously they don't know that, or why would they be after you?' Clive countered.

'Fair point,' Sean conceded.

'So,' Clive started again, 'we need to work out what it is we do know, and then what they might think we know. Firstly, what do we know? Facts only,' Clive cautioned.

Liz spoke first. 'That Charles Barker-Willet, the CEO of BW Corp, wasn't born with that name.'

'Good,' Clive said. 'Now, do we think that is enough for him to kill you?'

Sean shook his head. 'Depending on what kind of psychopath he is of course, I would say no, not in itself.'

'Given he is a fully functioning CEO, we have to assume that he is acting rationally. So what would make a man like that want to kill somebody?'

'If we were going to expose who he really was,' Liz said.

'Maybe,' Clive said. 'But who, or what could he be, that it had to be hidden so well?'

'Maybe the son of a London mobster?' Liz added.

'I don't think so,' Sean answered. 'In today's environment that would probably only boost his street cred. You know, bad boy done well and all that crap.' Sean couldn't help thinking that Clive already knew the answers to his questions, but was making sure he and Liz thought it through properly.

'A wanted criminal then?' Liz questioned.

'Or an escaped prisoner,' Sean added.

'I think we have to consider that they are two possibilities,' Clive said. 'Are there any more that you can think of?'

The room fell silent for a couple of minutes while Liz and Sean wracked their brains for something. Both went to speak and then stopped themselves.

'No,' Sean said.

'Ditto,' Liz added.

'Do we rule him out from the Thai rape?' Clive asked.

Neither Sean nor Liz spoke. Then Sean said. 'I guess we have to? The DNA leads us to Franky Findlow, or one of his sons. One is dead and the other says that he can prove that he was in Bosnia when the rape happened.'

'If we were investigating the rape, we wouldn't rule the Brigadier out so easily. But we aren't: we're trying to find out who Charles Barker-Willet really is, and why he is trying to kill you. I think the Franky Findlow link is just a distraction. Agreed?' Clive asked.

Sean and Liz both nodded their agreement. It was hard not to agree with Clive's logic.

'If Barker-Willet is an escaped con or a wanted villain there's a good chance that his DNA will be in the database.' Clive paused. 'So our priority needs to be harvesting some of his DNA. I'll also check on any escaped cons between 1989 and 1992, to see if any of them fit the bill.' Clive paused again. 'Okay, what else do we know?'

Sean and Liz looked surprised. They had both thought that was about it: they had a plan, why not get on with it?

'I learned a few things in my thirty years as a detective,' Clive said. 'The most important was that things are almost always not what you think they are. The old adage "if it looks like a duck and quacks like a duck . . . it's a duck", almost never applies to serious crimes. Where serious criminals are concerned, a better saying would be; "If it looks like a duck and quacks like a duck . . . it wants you to *think* it's a duck. Why?"'

Laughing at Clive's words, Sean couldn't help thinking how far out of their depth he and Liz were. He wasn't even an investigative journalist and yet here he was discussing how to catch a serious criminal, with an ex-detective superintendent from Scotland Yard.

'What about the Australian Charles Barker-Willet? Is he involved?' Clive asked.

'I don't think so. I think he was just a convenient identity; someone willing to go along with whatever he was asked to do,' Liz responded.

Clive nodded. 'I tend to agree. I think he's a peripheral character in our plot. What about this other journalist that you mentioned from Hong Kong?'

'The older Barker-Willet said he was dead; murdered by his wife for asking the same questions as me,' Liz said.

153

'Are you sure they were just the same questions?' Clive asked.

Liz shrugged. 'Not really. That's just what he said. What are you getting at?'

Clive frowned. 'I'm not sure, but let's just play out a scenario. I'm Charles Barker-Willet. I changed my identity because I was on the run from the police back in the early 1990s. Since then, I established a very successful business empire. Now, some twenty years later, two nosy journalists are threatening to expose me, so I'm going to kill them.' Clive looked at Sean and Liz.

'That sounds about right,' Liz said.

'But what's missing?' Clive asked.

Both Sean and Liz just looked blankly at the ex-detective.

'Sean, how many CEOs do you know?'

'Hundreds,' Sean said honestly.

'Of those hundreds of CEOs, how many do you think have their ears so close to the ground that they would know if somebody asked about them in a Bangkok brothel?'

'Well, none, but I don't think that was random. There has to be some connection to Lilac in Bangkok.'

'Agreed. And I think that will bring us circling back to his real identity and his time in Bangkok, prior to adopting his new identity,' Clive paused. 'But how many of those CEOs could put armed hitmen on the street in seconds, in two different countries, plus get people falsely arrested in England?' Clive asked.

Sean's eyes widened at the obvious point. 'None,' he said.

'Then I think we have to conclude that whatever it is that Mr Barker-Willet is trying to hide, may not only be his identity from the past, but something from the present.'

'What though?' Liz asked.

Clive sighed. 'I don't know, but whatever it is, I think it's big and it's scary. I doubt the US Government could mount kill operations in Australia and Thailand that quickly.'

'What do you think it could be?' Sean asked.

'To be honest, I have no idea, and I'm not sure I want to find out.'

'What do you mean?' Liz asked.

'Information like that is almost certain to get us all killed,' Clive said, somewhat morbidly.

'So should we just back off and call it a day?' Sean asked.

Clive shook his head. 'That horse has bolted, I'm afraid. They obviously think we already know more than they would like us to.'

'Shouldn't we go to the police?' Liz asked.

'With what?' Clive answered quickly. 'All we have is pure speculation. We have no link to Barker-Willet. We don't even have proof that anybody tried to kill you, let alone that it was him.'

'So what do we do?' Sean asked.

'My gut tells me to run as far away as we can get, but I doubt that there's anywhere in the world that we'll be safe from him. I think finding out his identity is still the priority. It might also shed some light on what he's up to now, so I'll focus my efforts on getting his DNA,' Clive said.

'Okay, what about us?' Liz asked.

'You should do what you are good at . . . research. God knows what we're looking for, but I'm sure it'll be something to do with that company of his,' Clive said as he started to pack his things, explaining that they would all have to get out of his office as soon as possible. 'Barker-Willet will know about my involvement from the previous evening, so I've rented a short-stay apartment in Knightsbridge for the three of us, under a false name.' Shortly afterward, they sneaked out of the building through the basement and into a waiting car being driven by Phil.

The apartment was on Raphael Street. It was modern and bright, with large floor-to -ceiling windows and four bedrooms. But the first thing Clive did was close all the curtains, taking away all of the natural light.

'This is the operations room,' Clive said, pointing to the large dining table in the open-plan kitchen-diner. 'You two take the master bedroom, I'll take the second one, and the other two are shift quarters for the guards, when they're on downtime,' he said nodding to the five bodyguards, who were already waiting for them when they arrived. With Phil still in the car, that made six in total.

'The rules are: no phones; no email, other than through the secure one that you will be provided with; no looking out of the windows; no going outside without clearing it with me first; and if the guards tell you to do something, you do it, and quickly,' Clive said.

Terror streaked across Liz's face, as she listened to Clive's strict rules. He was obviously seriously concerned that they would be attacked. She clung on to Sean's hand tightly, not daring to move.

Noticing this, Clive did his best to calm her down. 'Welcome to life in a covert investigation team. Don't worry, Liz, we've all done this before. Just do as you are told, follow the rules and you'll be okay.' He smiled warmly at her and then went into his bedroom.

Chapter 20

At one end of the long dining table, Sean and Liz were huddled close together behind Liz's laptop, while Clive, Colin and Phil were using the other end. 'His house is like Fort Knox,' Colin said. 'He leaves at eight every morning, including weekends, in a chauffeur-driven Bentley and doesn't stop until he gets to the office, where he enters a secure car park. At night, we haven't even seen him go out yet.'

'How does he travel?' Clive asked.

'Private jet. We won't get near it,' Colin answered.

'Doctor?' Clive asked.

'No record. My guess is a private GP that visits his house.'

'Do you think we can get to the driver?' Clive said.

'Don't know. I'll look into him,' Colin said. 'I'll look at the household staff too.'

'It doesn't make sense,' Clive said. 'Why does he want all that money, if all he does is go to work and stay in at night watching TV? There must be something else. Is he disguising himself, slipping out of the back door and hitting the town?'

'Could be,' Colin conceded. 'We've only been on him for three days. It's not enough time to establish a pattern, but I have a feeling he's careful and not in a normal way, but in a paranoid way.'

'Okay, stay on him,' Clive said. 'If you get the chance, take it. Otherwise let's meet here tomorrow morning at nine and discuss options.'

Sean watched on impressed, as Clive checked on the guards and marshalled his troops expertly. It felt safe with Clive around and he was convinced that, with Clive's help, they would find a way out of this mess.

'How are you two getting on?' Clive spoke to Sean and Liz.

Liz shook her head. 'Nothing obvious. We're still looking. They pay their taxes, file their returns, have never had an audit quali-fication. They don't seem to go in for marginal accounting treat-ments. They don't overpay themselves and their banks didn't even miss a beat during the liquidity crisis.'

'Really?' Clive asked. 'How's that, when banks all over the world were collapsing like skittles?'

'Well, according to their company information, they follow a very conservative investment plan, with no exposure to high-risk debt or assets. When asset values fell in 2008, they were in a very strong liquidity position, so they just sat it out until values returned. They didn't even come close to breaching any banking capitalisation rules,' Liz said in response.

'Seems too good to be true,' Clive said, 'which is why we need to keep looking.'

'Where are their banking assets based?' Sean asked.

'Zurich is the head office, but they have satellite offices all over the world,' Liz said.

'Surprise, surprise, Switzerland,' Clive said. 'Do they have a branch in London? Could I go in and open an account?'

Liz put her head to one side. 'Yes and no: yes, they do have an office in London, in Berkeley Square; but no, you couldn't go in and open an account. BW Banking Group is a private bank.'

Clive looked puzzled. 'Forgive me, my background is in murder investigations, so I never spent much time with the financial crimes mob. What's a private bank?'

'Okay, forget what you know about Barclays and Lloyds, although both have private banks, they are High Street banks; i.e., you deposit your salary, they give you money at the cash machine, issue you with a credit card and give you a car loan or mortgage, etcetera. Pretty much anybody can go into a High Street bank and open an account, right?' Liz paused.

'Well, private banks are the exclusive enclave of the wealthy. They have strict wealth criteria that must be achieved before you are allowed to open an account with them. Although most can handle transactional banking, they rarely do. They specialise in managing their client's wealth, by investing their money. They don't operate out of branches like other banks, so they're not something you will stumble across. They work out of offices, like yours or ours.'

Clive considered what Liz said. 'So they don't handle cash?' he asked.

'On the contrary, they can handle large sums of cash,' Liz said.

'How, if they don't have a branch, and thus a safe?' Clive enquired.

'Well, they will all handle cash drops differently, but in the case of BW, their offices are just agencies for the bank, which is based in Switzerland. So all accounts are actually held in Switzerland, regardless of where the client relationship is. If somebody drops a large pile of cash at say, their London office, they will simply deposit it in an account they hold with another bank, such as Barclays, and then wire the funds electronically to their own bank in Switzerland.'

Clive shook his head. 'The bloody rich! They always have to

have something different. Why would somebody want one of these private bank accounts?' he asked impatiently.

'Mainly because they get a far better range of services than normal banking offers them. In the case of Swiss private banks, privacy is obviously a draw as well,' Liz answered.

'Privacy. So they could be banking all kinds of villains?' Clive said.

'Yes, them and every other Swiss bank,' Liz said, 'but banking villains isn't illegal. If it was, the Swiss economy would collapse. The worst it would cause them if it got out would be some minor embarrassment. Hardly worth killing me for,' Liz smiled.

'Makes sense,' Sean added. 'If they were just about banking a few crooks, then why all the other stuff? They have more household consumer products in China than any other company. Why make mopeds in Vietnam, clothes in Nigeria? What about the tuna factory in Bangkok? Casinos in Vegas and Macau?'

'Sounds like we are spinning our wheels and getting nowhere,' Clive said.

'There's just not enough solid information to draw any kind of conclusion, other than that the company is completely legit. Sorry,' Liz said

'Don't get frustrated just yet. If being a detective was easy, everybody would be one. Why don't we try a different approach? Didn't you say you had the business card of the journalist from Honk Kong that was murdered in Australia?' Clive asked, trying to encourage the small team.

'Yes, David Chan. He worked for the *Hong Kong Courier*. Why?' Liz asked.

Clive shrugged. 'I don't know. He obviously knew enough to get himself killed. Maybe he knew more than us. You should try to get as much information on him as you can.'

Chapter 21

It was approaching 9 p.m. and the small team of unlikely investigators were getting restless. They had been cooped up in the rented apartment together all day, without natural light or exercise.

Liz and Sean looked into the background of David Chan and found that he had been the China business reporter for the *Hong Kong Courier*. During his tenure with the *Courier*, he'd written a number of articles about BW's acquisitions in China, none of which seemed to say anything of great interest. A Facebook profile in his name, was now dedicated to his memory and Liz scanned the people who had left messages, but none had been left for some time. He also had a LinkedIn profile, which nobody had thought to take down, giving Liz some ideas.

A shortlist of three people that were obviously close to David Chan was drawn up by Liz. Then without disclosing exactly how she did it, she managed to harvest email addresses for each of them. Using her new encrypted email account, she sent each of them the same email:

Hi, I know this may come as a shock after so long, but I have been investigating something that may

provide some insight into the death of David Chan.
Please contact me by return email. Elizabeth.

It was still only 4 a.m. in Hong Kong, so they didn't expect an immediate response, but they had little else to do but wait, so they sat around sipping coffee and fidgeting nervously. Clive decided to head to bed early, so Sean and Liz opted to hit the couch and watch TV. Terry, one of the bodyguards sat on a kitchen stool, looking at his iPhone and flicking between the security cameras that they had rigged around the building.

Terry suddenly stood up and walked towards Clive's bedroom, triggering a nervous response from Sean and Liz. 'Shit, what's wrong?' Sean said quietly.

'Clive, Colin's on his way up,' Terry said, standing outside the door of Clive's bedroom.

Clive came out immediately, looking a little ruffled, but still wearing the same clothes. Then a brief identification procedure, which was really a ploy to make sure he wasn't at gunpoint, was performed by Terry, when Colin knocked on the door. Once satisfied that everything was okay, Terry let Colin into the flat.

Not wasting any time of formalities, Colin produced two plastic tubes, each containing a cotton wool bud on a plastic stick.

'What are they?' Clive asked.

Colin held up the first tube. 'This is a swab from a bite mark on a prostitute's back.' Then he held up the second tube. 'This is a swab from the same girl's anus.'

'Barker-Willet?' Clive said.

'Yes. You were right. There was more going on that we initially thought. I tailed his car to a shitty tom house in Shadwell. He got out and went inside, leaving the driver in the car. He had a false moustache and was dressed in ripped jeans, with a black hoodie. It really didn't look like him, but it was him. I could tell by the way he walked. He was in there for two hours before he finally came out, got back in his car and they drove away,' Colin paused. 'I decided not to follow him, but to check out the brothel.' He looked at Liz. 'I don't know if you want to excuse yourself, Liz?' he asked.

'No,' Liz said firmly, 'I don't.'

'The place was one of those underground cat houses run by the Russians. It was dark, dirty and frankly a bit scary. There were two huge Ruskies in armchairs watching TV in the reception area, and I thought they were going to kill me there and then. But I told them I wanted a girl and the mood lightened a little.'

'"All girls are busy, come back later",' Colin mimicked a Russian accent, 'this man mountain of a bloke said. So I told him I liked them freshly fucked, still dirty and flashed him £500. The sick bastard smiled, took the money and escorted me to a room,' Colin stopped, shaking his head, clearly disturbed.

After downing a glass of water, he carried on. 'When I went into the room, there was a young girl and I mean very young, maybe eleven or twelve and oriental. She was curled up on the bed naked, crying quietly so nobody could hear her. When she saw me, she sat up and smiled, stretching out her arms. She obviously thought I was her next customer. She had blood running from her nose, scratches across her breasts and bite marks on her vagina. She was also bleeding from her anus and had semen running down her leg. I wanted to wrap her in a blanket and run for the door, but I wouldn't have got more than five paces. Instead, I held my finger to my mouth to hush her, gave her another £500 and took the samples.'

Sean saw that Liz had her eyes closed and tears were starting to drip from the corners.

Colin continued. 'Then I sat on the bed and tried to talk to her. She was Thai and didn't speak much English, but we could communicate well enough, so that I could confirm it was him; Barker-Willet I mean.'

The horror of what he had seen had clearly upset Colin and he sat down at the table, with a distant look in his eyes. 'It was fucking horrible, Clive. We can't leave that kid there like that. She'll be dead within a week.'

'If we do something, he'll know that it was us and he'll know we have his DNA. Are we prepared for that? Clive said.

Both Terry and Colin nodded. 'Yes.' Clive turned to Sean and Liz. 'You?'

'Yes,' they said at the same time.

'What are you thinking? A call to Vice?' Colin asked.

Clive shook his head. 'No, that will take too long. By the time they got a warrant, a few days would have passed. You know how they work. She could be dead. Where's Phil?'

'Outside in the van,' Colin replied.

'Good. Get the guys together. We're going to have to do this ourselves.'

The next hour was taken up by planning. Colin went through the details of the brothel and how many Russians there were and where they should expect to find them.

As they checked their weapons and then holstered them, Sean was mesmerised at the speed with which such a life-changing decision could be made. In the much hailed corporate world, important decisions routinely took weeks to make, but in the deadly world occupied by the likes of Clive Miller, they only had minutes to make a decision that would dwarf any made by a corporate board.

'You two stay in the bedroom and don't answer the door to anybody. If somebody breaks the door down, climb out onto the balcony and drop down to the balcony below. From there you should be able to drop into the garden. Take one of the secure phones with you and I'll be in touch,' Clive said holstering his pistol.

Liz looked angry. 'No way. I'm coming,' she said.

Clive looked down at her. 'You'll be safer here,' he said.

'I know that Clive, but which of you speaks Thai? I do, and to a little girl like that, one set of angry men with guns is just the same as the next,' she scolded.

Clive again looked at her, ready to argue.

'She's right Clive. It could be a big help with the girl,' Colin said. 'It could save some vital time, so we can get out of there before half of the Russian mafia descends on us.'

'Okay, but not a word of this to your grandfather, and you do exactly as you're told,' Clive said bowing his head.

'Okay,' Liz agreed.

Sean stood up also. 'Of course, I'm not letting her go alone,' he said.

The black transit van was lined with seats down both walls. For safety, Liz and Sean sat facing each other at the driver's end of the van, while Clive and four of the bodyguards climbed in next to them, leaving Phil to drive and Colin in the front passenger seat.

'When we get there, you don't get out of the van until I give you the signal. Then you come inside, tell the girl to come with us and we get out. It all needs to be done in less than two minutes,' Clive's instruction was clear and didn't require feedback from Liz.

The same fear mixed with excitement that he had experienced when he approached Bill's house in Hua Hin coursed through Sean's body.

It took them about twenty minutes to get to Shadwell and once there, Colin turned around. 'Third house on the right,' he said. 'The black BMW on the driveway.'

As they drove past the house, everybody scanned the shabby semi, with boarded-up windows. About fifty metres further on, they stopped. 'Okay guys, you know your roles. Let's go,' Clive said.

Five of the guards and Clive immediately jumped out of the

van, leaving Phil in the driver's seat, and Sean and Liz in their seats, as instructed. Within seconds the six men had disappeared into the driveway of the house. Sean watched as Clive pushed open the front door and entered the grotty Russian brothel, with Colin and Terry close behind him. As planned, two other guards went around to the rear of the house and one man stayed outside on the porch.

Sean held his breath, waiting for gunfire, but none came. Thirty seconds later Clive appeared on the road and signalled to the van. Following the earlier instructions, Liz and Sean jumped out and sprinted toward the house, with their pulses racing.

Inside the front door, the house opened out into a small dark reception area. The room was disgusting, with a threadbare carpet covering the rotten floorboards. Four dangerous looking men lay face down on the carpet, with their hands tied behind their backs and their noses pushed into the filthy pile. The black plastic cable ties effectively taking away any threat they posed, but Colin and Terry still hovered over them, with pistols at the ready.

'Third door on the left,' Colin said.

Taking her hand, Clive quickly guided Liz down a dark corridor to the door indicated by Colin, leaving Sean to follow behind, trying to keep up. The door to the room was almost off its hinges and it didn't take much to open it, though Clive still opened it with enough force to break a double-glazed window. The inside of the room was filthy and dark, with a metal bed supporting a dirty mattress pushed against a grey wall. The revolting stench of unwashed fabric and sweaty sex filled Sean's nostrils as he entered the room.

On the bed, a tiny, skinny, pre-teen Asian girl was kneeling, naked, as a fat man, who was sweating profusely, pushed his penis into her mouth. The sight of Clive entering the room forced her to scream and let the erect penis out of her mouth.

Without any hesitation, Clive ran forward and pushed the disgusting fat pig off the bed and onto the floor. 'Move and I'll fucking kill you!' Clive said in a commanding voice to the obese pink ball of sweaty flesh on the floor.

Liz quickly ran to the girl. 'It's okay. We're going to take you away from all this,' she said in Thai.

Clearly surprised to hear her own language, the girl surveyed Liz. 'Who are you?' she said. 'Go, they'll kill me,' she pleaded.

'We are your friends. They can't harm you with us,' Liz said calmly.

Still suspicious, the young girl stared at Liz again, examining her carefully, looking for the lies that she had been told everyday of her life. 'They don't let us have clothes,' she said, as she took Liz's hand.

'I'm Liz. What's your name?' she asked, taking off her coat and covering the young Thai girl.

'Praew,' she said, clutching Liz tightly as she was steered towards the door. Where Liz immediately turned, to head out of the building.

'No,' the young Thai girl shouted. 'The other girls, you must help them too.'

'There are more of you?' Liz said startled.

'Yes, there are four of us,' she said and then shouted instructions in Thai at the top of her voice, telling the girls to come out. Within seconds, three naked young Thai girls appeared in the dingy corridor. They all looked half-dead, beaten and scared. 'It's okay. They are here to save us. This lady is Thai like us,' Praew said proudly.

Behind one of the young girls, a man appeared from the shadows and grabbed her shoulder aggressively. 'Hey, I've not finished with you,' he said in an angry tone.

Only a metre or so away, Sean could see the vile face of the wrinkled middle-aged pervert. Mustering all his strength, he smashed his fist straight into the paedophile's face, sending him crashing backwards into the filthy room, clutching at his nose.

'*Khob-khun-krab,*' the young girl said, taking Sean's hand.

'That means thank you,' Liz said, smiling at Sean as he put his jacket around the girl.

They hurried quickly down the corridor and back to the van. As they were leaving, Sean heard Clive shout. 'If any of you perverts come out of these rooms in the next hour, I'll shoot you dead.'

They were all back in the van in no time. The young Thai girls were looking around furtively from under the huge coats they had been given to cover themselves up.

'It's okay. You're safe now,' Liz said in Thai. The four young girls took turns to stand up and hug Liz, as tears streamed down their bruised cheeks.

A tear trickled down Liz's cheek also, as she hugged them back and Sean wiped it away. 'I love you,' he said quietly into her ear and although he couldn't be sure, he thought he saw Clive wipe a tear from his eye.

Chapter 22

They sneaked back into the rented apartment through the car park, carrying the young girls in one at a time, in order to avoid any unnecessary questions. Phil stayed with the van and two of the other guards stayed outside to secure the area.

The couch looked crowded as the four young Thai girls sat next to each other, with Liz on the end Liz, her arm around Praew's shoulder. 'What now, Clive?' she said.

Clive laughed. 'I didn't think that far ahead. Sometimes you just have to act. Well done in there by the way, both of you,' he turned to Sean. 'Do you need somebody to look at that hand?'

Sean had been clutching his hand since they left. He hadn't punched anybody for a long time and he had forgotten how much it hurt. 'No, a bag of frozen peas ought to do it,' he said. 'Shouldn't we get the police involved now?'

'And tell them that we just carried out an armed raid in London? I don't think that would be a good idea. We'd get ten years each, regardless of the motive,' Clive replied.

'What about Praew? Isn't she walking evidence? Wouldn't she be enough to put Barker-Willet away?' Sean said.

'If you mean DNA evidence, would it make any difference if she'd been washed with bleach, in all of her orifices?' Liz said.

Clive lowered his head slightly. 'Has she?'

'Yes, after Colin left,' Liz said. 'They're fucking barbarians. We should've shot them.'

'Then there will be no DNA evidence to link Barker-Willet to her. I was going to suggest that we get a Home Office doctor to come out with a rape kit, but that that would be pointless now. How are they feeling?' Clive asked.

'Scared but grateful,' Liz said.

'They're right to be scared. When Barker-Willet finds out about this, which he will, we will be elevated from a minor irritation to a major problem and we can expect his full attention. We can also expect to have the Russian Mafia looking for us.'

Clive's words echoed around in Sean's mind like ricocheting cannonballs. How could they possibly hide four young Thai girls from the same people who had managed to find them in Bangkok, Hua Hin, Melbourne and London?

'We need to get them into a safe place until this is over,' Clive said. 'First we need to get them some clothes and get them cleaned up. They can sleep in my room tonight, I'll take the couch. Colin, could you nip down the 24-hour Tesco and buy some clothes. Liz, you look after cleaning them up. There's a first-aid kit in the kitchen drawer, if any of them need it.' Clive was regaining his composure after the violent and impromptu outing.

Colin quickly left to get clothes and Liz took the four girls into the en-suite bathroom, which belonged to Clive's bedroom, leaving Sean feeling useless. There was nothing he could do to help, so he logged on to his laptop and checked the encrypted email address they had used to send the emails to Hong Kong. They had received one reply from a Rose Abaya.

Hello,

I hope your note is not some kind of sick joke. David was very dear to me.

Rose

Sean noticed that Rose was still online. 'Are we okay to use instant messaging on this, Clive?' he asked.

'Yes, all messaging is encrypted now,' Clive said. 'Why?'

'Could be nothing, but I'll let you know later.'

Sean opened up an instant chat with Rose.

Sean:	Hi
Rose:	Hi
Sean:	Thanks for getting back to us. I'm Elizabeth's partner. How did you know David Chan?
Rose:	He was my fiancée. Are you from the Australian police?
Sean:	No
Rose:	Then I don't think I should be talking to you. Who are you?
Sean:	I'm a journalist. I was looking into something and some people tried to kill me. I think that David might have been looking at the same thing and that is what got him killed. Do you know what he was working on?
Rose:	No, he was always very secretive about work. He did say he was on to something big. Pulitzer time, he said.
Sean:	Did you live together?
Rose:	No, he lived in the Mid-Levels, I live in TST. Why?

Sean: Did you go to his apartment after he was killed? If so, had it been ransacked?

Rose: Yes and yes. How did you know?

Sean: Just a guess. Mine was too. Did anybody contact you after his death?

Rose: No.

Sean: Not even the police?

Rose: No. Nobody knew about us. I'm Filipina David was Hong Kong Chinese. His family wouldn't approve.

Sean: Did he leave anything in your apartment?

Rose: Yes, all kinds of stuff. He stayed here more often than at his own apartment. It was easier to get to the train station.

Sean: Train station? I thought he worked in Hong Kong?

Rose: He did, but whatever he was working on took him into Mainland China often and he used to get the train to Guangzhou from TST.

Sean: What kind of stuff did he leave there? Do you still have it?

Rose: Well, clothes mainly and bits of work stuff. I still have it all.

Sean: What kind of work stuff; a computer?

Rose: I don't know. One minute, I'll check. He kept it all in a box under the bed and I haven't been able to bring myself to look at it.

There was a short delay, as Rose went away from her computer.

Rose: No computer, sorry. Just a pile of papers and an old iPhone 4.

172

Sean: *What kind of papers?*

Rose: *Just a whole load of printouts and some bank statements, I think. I'm not really up on that kind of thing. I'm a singer.*

Sean: *Would it be possible for you to post me the box to London?*

There was a long pause on the other end.

Rose: *I don't think so. I don't know who you are.*

'Damn,' Sean said aloud.

Sean: *Could you scan a small sample of the documents and email them to me then?*

Another pause.

Rose: *Okay.*

After thanking Rose, Sean said that he would be in touch once he had looked at the documents. The fall in adrenalin levels from their earlier escapades was making him drowsy, so he went into the kitchen and made himself a coffee.

As he was pouring the steaming hot pick-me-up, Liz appeared at Clive's bedroom door, beckoning for him to come over, with her finger against her lips to keep him quiet. When he got over to her, she showed him the four young girls asleep in the same bed, holding onto each other. They looked so innocent, but god only knew what hell they had been put through in their short lives.

'You'd make a good mum,' Sean said, as he held Liz by the waist and kissed her. Trying not to wake the sleeping girls, they closed the bedroom door and returned to the table, where Sean told Liz and Clive about his IM chat with Rose. The revelation caught their attention and they all waited eagerly for her email.

They didn't have to wait long before an email arrived with four .pdf documents attached. The first of the documents appeared to be an internal bank transcript, for the transfer of 145 million Yuan on 25 April, 2003, from an account owned by a company called Mr Chan's Sauces, with the Workers Guangdong Bank Co. The payment was made to Gruppe BW Banking AG in Switzerland.

'What do you think?' Sean asked Liz.

'It's nothing in itself; just an intra-company cash transfer. Assuming it *is* a BW group company,' Liz said. 'Any global company would have the same type of transactions.'

'145 million Yuan, is that a lot?' Clive asked.

'It's about £14 million, which might sound like a lot, but BW's global turnover last year was £862 billion, so it's peanuts to them,' Sean said.

The next document appeared to be a set of statutory accounts made up to 31 December, 2002. They showed a company that, despite a 2-billion Yuan sales revenue, lost nearly 5 million Yuan and had a negative cash flow of 10 million Yuan. There was a hand-written note in Cantonese on the front.

It says: 'Acquired 4 April, 2003,' Liz said. 'I'm guessing by BW. If so, it does beg the question where a company that was bleeding cash suddenly got 145 million Yuan from.'

'They could've sold assets after the acquisition. The timing would be right,' Sean said.

'This should tell us that,' Liz said studying the next document. It was the next year's statutory accounts. 'No movements in fixed assets, but look at this. Liz pointed to the line marked 'Net Profit Before Taxation'. Only eight months after the BW acquisition, the company had made a tremendous turnaround, making a net profit of 260 million Yuan, with a positive cash flow from operations of 240 million Yuan.

'Unbelievable,' Sean said.

'Impossible more like!' Liz said. 'Look, it all came from sales growth. Sales are twenty per cent up with no corresponding increase in cost of sales. How could they do that?'

Sean shrugged. 'A price increase is the obvious answer, but . . .'

'But what?' Clive asked.

'Well, a consumer products business that takes a twenty per cent price increase, would normally expect a substantial volume decrease,' Sean said.

Clive didn't look any more informed, but nodded anyway.

'It is, of course, mathematically possible for them to have increased prices, lowered costs per unit, but increased volume, which would produce the same result,' Liz said.

'Mathematically yes,' Sean said, 'but they are carrying about five months of inventory, and it only operated under their ownership for eight months. So for costs to make any material impact, they would have to be not only dramatic, but instant upon acquisition. I'm still thinking that sales price is the answer and by adding that to the BW Group in China, they were able to stave off any volume decline.'

Liz pulled up the next document. 'Hmm, I guess that puts paid to that theory,' she said, showing the price comparison of the company's top twenty products, before and after the acquisition, noting that there was no change.

'David Chan obviously thought the same as us, that it could only be price,' Sean said.

'What could it be then?' Clive asked.

Liz looked at Sean and shrugged. 'Accounting fraud?'

'The obvious candidate,' Sean said. 'Some dodgy acquisition accounting most likely.'

'Wait a minute,' Clive interrupted. 'I know this is your field, but are you suggesting this whole thing is to cover up an accounting fraud?'

'Maybe multiple accounting frauds. Why not?' Liz said. 'There's real money in it. If it makes the company look better than it really is, the share price goes up. Barker-Willet has a mass of shares, so he makes a fortune.'

'Yes, that's certainly a powerful motive,' Clive said.

Sean sensed something in Clive's tone that indicated he doubted their conclusions. Was he was pushing them towards a more logical conclusion?

'It would fit with what Boonsong said: that the first thing they did was clean out the whole finance department and bring in their own people,' Liz commented.

Clive obviously thought he had let them go far enough down this line of enquiry. 'I know that I said I didn't get involved in financial crime, so I don't know much about it, but I know enough to know that the people who usually perpetrate it carry laptops, not guns. I don't think any of this would require a global army of armed thugs, do you?'

Sean and Liz thought for a moment. 'No, you're right. There must be more to it.' Sean said. 'The other flaw in that theory is the money,' he carried on. 'You can cook the books as much as you like, but you can't magic the cash out of nowhere. BW's cash flow matches its profit gain and we know that they have been paying down debt quickly, so real hard cash is coming in from somewhere.'

'In English, please,' Clive said.

'BW has been getting huge increases in its cash receipts after it buys a company. That's something that you can't cheat the books on: cash is real, whereas accounting fraud is just paper muddling; the gains made are external to the company itself, like share price increases or tax evasion,' Liz said. 'The only problem is, in this case, we can't see how they could have done it.'

'Thanks, that was helpful,' Clive said honestly. 'If we use this acquisition as a guide, how much money would we be talking about, if they did this in every one of their businesses?' he asked.

'Good question,' Sean said, pulling out his laptop and stroking the keys a number of times quickly. '£150 billion a year, give or take,' he said after a couple of minutes, waving his hand in the air, indicating the vagueness of his answer.

The huge sum stunned both Liz and Clive. '£150 billion, are you sure?' Clive asked with his mouth open.

'Well, it's only an extrapolation,' Sean said quickly, holding his hands up to emphasise the point. To be sure, we would need to review all of the acquisitions.

'We can't do that. It would take forever,' Liz said.

'I'll ask Rose to send a few more through as a sample. If they're the same, it's probably safe to assume that it's like that across the board,' Sean added.

At the end of the table, Clive had lost his usual cool demeanour and was holding his head in his hands, with a worried look stretched across his face. 'What's wrong Clive?' Liz asked.

Clive slowly pulled his hands away from his face. 'If that estimate is even close to being right, then we are dealing with something bigger than any of us could imagine, and I don't know what kind of criminal activity could possibly generate that kind of money. Unlike you corporate types, the criminals still deal in millions, not billions.'

'So the question we should ask ourselves is, what could they be doing that generates £150 billion per year in cash?' Liz said, picking up on Clive's point.

'Drugs?' Sean queried.

Clive had returned to holding his head, but looked up to respond. 'Not even close,' he answered. 'To get even a fraction of that, they'd have to control the whole world market for heroin, cocaine and ecstasy, at every level of the supply chain. If they did that, they would have every Columbian drug cartel, Afghan syndicate and two-bit thug from here to Sydney out to kill them. Not to mention the attention they would be getting from every drug enforcement operation around the world. No, it's not drugs.'

'How about people smuggling?' Liz suggested.

'Not unless they've found a way to smuggle the whole population of Mexico across the US border,' Clive said.

'Then what is it? What's big enough to generate that kind of cash?' Sean asked.

Clive shook his head. 'That's the problem. I just don't know of anything that would get even close to that scale. If it is that big, we're dealing with something the world has never seen before.' Clive paused. 'And there are only nine of us.'

'I guess we need to know what else is in David Chan's box before we get carried away. This could be an isolated case. As said, I'll ask Rose to send through some more documents,' Sean said, trying to lift the mood.

'Good idea. Now let's get some sleep. We need to work out what to do with the girls in the morning.' Clive instructed, as he shuffled to his room, still clearly distracted.

Chapter 23

Sean woke early and checked to see if there was any response from Rose. There was:

> *Dear Sean,*
> *I have attached four groups of papers. They are like the first one I sent, i.e., they were paper clipped together.*
> *Good luck*
> *Rose*

The documents showed a similar story to the company from the previous evening: companies losing money prior to acquisition, then a miraculous recovery following acquisition, driven by a twenty per cent lift in sales. There were four companies covered in the documents: another in China; one in Ecuador; one in Chad; and one in Indonesia.

Sean noticed that Rose was again online.

Sean: Hi Rose, thanks for sending documents
        through, they were very useful. How many
        batches of documents like this are there?
Rose: Hi Sean. I'm not sure 200–300 maybe. I
        can't scan them all: too many!
Sean: I understand. You've already done enough.
        Thank you for your help and take care. If
        we find anything more out about David,
        I'll let you know.
Rose: Thanks. Catch those bastards!

While Sean was chatting on IM, Clive came out of his room and was making a coffee. 'It looks like it could be as big as we thought,' Sean said. 'David Chan had looked at 200–300 similar stories. I have four here: all show a twenty per cent lift in sales, falling straight to bottom line in the first year after acquisition.'

Clive stopped his coffee making instantly and stared at Sean. 'You do know that is more than the GDP of most countries,' he said, his face creased with worry.

'Yes, but I'm not sure I see the relevance,' Sean responded.

Seeming to snap himself out of a trance like state, Clive carried on with his coffee. 'It's a scale thing. That kind of money could buy them an army bigger than any in the world, except the US,' he said. 'It's four times more than our government spends on the military each year.'

'What are you suggesting?' Sean said, still not fully following Clive.

'That we're in deep shit. An investigation of this size should involve thousands of detectives around the world, utilising the latest technology and with access to classified government information. We've got nine people, a couple of laptops and a few 9mm pistols. Barker-Willet has probably got an operation the size of the Chinese army, something that resembles GCHQ and nuclear missiles.' Clive commented.

Overhearing the conversation, Liz came out. 'If you're making one, Clive, black, no sugar,' she said, joining Sean at the table. 'Unlike you, we've been out of our depth from the start. A few more fathoms won't make any difference: drowning is drowning, however deep the water is.'

After following the usual security procedure, Colin entered the apartment, breaking the tension. 'Got the DNA results,' he said.

'How?' Clive asked.

'Paid somebody extra to do them overnight,' Colin replied.

'If you email them to me, I'll call in some favours and get them checked against the database,' Clive said.

'I already have emailed them to you and there's no need to check the database. I already know who it is,' Colin smirked.

Every bit of activity in the room suddenly stopped. Colin had the floor.

'David Findlow,' he said. 'Franky's son. The DNA was a 'Y match' to the one we pulled from the database a few days ago. The lab ran the DNA against the hair samples as well, the Thai girl's his kid alright, the lab were certain this time. So knowing that he was related to Franky, I pulled out some old photos of David Findlow and of Barker-Willet, and the lab enhanced some images of his eyes. It's definitely him, there's no doubt about it: the eyes don't lie.'

'What? I thought he was dead?' Sean said.

'We all did,' Clive added. 'I guess that's what he wanted us to think.'

'Isn't that good news?' Liz asked. 'We have evidence that he raped a girl in Thailand, plus what he did to Praew here.'

'You're right,' Clive said. 'The evidence for Praew wasn't obtained legally, so she can only be a witness at best, but for the Thai rape, the evidence is walking and talking. Will they testify?'

'What here, in London?' Sean asked.

'Yes, here. We need to get both the mother and the daughter to the UK without Barker-Willet knowing. I'm guessing he doesn't know about them, or they would have been dead years ago. That gives us an advantage.'

'They won't just come like that,' Sean said. 'Somebody will need to go there and convince them. They'll be scared.'

Clive didn't take his eyes from Sean. 'Only you can do that, Sean.'

'But I'm wanted for murder in Thailand. I can't go.' Sean sat bolt upright.

'I can get you a new ID, a fake passport, change your hair colour, etc. The Thai police won't know you're there,' Clive said.

Sean looked at Liz, closing his eyes. 'Okay. I don't think I have a choice. This is our only weapon against him. Otherwise we just sit around here and wait to be found and killed.'

'I'm going too,' Liz said.

'No way,' Sean responded quickly.

'I want to take the girls home. That's what they asked for last night. To be taken home, back to their families in Thailand,' Liz added.

'What? Back to the bastards that probably sold them into slavery in the first place?' Clive said.

'That's what they want, and after what they have been through, I would like to make their dreams come true.' Liz looked sternly at Clive.

'No,' Sean said again. 'It's too dangerous.'

Clive nodded. 'It will be dangerous, but on balance, given what we have just found out. I think you'll be safer out of the country under a false ID, than you will be here for now,' he paused. 'The girls will be safer there too. God knows we can't protect them here and I wouldn't trust Child Services to protect them from Minnie Mouse, never mind whatever deadly thing it is that we've uncovered.'

Sean huffed loudly. 'Okay, you win.'

'Good. You leave tomorrow night then,' Clive said.

'You can get false IDs that quickly?' Sean asked.

'Yes, I can,' Clive said, smiling, then turning to give some quick instructions to Colin about where to go to buy hair dye, scissors for cutting hair and a polaroid camera for the pictures.

'I'll get the passports sorted,' Clive said. 'In the meantime, remember the rules.'

Chapter 24

It was 3 p.m. on the day of the flight before Clive turned up with eight passports, two each for Liz and Sean, one British and one Australian each, with separate identities. Sean had to admit, that he didn't even recognise himself with short cropped dark hair and he was happy that he wouldn't be recognised in Thailand. With shorter, wavy hair, Liz looked different too. *She still looks perfect though*, Sean thought.

The four Thai passports Clive had obtained for the girls came complete with entry visas and letters from the American International School in Bangkok, that explained their cover. It explained that Liz and Sean were their teachers and had escorted them on an exchange trip to Malvern College in Worcestershire. For the trip home, the girls had all been dressed smartly in new clothes, from Next on Brompton Road, and Liz had done her best to cover up any exposed bruises with make-up.

'You're ready,' Clive said. 'You're on the Thai Airways flight leaving at 9:30 tonight.' Sean was surprised at how quickly Clive's

184

mood had improved from just two days ago, when he had been incredibly pessimistic about what they were up against. The revelation that Barker-Willet was indeed David Findlow seemed to lift his spirits and give him a sense of purpose, and perhaps the rape allegations gave him a glimmer of light at the end of the tunnel.

'Cool,' Liz said. 'The girls are looking forward to getting home and wanted me to thank you on their behalf.'

Clive smiled, then quickly changed the subject. 'I went to the police archives this morning and got this.' He pulled out a manila folder. 'It's the original case notes for David Findlow's murder in Hamburg. It looks like the identification of the corpse was nothing more than personal effects, watch, jewellery etc. It's pretty weak evidence, but the pathologist in Hamburg claimed that there was no DNA available after the fire.'

'That's it? Jewellery?' Sean commented.

'Yes, it would appear so. I'm surprised as well. In a high-risk case like this, dental records would be a minimum requirement, but there are none on file.'

'Sounds like somebody paid off the doctor,' Liz said.

'Yes, but the investigating officer would normally check the details, just to be sure.' Clive said, flicking through the file. Then he stopped. 'Shit!' he exclaimed loudly. 'Peter Dawson was the investigating officer. I should've checked.'

Just then Colin interrupted. 'Clive, take a look at this.' He was looking at the small TV screen.

After viewing the screen, Clive turned to Liz and Sean. 'Grab the girls and get your stuff. We've got to get out now!' Liz immediately headed for the bedroom to get the girls together and Sean started throwing things into a bag.

'Hurry, Liz, there's no time!' Clive shouted.

'They're just getting dressed,' Liz said.

'There's no time. Just get them out. Emergency plan one,' Clive shouted, referring to the procedure that he had taken Liz and Sean through should they need to get out quickly.

'What's happening ,Clive?' Sean asked.

'I arranged to meet Dawson here. I trusted him and I shouldn't have.'

A crackle of speech came over Colin's radio. 'It's on, Clive. About twelve of them gathering under the bridge, dressed as road workers, but they look like military to me. Here they come: two minutes max.'

The four girls were still getting dressed when Liz pulled them from the bedroom. Seeing this, Clive picked up one of them and Colin followed suit. Sean and Liz copied, following Clive into the stairwell. The others followed stepping down the stairs as quickly as they could, with the half-dressed girls clinging to them, crying.

In the basement car park, Phil was already waiting by the stairwell with the engine running. The small group quickly bundled the girls into the van, Sean and Liz followed. Colin climbed into the front. 'I'll be behind,' Clive said to Colin, before he ran across the small car park and climbed into a green Subaru station wagon, quickly pulling in behind them. 'Okay, let's do it,' Clive's voice came over the radio.

The transit van raced forward as Phil put his foot to the floor, with Clive a few metres behind in the Subaru. When it smashed through the flimsy barrier that protected the car park during the day, Liz was still trying to get seatbelts onto the girls. As they swerved right onto Raphael Street, against the one-way system, Sean saw a group of men in workers outfits begin to run in the opposite direction.

'They're moving.' A crackle came again over the radio.

The van seemed to corner on two wheels, as they took the right turn onto Trevor Square and Sean saw a white BMW 5 series take the corner behind the Subaru.

'White BMW and two white transits to follow,' the message came over the radio.

'Go north. A40. I don't want them to think we might go to Heathrow,' Clive's distinct voice said over the radio.

Following Clive's instructions, Phil screeched left into the traffic on Knightsbridge, followed by the two cars, as horns blurted out from angry taxi drivers.

'Any eyes on the vans?' Clive said.

'Yes, we're behind them,' Terry's voice crackled over the radio. 'Just pulling onto Knightsbridge now.'

Sean couldn't see the two vans, as they turned right into Kensington Church Street. The moderate traffic was stopping them from speeding away and the three vehicles were spaced about forty metres apart from each other, with a few cars separating them.

'Okay, eyes on you now,' Terry's voice came over the radio.

Looking back, Sean saw two white transit vans pull onto the street, closely followed by a blue Audi A4. Phil continued at a steady pace in the lead van and made his way up through Ladbroke Grove, before turning left onto the A40. Now on a dual carriageway, the cars between the vehicles pulled out and sped past, as Phil slowed deliberately.

'What's going on,' Sean said.

'Cat and mouse,' Colin replied. 'They're not going to start shooting here; the police would be here in seconds. They're waiting for us to make our move.'

'Why don't we shoot a bit, get the police here?' Sean said.

Colin looked waved his arm around the van. 'And explain this? No, neither of us can afford the police to come. Besides, at the moment we don't know who in the police is on the payroll.'

'Bowes Road, Acton. You know it?' Clive's voice came over the radio.

'Yes,' Phil replied.

'Yes,' Terry said also.

'Okay, shit sandwich. Let's do it.'

Suddenly the van sped up. Phil was now putting his foot to the floor, accelerating sharply. The others followed suit. Clive was only a few metres behind the van and Sean could see the concentration on his face, as he maintained the small gap, with the other vehicles right behind him.

'Hold tight,' Phil said, suddenly jabbing the brakes and mounting the kerb, throwing the van to the left, across the pavement and onto a residential street. Once over the kerb, he floored the accelerator again, as the others followed, then he screeched to the right, just as Sean saw the street sign for Bowes Road. It was a street of 1930s semi-detached houses, lined with cars on either side, so that there was only enough room for one vehicle to fit through. Once between the two lines of cars, Phil slammed his foot to the floor again. The following vehicles rounded the corner behind them one by one and accelerated quickly. The gap closed between the five vehicles, to a point where there was no more than five metres between each of them.

'Now!' Clive said down the radio sharply.

A sudden screeching sound rung out as Clive slammed the Subaru into a hand-brake turn, blocking the street, followed by an ear-shattering bang, as the BMW slammed straight into the passenger door at speed. Three more bangs followed as the other chasing cars careered into the each other.

In order to avoid the collision, Phil continued driving for fifty metres, then jammed on the brakes, as Clive jumped unsteadily out of the driver's seat of the Subaru and started to run in their direction. The front door of the first white van fell open and a young man carrying a pistol climbed out, he was covered in blood and waving the pistol unsteadily.

Slamming the van into reverse, Phil accelerated towards Clive as the attacker took aim. 'Get ready to pull him in,' he said to

Sean. Just then, a loud crack came from the pistol, its deadly contents knocking Clive to the tarmac, clutching at his shoulder. Then another piercing crack, which seemed to move Clive's body along the ground as the bullet hit his side, rendering him motionless on the black road, with a growing blood pool forming around him.

The attacker suddenly changed aim and pointed the pistol to towards the van. 'Get down,' Phil shouted, as he pulled up alongside Clive's bleeding and unconscious body. Looking straight into the barrel of the pistol, Sean pushed the four young girls and Liz onto the floor of the van, then opened the door to get Clive. As he did, another crack rang out and Sean, noting that he had not been hit, turned around to the four girls crouching down in the van, sheltered by Liz.

Although the girls were screaming, there was no sign of blood, so Sean swung his head back to the shooter. Just then, Terry appeared from behind the first mangled transit van and the shooter fell to the ground in a crumpled pile. Terry's gun was smoking from the single shot, as he sped past the carnage, holding his weapon up ready, but not needing to fire again. They both reached Clive at the same time.

Clive was unconscious and bleeding badly as Sean and Terry helped him into the van, both putting pressure on his wounds with their hands, as the van sped away. The scene they were leaving was one of complete devastation. Three cars and two vans were smashed beyond repair in the street. Motionless bodies were slumped through windscreens, covered in blood and a body lay on the pavement, still clutching a pistol, with a portion of its head missing. Observing the mess, Sean suddenly realised what a shit sandwich was. When Clive had given the signal and handbrake turned the car, so that the full impact of the collision hit his passenger door, it allowed Terry to brake also, ensuring that his head-on collision was minimised and he hit just hard enough to

189

ensure that nobody could escape via the rear door of the van. *The bread*, Sean thought. The three vehicles in the centre, however, didn't get any warning and collided at full speed, head-on, giving the passengers little chance of survival. *The filling, in this case: shit*, Sean thought.

As Phil sped the van under the A40 on Park Common Lane, Clive was losing blood at a dangerous rate. 'He's not going to make it,' Terry shouted to Phil. 'Speed up.'

The van tore right onto Du Cane Road at full-speed, then Phil jammed on the brakes and swerved left into the hospital slip road, pulling it up outside the emergency entrance to Hammersmith Hospital. Colin jumped out and he helped Terry get Clive out. When Sean went to help them, Colin stopped him and said quickly. 'Go to the airport, get out of here, or this was all for nothing. You can't do any more here.'

Feeling like he had betrayed Clive, Sean sat back in his seat, as Colin shut the van door and Phil accelerated away. Out of the window, he saw Colin and Terry carry Clive's limp body into the hospital entrance.

Chapter 25

During the long wait at Heathrow's terminal three and then on the overnight flight to Bangkok, Sean had been plagued with worry about Clive. Both he and Liz had become dependent upon Clive's knowledge, intelligent intuition and experience, and they had both grown to like him immensely. They had no way of contacting him that would be acceptably secure, so all they could do is speculate about his condition and hope that he was okay.

After Clive's comment in the kitchen, Sean had become paranoid about what they were up against, and saw Barker-Willet's men everywhere. They were the immigration officials, the police, even the pilots on the plane. He eyed everybody that came near him with suspicion.

Sharing their thoughts, Liz and Sean both admitted to each other that they were terrified about their return to Bangkok, but agreed to try to hide it, for the sake of the girls, who had witnessed too much fear already for one life. At twelve, Praew was the eldest and had become the de-facto leader of the girls, relaying their thoughts to Liz, who had become their surrogate mother. It was obvious the girls adored her and they took every opportunity to show it. They were more wary of Sean, but that was understandable, given their experience of white men so far in their lives. The good feelings were reciprocated by Liz, and Sean could tell that she was becoming very attached to Praew. It was hard not to admire her, at just twelve years old she had seen more of the vile side of human behaviour than most would in a lifetime, but somehow she still managed to smile and put the needs of the other girls before her own.

They chose not to stay in the same hotel as before, in case they were recognised, but chose one close by on Soi 2. The Grande was a Thai hotel and less salubrious than the Sheraton, but adequate for their purpose. Their two-bedroom suite on the top floor also allowed the girls to stay in the same room as them.

'Priority number one is to get the girls home,' Liz said.

Sean agreed, but was surprised when Liz said that they were all from small villages dotted about the Thai countryside. After studying the map, they arranged through the concierge for a driver with a people carrier to collect them the following day. All of the villages were within two hours' drive of Bangkok and the concierge told them that they should be able to get around all four places in one day.

That evening, Sean decided that he should visit Soi Cowboy, as he thought Ping might take some convincing to come to London and testify against a man she had been terrified of her whole life. He waited until midnight before venturing out of the hotel, Soi Cowboy would be busier at that time, so he would blend in more. Soi 2 was a small street below a flyover. It was quiet, but Sean could see that Sukhumvit Road, which was only metres away was teaming with people. The walk to Soi 21 was slightly longer than it had been from the Sheraton, and Sean hoped that he didn't have to sprint back again, as he did on his first visit. It took him about fifteen minutes before he rounded the corner onto Soi Cowboy and was greeted by the familiar neon cowboy sign.

As on his previous visit, he modified his behaviour to blend in with the sex tourists, skirting the outside of the go-go bars, looking at the girls, undressing them with his eyes. Outside Lilac, he turned away and moved a little quicker, then went into Girl House. Nothing had changed in the few days since his previous visit. He caught sight of Ping behind the bar, but she didn't recognise him. Nok was talking to a customer, obviously negotiating with him, so Sean ordered a beer from the same waitress he had ordered from the first time he was there. Within seconds, he was approached again by a young girl asking him to buy her a drink. This time he declined politely. *Is this the life we're returning Praew and her friends to?* he wondered.

Nok's negotiation with the seedy customer was soon over and she slipped behind the curtain to put the money, which she had extracted from him, into the till, while the customer prepared to leave with his purchase: a young girl that was probably no older than fourteen, which was at least fifty years the customer's junior.

'Hello Nok,' Sean said, as he pulled the curtain back.

She looked at him. 'Pay bar fine outside. Don't come behind curtain.'

'Nok, it's me, Sean,' he said.

She looked up. 'Oh yes. You changed your hair. I thought you were in London,' she said, sounding surprised.

Sean quickly explained to her why he was there, causing Nok to eye him suspiciously, before she went away to talk to Ping. A few minutes later she returned. 'She needs to think about it. Where are you staying?' Nok asked.

The same question again made Sean freeze, but he remembered that Nok had arranged his exit to Yangon with Bank and had not given him away. 'The Grande,' he said.

The mention of the hotel made her look at him curiously, but she didn't say anything about it. 'Okay, I'll get a message to you tomorrow.'

Swilling down what was left of his beer, Sean made his way out of Girl House and out of Soi Cowboy for what he hoped would be the last time. He didn't hold out much hope of Ping coming to London, but he had tried. Although Nok didn't openly say anything, he could tell from her body language that she didn't think it was a good idea. *She's probably right,* he thought.

Back on Sukhumvit Road, Sean took the time to amble down the busy street and take in the sights. For the first time since he had arrived in Bangkok, almost two weeks ago, he felt like he could just behave like all of the other tourists.

The high pavements were filled with market stalls, selling everything from DVD's to t-shirts. Tourists crammed the small gap between the stalls and the shop fronts, as bars and restaurants spilled out onto packed verandas. The sound of thousands of people speaking at the same time filled the humid night air. If it wasn't for his previous experiences, Sean conceded that he would have probably quite liked Bangkok.

When he arrived back at their suite in the Grande, Liz hushed him at the door and indicated that the girls were asleep. She then escorted him silently to their bedroom and undressed seductively in front of him, before taking his hand and leading him to the bed.

Chapter 26

The first stop of the day was in a small rural hamlet in the Sam Chuk district of Suphan Buri Province, two hours north-east of Bangkok. They arrived at 9 a.m. just as the two stores on the crossroads that made up the town were opening. Bow, the first of the girls to be dropped off, was pointing places out to the other three girls and Liz. Although Sean didn't understand what they were saying, he could still get the gist of it.

Then Bow pointed down a dirt track on the edge of the town and the driver pulled into it. The tight street was lined with corrugated tin shacks and people were washing their clothes in basins outside them.

'Stop!' Bow yelled in English, as she scrambled forward and pulled the car door open. 'Grandpa,' she shouted in Thai again. An old man carrying a basket of rice stopped and looked around towards the origin of the voice.

'Bow? Bow?' he stared at her in disbelief, as she ran into his arms, both of them weeping with joy, holding each other tightly.

Then her grandfather lifted his head and started shouting loudly and indiscriminately into the street. Soon people started to come out of the tin shacks all around them. When they saw Bow, they ran to her screaming with joy, crying her name.

When she climbed out of the car, Liz was crying uncontrollably. She was instantly greeted by Bow's grandfather, who hugged her so tightly Sean didn't think he would let go. Then each person from the small hamlet came and hugged Liz, Sean, then the driver and the other girls, thanking them for bringing Bow back. Within minutes, the joyous villagers were setting up small tables for a street party.

Declining the offer to stay for the festivities, Liz pointed towards the other girls. 'I have to get them back to their families also.'

Just before leaving, Liz pulled Bow to one side and gave her US$3,000. 'It's for your education: spend it wisely,' she counselled, as they hugged one last time. Liz then jumped in the car and they pulled away, to the sight of everybody in the village waving at them, jumping up and down joyfully.

The next two stops were about an hour apart. Pim and then Muk were dropped off to similar scenes of jubilation and thanks. Sean was so proud of Liz. He could see the rawness of the emotions she was experiencing, yet she soldiered on and was always there for each of the remaining girls when she got back in the car.

Praew was from a village about two hours away, on the way back to Bangkok. The town of Nakhon Pathon was much bigger than the previous villages they had visited, which had been nothing more than hamlets. When they arrived, Praew was looking less jubilant than the other girls, as she scanned the familiar streets.

'Just drop me here,' Praew said, as they approached some traffic lights.

'What's wrong, Praew?' Liz asked, seeing that she wasn't happy to be home.

'Nothing,' she said, shaking her head bravely.

'Then we'll take you home,' Liz said.

Praew just conceded the issue without further discussion and pointed to the left for the driver to turn into a side street. The dirty alley was made up of two-storey concrete buildings, with electrical cables slung between them like spaghetti. Children sat in gutters on the street, whittling at wooden sculptures, while men, dressed in dirty polyester clothes, drank beer from oversized glass bottles.

'Here,' Praew said without emotion.

She climbed out of the car, followed closely by Sean and Liz, while the driver stayed in the car, with a look of distrust on his face.

When he saw Praew, a young man in his late teens shouted something into one of the scruffy buildings. Moments later, a man appeared at the door, wearing a pair of loose-fitting jeans and no top. He had needle marks along the length of his inner arm. On seeing Praew, he nodded and went back inside.

'How did you get back here?' the young man said in Thai.

'By plane. I was in England,' Praew said.

'Why did you come back then, if you were in England?' he said dismissively.

Praew didn't answer. She just kissed Liz goodbye and walked forlornly into the house, tears welling in her eyes. She was followed quickly by the young man, who was presumably her brother. Just then, an argument erupted from within the house, between Praew's father and brother.

'You know you will have to tell them. We took 20,000 baht for her. They'll kill us if they find out she's back,' Praew's brother said.

'Then I'll sell her again,' her father said. 'She's still young. She'll get a good price in Bangkok.'

Hearing the argument, Liz climbed back into the car and sat down silently, shaking with loathing for the two men.

'What's wrong?' Sean asked.

As Liz was explaining what she had heard, Sean felt the physical and emotional disgust rising in his body. He too had grown fond of the young Thai girl, who had shown such personal strength to shrug off the horrors of her difficult life. There was no way he could just watch, as she re-entered the same horrific cycle.

'Wait here,' he said and climbed out of the car, walking straight into the filthy house. Praew's father was sitting on a threadbare couch, drinking beer from an oversized bottle, while her brother leant against an adjacent wall, also holding on to a beer bottle. The faint sound of Praew's crying could be heard from another room. Resisting the urge to punch them both, Sean walked straight past the two Thai men and into the room where Praew was curled up on a disgusting foam bed, which looked like it hadn't been cleaned in years. As Sean bent down to picked her up, she looked into his eyes and then placed her small arms around his neck.

Holding Praew gently against his shoulder, Sean turned around and walked out of the room. Instantly, her brother moved forward threateningly to stop him, but he was half Sean's size and he pushed him out of the way with ease. When he stood to try again, Sean just clenched his fist to hit him and he backed off.

'20,000 baht, you bastard,' her father shouted in English, but didn't dare move from the couch. His words made Sean want to kick him, but again, he resisted and just walked out of the open front door, placing Praew back in the car next to Liz.

Liz leant towards her and said, 'Do you want to come with us?' in Thai.

Praew's face lit up instantly. She didn't need to speak as she wrapped her arms around Liz's waist and beamed a beautiful smile.

Suddenly her brother appeared at the side of the car, wielding a baseball bat. As he pulled his arms back to swing it into the windscreen, the driver appeared from nowhere and punched him firmly in the face. The bat fell from his hands and the driver picked it up, threatening the brother with it, as the young man ran back into the house swiftly. The driver then climbed back in the car and drove away laughing, as he mumbled something in Thai, before pulling back onto the main road.

'What did he say?' Sean asked Liz.

'Scum!' would be an approximate translation, Liz smiled.

It took them an hour to get back to Sukhumvit Road and the Grande. As the driver pulled the car up outside, Sean pulled out a wad of notes to pay him. Taking one look at the money, he shook his head. 'No charge,' he said in English.

'Please,' Sean said, offering the money again.

'You good people; do good thing; not charge; is pleasure for me,' the driver said, pushing Sean's hand away.

Sean and Liz walked through the glass doors of the hotel, with Praew between them, hanging onto their hands. 'What now?' Liz said.

'No idea,' Sean answered. As he did, he caught sight of Ping sitting in a chair close to the reception desk. She was with her daughter and they had two small suitcases with them.

Chapter 27

Once they had all settled in to the rooms, Liz and Praew both complained about feeing hungry, so Ping offered to show them one of her favourite places. May, Ping's daughter, led the way up Sukhumvit Road to Soi 24, where they made a right turn and came upon a huge warehouse style building, with a neon sign above, announcing it as the 'Seafood Market'. Inside, it was the size of a football pitch, with hundreds of round tables surrounded by plastic chairs. A waitress quickly escorted them to one of the few free tables and took a drinks order. Strangely then, Ping and May stood up. 'Follow,' May said in English.

Beyond the huge seating area, there was a raised platform with a fish counter, which must have been 50 metres long, on it. The display cabinet contained every conceivable type of fish and crustacean, presented on ice and fresh from the ocean. Having acquired a shopping trolley from somewhere, Ping started to put fish into it and Liz quickly got the idea, selecting things as well. Sean just watched in awe at the incredible display. At the end of the fish section, there were mounds of vegetables, herbs and spices, a good helping of which ended up in the shopping trolley.

After filling it with enough food to feed an army, they took the trolley to a supermarket style checkout, where Ping spoke for a while to the assistant. 'She's telling her how she wants each item cooked,' Liz said, as they returned to their seats, where four fresh cold beers, and a lemon lassi for Praew, were waiting for them.

By the entrance, Sean could see two huge open kitchens, with woks burning away and at least thirty chefs cooking various dishes. In no time at all their food started to arrive. Sean had never seen such an array of perfectly prepared seafood, mounded into the centre of the table. As they tucked in, every bite going part way to satisfying their hunger, Praew laughed and giggled with Liz, making funny faces at her, while May cut some difficult-to-handle squid. An onlooker could have been forgiven for thinking it was a family outing, not a dinner between people who barely knew each other.

The conversation soon turned to what they were going to do. Sean had been surprised to learn that both Ping and May spoke English well enough to get by. 'Do you have a passport?' he asked Ping.

She smiled. 'Yes, and we both have British visas. We went there on holiday two years ago and the visa lasts for five years.'

Sean was surprised again and obviously it showed.

'Working for Nok is not so nice work, but it pays okay,' Ping said, picking up on Sean's expression.

'Nok owns Girl House?' Liz said.

'Yes, she bought it from a pig of a man who abused the girls. It is her way to protect them. She pays them fairly and doesn't treat them like slaves. She borrowed the money to buy it from your friend Boonsong.'

'You don't have a Hong Kong visa by chance?' Sean asked

'Why?' Liz said.

'I think we should call into Hong Kong on the way home if possible, to get the rest of David Chan's things.'

'We don't, but we don't need one. Thai's get a thirty day auto-matic visa on entry to Hong Kong,' Ping responded.

'Okay then. Hong Kong it is,' Sean said, clinking his glass against Ping's.

Chapter 28

The 6:35 a.m. Air Asia flight landed in Hong Kong at 10 a.m. on the same day. Sean was tired: the previous night he and Liz had stayed up late, filling Ping in on the details of what had happened so far in the investigation, and telling her what her role would be, while May and Praew slept silently in the other room. Throughout their discussion, Ping had showed a steely determination, never suggesting that she would walk away from the difficult situation.

Sean explained that it would be dangerous for them and that they could leave scot-free if they left now: nobody would know and they could return to their lives in Thailand.

'What lives?' Ping said angrily. 'I want him to suffer, the way he made me suffer; the way I have suffered my whole life because of him.'

At Hong Kong airport, they were picked up by a hotel limousine, which whistled them through the tunnel to the hotel on Hong Kong Island. They were safely in their rooms in the Four Seasons

Hotel by 11 a.m. and while the women settled in, Sean immediately went out again to find the business centre. He had sent an email the night before from a new Gmail address, trying to get hold of Rose, as they had lost use of the encrypted address when they left London.

They had also used the opportunity to email Liz's mother and father. In their messages, they told both parents what had happened to Clive, but in separate messages, warned Liz's dad to get as far as he could away from anywhere that they might find him. and asked Liz's mum for an update on Bill. Neither parent was told that they were no longer in London.

The first email was from Liz's father:

Liz,

It's okay. Clive had been keeping me up to date. He warned me to get out 3 days ago. I'm not going to tell you where I am on here, but I'm safe. Sorry to hear about him, he was a good man.

Dad

The second was from her mother:

Hi Liz,

Glad you're safe. Sorry to hear about Clive.

The situation with Bill is worse. They are planning an accelerated trail now. It is due to start on Monday. If we can't get your side done in the next couple of weeks we'll have to go to plan B. He has been moved to a military prison, so plan B won't be easy.

Mum x

The last one was from Rose:

Sean,

I'm confused. Are you saying that you aren't coming over this afternoon to collect David's things as we arranged?

If you are still coming then I'll see you in a couple of hours, if you can't make it now. I'll be in Como Bar on the Island at 7 p.m. Wear a yellow shirt and I'll find you.

Rose

'Shit!' Sean said aloud. 'They must have Clive's computer with the encryption information.' He put his head down. That could only mean one thing . . . that Clive was dead.

He hit reply:

Rose,

I don't know who contacted you, but you're in danger. Get out of your apartment now and don't go back there.

Sean

After sending the email, Sean sprinted to the lift and then crashed into the room. Liz was sitting upright on the bright yellow couch. 'Can you find an address from a Facebook page, or LinkedIn page?' Sean blurted out.

'If you mean physical address, no,' she said wearily.

'Shit! Our encrypted email has been compromised. They're on to Rose. I need to get to her apartment in the next hour and a half, or they'll kill her,' Sean said, breathing heavily.

'Damn, you know that means they must have Clive,' Liz said.

'Yes, but I can't think about that right now. I have to find Rose. She's arranged to meet somebody claiming to be me at her apartment at one o'clock.' Sean glanced at his watch.

'We need a computer,' Liz said.

'I have an iPad if that will help?' Ping came into the conversation.

Liz quickly logged on to the hotel Wi-Fi and began searching address databases for Hong Kong. 'So what do we know?' Liz asked Sean.

'Just that she is called Rose Abaya and she lives in somewhere called TST,' Sean said.

Liz shook her head, 'There will be thousands of Rose Abaya's in Hong Kong. It's a common Filipina name. Did she tell you what her job is?'

'Yes, she said she was a singer,' Sean remembered.

'Great, that might help. I'll try band sites,' Liz responded positively.

Although Liz was tapping away at the screen rapidly, she was also constantly shaking her head. A further fifteen minutes went by, until she looked up defeated and said. 'I can't find anything, sorry.'

'Shit!' Sean hit his fist against the wall. 'God, how many more people are going to get dragged into this terrible mess because of me?' He looked up at Liz. 'How do I get to TST? I'll try to find her.'

Liz frowned and pointed out of the window. 'Do you see the area on the other side of the harbour? From the tall new building on the left, right over to the hotel on the right and then ten blocks back? That's Tsim Sha Tsui, one of the most populated areas in the world; home to more than half a million people.'

At the sight of the vast area, Sean slumped onto the sofa next to her, his body limp with dejection. 'We need to check the Gmail account every ten minutes, in case she responds to my warning. It should be okay if we use Ping's iPad. Nobody's looking for that.'

Liz put her arm around his shoulder. 'Hey, Sean, there are some very bad people doing very bad things. None of that's your fault. You're just the brave person trying to stop them; a force for good. Look at the things you've already achieved: Praew and the other girls; Ping and May . . . me.' She kissed him softly on the lips. 'We need you to be strong,' she said quietly.

That's just the problem. I'm not strong, Sean thought, shaking inside. He knew that he had come this far by just blindly following his instincts and somehow overcoming the ever-present fear that he felt. But now, all his insecurities were coming home to roost. Now that they were relying on him to keep them alive, rather than Clive, he didn't know what to say, or do. He opened his eyes and stared into Liz's deep black eyes. To have her soft lips on his was everything he had ever wanted, but would she still want him if she knew what he was really like? If she knew that he felt like a small boy drowning, helpless and ready to give up?

The answer to that question was simple: no, who would? And the one thing he couldn't bear to lose right now was Liz. So he dug deep within himself and mustered up some resolve. 'Thanks, I'm okay,' he whispered back to her. 'Could you check the email, please?'

There was no response from Rose, when Liz checked the account.

'Is there a shopping mall around here?' Sean said, trying to be more upbeat.

'You're sitting on one. This hotel is part of the IFC complex. There's a huge mall downstairs,' Liz said. 'Why?'

'I need a yellow shirt. I'll explain later. Could you keep checking the Gmail account. I'll be back in half an hour. Thanks.' He pecked Liz on the cheek and walked out of the room.

An hour later, he returned with two shopping bags. All four of his female companions were asleep, so he slid onto the sofa next to Liz, pulled the iPad from her lap and checked the Gmail account. There was still no response from Rose. 'Damn!' he said quietly and put his head on Liz's shoulder. Within ten minutes, he was asleep himself.

Chapter 29

Como Bar was on top of a large office block in Admiralty, one of the main business districts in Hong Kong. Sean decided it was safer if he went alone, so he put it to Liz that she was needed to look after Praew and she reluctantly agreed. All five of the group had walked out of the hotel together and stayed together for most of the walk, but Liz broke off near the end with the three Thai women. She had promised to take them for a treat at her favourite Hong Kong restaurant, which was in a shopping mall close to Como.

When he stepped out of the lift and into the bar area, Sean was taken aback by the opulent decor. A crystal chandelier hung from the ceiling, over white leather seats, which sat on a thick black carpet. The bar area was full with the afterwork crowd, still in business suits, knocking back cocktails. He walked through some glass doors and out onto a huge wooden deck. The view was breathtaking and he could see the whole of Victoria Harbour, with its mesmerising array of skyscrapers scattered before him.

There was a lone singer at one end of the deck singing 'Someone like you' by Adele. If he closed his eyes, Sean would swear that it was the real Adele, her voice was so similar. But he could see her: she was of Asian origin, adorned in a glittering full-length black dress, and clutching a silver microphone, as she sang with her eyes closed. A floating waitress passed Sean and he ordered a beer, settling into a seat with a good view of the deck.

It was 6:45 p.m., he still had fifteen minutes before Rose had said she would be here, but he knew the chances were slim, given that she was meeting the person who used his email address at her apartment. It didn't matter. He had to be here anyway, just in case.

The singer moved on to 'It's hard out there,' by Lily Allen. Strangely, she now sounded just like Lily Allen. Sean examined his bright yellow shirt. It wasn't something he would wear normally. *But I guess that's the point*, he thought. *Nobody else will be wearing one.* He looked around the other customers of Como. Most of the men were young, both white and Asian, in their twenties and wearing business suits, with white shirts. There was a smattering of other people wearing jeans and shirts, but all were white, blue or pink, none yellow. The girls were roughly the same age, again a mix of whites and Asians, and were either wearing business clothes, or short dresses with high heels.

Continuing to sip on his beer, Sean sensed the carefree and out-for-fun atmosphere that surrounded him, and he longed to be part of it again, his biggest concern, a deadline for a piece he could write in his sleep. He closed his eyes and wished everything could be back to normal, as the singer moved on to 'The Closest Thing to Crazy' by Katie Melua, showcasing her ability to mimic the voice of the famous artist.

It was 7:02 and there was still no sign of Rose. He was losing hope as he looked back towards the bar to see a man walking in, wearing a faded yellow shirt outside his tight jeans. The new entrant was in his twenties, athletic in build and had short cropped blonde hair. 'Sods law,' Sean thought, watching as the yellow shirt took up a position close to the railing, in the centre of the deck, ordered a drink from the waitress and turned to look at the view. In his line of sight, there was a huge laser light show happening, which spanned nearly all of the buildings in Hong Kong, working in sync, to spectacular effect. *Amazing*, Sean thought. *They could never coordinate that in London, they'd spend the whole time arguing about who paid the electricity bill.*

When the singer had sung her way through three more songs, Sean was ready to give up. Rose obviously wasn't coming. He kept an eye on the other yellow shirt, in case she approached him by mistake, but he knew it was only a remote hope. 'I'll wait until eight,' he told himself, as the sense of extreme guilt welled inside him. Strangely, when he had killed a man in Thailand, he had felt no such guilt and would have done it again without hesitation, but being responsible for the death of an innocent women was a totally different prospect and his sense of remorse was palpable.

After two more pitch-perfect cover songs, Sean moved on to his second beer and the singer announced that she would be having a short break. Funky DJ music replaced her cool, laid-back singing and Sean couldn't help but feel disappointed. He watched as she walked towards the bar and grabbed a bottle of water, smiling at customers as they made comments to her. She was about thirty years old and incredibly beautiful, with long dark wavy hair, a perfect figure and a face that could adorn magazine covers.

She gracefully walked over to the railing to look out at the view and was standing right next to the other man in the yellow shirt. After taking a big gulp of water, she said something to him subtly, still looking at the view. Sean saw the yellow shirt's head move as he replied.

'Of course, a singer,' he said to himself, as he watched the interaction between the yellow shirt and the beautiful singer, waiting for the point when she would move on, realising that she had the wrong man. He made himself more prominent by sitting upright, but oddly, the two of them seemed to be getting deeper into a conversation. *Shit, he's chatting her up!* Sean thought, resisting the urge to stand up and wave at her.

The two new acquaintances were chatting away and laughing casually, as if they had known each other for years. Sean suddenly started to doubt his conclusion that the singer was Rose. *Maybe it's his girlfriend and that's why he arrived alone?* he thought. Finishing her water, the singer said something to the yellow shirt and moved back towards her mic. Then, thankfully the loud DJ music subsided and her beautiful voice filled the air again. This time she was Nina Simone.

By the time three more songs had gone by, Sean had convinced himself that the yellow shirt and the singer were partners, as they seemed to be exchanging fond looks throughout her performances. He washed his sorrows down with another beer and checked his watch. It was 7:30: Rose wasn't coming, he was sure. Suddenly he felt sick to the stomach, as the combination of three beers and the overwhelming guilt, hit him hard. Getting carefully to his feet, he made his way inside, looking for the toilet. When he passed through the glass doors, the singer was still blasting out perfect imitations and the yellow shirt was still watching her adoringly, swaying from side to side.

Thankfully, the toilets were empty, as he rushed into a cubicle and locked it behind him, barely having time to crouch down, before the vomit ejected from his stomach. His aim wasn't good and he mostly missed the toilet, the disgusting contents of his belly spilling out around the cubicle. To avoid the spreading puddle, he slid his feet to one side of the pan and wiped the remnants of the sick from his mouth with toilet paper. He looked at the mess that he had created in the only cubicle. *I need to get out of here before somebody sees that it was me. They'll throw me out and what then, what if Rose does appear?*

As he went to open the latch, somebody came into the toilet

and Sean took his hand away, moving as far away from the cubicle door as he could, hiding his shoes from the customer.

'Fuck! Somebody's puked in here!' he heard the man say in a southern English accent. 'Fuckin Honkies can't take their beer,' Sean only heard one set of footsteps and concluded that he must be on the phone. 'Yes, she's here. Shirt worked a treat, like a lamb to the slaughter. You should see her, man, she's fucking hot.' There was a pause. 'Yeah, he's here too. Just sat watching us, going nowhere. He hasn't paid his bill yet.'

There was another longer pause and Sean held his breath, trying not to make a sound. 'No, too many people here. Just wait outside in the car. I'll bring her down when her set finishes. Around eight, she said. Jonny and his team can come up then and grab him. Easy.'

Another pause. 'Naw, man. She's mine, you'll be lucky to get sloppy seconds.' Then, 'Okay, dude, it's under control.' The conversation finished and the man relieved himself in the urinal. Sean leant forward slightly to glance through the small crack surrounding the door. He couldn't see much, but he caught sight of the faded yellow material on the man's shirt, before the door swung open again and he walked out, leaving Sean alone in the toilet.

His emotions were a mixture of elation and panic. On one hand, Rose was alive; on the other, they were both in imminent danger. He stayed in the cubical for enough time to allow the yellow shirt to get back outside and onto the deck, before he ventured back into the bar area, making sure that nobody was watching him. A shudder of fear ran though him when he realised that they must be reading her emails, giving away the yellow shirt plan. *It means that they'll be on to mine too*, he concluded, noting that he needed to warn Liz's family not to use the account any more.

It was 7:45 and the yellow shirt had said that Rose would finish up at 8 p.m. He had fifteen minutes to come up with a plan, before she was whisked away to a horrible fate and he was taken somewhere to be disposed of. The same adrenalin surge he had experienced before started to kick in, making him think back to that night in Hua Hin and how he had overcome his fear by just acting, and not thinking the consequences through too much. A light came on in his mind. He had used the fire alarm as a distraction that night in Hua Hin. Could the same trick work here in Hong Kong? The bar was packed, with hundreds of people making merry. A fire alarm would certainly create chaos and panic twenty-five floors above the city, and it might just give him a chance to get Rose away from the yellow shirt.

He scanned the bar area for the familiar red box. Unable to see one, he moved back towards the bathroom. There, under a dimmed light by the emergency exit, the small red box clung to the wall, a tiny lead hammer dangling from it on a chain. The area was quiet, so he moved forward quickly and smashed the glass, then backed away just as quickly to avoid detection.

The ear-piercing alarm sounded before he could get back to the main bar. As it did, he saw the look of disappointment on the face of the people drinking at the bar. Their night ruined, they put their drinks down and gathered their things, then slowly started drifting towards the emergency exit.

Sean fought against the swelling crowd that was now moving towards the stairwell. By the time he managed reached the doors to the deck, Rose had gone from the place where she was singing. He panicked, craning his neck to survey the area, then he caught sight of her. She was walking next to the yellow shirt, laughing. He hid behind the door and pulled the thick velvet curtain around himself.

Waiting until Rose and the imposter had passed, he let a few more people through then slipped out of the curtain to join the queue. As they entered the emergency stairway, he positioned himself one flight behind Rose and her would-be assailant, so he could only see only their shoes and they couldn't see him.

The movement of hundreds of drunken people down twenty-five flights of stairs was slow. Clearly none believed that there was any real emergency and this was nothing more than an unwelcome inconvenience to their night out. In the middle of each flight, Sean caught a glimpse of the two pairs of shoes: Rose walked in front, the imposter behind.

As they passed the large number 4 on the wall, Sean lifted a fire extinguisher from its hook.

'There's no fire, man,' a drunken Asian man said to him.

Sean just smiled, as he slowly pushed past somebody on the stairs, not speaking. Then he pushed past another person. When he the hit the first floor, he was only three people behind Rose and the yellow shirt. On the last flight of stairs, he pushed past the final three people, until he was right behind the yellow shirt. He could smell the imposter's aftershave as he noticed just how muscular he was beneath the tight fitting yellow shirt. *One chance only,* he thought.

As Rose stepped through the fire exit and out onto the street, a voice called out from behind Sean. 'Hey, man, two yellow shirts together. That's weird,' It was the same drunken man who commented about the fire extinguisher. The comment made the imposter turn around to face Sean, but before he registered what was happening, Sean swung the fire extinguisher above his head and brought it crashing down into the imposter's skull with all his force. The imposter just crumpled to the floor, as screams burst out from the stairwell behind.

Sean dropped the fire extinguisher and jumped over the body, grabbing Rose by the arm. She spun around and screamed. 'Sean.'

Sean pulled her to face him forcefully. 'Rose, I'm Sean. That man wanted to kill you.'

'No, he's Sean, he told me,' she struggled against his grip, before she realised that Sean was also wearing a yellow shirt. 'Why should I believe you?' she said, suddenly not struggling anymore.

'The IM discussion we had. You said David was your fiancée,

214

but nobody knew because his family would not approve,' Sean said thinking on his feet.

'So?' Rose said.

'Nobody else could know that. IM chats are deleted as soon as you log off,' Sean concluded.

People were now gathering around Sean and Rose, clearly not sure what to do. They had seen him smash a man's skull, but nobody seemed game to take him on. Sean knew that it wouldn't last for long. He shook Rose. 'We have to go, now Rose Abaya.'

She grabbed his arm. 'Okay, but you'd better not be fucking lying to me.'

'I'm not. Does he look like a journalist?' Sean pointed to the motionless body blocking the emergency exit. One sleeve of his yellow shirt had ridden up his arm, revealing a military style tattoo, etched upon an incredibly muscular forearm.

'No,' Rose agreed. 'What now?'

'Follow me,' Sean said.

He ran, holding onto Rose's hand in the direction that looked like it was away from the front of the building. The crowd parted and let them go, still not wanting to tackle him. When they rounded the corner at the end of the tall building, Sean breathed a sigh of relief. He was right, they were at the back and nobody was there waiting for them. Their would-be assailants had been complacent, thinking that they already had their prey.

Speeding across a quiet road and up a side street, they soon emerged onto a busy road, with taxis going by and double-decker trams stopping and starting. 'In there,' Sean said and ran still holding Rose's hand into a shopping mall.

Inside the mall, the shops were still trading and customers were wandering in and out with arms full of new purchases. As Sean scoured the area for a good spot, he found a bench in the middle of the walkway, with a good view of the doors, but not prominent enough to make them stand out and sat Rose onto the bench.

'We need to wait here to check that we aren't being followed,' he said, looking at her. 'I'm sorry for getting you in to this,' he added.

'If you can find the people who killed David, then that's okay. Was he one of them?' Rose asked, linking Sean's arm.

'Yes, but there are a lot of them,' Sean said, without taking his eyes from the revolving door. They stayed on the bench for five minutes before Sean felt it was safe to move. 'Okay, we're clear. Let's go,' he said, steering Rose into a unisex clothes shop. 'Choose some clothes quickly: casual and comfortable would be good.'

Getting the point quickly, 'You don't have to tell me twice to buy clothes,' she said, winking at him.

When they emerged from the store, Rose was wearing a pair of white jeans, a pink blouse and flat shoes. Sean had changed his shirt to a white tailored polo shirt and when they passed a bin, Sean slipped the two shopping bags containing their old clothes into it.

'What now?' Rose said.

'You can't go back to your apartment. They'll be waiting there for you. Do you have anywhere to stay?' Sean asked.

Rose nodded. 'I have a room at the Mandarin Oriental tonight. I sing in the bar there on late shift, till two and part of the deal is that they provide me a room for the night. After that, I don't know. Maybe I'll go back to the Philippines for a while, catch up with my family.'

'I'll walk you to the hotel. Where is it?' Sean said.

'Not far. Anyway, you'll need to come so that you can collect David's things. I didn't lug that heavy suitcase all the way from TST for nothing,' she grinned.

Sean looked at her puzzled.

She smiled. 'When I got your email I put it all in a suitcase and ran out of the apartment, just like you said.'

Sean still looked puzzled. 'You got my email? Why didn't you reply?'

'I did. I reminded you about Como and the yellow shirt,' she said, then stopped, putting her face in her hands. 'Shit! I was in a hurry and opened up a new email stream. I must have sent it to the email address you used to contact me from London. Is that how they knew about the yellow shirt?' she looked at Sean with a sad face.

'Surprisingly, that's good news. It means that my other email address isn't compromised,' he said, pulling her into his chest and hugging her tightly.

As they made their way through the polished black and white marble lobby of the Mandarin Oriental and into the lift, Rose linked Sean's arm, making them look like any other romantic couple. They continued the charade as they walked down the wood panelled corridor, to her room on the twentieth floor. Once inside, Rose broke away and pulled out a large suitcase on wheels. 'It's all in here,' she said.

Sean sat the case on the floor and opened the zip, while Rose went into the bathroom to freshen up. There were three neat piles of papers, with paper clips grouping some together. An iPhone 4, in a Union Jack case, was sitting in a pocket in the lid. After quickly flicking his thumb through one of the piles of papers, he closed the case.

As he was zipping up the case, Rose came out from the bathroom, wearing nothing but a tiny black silk G-string. Above the flimsy material, her flat stomach sparkled from a stone set into her pierced belly button and her dark erect nipples protruded at an angle from her ample breasts. Sean's jaw dropped, he had never seen such a perfect body and he felt a twitch in his jeans as his penis hardened.

When she walked past him slowly and crawled onto the bed, provocatively showing her round firm buttocks under the G-string, which barely covered the hump of her vagina.

'I don't want to be alone tonight, Sean, I'm scared,' she said holding out her arms, beckoning him to join her.

217

His erection was sitting painfully against the zip on his jeans and his breath was getting heavier, when he eventually dropped his head, trying not to stare at her perfect form. 'I can't,' he said. 'I'm very flattered, but I'm in love with somebody else and it wouldn't be fair to her.'

Immediately understanding, Rose stood from the bed and went into the bathroom, returning a few seconds later in a bathrobe. 'I'm sorry,' she said. 'Whoever she is, I hope she deserves you.'

Sean smiled. 'She's called Liz and she's wonderful. The question is more do I deserve her?' he said, glancing down at the obvious bulge in his trousers.

Rose laughed. 'I'd be disappointed if that didn't happen,' she said cheekily.

A thought crossed Sean's mind quickly. 'Why don't you come and meet her? She's here with me in Hong Kong. You can stay in our room for the night and fly out tomorrow. I'm sure she'd love to meet you.'

Rose tugged at the lapels of her bathrobe exposing her deep cleavage. 'You're not looking for a threesome are you, Sean?' she winked, laughing.

'Don't tempt me,' he said laughing in response. 'Anyway, it would be more like a sixsome. We have other guests.'

Chapter 30

A glamorous hostess smiled at Sean and Rose, as they came into the Japanese restaurant through the sixth-floor entrance. 'Can I help you?' she asked, eyeing the suitcase suspiciously that Sean was pulling. After letting her know that they were meeting people, Sean surveyed the area. A funky square bar sat on the opposite side of a huge glass atrium and when he moved to the rail, the shimmering restaurant below came into view. It took him a while to locate Liz and the other girls, but they were at a wooden table against a wall of glass, which contained another room full of diners.

'This is Rose,' Sean said beaming, as they arrived at the table. He and Rose pulled up seats and began picking at the delectable food, while Sean quickly filled the group in on the events of the night so far.

Liz immediately looked concerned. 'How many people saw you hit the man with the fire extinguisher?'

'I'm not sure, but quite a few,' Sean answered.

'Not to mention CCTV. Hong Kong is full of it,' Liz added. 'We need to leave Hong Kong as soon as possible. The police will be looking for you.'

Liz's comments brought Sean back to earth quickly. 'God, you're right! I wasn't thinking straight. We should get morning flights.'

'It's only 8:30 now. If we're quick we can get the midnight flight to London on BA,' she said, glancing at her watch.

'Are you really sure we should be going back to London after what happened there?' Sean asked.

'I don't think we have a choice. If we don't stop Barker-Willet, the attacks will just keep coming, until he eventually succeeds. Taking Ping and May to the police in London is our only way out. It's the only way we can get him arrested.'

'What about the police, can we trust them after our last experience?' Sean queried.

'Clive seemed to think so. He thought that they were just a few rotten apples and that the best chance we had was to take the rape case to the police.'

'You're right, let's go,' Sean agreed.

'I'm coming too,' Rose said, as they were standing to leave. 'I'll leave you at the airport and get a flight to Manila, but I'm not staying here alone.'

As five of the six guests stood to leave, Praew remained seated, grabbing at the food on the table. 'Are you mad?' she said in Thai. 'You can't leave food like this.'

Answering in her native tongue, Liz said, 'It's okay, they have the same restaurant in London and I promise I'll take you there for your birthday.'

After grabbing a few more pieces and putting them in her pocket, Praew smiled and stood up, taking Liz by the hand. 'It's my birthday tomorrow, and the day after and the day after that,' she said, giggling happily.

On the walk back across Central, the main business district of Hong Kong, Liz held one of Praew's hands and May held the other, while she jumped up and down excitedly, talking about each different piece of the food they had eaten. Sean couldn't help but admire her, she was such a contradiction: On one hand she was just like any other twelve year old girl, giggling and playful; on the other she was a determined young woman, who marshalled three other girls out of a deadly situation and never showed a sign of feeling sorry for herself.

Back at the hotel, they quickly gathered their belongings and hopped into two taxis, arriving at the airport just in time to get seats on the late flight to London. Unfortunately, Rose couldn't get a flight to Manila until the morning. 'I'm okay, I'd rather sleep on the floor in the departure lounge, than a bed where they might come to get me any moment,' she said.

When they were leaving, Sean hugged Rose tightly and helped her create a Gmail account, so that they could stay in touch without risk of being spied upon. 'I'll let you know how we get on and if anything specific to David comes up,' he said, kissing her on the cheek.

They had split the large suitcase containing the documents down to three smaller cases, so that they could take it as carry-on luggage and not run the risk of losing the information.

Once on the plane, Ping, May and Praew sat together, while Sean and Liz sat on two seats adjacent to them. Ping put one arm around May and one around Praew, and they were soon fast asleep, looking like conjoined triplets.

'I'm not so tired. I might take a look at some of the documents,' Sean said.

'Me either,' Liz said. 'Why don't you pass me that iPhone, and I'll see if I can get into it.'

Sean passed Liz the iPhone and began scanning the documents to see what was there. 'They're all pretty much the same thing: pre- and post-acquisition accounts and print-offs of pricing from the Internet. Every single one shows the same picture: a roughly twenty per cent lift in sales in the first year, falling straight through to profit and cash flow. There're ones from Liberia, the Congo, Zimbabwe, Venezuela, Myanmar, Ivory Coast, Yemen, Libya, Sudan, East Timor.'

'Wow, that's an interesting list of countries. I guess BW always says that its strategy is to do business where others don't dare,' Liz said. 'This iPhone's dead. It'll take a while to get enough charge into it from my laptop to get anywhere.' She picked up a bundle of the papers from Sean and started to scan them herself. 'Uzbekistan, Algeria, Angola, Iraq, Pakistan, Columbia,' she said, flicking through them. 'It reads like a list of the most dangerous countries in the world.'

'Yes, but how would Thailand and China fit that list? They're not so dangerous,' Sean replied.

Liz thought for a little while. 'Corruption,' she said laughing. 'If we were doing a word-association test and you gave me a list of countries like that, I would say "corruption", as it is the common link. They're all highly corrupt countries.'

'So BW Corp is aiming to maximise its political risk. It's an interesting model. I wonder if it's factored into the share price.' Sean laughed.

Just then, the screen lit up on the iPhone and Liz flicked at it. 'Great, it's locked,' she said.

'Can't you hack it or something? You're a bit of a computer whiz, aren't you?' Sean asked.

'No, you only get ten attempts at the code, and then it fries the data if you get it wrong. We can email Rose when we get to London, maybe she'll have some idea,' Liz said. 'I think I'll try to sleep now. What are we going to do when we land?'

'I don't know, but no more 5 star hotels, I'm afraid. We're running out of money. We only have $3,000 left,' Sean replied.

'I can get more from my family,' Liz responded.

'Okay, but until you do, we need to be more careful.'

Chapter 31

The dingy B&B on Woodville Gardens in Ealing was a far cry from the Connaught, but they had managed to get two rooms for a week, for the same price as the nightly room rate they had paid at the prestigious Mayfair establishment. The rooms had the basics: bed, shower and the added bonus of a decent home Wi-Fi service, rather than the slow systems most hotels have. Liz and Sean took one room, while Ping, May and Praew took the other.

'We have to find out what happened to Clive,' Liz said, as they sat on the bed.

Sean agreed. 'They could be watching the hospital though. We should call from a phone box,' he said. 'If we can find one that works that is,' he added.

They left the hotel and walked for half an hour through the residential streets of West Acton, before stopping at a phone box that they considered far enough away from their Ealing hideout. Liz dialled the number for Hammersmith Hospital Admittances Department and waited.

'I'd like to check on a patient that was admitted last week. A Mr Clive Miller; he's my uncle,' she said into the sticky mouthpiece, while avoiding the urine stain on the floor of the box.

'We have nobody by that name, I'm sorry,' the polite female voice replied.

'Are you sure? He was admitted on Tuesday, through A&E, with multiple gunshot wounds?' Liz persisted. She heard a few keyboard clicks, as the receptionists rechecked the information.

'No. Nobody by that name, sorry. Try the Charing Cross Hospital. People often get us confused.'

Liz replaced the receiver and relayed the information to Sean.

'Impossible,' he said. 'We saw him go in.'

'I think we have to assume Barker-Willet got to him,' Liz replied. 'We're on our own now,' she added.

As they were walking back towards Ealing, Sean said. 'You know, we're due back at work in two days. Have you thought about what we are going to tell John?'

'I don't care. I'll just tell him I quit,' she laughed.

Sean didn't laugh and looked at her seriously. 'Without notice, you won't get a reference.'

Picking up on Sean's seriousness, Liz changed her tone. 'I can live with that,' she said.

'Unfortunately. I can't. I really need a job and if I leave the *Daily* on bad terms, I'll never get another job in London. You know how it works.'

'Then we've got two days to get this sorted out,' she said, squeezing his hand.

After a broken night's sleep and a greasy breakfast, they made their way with Praew, Ping and May to the Ealing police station. It was a short walk through the gardens by Ealing Broadway and onto the Uxbridge road.

Ping and May were clearly nervous as they approached the

Metropolitan Police sign, so Sean stopped and asked them again whether they were sure they wanted to go through with it. After speaking to May briefly in Thai, Ping turned to Sean. 'Yes, we're sure,' she said through gritted teeth, showing the same steely determination she had previously.

'Are you sure they deal with this type of thing?' Liz asked, looking at the five-storey office block that made up the police station. 'Shouldn't we go to Scotland Yard?' she suggested.

Sean shrugged. 'I don't know, but I think we can make the complaint at any police station. They'll tell us where to go after that. I just hope Clive was right and we aren't just walking straight into a trap.'

The first part of the formalities was relatively straight forward. They all entered the small reception area and Sean explained to the duty officer that they would like to make a rape complaint. The officer didn't ask any details, just the name of the complainant and asked them to wait for a CID officer to join them.

Detective Sergeant Rhonda Banford appeared after about ten minutes of waiting. Her dark brown hair was tied in a tight bun, accentuating her hardened facial features, attained through a difficult life. After confirming that the complainant, Ping, was happy to have the rest of them in the interview room with her, she escorted the group of five through to a small office at the rear of the police station.

To avoid any loss in translation, Sean explained the complaint against Charles Barker-Willet, showed the ID card evidence and produced two printouts of the DNA evidence from Korea, explaining that May's would show a paternal match to Charles Barker-Willet, if they checked, and the ID cards proved that Ping was only twelve years old when she conceived. As Praew was currently on an illegal passport and at risk of being deported, Sean didn't mention her to the female DS.

Throughout the interview, DS Banford took notes efficiently, until Sean mentioned Barker-Willet, when she looked up sharply. '*The* Charles Barker-Willet?' she said emphatically.

'Yes, the CEO of BW Corporation,' Sean said confidently.

'And the rape took place in Thailand, in 1992?' She questioned again.

'Yes,' Sean added.

'Then why only report it now? And why here? Why not in Thailand?' The DS was speaking to Sean, but looking at Ping.

'Because she only just saw a picture of him and recognised him. And because he's here, not in Thailand,' Sean responded.

'And your involvement?' the DS continued with her questions.

'I'm a journalist. While working on an article about Charles Barker-Willet, I came across Ping and thought that she should report the crimes committed against her,' Sean told the truth.

'Do you intend to publish this story?' The DS eyed Sean suspiciously.

'Eventually, yes,' Sean thought there was little point in saying no, it wouldn't be believable.

The DS suddenly stopped writing and surveyed the five people in the room with her. 'Look, I'll be honest. This is way above my level, not just because of who the alleged perpetrator is, but because the crime was committed so long ago and in another country. I'm just the local rape officer here in Ealing. I deal with people that were raped yesterday normally.' The detective sergeant looked apologetically at the group.

'And?' Sean shrugged. 'What do we do now?'

'I'll have to refer your case to a specialist in Scotland Yard,' the detective said.

'How long will that take?' Liz spoke for the first time.

'With a name like that on the complaint, not long I wouldn't think. It is Sunday though, so we'll have to get somebody in from home,' DS Banford said, as she stood to leave the room.

'That was easier than I thought it would be,' Sean said, blowing a sigh of relief.

The others smiled nodding their agreement.

'With any luck, we'll have Barker-Willet behind bars by this afternoon and we can all go back to living our lives.' Liz added.

Ten minutes later, DS Banford stuck her head around the door of the room. 'DCI Jenkins will be with you in about half an hour. Can I arrange a coffee while you wait?'

Detective Chief Inspector Jenkins came into the small interview room, accompanied by DS Banford, about forty-five minutes later. He was a stocky man in his mid-thirties, with an untidy mop of curly ginger hair and an unshaven face. 'Right. DS Banford hasn't told me much; just that you have rape allegations against one Charles Barker-Willet and that it was in Thailand. Can you fill me in on the rest, please?' The DCI's northern accent made him sound aggressive.

Trying not to leave anything out, Sean gave him exactly the same explanation that he had to DS Banford. Then he produced the evidence by way of IDs and DNA results.

After briefly scanning the material, DCI Jenkins placed it back on that table. 'Now, what I'm going to say in no way means that I think Mr Barker-Willet should get away with it,' he paused. 'But the ability for us to prosecute people in the United Kingdom, for sex offences committed overseas, was a part of the Sexual Offences Act 1997, which came into effect in September that same year. Unfortunately, this looks like an offence committed in 1992 and we have no power at all to do anything about it.'

Sean felt as if a falling hammer had just landed on his head. All of his hopes had been pinned on this being the final chapter in the story; something that would put Barker-Willet in jail and get him away from them. Shock was written on Liz's face too. Her uncle was languishing in a Thai jail, with the threat of

State-sponsored execution hanging over him. She needed this to work even more than Sean did.

The real horror was etched into Ping's expression though. She had agreed to come all the way from Thailand, seeking her revenge on an evil man, who had stolen her childhood and that of her daughter. Now she was being told that, although the British police believed the story, there was nothing they could do.

'So that's just it? He gets away with it?' Liz said angrily.

'Unless you have information on a more recent crime, or one committed in the United Kingdom, then yes, I'm afraid so,' DCI Jenkins said apologetically. 'I'm really sorry,' he added, 'but we'd just get nowhere with it.'

Every nerve in Sean's body tingled, as he wanted to mention Praew and how they found her, but he couldn't betray her. Any mention of that crime would lead to her return to the heartless family, in the dingy concrete house, North of Bangkok and her certain resale to the people traffickers that had got her into this sordid mess in the first place. Sean simply nodded and didn't speak.

DCI Jenkins seemed to appreciate the level of disappointment in the group and started to come up with ideas. 'The Thai police may prosecute this, but they would need to catch Barker-Willet on Thai soil. Although, we do have an extradition treaty with Thailand, so far in its 104 years of existence, we've only ever extradited one man and that was to face murder charges with strong evidence to suggest his guilt. I don't see any chance of getting this approved, even if we could get the Thai authorities to request his extradition,' the knowledgeable DCI added.

Ping shook her head violently. 'No Thai police, please,' she said to Sean.

'Okay,' Sean said, placing his hand gently on her shoulder.

Witnessing Ping's disappointment, DS Banford whispered something into the ear of the DCI, who nodded his agreement.

'Now far be it from me to tell you your job, but you did say to me that you were a journalist yes?' the DCI asked.

'Yes, with the *Financial Daily*,' Sean said.

'Okay, I'm assuming then that you have further proof of this crime; i.e., you have managed to harvest some DNA from Mr Barker-Willet and have a match?'

Admitting that they had harvested and tested Barker-Willet's DNA would implicate them in a crime, so Sean and Liz said nothing.

'Yes,' Ping said, 'we have.'

Sean lowered his head, waiting for the barrage of questions that could follow such a revelation.

'It's okay, Mr McManus, I have no interest in how you got it. I just wanted to be sure you had conclusive proof of the crime before I made any other recommendations,' the stocky DCI said, noting Sean's change in demeanour.

Still wary of admitting any personal involvement in the DNA harvesting, Sean simply looked the DCI in the eyes.

'Why don't you just publish the story? A story like that in the newspapers will do just as much damage to his reputation as a legal case will,' Jenkins said enthusiastically. 'And your newspaper is only bound to prove that it is true; it doesn't have to worry about being tied by the dates of the legislation like us, or the admissibility of evidence for that matter.'

Although Sean agreed that publishing a story like this could have the same effect upon Barker-Willet's reputation as the charges being laid, he also knew that it wouldn't get Barker-Willet locked up, which was his real aim.

Sharing his concerns with Liz, they concluded that, although it wouldn't make them fully safe and may, in fact, redouble Barker-Willet's efforts to kill them, it may just help Bill. Exposing Barker-Willet in this way could start to put pressure on whoever his powerful friends were in Thailand and might force the Korean's to begin diplomatic efforts to free Bill. Above all though, Sean thought that it would be a battle won: not the war, but an important victory on the way. It would make the arrogant Barker-Willet realise that he couldn't have it all his own way. So far they had been running from him, hiding. Now it was their turn to be the hunters.

The two police officers again offered their encouragement, DCI Jenkins even offering to make a statement for the story, if required. Taking him up on the offer, Sean quickly took his statement, which read: ' . . . *that although there was enough evidence to warrant further investigation in this case, the law as it stands prevented him from doing so*'. Sean wrote the words down verbatim and checked the details of DCI Jenkins' rank and position.

The short walk back to the B&B in Woodville Gardens was peppered with a mix of bitter disappointment at the lack of legal ability to bring Barker-Willet to trial, and a strong sense of purpose to get the piece written; something which was now in their control. Sean gave each of them tasks that he needed to be completed prior to submitting the piece. All except Liz were surprised at the level of checking that needed to be undertaken, before it could be submitted to the newspaper.

'Do you think they'll go for it?' Liz asked.

'Why not? We've got cast-iron proof. It's a great scoop. It'll go over to the *Daily* – it's not the kind of story for the *Financial Daily* – but John can arrange that. We're all the same company after all,' he said energetically.

'You don't think Barker-Willet's lawyers will threaten all kinds of horrors and our lawyers will just wimp out?' Liz frowned.

Sean shook his head. 'No. I've been in the discussion between editorial and legal before. Our lawyers are wimps alright, but the editor has the final say and with a story this big, with irrefutable proof, he'll override any legal concerns. The commercial people are bound to back him as well, as this type of story sells papers.'

'Great. Let's get it done then,' Liz said with purpose.

Chapter 32

The remainder of the day was spent piecing together the story, editing and re-editing, until the final copy was ready. Liz proved invaluable at documenting all of the background evidence and making it easy to follow for the lawyers. While Sean spent every waking moment focusing on the perfect wording, in order to get the tone right. As crime wasn't his speciality, he read hundreds of genre articles, before finally announcing that it was ready.

At 7 a.m. on Monday morning, Sean looked at the two bundles of paper on the small sideboard in their tiny room, visualising the front page headline.'CHARLES BARKER-WILLET CHILD RAPE ALLE-GATIONS'. He grabbed one bundle and placed it carefully in his backpack, before heading to the door.

'Be careful,' Liz said, as she kissed him softly on the lips.

'I think it's the last place they'll expect me to be,' he said, holding her tightly by the waist. He was glad when Liz decided that she was not going in to work, preferring instead to look after Praew,

Ping and May. Despite his previous comment, he knew that it could be dangerous, but it was a risk worth taking if it finally got something back at Barker-Willet.

'If I get fired, then that's life,' Liz said. 'I'll see if I can get into David's iPhone with the code Rose sent through,' she added.

On the short walk to Ealing Broadway Tube station, Sean was relaxed and enjoying the normality that came with a morning Tube ride to work, even though he normally walked to work from his Whitechapel flat. He found a seat on the District Line Tube, one of the advantages of being the first stop on the line, and settled in for the forty-five minute journey to Aldgate East Tube station. By the time they reached Chiswick, the Tube was already heaving with people and at each stop more poured on, until some light relief came as people hopped off to change lines at Earls Court. The packed Tube gave Sean comfort that he was safe and he let his mind drift off to the effects submitting a piece like this could have upon his career.

He had been overdue a promotion to assistant editor for some time and doubtless, his attitude was probably partly to blame for that, but a simple promotion wasn't what interested him now: penning a story as big as this could propel him out of financial journalism and into more interesting fields, such as crime, possibly into one of the very few investigative jobs still available in the world of newspaper journalism. Maybe he could even make the move to TV journalism, with a role on *Panorama* or similar. The opportunities would be endless. This was the break he had been looking for, but he had never appreciated the price he would have to pay to get it.

When the tube pulled in to Aldgate East station, Sean's dreams were cut short. He went with the crowd up the escalators and out onto Whitechapel Road, turning immediately left onto the wide street. From there, he could see the glass and concrete facade of the newspaper's offices, some 150m ahead of him. It was 8:30, and people would be drifting into the newsroom about now, so he made his way towards the front door.

When he reached a spot about 50 metres away, something odd caught his eye. He couldn't be sure, but he stopped to check anyway. Then he saw him again, standing about twenty metres beyond the entrance to the newspaper's offices: Peter Dawson, the ex-policeman who had betrayed Clive. Sean froze. They were obviously staking out his office. Did they somehow know that he was due back in work today? If so, how? Or was it just that they were staking out lots of places hoping that he might turn up?

Searching for an answer to his questions, he crossed the road quickly, using a fellow commuter as cover and slipped into a coffee shop, which occupied a spot almost directly opposite the office. He ordered an espresso and took a seat close to the window, with a view of the main entrance to the office block.

Dawson was still there, pretending to read a newspaper, but observing everybody that came or went through the revolving doors. Two other people were loitering without reason: they were in their twenties, with close cropped hair and muscular builds. *They all look the same*, Sean thought. *Like soldiers.*

There was no way that Sean could get into the front entrance without being spotted, but he wasn't going to let that stop him; not now; not after he had come this far; not when he could finally see the finish line. So he finished his coffee and left the café.

He turned sharp left and went under the protective cover of the scaffolding, which was covering the building next to the coffee shop. Staying under the cover, he made his way back to the Tube station entrance and crossed the road onto Leman Street. A little way along Leman Street, he turned onto a tree-lined footpath, which led to the rear door of the newspaper's offices. Only ten metres up the path, he stopped abruptly. Two men with the same cropped hair and military style precision, were lurking outside the rear entrance. Sean moved in towards the treeline and backed away onto Leman Street, where he turned right and headed away from the office.

Further along he cut quickly into Alien Street and circled around the back of the office, then back around onto Mansell Street, bringing him to the side entrance. He needed a place to think; somewhere that he wouldn't run any risk of being seen; but he also needed to get into the office. As he suspected, the side door from Mansell Street was also covered by BW's soldiers.

Realising that there was no way he could get into the office, Sean glanced at his watch. It was 8:45 a.m. He still had time to head John off before he got to the office. John always arrived at the office at 9:10 a.m., and came in via Fenchurch Street mainline station. Sean knew that he walked from the station, which must mean that he would walk up Aldgate High Street. So he quickly crossed Mansell Street and ran up the small back alley, that led to Aldgate High Street, coming out opposite Aldgate Tube station, onto a pavement jam-packed with people heading to work. Nearly everybody wore the same long black coats and carried slim leather briefcases along with umbrellas. How was he going to pick out one person in the crowd?

Narrowing his search down to the southern pavement, as he knew that there was no reason for John to cross to the northern side, Sean found a suitable spot outside a pub, on a corner where John would need to cross the road. If John did come that way, he would get a good view of him approaching. There was an old church opposite and the Gherkin building dominated the skyline to the left of it. Sean marvelled at the odd juxtaposition, as hundreds of people walked passed him in both directions. Still he didn't see John. When it reached 9:00 a.m. and John still hadn't appeared, Sean was beginning to think that it was a bad idea and that he had somehow missed him.

Just when he was ready to give up, John's familiar face appeared, carrying a coffee from the café on the junction. 'John,' Sean called out, as he stepped onto the pavement.

John looked up, startled. 'Sean, welcome back. I didn't know you walked this way,' he said. smiling, taking a sip of his coffee.

'I need to talk before we get to the office,' Sean said.

'I don't really have any time. I've been summoned upstairs for a meeting; some big announcement apparently. Can't it wait until later?' he asked.

'No, it can't wait. Just ten minutes, please. It's important,' Sean pleaded.

John obviously picked up on the sincerity of Sean's tone. 'Okay, just ten minutes. I really do have to be at this meeting though.' He led Sean to the a small café, further along the street and closer to the office. For a moment Sean thought that he was leading him straight to Barker-Willet's men, but he controlled his paranoia. They found a seat and ordered two coffees, as John disposed of his takeaway coffee in a bin. 'What's so important then, Sean?' John said, impatiently glancing at his watch.

Without speaking, Sean produced the bundle of papers from his backpack. John immediately opened the manila folder and looked at the front page, then closed it again quickly. 'I thought I gave you instructions to back off Barker-Willet?' he said.

'Well, I didn't, and this is what I came up with,' Sean replied dismissing John's reprimand.

'Child rape? Are you sure. It's way off your patch,' John asked.

'Fully documented and evidenced with DNA, ID cards and witness statements, inside the pack. It's irrefutable,' Sean said confidently.

John fell silent briefly. 'Fuck! If you're right, this is big,' he said, shaking his head slowly.

'I'm sure, John. It's all there and Barker-Willet isn't his real name. He's called David Findlow and he's the son of an East End gangster named Franky Findlow.'

'Fuck!' John said again.

'Can you get it out?' Sean asked.

John lifted his head and looked at Sean directly in the eyes. 'If I can't then why the fuck did I become a journalist? You're damn right I can get this out. It will need to go over to the *Daily*. Let's go and see Morris Greene. I think you'll be his new poster boy.'

'Thanks, but I can't come.' Sean explained that Barker-Willet knew he had the story and was trying to kill him.

'If you could give any evidence of that, that would make the story even better,' John said.

Sean shook his head. 'Be careful, John. This is serious; this guy's dangerous.'

John immediately changed his demeanour. 'Okay, I'll get the story out. How can I get hold of you?' he said in a serious tone.

'I'm in hiding with Liz. He's trying to kill her too, and the woman he raped. I'll get hold of you. I can't come in to work until it's safe; Liz neither,' Sean said.

'Okay, I'll cover for you until you think it's safe to come back,' John nodded.

'Once the story is published, it will make it a lot more difficult for him, as there will be a direct link to him if we're killed. So we may be okay later this week,' Sean said optimistically.

'Take your time. I doubt you'll be working in my shitty department anyway after this gets published,' John smiled.

'Watch the news. This will hit the TV news before the papers if we play it right. You'll need to queue for a copy of the paper in the morning. Stay safe, Sean, and let me know if there's anything you need.'

Before walking out of the door, John patted Sean on the back warmly and then turned right towards the *Daily News* offices. Two minutes later, Sean left in the opposite direction, his pack considerably lighter without the thick manila folder that made up one of his two copies. But the real weight had been lifted from his mind, and he felt like jumping for joy.

Chapter 33

Monday, 2nd March. London, England

Sean sprinted excitedly into Aldgate Tube station and hopped on a Hammersmith and City line train to White City, where he changed to the Central Line for Ealing Broadway, making his way across London, as he couldn't wait to tell Liz the good news.

When he arrived at the small B&B, he found all four of the women sitting in the same room, playing some kind of Thai board game that they had made with paper. Liz jumped up and put her arms around him. 'I was so scared,' she said. 'What happened? Why are you back so quickly?'

Sean explained the morning's events and told everybody to get ready, as they were going for a celebratory lunch. 'We'll need to find a place with a TV though,' he said. 'John told me to watch the news, as they'd probably release the story through TV, to boost paper sales tomorrow.' He was beaming and his excitement flowed through to everybody else, as they scrambled to get ready.

Automatically packing up their important things – it was becoming a force of habit now to carry everything with them

– they made their way out of the B&B. After counting the remaining cash, Sean announced that they still had enough for a good slap-up lunch and then they would need to get more.

'Oh, I got into this, but haven't really looked at it yet,' Liz said waving David Chan's mobile in the air, then throwing it into the backpack with the passports and laptops. After a short tube ride and a long walk, they found a table at a waterfront eatery in Chiswick. The TV was on in the background and Sean asked if it could be turned to the *BBC news*. The restaurant was quiet and the owner gladly obliged, as Sean ordered a bottle of Krug.

When the mountain of food that they had ordered arrived, they all ate like they had never eaten before. Keeping one eye on the TV throughout the early lunch, Sean's pulse was racing with excitement, but nothing appeared. At 12 p.m., they had already finished eating the main course and were tucking into puddings, washed down with a bottle of sticky wine.

The main news items covered the continuing problems in the Middle East, but nothing was mentioned about Sean's story. *Maybe John couldn't convince the lawyers?* Sean thought. Then, at the end of the regular news, the business news came on. Sean dropped his glass to the floor, as the headline appeared behind the grey-haired news anchor. 'BW CORP BUYS DAILY NEWS GROUP.'

When the anchor started to speak, the whole group went silent, staring at the screen in silence. 'Yes, this is an emerging story, apparently BW struck a deal in the late hours of Sunday evening to acquire the struggling Daily News Group from the Moretti family, who said they were delighted with the £2 billion price tag.'

The camera panned to 'an expert', that they had found quickly from a London-based business college, which Sean had ever heard of. 'It would seem an enormous price to pay for a company that hasn't made a profit for ten years and only has a net asset value of £100 million?' the anchor asked.

'Well, when you put it like that yes, it would seem excessive, but . . .'

The anchor interrupted. 'Is there another way to put it? It's twenty times the value of the assets and as it doesn't make a profit, what other way to value it is there?'

'Well, Charles Barker-Willet didn't get to be as rich as he is by overpaying for companies. He'll have a plan for it. He always does,' the expert said, pompously implying that he knew more than the perplexed anchor.

None of the group moved, their eyes transfixed on the TV. A wave of nausea suddenly hit Sean and he stood quickly, weaving his way to the toilet, where he vomited the contents of his stomach into the bowl. The feeling of loss and desperation he felt encompassed his whole body. 'How could he beat us again?' he said aloud. After cleaning up his face, Sean went back out into the restaurant to see that the news item had finished and the four women were talking heatedly around the table.

'What does it mean, Sean?' Ping asked.

'That it's over: they've won; we've lost,' he said quietly.

'No,' Ping said adamantly. 'There are other newspapers, we go there.' She banged her fist on the table.

'It's not that easy,' Sean said. 'They won't take a story like that from somebody who just walks in off the street, it's too risky for them. Our only real chance was the *Daily*, where they know that Liz and I would have checked our facts properly.'

'So what do we do now then?' Liz asked.

Sean started to speak, but was interrupted by Liz as the news returned to the BW story.

The news anchor had just transferred to somebody on-site at the Daily News Group building. Sean looked at the picture of the building on TV that he had been stood outside not three hours before. The reporter was holding a microphone in her hand, speaking into the camera. 'Yes, Connor, the police have just confirmed that there has been a suspicious death in the building. They are not saying whether it is related to the acquisition announcement, but they have asked us to appeal for help from the public.'

'Okay,' the anchor said.

The female reporter continued with her piece to camera. 'The victim has been named by the police as John Hammond, a forty-five-year-old assistant business editor in the *Financial Daily* division of Daily News Group. He was apparently stabbed repeatedly in the emergency exit stairwell and died before he was found at 11 a.m. this morning, by the cleaner.'

'You said the police are making an appeal for information. Jane. What is that?' the anchor asked.

The story hammered Sean's already weakening resolve, and he began to tremble and shake. He was responsible for John's death; he had given him the story and John had been killed because he knew too much. Sean's loathing for the corrupt CEO had grown so strong that it had twisted his own moral fabric to the point where, at that moment and given the opportunity, he would have killed David Findlow, aka Charles Barker-Willet with his own bare hands.

The reporter continued. 'Well, they already have a suspect: a rogue employee named Sean McManus. A large photo of Sean was put onto the screen. Apparently, Mr McManus's security card was used to enter and leave the building around the time of the murder, and he was known to bear some kind of grudge against the deceased,' she said, reading from a script.

'Really, a disgruntled staff member?' the anchor added some pre-staged drama to the story.

'Yes, but in a further twist to this story, the police have received information that the same staff member, Sean McManus, is wanted by police for murders in both Thailand and Hong Kong,' the reporter added, faking a serious frown.

'So this man is on some kind of killing spree? Do the police know why?' the anchor asked.

'Not at this stage, no. But he is believed to be working with an accomplice, who is also an employee of the Daily News Group: Ms Elizabeth Channing, a thirty-two-year-old woman of Anglo-Korean decent. She is also wanted by police in relation to the murder in Thailand.' A picture of Liz was placed alongside that of Sean, before the female reporter continued her piece.

'If anybody has seen either of these two people, they should not approach them. The police believe them both to be armed and dangerous. Please contact the investigation team on this number, if you have any information as to the whereabouts of Sean McManus or Liz Channing, or dial 999.'

The restaurant owner was now staring at them, clearly unsure of what to do. To appease him, Sean reached into his backpack, pulled out £500 for the food and wine and placed it on the table. Upon Sean's signal, the previously jubilant group then sprinted out of the door, running as fast as possible, until they were well into Ravenscourt Park, some 700 metres from the restaurant. Observing that the park was quiet, they stopped to regain their breath, next to an ornamental lake.

'What now?' Liz said, breathing heavily and mopping sweat from her forehead, her face etched with fear.

'We can't go back to the B&B in Ealing, it's too risky,' Sean responded. 'What have we left there?'

'Only clothes and the accounts for the BW companies from David Chan. I already made a list of them, along with the major details, it's on my laptop and yours, so it's okay,' Liz replied.

'We need to find somewhere safe to spend the night, while we think of a plan,' Sean said, breathing heavily.

'This place will be crawling with police any minute,' Liz added.

'Manchester,' Sean said. 'I keep a rental house there; it's empty at the moment and I can get the key from the key safe. We should be okay there for a couple of days at least.'

'Okay. We need to travel there separately though. It's too risky for us to be seen together. I'll meet you outside WHSmith in Manchester Piccadilly train station at 7 p.m. tonight. You get there alone. I'll take the others. The police are looking for a white man with an Asian woman, so you'll stand out if you travel with any of us.'

Sean gave Liz £300 of the remaining money and she quickly went north, steering the small group towards Goldhawk Road. Sean went south towards King Street, where he managed to get a cab quite easily, directing the driver to Euston Train station. As they drove east towards the Hammersmith Apollo, a stream of police cars went in the opposite direction, with their sirens blaring out.

'Bloody hell!' the cab driver spoke. 'They're in a hurry. Must be a sale on at Dunkin Doughnuts.'

Sean laughed reluctantly at the joke, trying to act normally.

'I bet they're chasing that Sean McManus geezer. He's a right bad bastard apparently,' the driver added.

'Who's he?' Sean asked hesitantly.

'Oh, it's been on the radio constantly for the last half hour. He stabbed a geezer to death in the city this morning. But then it turns out him and his missus are wanted all over the world for other murders. They reckon now that he's the top dog in some kind of international paedophile people-smuggling ring. They got pictures of 'em both, with a young oriental girl that they kidnapped.' The taxi driver's accent became more and more cockney, as he became more agitated.

Sean could do nothing to quell the growing sense of panic in his stomach. Being a wanted killer was one thing, the general public would barely take notice. Being a wanted paedophile was another. Every deranged vigilante with a TV set would be looking to lynch him. Of course Barker-Willet knew that and was tightening the noose with each piece of information he released.

Chapter 34

Monday, 2nd March. Manchester, England

'Ping and May decided to go it alone,' Liz said, as Sean arrived outside WHSmith and noticed that only Praew was with her.

'God,' Sean said. 'I feel so responsible for putting her in this situation and I've let her down. She'll never get justice now.'

'On the contrary,' Liz interrupted. 'She was so grateful that somebody had at least tried. She doesn't blame you at all. She can see that you did everything you could for her. She said that she's going to stay in Europe somewhere and try to make a life as an illegal immigrant.'

'I wish I could've done more,' Sean said, shaking his head.

Praew was smiling at Sean, tugging his arm excitedly. 'She saw herself on the TV with us. She has no idea why, but she thinks she's a celebrity now,' Liz said, kissing Praew on the forehead. 'I didn't have the heart to tell her the truth.'

The small 1930s' red brick semi-detached house in Failsworth, an inner-city suburb in North Manchester, had belonged to Sean's grandmother, who had died a few years before. It had been tenanted when she died and the tenants had moved out a month earlier. As far as Sean knew the title was still in his grandmother's name, which wasn't McManus and as nobody knew him in the area, he was happy that it would be a while before they found them there.

Parkside Avenue was a quiet cul-de-sac, leading onto open parkland and the house was at the end of the street, in a secluded corner plot. Inside, the furniture had been left, as it was a fully furnished rental and although the old style furniture wasn't exactly tasteful, it had everything that they needed for a couple of days to collect their thoughts. Sean quickly turned on the TV and tuned in to the *BBC news* channel. Photos of Liz, Praew and himself behind the anchor immediately came onto screen, with a heading at the bottom of the page stating: 'BRITAIN'S MOST WANTED'.

'How did they make us look so depraved?' Liz asked, examining the photos on screen, in which she and Sean looked like hardened criminals.

'It looks like they've added pockmarks to your face and a five-o'clock shadow to mine. They must've used Photoshop to make us look more like criminals, without making us unrecognisable,' he said, still in shock at the latest twist in the saga.

The anchor started to speak. 'We have further developments in the Sean McManus and Liz Channing story. This very morning, they allegedly ran out of a Chiswick restaurant, after drinking a £300 bottle of champagne, without paying.' The *BBC News* then showed a clip of the restaurant owner holding up a bottle of Krug. 'Mr Sachetti was just pleased to get away with his life, after Sean McManus became angry and started throwing glasses around,' the anchor said.

'Lying arsehole,' Liz commented.

'They also left a B&B in Ealing without paying their bill.' A clip came on of the owner of the grotty B&B.

'I thought they were suspicious. They passed the kid off as

their own, but there was something about them that I didn't like.'

'Fuck!' Sean said. 'I'm glad that I've got no family left to watch this shit. What will my friends think?' he said holding his head.

'Exactly what Barker-Willet wants them to think: that you're a dirty twisted pervert and a murderer,' Liz said coldly, telling the truth.

'In a new twist to the tale, it appears that Liz Channing, Sean McManus's partner in crime, comes from a family of criminals. Not only is she wanted for murder in Thailand, but her uncle is currently in a Bangkok prison awaiting for trial for murder.' The anchor paused. 'There are many theories about the killing spree these two young people have embarked upon, but the police believe that they run an international prostitution and people-trafficking ring, which deals in young Asian women and children.'

A CCTV footage clip of Sean pulling Rose away from the fire exit at Como came onto the screen. 'This clip from the Hong Kong police shows Sean McManus dragging a young Filipina woman, believed to be a prostitute, away from a place where he had, just seconds before, viciously killed an undercover police officer.' The anchor shook his head in staged disgust.

Another clip then came on, showing Sean, Praew and Liz holding hands. They were at Hong Kong airport. Sean remembered the moment, when Praew had been playing and pulling on their arms. The grab taken from the footage though made it look like they were dragging her, against her will, through the airport.

'This footage, also from the Hong Kong police, shows the couple abducting a young girl, probably to bring her to London to work as an unpaid prostitute and slave,' the anchor said, shaking his head in a rehearsed manner again. 'The police believe that the couple are in hiding, somewhere in London. If you have any information regarding their whereabouts, please call this number.'

'How does it feel to be the most hated woman in England?' Sean joked.

Liz didn't laugh. 'Honestly? Scary,' she said and started to cry on Sean's shoulder.

The anchor then changed tack and became more upbeat. 'In a slightly related story, the Prime Minister let slip a name that will definitely be on his Queens Birthday Honours list this summer; Charles Barker-Willet. The PM said this morning, that Mr Barker-Willet has done more to put this country on the map, than could ever be expected, and the country needs to recognise his outstanding contribution.' When Barker-Willet's face came onto the screen, Praew stopped moving, her body rooted to the spot with fear at the sight of his image.

'Turn it off,' Liz screamed. 'I can't stand it. I wish he was dead.'

After trying to convince her that she would be okay, Liz put Praew into bed in the spare room and kissed her on the forehead. 'She's such a sweet kid. She doesn't deserve this,' Sean said, when Liz returned the lounge.

'I know, but what's going to happen to her when we get arrested?' Liz said.

'I've been thinking about that,' he said tentatively. 'I think you should get out of the country and go back to Korea. You'll be safer there. We still have a passport for you that hasn't been used.' Sean held her as tightly as possible.

'No way, and leave you here to face that lot?' Liz said.

'You need to do it for Praew. Take her with you,' he said quietly, knowing that it would make it difficult for her to refuse.

When Liz realised that he was serious, she didn't speak for a while. 'Okay, as long as you promise to make love to me, like it is our last time, right now,' she said, as tears welled in her eyes. Sean reached over and kissed her passionately on the lips, before he guided her up the stairs to the master bedroom.

Chapter 35

Parting from Liz was the hardest thing Sean had done in his life. He told her that he would join her in Korea soon, but they both knew that he had to bring the conflict with Barker-Willet to a conclusion first, or it would never go away and they would never be safe. Although neither spoke about it openly, they knew that Sean's chances of winning against Barker-Willet and his army were almost non-existent.

Liz opted to take a complex route to Seoul, in order to hopefully avoid capture. She would take the train to Hollyhead, in Wales, then the ferry to Dublin. From Dublin, she would fly to Munich and then on to Seoul. Her parting gesture to Sean was to give him £2,000 that she had obtained from a cash machine, before leaving London. 'It was the maximum my cards would let me have and I thought that it would make the police think that we were still in London,' she said, shoving the money in his backpack.

When it was finally time for her to leave, Sean held her so tightly

247

he thought he might injure her. The sight of Liz and Praew walking up Parkside Avenue towards the bus stop, hand in hand, had brought tears to his eyes for the first time since this mess had started two weeks earlier. Deep down, he knew that there was a strong probability he would never see Liz again and it hurt more than anything Barker-Willet had done to him so far. A determined resolve overtook his body, as he sat at the kitchen table to plan his next move.

Now that the rape plan had failed, he knew that he needed another approach to get at Barker-Willet. He was sure that the key was in the BW Corporation's operations. Clive was right that the actions of Barker-Willet had been too over-the-top for just the rape allegations and he still didn't understand why they needed a private army.

He had to find the answers to his questions: it was the only way he could take on Barker-Willet and the only way that he might find his way back to Liz.

Still considering his approach, he toyed with the iPhone that was now successfully unlocked. *Did David Chan get further than us into the company's affairs?* he thought. He started with the text messages: there were thousands of messages, from hundreds of people. Most were in English and it took him about two hours to scan them all, but he found nothing, just the usual collection of short personal messages to friends, family and colleagues. By far the most were between Rose and David. It was clear they had been very much in love.

The next obvious place to check was his email. David Chan operated six email accounts from the phone. The work email wasn't responding and hadn't had any activity on it for years. The other Gmail and Yahoo accounts were still live and receiving piles of spam daily. He changed the password on each of the accounts and then logged on to each of them individually, using his laptop in order to get far enough back in history, that he could see the activity around the time of David's death.

David clearly compartmentalised various parts of his life. He had one account for social media, one for family, one for friends, one for Rose, one for Internet shopping and one for work. None of them contained anything remotely connected to the BW Corp, and Sean was beginning to despair.

When he clicked on the photos icon, there were scores of photos of David and Rose together in various places: out with friends, on holiday in Beijing, etc. Then he saw a picture of David Findlow, in the forecourt of the Peninsula Hotel in Hong Kong; he appeared to be waiting for somebody. Sean quickly flicked to the next photo. It was David Findlow again, this time climbing into the back of a green Rolls Royce outside the same hotel. Sean could just make out the face of another person in the car, waiting for him, but he didn't know who it was.

There were no more photos of interest in the phone and Sean put it to one side, his frustration mounting at his lack of progress. Then he thought of Clive's wise counsel. 'If being a detective was easy, everyone would be one.'

'What would Clive do?' he said aloud, as he laid a blank piece of A3 paper out in front of him and wrote David Findlow/Charles Barker-Willet in the middle of it, making a large circle around the name. He didn't know whether playing at being a detective would help, but he had to try something.

The next name he placed on the page was Franky Findlow. He wrote the name at the top right of the page and circled it, then entered Charles Barker-Willet (Elder) into the top left corner.

He continued thought-mapping, until he had circles covering Lilac Bar, David Chan, Anthony Findlow, Hong Kong, soldiers, Peter Dawson, BW Corporation, Ping, Swiss banking and Thai general. The circles orbited around the centre: David Findlow. But what was the connection?

Drawing a red line between the circles for Franky Findlow, David Findlow and Anthony Findlow, indicated the family link, and then Sean studied the boxes further. Following the same process, he drew a green line between BW Corp, Swiss banking and David Findlow, highlighting the company relationships.

The next line was drawn in orange, linking Ping, Lilac Bar and David Findlow, showing the rape connections.

Sean stared at the page, then linked David Chan to Hong Kong and Charles Barker-Willet (Elder), in yellow. Still nothing stood out that he thought could take him further in his understanding of what was behind BW Corp.

Scrambling for ideas, he pulled out a black pen, checking the entries that had no connecting lines and drew a dotted line from soldiers to Thai general, then drew a question mark. The link was a little tenuous, but they were both military, he thought. Under the same premise, he continued the dotted line to Anthony Findlow and adjusted his name to Brigadier Anthony Findlow.

Happy that he had covered the military connections, he drew a pencil line from Anthony Findlow to Peter Dawson, David Findlow and Franky Findlow, noting that the corrupt policeman knew all of them.

When he sat back and studied the page. Other than David Findlow, the person with the most connecting lines coming from their circle was Anthony Findlow, the Brigadier. 'Why did we originally rule him out?' Sean said aloud. Then he remembered the meeting with Peter Dawson in Clive's office. 'But Dawson turned out to be corrupt,' he said to himself.

Sean put a double red line around the circle of Brigadier Anthony Findlow.

A Google search on Brigadier Sir Anthony Findlow returned a surprising number of hits. A mass of newspaper articles had been written about him. Some claiming that he was the most well-connected military man in the world, and that he was the personal confident to most of the world's military leaders. Other articles claimed that he had personally stopped more wars than the whole of the United Nations put together, simply by making a phone call.

In 2008, he had been knighted for 'services to peace' and his current role in Whitehall made him the key link between foreign military forces and the British Government.

Dawson was right. This guy walks on water, Sean thought. *But Dawson was in some way linked to BW, so why should I believe him?* he countered his own thinking.

When he clicked on one of the newspaper articles, the heading 'BRITISH MILITARY DELEGATION VISITS ANGOLA', came up. David looked at the picture beneath and zoomed in on it. A group of senior military officers were shaking hands with their foreign counterparts. Sean scrolled down to the photo caption: *General Lukamba greets Brigadier Sir Anthony Findlow of the British Army and welcomes him to Luanda.* The faces were too pixelated to make out in the grainy black and white photo.

Sean flicked onto the next article. This time it was of Brigadier Findlow visiting Ghana, then another of him visiting Paraguay. There were thirty or so articles in all about Anthony Findlow, at various ranks, visiting foreign military officers. 'But so what?' Sean said. 'That's his job surely?'

Then a photo came up of Anthony Findlow being interviewed following his knighthood. Sean instantly recognised the face and pulled David Chan's phone out. The mysterious photo on David Chan's phone was of a meeting between Anthony Findlow and David Findlow, in the back of a green Roll Royce in Hong Kong. It triggered alarm bells in Sean's head. 'So much for him disowning his family. And how would he know that David wasn't dead, unless he's involved?' he said to himself.

He quickly found the spreadsheet that Liz had left him, of her workings on the BW acquisitions, remembering that there was an acquisition in Angola. The spreadsheet noted it as taking place in August 2002. When he flicked back to the photo of Anthony

Findlow and the Angolan General, the article was dated February 2002.

Then he found an acquisition in Paraguay from November 1999, and noted the article showing Anthony Findlow's visit was in April 1999.

He cross-referenced ten more of the articles to the acquisition dates. In each case, Anthony Findlow had visited the country in an official capacity, between six and nine months before the acquisition by BW Corporation. But why?

Was he just smoothing the way for a BW acquisition, making sure that the local military weren't about to burn the company to the ground? It would certainly make sense to check out the political and military situation, in the unstable countries where BW operated, before buying a company. But if that was what the Brigadier was up to, it wouldn't even be a scandal. He would just be seen to be promoting British trade. And still, Sean came back to Clive's comment: 'Why does Barker-Willet need an army?' He added his own line to it. 'Where does that army come from?' The Brigadier would certainly have access to soldiers that were leaving the service, and would be in a prime position to recruit them. Then he again came back to 'why?' as the missing link.

Sean spent the rest of the day researching the Brigadier, and although by midnight he thought that he knew him well, he had nothing more to go on than what he had already found. He went to bed frustrated and lonely, hoping that Liz was okay. *She should be on the ferry to Dublin now*, he thought, having not seen anything on the news that would indicate that she had been caught.

In the morning he would need to leave the comfort of the small house in Manchester. The risk that the police or Barker-Willet would find him there was too great for him to stay. He had nowhere to go, but had decided that he should head back towards London, to confront the enemy and try to bring the terrifying ordeal to an end.

Chapter 36

Wednesday, 4th March. The Irish Sea

It was 2 a.m. and Liz couldn't get to sleep. She had tossed and turned in her bunk since 8 p.m. and couldn't stop thinking about the danger in which she had left Sean. Her growing feeling of shame and cowardice was compounded by fact that she had no way of contacting him. She resolved that as soon as Praew was safely with her family in Seoul, she would return to the UK and help Sean in his fight against Barker-Willet's evil empire.

Praew was also awake and complaining about feeling seasick, as the boat had been rocking steadily from side to side since they left the harbour in Wales.

'Let's go for a walk,' Liz said, snapping herself out of her gloom for Praew's sake.

The cold air hit them hard as Liz forced open the door to the deck, but Praew, who was looking pale, went through regardless. She immediately stopped at the rail and vomited over the edge of the ship. As soon as she had finished, she stood upright and faced Liz. 'That's better,' she said, with a bright smile on her face.

They walked slowly around the deck linking arms, until they reached the rear of the ship. Praew marvelled at the huge wake left by the ferry, as it ploughed through the cold Irish Sea, but it wasn't long before they felt the chill from the stiff breeze and decided to head back to their cabin.

Praew walked in front, with Liz holding on to her shoulders playfully. She giggled as Liz danced down the narrow corridor that led to their tiny cabin. After Liz unlocked the door, Praew entered the cabin first, followed by Liz, who immediately locked the door behind her and moved next to her bunk. As she did, the toilet door swung open and a young man stepped out carrying a pistol.

Praew screamed, but the dull roar of the engines and the vibration from the ship muffled out the sound, so that it would be nothing more than a whimper outside the cabin.

'Sit down,' the man barked aggressively.

Both Liz and Praew followed the instruction and sat on the edge of the lower bunk.

'Where's McManus?' the gunman asked.

Liz didn't speak.

'Tell me where he is or I shoot the girl now!' He waved the pistol at Praew, who immediately stuck her tongue out at him defiantly.

'He didn't come,' Liz said.

The gunman shook his head angrily. 'I know that, but where's he hiding?'

'I don't know,' Liz answered.

'I don't believe you,' he waved the gun at Praew again and she repeated her defiance.

'I really don't know. We were staying in a house in Chester. I have no idea where, but he moved on when I left this morning. He didn't say where to.' Liz stared at her attacker, without showing any emotion.

'Then I'll just have to kill you. You're of no use to us,' he said angrily, through gritted teeth.

'Okay,' Liz said casually, gambling that it was a hollow threat.

'If you tell me where he is, I'll let you and the runt live,' he said, as his anger increased at Liz's faked nonchalance.

'I don't know, so you'll just have to kill us; won't you,' Liz said again. She was still gambling that he wasn't there to kill them, or they would already be dead. They wanted to know where Sean was, but if she told him, she knew the attacker would kill them both.

She drew a sharp breath of air when he raised his pistol to the side of Praew's head, but held her nerve and continued her dangerous wager. *As long as they don't have Sean we should be okay*, she thought. *They won't kill Praew, as risking it would just push me over the edge and I would never cooperate*, Liz reasoned. She hoped she was right.

The sight of the pistol didn't make Praew flinch at all. Liz thought that she had probably seen them many times before, from her dingy cell at the gruesome Russian brothel. Instead, she looked at the man holding the gun to her head with disdain, and smiled proudly, as if to say, 'Okay kill me. It's not the worst thing that has ever happened to me.' At that moment Liz felt so proud of the plucky young Thai girl, she committed to herself that, should they get through this ordeal alive, she would do everything she could to ensure that Praew had the best life possible.

While the attacker tried to work out why Praew wasn't intimidated by him, Liz looked for an opportunity to tackle him. But he was muscular and young, she would have no chance in the tight cabin space.

The Mexican stand-off continued, as the group of three people sat out the remainder of the voyage in Liz's tiny cabin. The young man didn't drop his guard, holding the pistol at the ready the whole time and Liz didn't take her eyes off him, waiting for an opportunity to pounce.

When they started to pull into the port of Dublin, the attacker suddenly stood up. 'Right, come with me,' he said, looking out of the porthole. 'Tell her to stay in front, and if she runs, I'll kill you. You stay in front of me. Any tricks and you're dead,' he waved the gun at her.

Liz said some words in Thai to Praew, who nodded her understanding, before they stood to leave. Outside the cabin, the ship's corridors were still empty, as the ship still had an hour or so before docking. They walked forward, with Praew in front carrying the backpack, followed by Liz and then the attacker, his pistol forced painfully into her back.

When they reached the end of the corridor, they turned sharply into the stairwell that led to the car decks. The staircase was narrow and steep and they stepped forward carefully, taking one step at a time. Halfway down, the stairs cornered and looped back on themselves sharply. As Praew stepped onto the narrow landing, with Liz and the attacker still in the tight stairwell, Liz suddenly stopped, wedging her body in the stairwell, her hands gripping the rails. 'Now!' she shouted in Thai.

Hearing the instruction, Praew sprang forward and around the corner out of sight, then she dashed down some more stairs. Fighting to get past, the attacker barged into Liz's back, but she clung on to the stair rails using all of her strength. When she heard the door to the car deck below open and then close, she knew that Praew had gone out onto the car deck, which would give her a lot of places to hide. She allowed the attacker to finally knock her to the floor and run past her, but when he did, she made a move in the opposite direction, forcing him to stop and make a decision between her and Praew. Making his call, he grabbed Liz by the hair and dragged her down the remaining stairs, then out onto the car deck. The searing pain in Liz's scalp felt as if her skin was being ripped from her head, when the attacker pushed the gun in her ribs and spoke. 'That'll cost you, bitch,' he said, but he still didn't shoot. Liz's realised that her gamble had been right: they needed her alive to get to Sean.

On the car deck, there was no sign of Praew and there were a million places to hide. The deck would soon fill up with people, giving the attacker no chance to search for her. Liz was pleased that Praew had escaped; it went someway to numbing her sense of guilt over leaving Sean to face Barker-Willet alone. As she was dragged aggressively by the hair to the back of a white transit van, she lashed out at her attacker with her fists, feeling a renewed sense of life. But he just ignored her, taking the blows, as if they were fleabites. When they reached the van, her attacker opened the rear door and pushed her in, stepping in quickly after her.

As soon as the door was closed, Liz felt a sharp kick to the back of her knees and she tumbled onto the floor of the van. The attacker was on her in seconds, tying her hands behind her back and taping her mouth shut with packing tape, before he put a sack over her head.

The sudden darkness scared Liz, as she rolled around on the floor of the van, trying to escape. Her fear then turned to abject terror, as the young gunman ripped open her blouse and roughly fondled her breasts, through her bra.

'I said I'd make you pay for that stunt, bitch,' he said, as he pulled her jeans open at the waist.

Suddenly realising what was happening, Liz wriggled and kicked, but he was strong and pinned her down again. Each time he tried to pull at her jeans to get them off, she opened her legs and twisted her torso, making it difficult for him. The fight went on for some ten minutes, before the attacker finally managed to rip her jeans over one of her feet. As Liz felt the cold metal of the van against her buttocks, he started to grab at her knickers, trying to tear the flimsy fabric. Unable to see, she raised her knee hard in hope that it might find a target. It connected into the assailant's groin, which made him stop for a few seconds. But in no time at all, he was back on her, grabbing at her vagina, ripping at her knickers again. She bounced her body up and down as much as she could, trying to stop him . . . but he wasn't stopping. Then she heard him unzip his fly and pull his trousers down. The warm prod of his penis against her leg made her feel sick to the stomach.

In a last-ditch attempt to stop him, she jolted up and smashed her leg into his testicles again, but it didn't deter him. He just pushed her down, hard into the floor of the van and ripped her knickers from her body. The rush of cold air against her vagina was soon smothered as his body descended onto her, and he positioned himself to enter her.

In that moment, as she lay pinned to the floor, helpless to stop him from raping her, Liz wished that he had killed her in the cabin. *Better that than this*, she thought, feeling his hard penis pushing against the outside of her vagina.

In the distance, outside the van, Liz could hear footsteps running across the car deck. They were approaching the van rapidly, as her attacker tried to force his penis into her unwilling vagina. Suddenly the back door of the van was flung open. Liz couldn't see what was happening, but the attacker was suddenly off her, shouting. Then she heard the sounds of a scuffle and the shout of. 'He's got a gun. Over there, stop him.' Then some more scuffling and more shouting, before the moving finally stopped.

Liz felt somebody pulling at the bag on her head lightly, as it came off she saw Praew's face. She had tears in her eyes, as she looked at Liz's half-naked, bruised body. Rape had been an unceasing part of her life, but seeing it happen to Liz seemed to break her normal cast iron resolve. Two uniformed security guards were holding her attacker on the floor and handcuffing his arms behind his back. One of guards kicked him fiercely in the ribs as he tried to get free, knocking the wind out of attacker.

The other guard quickly untied Liz's hands and passed her clothes to her. They were torn and dirty, but she took them gladly. 'I'm sorry about this, ma'am,' he said, 'but if you could just wait in the van for five minutes with the young girl, we'll get him locked up, then come and get you. Is that okay?' he asked in a soft Irish brogue.

Liz looked at the young security guard. He was shaking, his nerves having clearly got the better of him. 'Thank you,' she said and nodded her agreement. The two security guards grappled with her attacker and dragged him over to the door, kicking him every time he tried to stop them.

'That's Liz Channing. She's wanted by the police,' her attacker shouted. Liz froze. She hadn't been expecting him to give her away.

'Aye, and Shergar's in the next van,' the security guard said, kicking the attacker again.

As soon as they went through the door, Liz quickly pulled on her jeans and did up her blouse, as best she could. 'Let's get out of here,' she said to Praew. They ran across the car deck and into a stairwell. By the time they reached the passenger deck, there was a queue of people waiting to disembark and they mingled in as well as they could, with Liz wearing torn dirty jeans and a ripped blouse. Although the people around her noticed, they didn't say anything. All were pushing for a place to get off the ferry.

Staying in the crowd, Liz walked hand in hand with Praew, down the gangplank and onto the docks in Dublin. They walked straight through the 'EU ARRIVALS' channel and out into the arrivals hall. Within five minutes they were in a taxi on the way to a shopping mall, where Liz went into the first clothes shop that she found and bought some replacement clothes. Then she guided Praew back out to the taxi rank and they took a taxi to the airport.

'I told you to run and hide,' she said to Praew in the taxi.

Praew just smiled and held Liz's waist, resting her head on Liz's shoulder 'Really? I didn't understand,' she said smirking shyly.

Liz kissed her gently on the forehead. 'Thank you. You saved my life.'

Chapter 37

Wednesday, 4th March. Manchester, England

Sean took one final look at the small house he had inherited from his grandmother and left for the bus stop. He had dyed his hair an odd shade of ginger, including his eyebrows and was again amazed at how different he looked. An email from Liz, saying that she was fine and at the airport had calmed his nerves somewhat. He was glad she hadn't specified which one, but he knew it was Dublin and he also knew that her passage to Korea should be much easier now that she was outside the UK. According to the news, the two despicable criminals were still hiding out in London, so the police wouldn't be looking for her in Dublin. It was a big weight off his mind. Since the start of this investigation, he had been plagued with guilt about involving Liz and he would never forgive himself if something happened to her.

Sean stopped in Debenhams for a change of clothes, before making his way to Piccadilly Station and boarding a train to London Euston. Two hours and seven minutes later, the train pulled into Euston. There seemed to be a substantially increased police presence there, but they were focused on people leaving, rather than arriving and Sean just walked straight past them and out onto Euston Road.

It felt good to be back on the crowded streets of London where, with his new disguise, it would be hard to spot him. In London, it was easy to be anonymous. He turned to the left and made the short walk to Kings Cross, where he found a small bed and breakfast on Birkenhead Street, which had a vacancy for £30 per night. Settling his bill for one week in advance, he didn't give a name and the Eastern European man on reception knew better than to ask for ID in that district.

The tiny room was cramped and dirty, and he had to share a shower with the room next door, but it was good enough for his purposes and it was in an area where people came and went all the time, without any questions.

Sean's research had highlighted two addresses for Brigadier Findlow: one a large house in the countryside, close to Aldershot, which was the home of the British Army; and another in Belgrave Square, in central London. He made the assumption that the country manor was his family home and the Belgravia house his weekday residence, required to accommodate his duties at the Ministry of Defence in Whitehall. It was Wednesday, meaning that if Sean's assumptions were correct, the Brigadier would be in residence in Belgravia. Sean made his way through the slum-like flats of Kings Cross, across London's busy West End and on to the affluent Edwardian terraces of Belgravia.

Belgrave Square was made up of a large private garden, surrounded on all sides by a road. On the other side of the road from the garden, grand white Edwardian terraces, with white-painted stone pillars and black iron railings circled around, like an elaborate amphitheatre. Sean jumped over the low iron gate and into the private gardens that were reserved for the residents of the grand mansions surrounding them. The driving rain ensured that the gardens were deserted and he found a well-hidden spot behind a privet hedge, kneeling on the wet grass out of sight, but with a good view of the house that belonged to Brigadier Findlow.

A number of the houses in the circle were now embassies or consulates; the £50-million-plus price tags on properties in this neighbourhood put them well out of reach of everybody but the richest people in the world and foreign governments. *He certainly didn't buy this house on an army officer's salary,* Sean thought, increasing his belief that the Brigadier was more than just a peripheral player in this story.

I wonder how he explains this house in the officers' mess? Sean wondered. But then he guessed the army was full of officers with family money; they would just assume the same of him.

The Brigadier's house looked just like all the other terraces in the row to the eastern side of the square, its plain white facade belying the vast opulence inside. Sean couldn't detect any activity in the house through the front windows, so he waited, chomping on the snacks he had taken with him.

It was four cold and wet hours before he saw the uniformed officer round the corner onto Belgrave Square, arriving in the direction of Whitehall. Sean had expected him to arrive in a military chauffeur-driven car, provided to senior army officers, but clearly the Brigadier preferred to walk, even in the driving rain. *Maybe to hide this residence from his colleagues?* Sean thought.

After hopping up the steps in front of his house, two at a time, the Brigadier entered a code in the front door panel and walked in. A light came on in the front room as he entered and laid his briefcase down on the table, before pouring himself a whisky from a small wet bar. Unsure of what he was actually looking for, Sean just watched the military man, wondering whether he would provide the key that unlocked the mystery behind BW Corp.

Just as the army officer was taking his first sip of whisky, a car pulled up outside the house: a chauffeur-driven black Bentley, so highly polished that the raindrops ran straight off the gleaming paintwork. The driver jumped out smartly with an umbrella and held the door open for the rear seat passenger, protecting him from the rain. Sean watched, not daring to move, as David Findlow climbed out of the car. He looked exactly as he had on the day of the shareholder meeting, dressed in a tailored chalk-striped suit, with a long trench coat over the top. His carefully coiffured hair, slicked back against his head. The sight of his adversary gave Sean a sudden urge to run out and confront him, but he knew that would be futile, and may just be what David Findlow wanted.

Carefully pulling the iPhone from his pocket, Sean started to take photos. David Findlow didn't ring the doorbell; he too entered a code and walked straight in. After a cursory nod to his brother, he helped himself to a whisky from the wet bar. The two brothers then sat in armchairs, with glasses of whisky in hand, but they seemed distracted and continually looked out of the large sash window, as if they were expecting somebody else.

A black Mercedes limousine soon pulled around the corner into Belgrave Square and cruised slowly up to the kerb outside the Brigadier's house. Sean continued to photograph the activities, as a uniformed chauffeur climbed out of the car and took in the surrounding area, before opening the rear door. Then a tall white man, perhaps in his early sixties, climbed out of the vehicle and also looked up and down the street, before making his way up the steps to the Brigadier's house.

Anthony Findlow was already opening the door for him when he arrived and he quickly ushered him in. David Findlow immediately closed the thick curtains to the front room when he entered. Seconds later, the car pulled away slowly and rounded the corner towards Buckingham Palace. Sean noticed the odd number plate on the limousine, and made sure that he got a clear picture of it.

Tired of the driving rain, Sean started to move back from the hedgerow. He was cold and wet and he had had enough for one night. However, as he moved another car arrived: this time a black Rolls Royce Phantom. The passenger didn't wait for his chauffeur to open the door, jumping out onto the pavement and running up the steps, to shelter from the rain. He also keyed in the code and entered the house. Sean took some quick photos of the older white man that he guessed was in his seventies and wearing a long overcoat and a trilby style hat.

Having something to work on, Sean backed away from the hedgerow carefully and ran out into the gardens before hurdling the gate on the opposite side of the gardens to the Brigadier's house. Freezing cold and soaking wet, he ran all the way to Sloan Street, before turning right towards Brompton Road and slowing down to hail a cab.

A short while later, he was back in his dirty room at the Kings Cross B&B, where he dried himself and wrapped a blanket around his shoulders in an attempt to warm up. As he waited for the photos to upload from the phone to his laptop, he collated his thoughts. He had seen what he needed regarding the meeting between Anthony and David Findlow: it confirmed his suspicion that the Brigadier was somehow involved, in whatever it was BW Corp was up to.

As his iPhoto acknowledged the completion of the upload, he turned to the photo of the older white man. He knew that he had seen the face before, but he couldn't place it.

Then suddenly it clicked and he opened a newspaper clipping that he had seen previously, of Franky Findlow during his murder trial. He zoomed in on the photo that he had taken earlier. The moustache was gone, but there was no doubt that it was the same man. Franky Finlow was meant to be in Portland Bill Prison serving twenty-five years for murder, but here he was, being chauffeured around London in a Rolls Royce. How could that be possible?

Perplexed by his findings, Sean turned his attention to the

fourth man. He was tall, with Slavic features, highlighted by a strong square jaw bone. *Could be anybody*, Sean thought, not recognising the photo and still shocked by the sight of Franky Findlow. He flicked onto the photo of the limousine that the mystery stranger had arrived in, making a note of the odd number plate. '463 X 116'. It was unlike any other he had seen, so he quickly entered it to google search.

There were a number of hits, but most weren't relevant. The one that interested him most was a Wikipedia hit for diplomatic plates in the UK. Following the link, he found what he needed and noted that the plate belonged to a diplomatic car from the Bolivian consulate. He searched quickly for the Bolivian Consulate; it was close to the Brigadier's house, in Eaton Square, but he couldn't find any information that might help.

Randomly, Sean entered 'Slavs in Bolivia' into his search engine. To his surprise, he got four relevant hits. The first two didn't contain anything that would help him, so he clicked on the third. It was a newspaper article from his previous employer, the *Daily News*, dated 12 December, 1997. The heading read, 'SERB WAR CRIMINAL HIDING IN BOLIVIA', and the body of the piece discussed the possibility that Milan Bratic, a Serbian General during the Yugoslav war, was hiding out in Bolivia, helped by the Socialist Government in Sucre.

Reading on, Sean discovered that Bratic was allegedly responsible for the ethnic cleansing of four Bosnian villages, and suspected of ordering the murder of more than 400 unarmed women and children. He was also suspected of looting banks and art galleries throughout Bosnia and Croatia during the conflict. The International Criminal Court had outstanding warrants for his arrest, on suspicion of genocide, war crimes and crimes against humanity. At the date of the article, he was still at large.

Noting that there was no photo with the clipping, Sean entered an image search for Milan Bratic. He breathed in sharply when the image came onto the screen. He was a few years older, but there was no mistaking the angular jawline and the hardened features. The man that had visited Brigadier Findlow's house earlier *was* Milan Bratic: a wanted war criminal and mass murderer.

The discovery made Sean both uncomfortable and excited. Bratic was one of the world's most notorious war criminals and his presence in the UK was newsworthy in itself, but how far would a man like that go to silence him?

Is this enough evidence to bring David Findlow down? Sean asked himself. He had photos of the meeting with a wanted mass murderer; it was also attended by his father, who was supposed to be in prison. It was certainly enough to create a scandal and cause an investigation, but he still didn't know what they were doing, or why. Why would they meet with a despot like Bratic? And what could be so important that Bratic would risk capture by coming to London?

Punching away at the keys on his computer, he started to draft a story, including the photos of the four men meeting at the Belgravia house, press clippings of the Brigadier's meetings in various countries, and notes regarding BW's acquisition shortly thereafter. Satisfied that he had completed as much as he could, he reread the piece.

'Damn!' he cursed aloud. Although the piece would certainly cast some doubt about the activities of BW Corp, maybe enough to trigger an investigation of some kind, it still fell short of a slam-dunk for publication, especially as the author was a wanted murderer. In order to guarantee publication, he still needed to answer the questions about why these people were meeting, and what it was that BW Corporation were so desperate to hide.

After hours of deliberation, he concluded that the half-finished piece was the best he could do for now and put the second part of his plan into action. He opened an anonymous cloud storage account, where he stored the piece, along with all of the back-up information – including the rape story and information regarding the Russian brothel – in the same account.

Once the information was stored, he sent Liz a short email with the access details to the cloud account, but told her only to release it if she didn't get an email from him every twenty-four hours. Making it easy for her, he included links to three reputable newswire services.

Chapter 38

Wednesday, 4th March. Dublin, Ireland

Liz saw the three men waiting by the entrance to the check-in hall, as the taxi approached the terminal building. She had thought that they would be there, but in the same thought process, she reasoned that they would neither attack them in a busy airport, nor hand them in to the police. If they wanted to hand them over to the police, it would have been easy to do so in Hollyhead, before the ferry left, rather than wait to kidnap them. Also, if they had wanted to kill them, the attacker could have done it in the cabin on the ferry. *No*, she thought. *They want to use us to capture Sean. They're afraid he can expose them, which means he must be getting closer to the truth behind BW Corp.*

Thinking of Sean made her tremble with fear, as she thought about him, alone, facing something that was so deadly Clive hadn't even been able to imagine what it could be. Again she reconciled herself to return to England, as soon as Praew was safe. *If any of us can ever be safe again*, she thought.

Plucking up courage, she climbed out of the cab with Praew

and walked straight past the waiting men, into the terminal. Making no pretence of not seeing them and even nodding cockily at one of them. They, in turn, followed her to the Air Lingus ticket desk and watched her closely as she bought two tickets to Munich, paid and went straight through security and immigration.

On the other side of immigration, Liz wasn't surprised to find another young man waiting for her. She simply held Praew by the hand and sat in the busiest café in the departure lounge, waiting for her flight to be called. When Praew wanted to go to the toilet, Liz said no, explaining that it was too dangerous and asking her to wait until they were on the plane. With her usual understanding, Praew smiled happily at Liz and waited, crossing her legs.

'It'll be okay,' she said taking Liz's hand.

When their flight was called, Liz waited until there was a large group of people walking towards the departure gate and mingled with them. At the departure gate, she looked back and saw the young man mouthing the words of her flight number into his phone.

Once on the flight she found her seat and let out a sigh. The first part of her plan had worked well. She knew they would be waiting for her in Munich, so she had made the decision that she couldn't go straight to Korea, as it would lead them straight to her family. Even though they were well-connected, she wasn't sure what kind of resources Barker-Willet had in Korea. The risk of exposing her family to a group of ruthless killers was one that she wasn't willing to take.

On arrival at Munich airport, as she suspected, two men were waiting for them by the gate. Liz took Praew's hand and walked straight past them, staying close to the group of people from the same flight, heading for the immigration hall. Again on the other side of the blue EU channel of German Customs, she saw another man waiting for her. She ignored him and walked out of the crowded terminal, straight into a large glass-framed courtyard with a beer garden in it. She waited by an old polished silver plane that decorated the courtyard, which linked two of Munich Airports terminals, getting her bearings and timing her next move. Her follower stopped and watched her, not making any advance towards her in the crowded area.

It was tempting to just run, but she knew it was pointless; there was no way they could outrun Barker-Willet's foot soldiers. Sticking to her plan of staying in busy areas, she guided Praew to the escalator, then down to the crowded S-Bahn terminal and hopped straight onto a train, terminating at Munich Hauptbanhof, the main train station in the Bavarian capital.

The S-Bahn carriage was busy with tourists and business people heading into the city, which gave her confidence that they would be safe, at least until they reached the station. The young soldier shadowing them sat three benches away and just watched, as she and Praew chatted in Thai. Liz was concerned that Praew might panic and run away, but each time they talked, she grew in confidence. The young Thai girl was, if anything, stronger than she was and never once let the situation get to her.

Munich Hauptbanhof was as busy as Liz had hoped, with people milling in all directions. *Is this our chance?* Liz wondered, as they went quickly up the escalator to the main station and out of the S-Bahn. Any hopes were dashed as the young man following them kept pace and stayed within sight.

The main concourse of the station was jammed with people, either arriving or leaving, pulling luggage or carrying briefcases. Again Liz thought about making a run for it, but it was pointless and worse still, might give him an opportunity to take them. She still believed that they were safest in busy places, but that feeling of safety would start to ebb as the night fell and the crowds dwindled. She would need to make a move soon, or become a sitting duck for her would-be attackers.

The constantly clicking departures boards showed trains leaving for what seemed like every major city in Germany and a number of other major European centres. Liz studied the board carefully: the next train to depart would leave from platform twelve in four minutes, and was bound for Innsbruck in Austria.

Liz quickly walked Praew down the platform, climbed into the second-class carriage and felt a wave of relief when she saw that the train was full of people heading to Austria for ski holidays. The doorways to the train were piled high with ski and boot bags, making it hard to squeeze through. Liz found two seats and they sat down amongst the holidaymakers. As the train pulled away, she scanned the carriage for Barker-Willet's man, but she couldn't see him. 'Had they lost him on the crowded train?'

Only seconds later she welled with disappointment, as their shadow entered the carriage.

The ÖBB train moved quickly through the rolling hills of South Bavaria, stopping at the major towns along the way. At the ski resort of Garmisch-Partenkirchen, Liz stood at the door with Praew. They stepped quickly onto the platform and watched Barker-Willet's man do the same. Liz watched his movements carefully, playing a dangerous game of cat and mouse. As the doors began to close for the train to leave, they jumped back into the carriage, only to be disappointed when the young man following them did exactly the same.

They repeated the same manoeuvre at the next stop in Mittenwald, but again it proved useless. The train was moving much more slowly through the high mountains now. Liz considered prizing the doors open and jumping out into the snow bank beside the tracks, but when she pulled at the door with all her strength, it didn't budge.

They were only forty minutes away from Innsbruck and Liz wasn't sure what to expect there. Would it be as busy as Munich, or would it be less crowded and thus more dangerous?

When the train pulled into Seefeld-in-Tirol, Liz descended onto the platform with Praew, as a large group of skiers got off the train. The young soldier followed suit as before. When the other passengers were clear and the train was ready to leave, Liz jumped back on leaving Praew on the platform. Barker-Willet's man hesitated, but then followed Liz. She then spun around as the doors were just about to close and pushed a suitcase into the doorway, wedging the doors open. She jumped over the suitcase and onto the platform, as Praew pushed the case back onto the train, allowing the doors to close.

At the next door along, Liz saw the frustrated face of the young man who had been following them, as he grappled uselessly with the door and the train pulled away from the station.

Chapter 39

Liz grabbed Praew by the hand and ran out of the small train station, straight across the road into a pedestrian shopping street. The area was busy with people shopping and sitting in cafés, surrounded by piles of snow. Praew shivered from the cold and Liz suddenly felt it bite into her skin too. The temperature gauge attached to the door of the Seefeld Casino stated that it was minus ten degrees centigrade. She only had enough cash to buy tickets to Seoul, but she couldn't let Praew freeze. 'What the hell. They know I'm here anyway,' she said to Praew.

Entering a quaint boutique, opposite the large church in the main square, she helped Praew chose a completely new outfit and then chose one for herself. Twenty minutes later, after paying by credit card, they both emerged wearing their new outfits, including heavy winter coats, gloves and hats. Scanning the area for a bank, Liz saw a Raiffeissen Bank branch about fifty metres away, still within the pedestrian area. At the ATM, she extracted as much money as she could from each of her three credit cards, then

€4,200 better off, she walked across to a main road with Praew.

The spectacular scenery of the snow-covered mountains around them seemed to hypnotise Praew, as she pointed to different highlights. They could see people, like ants, skiing down the mountains in the distance and Liz wished that she could just join them and be normal for a day. But she knew that they had to get out of the quaint ski resort as soon as possible. The use of her credit card would have alerted Interpol to her presence there and it wouldn't be long before they alerted the local police, although that was the least of her worries. Barker-Willet's men already knew they were there and would be sending people as soon as they could.

A bus swung around the tight corner and stopped ten feet from them. It had a sign in the window, indicating that it was going to Telfs. Liz had no idea where that was, but made a quick decision and they boarded the single-decker bus.

During the twenty-minute journey down the steep windy road to Telfs, Liz and Praew sat quietly admiring the spectacular view, as the road swept down into the Inn valley below. When they got off the bus at the train station, Liz had a chance to view a map. Fifteen minutes later, she and Praew boarded a local train to Otztal, then changed to a high-speed train to Zurich, the closest city Liz could see, which she thought would have a good range of international flights.

As they alighted the train at Zurich Hauptbanhof, Liz reflected upon how easy it was for a fugitive to move around Europe, since the Shengen agreement had removed any immigration control from the borders.

They made their way out of the modern Zurich train station and across the bus depot. A large neon sign for the Hotel Schweizerhof enticed Liz and they walked into the small marble lobby. Using her false passport, she booked a room and paid cash in advance. The room was compact, with a small double bed, but it was clean and well-decorated. After a room service dinner of *raclette* and potatoes, which Praew didn't seem to like, the two of them settled in to get some sleep.

Before sleeping, Liz checked her email: there was a message from Sean letting her know he was okay and telling her about the information in the cloud account. Curious, she downloaded the file to her laptop and read the story. The mention of Milan Bratic made her shudder. What could BW be into that would bring them into contact with people like Bratic? The revelation that the Brigadier was involved came as a surprise too. But when she thought about it, it had been Dawson who had claimed his innocence and protected him, and Dawson had later turned out to be a traitor.

She scribbled a note back to Sean:

Hi Sean,
Amazing findings. I'll wait for your emails every day until you're with me again in Korea.
We're safe. In Zurich would you believe!
Love you
Liz xx

She chose not to tell him about her planned return to the UK, knowing that he would object.

Chapter 40

Sean woke in an uncomfortable position, still dressed, on the hard single bed in the dirty little B&B room. It was 6 a.m. and still dark. He grabbed a threadbare towel, went out into the cold corridor and into the mould-ridden shower. After making the best attempt he could to dry himself, he put the same clothes back on and grabbed his small backpack. The cold air bit into his still wet body, as he stumbled half-asleep onto Birkenhead Street, turned right, walked the short distance to Kings Cross station and climbed in a cab.

Sloane Street was deathly quiet, as it was too early for people to be hitting the designer stores that ran its length. Sean walked quickly and turned left towards Belgrave Square. Once there, he jumped over the same gate he had done the previous evening and made his way back to the same vantage point, behind the privet hedge. As he crouched down, the ice-cold rain started to run down his back, making him shiver uncontrollably.

The Brigadier's house was quiet, the curtains still drawn to the room at the front, where the previous night's meeting had taken place. Sean settled in for a long wait, making himself as comfortable as possible in the freezing rain.

He didn't have to wait long. At 7 a.m. precisely, the Brigadier came out of the front door, wearing full uniform and a great coat and carrying a green golf umbrella, in a brown-gloved hand. The Brigadier turned right and walked along the square to Upper Belgrave Street, where he turned into a wide street, with the same type of Edwardian terraced mansions as Belgrave Square. Staying in the shadows, Sean followed about fifty metres behind.

When the Brigadier turned into Hobart Place and walked along to Buckingham Gate, it confirmed to Sean that he was on his way to Whitehall and he quickly cut into a side street and started to sprint. Keeping up his pace, he ran down Wilfred Street and onto Petty France, behind the army barracks, and continued to sprint down Queen Anne's Gate, until he finally came onto Birdcage Walk, by Storey's Gate. Slowing down to a walk, he crept down to the entrance to St James's park and slipped in.

Banging his feet on the floor to keep them warm, Sean waited by the railings, away from the gate, watching the footpath that led back towards Buckingham Gate. It was still very quiet and too early for the morning commuters. The solitary figure of the Brigadier soon came walking along by the park fence, his umbrella held forward against the driving rain.

As Anthony Findlow approached, Sean stepped forward and called out to him from behind the fence. 'I know what you're up to, Brigadier,' he said, just loud enough for the passing soldier to hear him.

The Brigadier continued walking for a few paces, then stopped. 'Are you speaking to me?' he asked in a pompous voice.

Sean felt the railings in front of him, confirming that he was protected against any attack by the Brigadier. 'Yes. I know about you and your brother David, aka Charles Barker-Willet. I know you met with Milan Bratic yesterday and I know that your father, Franky Findlow, was there too. I also know that you have been meeting with deranged war criminals all over the world, setting up dirty deals for BW Corp.' Sean embellished his knowledge a little, in an attempt to provoke a reaction from Findlow.

As the Brigadier turned around, Sean saw his face properly for the first time. He wasn't handsome like his brother: his face was gaunt and lowered into a narrow chin. He stared at Sean from underneath the brim of his peaked army hat without blinking. Holding his nerve, Sean returned the stare back into the bright green eyes, which seemed to be burning holes into him.

'And what do you think you can do with that meaningless and circumstantial information . . . Mr McManus, I assume?' The Brigadier's voice carried no discernable accent, belying his East London roots.

Sean was lost for words. He had expected the Brigadier to deny any knowledge of the information and he had prepared himself for that. But he could tell now that the Brigadier was not a man who would enter a debate with him. He wore his pompous arrogance on his sleeve, like a badge of honour. People like Sean were beneath him, not worthy of debate.

Kicking himself for not using the record function on his phone, he continued with his plan. 'I've placed the information and supporting evidence in a safe place. If I don't stop it every twenty-four hours, it will be released to a newswire service,' Sean said, as confidently as possible, still haunted by the Brigadier's eyes.

'So?' Findlow said, arrogantly shrugging.

'So, if I go missing, or you harm a hair on the head of Liz Channing, or the young girl she's with, the information will be released,' Sean paused for breath. 'If you leave us alone, then you can go about your business and we can get on with our lives.' Sean held the Brigadier's stare for as long as he dare.

Findlow didn't speak. He simply turned and started to walk away

278

towards Whitehall, pulling a phone from his pocket. Was he communicating the deal to his brother, or calling for re-enforcements? Sean didn't know, but he didn't want to stick around to find out.

He ran across the park, over the bridge which spanned the lake and out onto the Mall. There he turned right, sprinted up through Admiralty Arch and into Trafalgar Square, where he slowed down and mingled with the growing crowd of people on their way to work. Trying to blend in, he made his way through the back streets of Charing Cross and into the Covent Garden area, where he found a small café on Floral Street and took shelter from the driving rain.

A full English breakfast, black coffee and warm air slowly lifted the numbness from his hands. He analysed every part of the meeting with the Brigadier, but he couldn't determine its outcome. He guessed only time would tell. Somewhere in the back of his mind though, he was confident.

The cold rain was still pounding against the pavement when he left the small café, but he felt a renewed sense of optimism as he walked without an umbrella, back towards Kings Cross. Putting himself in David Findlow's shoes, why would he risk the information getting out, when he had the simple solution Sean had offered? He wandered through the streets, watching the people taking shelter from the rain. To him it felt cleansing, as if he was washing away a dirty chapter in his life. Soon he would make his way to Korea to be with Liz.

Outside Great Ormond Street Hospital, he stopped as an ambulance pulled up in front of him. The rear doors opened and he stepped to the side to let the paramedic out. As he did, the burly young man, with short cropped hair, grabbed him and pulled him into the ambulance. Sean kicked and lashed out screaming, but it was no use. The two men dressed as paramedics subdued him easily and gagged him, before tying his hands behind his back.

Chapter 41

When Sean regained consciousness, he found himself in a luxurious office, surrounded by wooden wall panels and expensive furniture. He was slumped in a Chesterfield wing-backed chair, with his wrists tied to the armrests and his head throbbing with pain. The metallic tang of blood in his mouth reminded him of his injury and he realised that the blood had run down his face onto his lips. He felt it with his tongue; it was dry and cracked when he touched it; he had been out for some time.

A voice came from behind him calling out into a corridor. 'He's awake,' the gruff cockney accent conveyed. Sean heard footsteps coming down a hard floor towards the office, a few shuffles then the door close behind them. Brigadier Sir Anthony John Findlow stood before him, still in full uniform.

'You really didn't think you could threaten me and get away with it, did you?' he said, looking down at Sean from his standing position.

Sean's head felt hazy and he struggled to think properly, but he fought the grogginess and spoke. 'Does this mean our deal is off?'

The Brigadier laughed. 'Deal? Who do you think you are to strike a deal with me? You have no idea what you're dealing with, young man.' He strutted arrogantly behind a large mahogany desk, sticking his chest out victoriously. He had won the battle and he was revelling in the glory.

Realising that his situation was hopeless, Sean gained a courage that he had previously lacked. 'You're right, I don't, so why don't you tell me?' he said, mocking the army officer.

A sharp punch cracked into the side of his head quickly, as a gloved hand flashed before his eyes. 'Cheeky bastard!' He recognised the voice as ex-detective Peter Dawson's.

'No need for that, Peter,' the Brigadier interrupted. 'He's about to meet his maker, he may as well know why.' He smiled sadistically. 'So what do you think you know, Mr McManus?' he asked pompously.

Sean's initial instinct was to tell the Brigadier to 'go fuck himself', but the reality was, he did want to know what he was going to die for; what had he inadvertently stumbled upon that was worth taking a man's life for. Delaying the inevitable couldn't do any harm either. He still might be presented with an opportunity to get away. 'I know that you and your family are in cohorts with war criminals,' Sean said.

'As you said this morning! Is that it?' the Brigadier asked.

'I know that your brother is a sadistic child rapist,' Sean answered.

The Brigadier laughed. 'Yes, David does have some eccentric tastes, but that's what you want when you have everything else: the things that are denied to you by a prudish and blind society.'

'I can't believe you could condone that. You're an army officer. Didn't you learn anything at Sandhurst?'

'On the contrary, I learned a lot at Sandhurst. One of my most important lessons was not to assume, or expect that other people's morals would be the same as mine.' The Brigadier used a lofty tone of speech; the type a person would use if he were giving a lecture.

The sick bastard is enjoying this, Sean thought. *He wants to prove that he's cleverer than me, before he kills me.* He chose not to speak.

The Brigadier laughed even louder. 'My god, you haven't even worked out what this is about, have you? What a shame. If I'd known you were so stupid, I wouldn't have needed to kill you. Unfortunately for you, that opportunity has passed.'

It was true; Sean had no idea. He'd only managed to scratch the surface of David Findlow's operation. He again chose not to speak.

'Let me put you out of your misery. A condemned man should always know what got him killed.' The Brigadier's tone was arrogant, and Sean could tell that he was getting some perverse pleasure from the moment. It was as if he was showing off, proud of his family's achievements.

Then it suddenly dawned upon Sean that the Brigadier never got the chance to tell anybody about how brilliant their scheme was. He couldn't brag about it over a beer with his mates, while pretending to be humble. The family that controlled the largest company the world had ever seen, couldn't boast about what really made their business tick; about the genius behind it. It would condemn them to life in prison, or worse.

Sean had seen the trait in many successful CEOs. The need to impress other people was a part of their DNA; a vital urge that they couldn't control. To be denied that right, when you had had the most successful idea in the history of business, would be like torture to man with an ego as aggressive as the Brigadier's.

Sean decided to play along. His natural curiosity was piqued and the longer he could string things out, the better.

'What's the most abundant commodity in the world?' the

Brigadier asked, like a school teacher would ask a pupil.

'Oil?' Sean suggested.

The Brigadier laughed churlishly, like a child who knew the answer to a teacher's question. 'Not even close,' he paused for effect. 'Cash, Mr McManus, cash.' He smiled arrogantly, as if revealing some deep hidden truth, while all the time his bright green eyes burned into Sean's, like lasers assessing their target.

'So?' Sean said indifferently.

'So?' the brigadier exclaimed loudly. 'Did you know that more than twenty per cent of the world's cash pile is trapped, unable to be used because lily livered, incompetent politicians create petty laws to stop the people who have earned it from using it?'

'So, that's what this is? Just a money laundering operation?' Sean shrugged his shoulders, feigning disinterest.

'Just a money laundering operation!' the Brigadier said, obviously insulted by Sean's comment. 'This is far more than just a money laundering operation. We provide an end-to-end solution to the biggest single problem faced by the leaders of over half of the countries in the world,'

'Which is?'

'How to use their hard-earned wealth,' he said callously.

'You mean you provide a banking solution for despots!' Sean said purposely to wind up the pompous soldier further.

Findlow took the bait. 'You belittle the greatest enterprise this planet has ever seen, yet you praise the companies that exploit thousands of underpaid workers in sweat shops across Asia. That's typical of the lazy middle classes that make up this country.' Findlow paused again to emphasise his point. 'To use a simple term such as money laundering shows that you cannot grasp the great enterprise and complexity behind it.' Findlow grandstanded, as if he had worked out how to split the atom for the first time. 'Do money launderers have the ability to collect cash from a dirty warehouse floor in Kaiping and then, the same day, allow that money to be gambled in a casino in Las Vegas?' the Brigadier carried on.

'I don't know, maybe,' Sean answered honestly.

'Let me assure you they do not, Mr McManus. Money launderers wear cheap suits and have gold teeth protruding from their ugly faces. They do their dealings behind dirty doors, in back alleys. We are the largest corporation in the world. We operate from luxury offices in Mayfair and sell our shares on the Stock Exchange,' the Brigadier said proudly.

'And the companies you buy?' Sean asked, seeking answers to some of the frustrating questions he had been asking himself since the investigation began.

'Just vehicles for the cash. We don't even look at them properly as long as they're close enough to break even,' he replied arrogantly. 'Every time we get a new customer, we buy a new company to create capacity for the cash. Then sycophantic middle-class investors like you buy up our shares and drive our share price even higher, giving us double the benefit of just the cash.'

'The twenty per cent increase in sales!' Sean said aloud, realising finally what BW Corporation had been up to.

'Ah, I see you have at least paid some attention,' the Brigadier said.

Sean switched tack. 'And what do you get out of it?' he asked.

'What? Besides massive deposits into our bank?' the Brigadier asked.

'Yes,' Sean persisted.

The Brigadier paused for a second, obviously wondering whether he had already said too much. Then his hubris got the better of him again. 'We, of course, charge a small fee for our services,' he said, as if discussing the delivery cost of a computer.

'Which is?' Sean asked, genuinely curious.

'That depends upon what level of service our clients require. For example, if you take our platinum package – which means that we collect cash from any location in the world, however remote or dangerous, in any currency – then we make that cash available to be used in a place of our client's choosing, in a currency of their choice. Plus, we arrange luxury transport to that location, entry and exit to any country in the world, and fake identification where required. For a service like that, Mr McManus, we take sixty per cent of the cash collected.' The Brigadier preened himself behind the desk, the way Sean had seen many CEOs act, when they revealed a secret behind a great deal.

Sean realised for the first time just how despicable David Findlow's company was. They weren't just morally challenged bankers, who didn't care how their customers earned their huge deposits, they were the driving force behind the crimes, because without BW's insidious services, plundering the wealth of nations would be pointless, the cash stolen just worthless paper, unable to be used for anything more than fire fuel.

Sean shuddered at what the revelation meant: BW Corporation was indirectly responsible for crimes against humanity and for promoting the corruption which caused the deaths of millions of people: from starvation, because their aid money was stolen; from bullets, caught in the crossfire between warlords; or from disease, inflicted on them by poverty, while their countries leaders pillaged anything of value; not to mention the billions of people that lived in misery and constant fear of their own governments, slaves to a corrupt machine which robbed them of any human dignity.

BW Corporation was indeed the most insidious creation that had ever been invented; a facilitator of famine and a paymaster of genocide.

'Don't you have a conscience?' Sean asked. 'Every penny of that is blood money, stolen from whole populations left to starve to death, or murdered by militia. You're meant to be a soldier; a person that defends the weak.'

The Brigadier straitened, angered by Sean's comment. 'Don't preach to me, young man. I've seen horrors that you couldn't even imagine. But do you think they'd stop, just because we didn't provide the service that we do?'

'Maybe,' Sean said. 'It would be a start.'

'Ha!' the Brigadier scoffed. 'Again, typical of the naïve, do-good middle classes in this wretched country. Do you know that we paid £30 billion in taxes last year alone? How many policemen, nurses and lazy dole-grabbers do you think that pays for?'

To any normal person, justifying BW's abhorrent activities, the facilitation of the evil enterprise of dictators and war criminals, just because they paid tax in the UK, would seem incredulous, but Sean realised that the Brigadier was serious. He actually believed that he was doing a good thing. He viewed himself as a hero of the nation. This was the perverse political reasoning of men like Adolf Hitler or Pol Pot, and David Findlow wielded as much power as both put together.

'My foundation made £11 billion in charitable contributions last year. Do you realise that's the same as the total UK foreign aid budget?' the Brigadier boasted further. Sean had read about the Barker-Willet foundation, which supported British-based charities and political parties, meaning that, in effect, it was stealing aid money from starving people in Africa, so that politicians in the UK could put their faces on billboards.

Then the truth suddenly hit Sean like a sledgehammer. He said, 'My foundation', and 'I.' He didn't know why he hadn't seen it before. David Findlow wasn't behind BW Corp: he was only the front man, indulged by his successful brother. BW was Anthony Findlow's masterpiece and he was desperate to tell somebody. He was tired of his brother getting all of the credit, while he took a back seat, unable to be even associated with the great company, and to a man with Findlow's obvious hubris that would hurt tremendously. He had created what he called 'the greatest enterprise on the planet', yet he was forced to watch silently from the side lines, as somebody else stole the glory. Sean knew that his ego would be tearing his insides out.

'Your foundation? I thought it was your brother's!' Sean said provocatively.

The Brigadier breathed through his nose angrily. 'In name only. David is an impulsive psychopath; he could never have devised anything this brilliant.'

'Doesn't that piss you off, if this really is all your idea? David is hailed as a business genius, celebrated the world over, while you . . . well you're just an army officer, unknown to most people,' Sean prodded the Brigadier's ego even more, knowing that he had struck a raw nerve.

'I bet you never imagined it was going to be so big, all those years ago in Sandhurst, when you met foreign army officers and devised your scheme.' Sean nodded towards a photograph of the young second lieutenant, with a group of foreign army officer cadets at Sandhurst, the British Officer Training School. He was just guessing that it was where it had all started, by the prominence given to the picture amongst the others.

The Brigadier gritted his teeth hard. 'Enough! How does it feel to have learned everything you've been searching for these past weeks, while knowing that you are about to die?' he asked, his green eyes burning once again into Sean's.

'What do you do with the money? How much is enough?' Sean asked. 'How many people have to die, so that you can add another digit to a number on your bank balance?'

The Brigadier laughed loudly. 'Is that what you think this is about, Mr McManus? Money? If money was all I wanted, I could have followed in my father's footsteps and been the king of the East End.'

'Then what is it about?' Sean asked.

'You wouldn't understand. Pampered liberals like you have never understood the aphrodisiac of absolute power. I, like any other good businessman, re-invest my profits in my business, ensuring that its expansion will carry on unhalted into the future.'

'Really? And how do you do that?' Sean was genuinely surprised. The Brigadier's business model was one which didn't seem to require heavy investment.

'Do you think we just gather our clientele at random, leaving our future to chance?'

'I just thought you looked through the who's who of despots and dictators,' Sean said, his imminent death taking away any fear or inhibition he possessed.

'It will surprise you to know then that I invest a lot of time and money in our client base. They don't just become the leaders of nations by mere chance. I finance their political campaigns, or their military coups. I put them on their thrones, and in return, I control their every move.'

The Brigadier's stare was chilling, boring into Sean as he revealed the innermost secrets of BW's strategy, boasting triumphantly about his atrocious accomplishments. The truth was more sinister than Sean had previously thought. BW Corp wasn't indirectly responsible for the billions of lives ruined by corrupt governments, it was *directly* responsible: Anthony Findlow was a kingmaker, a puppet master of dictators, using his wealth to spread untold misery across the world.

'And Bratic, where does he fit in?' Sean asked, still reeling from the previous revelation.

'Since you ask, Mr Bratic is looking for somebody to finance his latest venture.'

'Which is?'

'The re-unification of the former Yugoslavia . . . under Serb control of course.'

The words echoed in Sean's head like a weird dream. He

couldn't believe what he was hearing. 'You couldn't ... you wouldn't, after what happened there.'

'I could and I would. In fact I transferred £50billion into Mr Bratic's account this morning. Quite a war chest don't you think?'

'You're sick. Luckily the UN will never allow it to happen.' Sean spat out.

The Brigadier let out a loud laugh. 'The UN no longer have the stomach for a fight like that. Anyway, I'll make sure the security council vote against any military intervention. If you have any friends in Bosnia or Croatia, I'd tell them to get out now if I were you.' He paused. 'Oh, but then again you can't, as you're about to die.'

'You're a maniac. No better than Amin, or Hitler.'

'Apparently both much misunderstood men,' the Brigadier said grinning evilly, before looking at Dawson. 'Kill him,' he said coldly.

Chapter 42

'If you kill me, I've stored enough information to make the authorities investigate your company. You know it won't stand up to close scrutiny,' Sean said quickly, hoping that it would buy him some time.

'And where have you stored this information, Mr McManus?' the Brigadier asked.

Sean sighed. 'I'm not going to tell you that, but if I don't stop it every twenty-four hours, it will be released to a newswire service.' Sean said, repeating his threat of the morning.

The Brigadier smirked. 'We've read your file in the Acorn Cloud account and replaced it with a Donald Duck cartoon. Do you think *Reuters* will like that?'

Panic shot through Sean's veins. How did they know the story was with Acorn? 'Bullshit!' he said, not so confidently.

'Indeed,' the Brigadier said. 'Would you be more convinced if I told you that the password to your account was 2gninnahc23? Which is, of course, your little Korean slut's name in reverse, isn't it? Pity about the South Koreans: they've become too honest for their own good. I much prefer to do business in the North, where things are more . . . orderly.'

Shit! My laptop! Sean saw the silver coloured device on the corner of the desk and realised that it was his. He had been unconscious for a while, which was plenty of time for somebody who knew what they were doing to work back through his internet pages, find his email account and hack his password. He convulsed, as he remembered the last email from Liz saying that she was in Zurich. 'Liz has the file. She'll release it,' he said bluffing as best he could.

The Brigadier laughed out loud. 'What after my brother has finished acting out one of his perverted fantasies on her and her little friend?'

'What?' Sean breathed in deeply.

'Yes, not so smart your girl, is she? Very pretty though. Well, she *was*. She probably has an arsehole the size of basketball ring by now, and as for that cute young Thai thing with her . . . well, she's just David's type of meat, if you know what I mean.' Findlow pulled an ugly face, showing his true character. The self-righteous pomposity was gone, replaced by pure evil.

Sean strained against his restraints, trying to get up 'You're bluffing!' he shouted, before Dawson's firm hand shoved him forcefully back into the chair.

The Brigadier laughed again. 'I don't bluff, young man. If she is so stupid as to stay in a hotel right opposite Zurich train station, then it's her own fault we caught her. Although I thought it was rather fortuitous that David was at the Zurich office today, and only had a short walk down to the hotel to meet her.'

Although Sean didn't know where Liz was staying in Zurich, he knew she was in Zurich. Was he bluffing to try to get him to reveal the hotel? 'Bollocks! She left Zurich yesterday,' he said, still attempting to throw him off.

'As much fun as this is,' the Brigadier chuckled, 'I'm afraid I have things to do. Why don't we have a little face time with David, so you can see the little bitch squirm,' he said coldly.

Dawson pressed a button on the desk to reveal a hidden TV screen in the wall. After hitting a few digits, the outbound call was made. The mobile phone on the other end was answered quickly, 'Anthony,' the voice said, as the picture was coming into focus. David Findlow was on the other end of the phone.

'David, I have Mr McManus here and I think he'd like to see Miss Channing and the Thai runt,' the Brigadier said.

Sean watched in dread, as the picture spun around to Liz and Praew. They were huddled together on a bed in a hotel room. David Findlow and another man were there with them. 'Liz!' he called out.

'Sean, is that you?' she replied.

Findlow leant forward and struck her hard across the face. 'Shut the fuck up, slag!'

The Brigadier smiled, as Sean tried to get out of his seat again, only to be met with a firm punch in the side knocking him back down.

'I think young Mr McManus would like to see you in action, David; apparently he is quite the voyeur,' the Brigadier said in a haunting tone.

'No!' Sean shouted at the top of his voice, before Dawson punched him in the face again.

On the screen, David Findlow handed the phone to the other man in the room. 'Make sure he gets a good view,' he said, as he moved towards Praew.

Sean watched in horror as Liz kicked out at David Findlow, catching him squarely in the mouth. Findlow just wiped the blood from his face and grabbed her by the neck, his hand spanning her windpipe. In an attempt to stop him, Praew leaped up and kicked him repeatedly in the side, but the other man grabbed her by the hair and pulled her off the bed and onto the ground. As she fell, she lashed out and caught him in the groin, making him drop the camera.

'Keep filming,' David Findlow said, breathing heavily, overtly aroused by the sudden violence.

When the camera came back into focus, David Findlow was still choking Liz and she was now struggling to breathe, gasping for air, as Findlow's other hand ripped at her blouse, tearing it open.

'Nice tits,' Dawson said, laughing at the screen.

Sean swung his leg up towards Dawson, but the ex-DCI just dodged it and punched him in the neck, crashing him back into the seat, painfully. 'Silly boy! Why don't you enjoy the show?' Dawson laughed again.

A feeling of utter helplessness was overtaking Sean and he felt sick to the stomach. He had to do something. He tried to get up again, but Dawson was strong and he just pushed him back into the seat heavily and smashed his elbow into Sean's cheek.

Naked from the waist up and desperate for a breath, as Findlow increased the pressure on her neck, Liz did everything she could to stop him. As he groped at her naked breasts with his other hand, Sean could see the sadistic pleasure etched onto his face. At that moment Sean knew that Anthony Findlow had told the truth: David Findlow was an impulsive psychopath and his fear for Liz re-doubled.

Somehow, in the heat of the moment, Praew had sneaked out of grabbing distance of the cameraman and she launched another attack on David Findlow, this time climbing on his back and biting hard into his ear. Findlow cried out in pain and Liz swung her leg hard into his groin again. But he didn't release his grip on her neck, seemingly enjoying the pain the kick had caused and the cameraman once again dragged Praew away by the hair, as she kicked, punched and bit any part of his body she could reach.

Liz's face had now turned dark red. She was running out of oxygen, while Findlow was biting at her exposed skin, making a sickly sound with his mouth. Back on her feet, but being held tightly by the hair by the cameraman, Praew continued to kick and punch wildly, but she couldn't get free.

Suddenly Findlow released his grip on Liz's neck and she breathed in deeply, coughing as she filled her lungs with air. He stood at the end of the bed and removed his shirt, revealing a muscular body, covered in tattoos. Sean shivered as he saw the depiction of torture scenes across Findlow's whole back, centred by a large swastika. The elegant CEO he had seen some weeks ago was gone and all that was left was a sadistic rapist, consumed with a vulgar lust.

David Findlow breathed heavily as he pulled down his trousers and underwear, revealing his elaborately tattooed buttocks. He swung quickly around the side of the bed and grabbed Praew by the hair.

'I thought he'd go for the younger one first,' Dawson said, laughing sickly.

Liz jumped up and lunged at Findlow, but he swerved her attack and the cameraman grabbed her hair, then moved his grip to her throat, before he placed the phone onto the bedside table, ensuring that it gave a clear view, but freeing his other hand up to subdue Liz, who was fighting like a wild cat.

The naked Findlow didn't seem to be bothered by the kicking and scratching of Praew and he suppressed her with his body, forcing himself on top of her, while tearing at her clothes. Desperate to stop him, Liz still struggled against the other man, but she was losing strength quickly, as her body was once again denied oxygen by a hand across her windpipe.

Sean struggled helplessly against his restraints, as Findlow won his vicious battle to get Praew's trousers and underwear off. The abject terror in Praew's eyes as he pushed himself on top of her burned itself into Sean's memory, the feeling of utter helplessness torturing his very existence.

Chapter 43

As Sean crashed his head back into the seat, in a failed attempt to butt Dawson in the stomach, he heard two sharp sounds, like a piston firing. Splinters of glass shattered onto the floor and then he felt blood dripping onto his head, before Dawson dropped to the floor beside him.

The door crashed open behind him and two men burst through holding silenced pistols up in front of them. The Brigadier reached for a drawer in his desk, but the first man ran forward and smashed him into the chair with his shoulder. Anthony Findlow was winded from the blow and he doubled over on his ornate desk. His attacker stood up and pointed his pistol straight at him. Immediately Sean recognised the intruder, it was Colin from Clive's team, Terry was with him and Phil was at the window still holding up his smoking pistol with a long silencer attached.

'Liz and Praew,' Sean shouted pointing to the screen.

Colin walked behind the Brigadier and pulled him into view of the camera, putting a pistol against his temple. 'Tell him to stop,' Colin said.

The Brigadier ground his teeth angrily. 'David!' he shouted.

David Findlow looked up. 'What?' he said, obviously angry at the disturbance.

'Look at the screen,' Anthony Findlow said.

When he saw his brother being held at gunpoint, David Findlow didn't stop trying to part Praew's legs, he just carried on pulling at them as Praew twisted away and kicked out. The cameraman immediately increased the pressure on Liz's neck. Her eyes had now rolled into the back of her head and Sean could tell she was losing consciousness.

'Let them go!' Colin said and pressed the barrel hard into the Brigadier's temple.

'Do as he says, David,' the Brigadier said, obviously concerned that his psychopathic brother may be too far gone to care.

After a brief pause, David Findlow stood reluctantly and backed away from Praew, who gave him one last kick as he backed away. In turn, the cameraman let go of Liz's neck. She instantly breathed in deeply and her eyes returned to the front, as she gasped for breath trying to get oxygen into her lungs. A deep red mark extended right across her neck where two hands had been starving her of air. The two women instantly reached for their torn clothes and began to dress themselves. David Findlow and the cameraman just stared at the small screen on the phone, waiting for the Brigadier to give them instructions.

'Now, here's what's going to happen,' Colin said. 'You are going to let Miss Channing and the young girl go. You are going to stay in the hotel room where we can see you, until I say you can go. Or I'm going to paint the wall with your brother's brains.' Colin's tone was calm and collected, letting Findlow know that he was used to violent situations and didn't scare easily.

'You wouldn't dare!' David Findlow said angrily.

Terry panned the camera down to Dawson's dead body on the floor and then back to Colin and the Brigadier. 'Really?' Colin said. 'We've got nothing to lose.'

'Do as he says, David,' the Brigadier said, clearly unsure whether his brother would comply.

'How do we know they won't kill you anyway?' David Findlow said.

'You don't,' Colin answered. 'But you can be certain that we will if you don't let them go.'

David Findlow looked confused, unsure of what to do, violent lust still coursing through his sweating body.

'David, listen to me. Do as they say; you'll get another chance,' Anthony Findlow pleaded with his brother, the man he had minutes ago called a dangerous psychopath.

'Okay, fuck it! Okay! But I'm coming for you, McManus, and when I find you, you'll wish you'd let me expend my sexual energy on these two worthless sluts,' David Findlow threatened, as he threw his arms in the air in frustration.

Deciding not to provoke the situation by speaking, Sean held his breath, hoping that Findlow wouldn't change his mind.

'Liz, get your things and get out of there,' Colin said.

Still fighting for breath, Liz quickly grabbed her coat and Praew did the same. She picked up her backpack and took Praew's hand. 'Sean, I'll see you for my favourite *gelato*,' she said hoarsely, as she left.

What did she mean? He had to get to her before David Findlow did. Sean was puzzled by the comment and wracked his brains for a clue.

The stand-off between room 211 in Zurich's Hotel Schweizerhof and Brigadier Findlow's office lasted for a further hour. None of the people spoke until Colin decided it was getting too risky to stay longer and announced that they were going to leave. As they were preparing to run, with Colin's pistol still pressed firmly into the temple of the brigadier, Sean reached down from his seat and pulled the pistol out of Dawson's jacket. It was covered in blood and was heavier than Sean had expected, but he levelled it at the Brigadier, aiming carefully between his eyes.

The Brigadier didn't react. He just stared at Sean, daring him to shoot with his bright green eyes burning holes into Sean's soul.

'Don't, Sean,' Colin said. 'That's not a line that you want to cross.'

'But you don't know what this man is; what he's capable of,' Sean responded, tightening his finger against the pressure of the trigger.

'Maybe, but I know that killing a man in cold blood is something that will haunt you for the rest of your life,' Colin responded.

'But he deserves it,' Sean said, still pointing the gun at the Brigadier's head.

'Maybe, but you don't!' Colin said calmly, as Terry took the pistol from Sean's hands. 'Bring him with us, we may need him,' he said to Terry, nodding towards the Brigadier.

Sean picked up his laptop from the desk and the four men then moved slowly into the hallway, with Terry bringing up the rear, pushing the Brigadier along. As he stepped through the office door, the Brigadier darted to his left and rolled onto the floor, sliding into a doorway under the stairs. The door quickly closed behind him.

'Shit, get him,' Colin shouted.

Terry ran to the door, but it was locked. He charged his shoulder against it, but it didn't even budge. Then he saw the array of electronic equipment and camera attached to the outside. 'It's a panic room, we're done,' he said.

Colin looked angry. 'Leave him, he'll be calling the troops, we have to go.'

They ran out of the front of the house and straight into the transit van that Phil had pulled around for them, before they sped away around Belgrave Square towards Chelsea.

'How did you know I was there?' Sean asked Colin.

'We were following Dawson and he led us to you,' he said.

'I can't thank you enough,' Sean replied.

Colin smiled. 'Let's nail these bastards for Clive.' he said.

Sean put his head down. 'I'm sorry about' Clive,' he said sincerely.

Colin laughed. 'Ah, he was shit at darts anyway!'

Sean pulled a puzzled face.

Colin laughed again. 'Clive's fine. He's lost the lower part of his right arm and only has one working kidney, but he's recovering quickly, under a false name in a private hospital in Scotland.'

'That's great,' Sean said smiling. Then immediately turning more serious. 'I have to find Liz before Findlow does.'

'I know,' Colin said. 'Any idea what she meant about gelato?'

'No,' Sean replied.

'Did you ever go to a gelato bar with her in London?'

'No,' Sean shook his head.

A flash of memory suddenly shot back into Sean's mind from the first night he spent with Liz. She had said that she spoke Italian and that her grandfather had a place somewhere in Tuscany, where they did the best *gelato*, but he couldn't remember where. 'I need a map of Tuscany,' he said.

Colin pulled out his iPhone and tapped a few keys. 'This okay?' he said, passing him the phone with google maps open. Quickly taking the phone, Sean scanned the screen. What was it called? He expanded certain parts and scanned each town name without recognition. Then he remembered she said it was on the Tuscan coast. Starting at Pisa, he worked his way up the coast. 'Forte dei Marmi, that's it!' he said, pointing to the screen.

'Heathrow,' Colin said to Phil.

'Already on the way, boss,' Phil replied.

At Heathrow, Colin jumped out of the van with Sean. 'Try to keep an eye on the Brigadier,' he said to Phil and Terry. 'But from a distance, I think he'll be well guarded from now on.'

'You should've let me kill him,' Sean said.

'No. I've never killed a man who wasn't trying to kill me or somebody else. There's a fine line between murder and self-defence, and for your own sake, it's best to steer well clear of it,' Colin answered thoughtfully.

'When I tell you what he's been up to, you may change that view.'

En route to the airport, Colin had booked two seats on a flight to Florence leaving in three hours using his phone. 'Best I could do,' he said. 'If Liz is travelling by train, it'll take her a while to get there anyway.'

Once inside the terminal, Sean opened his laptop and began crafting his piece as quickly as he could, while taking care to make it professional in quality. He explained it to Colin while typing the last sentences.

'Shit!' Colin said, trying to grasp the enormity of the Brigadier's vile empire.

'Yep, that about sums him up,' Sean responded.

'In your piece does it mention Bratic and the £50 billion?'

'Yes, of course, why?'

'You need to take it out. We can't let the people know that he has that kind of money, it will bring mercenaries out the world over looking for a payday.' Colin shook his head. 'Maybe I should've let you kill him.'

'It would be nothing compared to the millions of deaths he's responsible for, but you're right. Men like that should be brought to justice, not murdered unarmed in their homes, and once this piece is released, he'll spend a very long time in prison anyway.'

As the flight started boarding, Sean made the changes to his piece. He was twitching as the queue passed through the gate and only three people remained. 'Done,' he announced, while hooking up his laptop up to Colin's phone. He sent an email with the piece and background evidence attached, to four different newswire services, in the hope that one would pick up the story.

They passed through the gate just as the attendant was closing the flight.

Chapter 44

It was midnight by the time the plane landed in Florence. Sean and Colin rushed through Customs and quickly made their way to the Hertz desk, where they rented a small Fiat for the journey to Forte dei Marmi. The drive through the beautiful Tuscan countryside took just over an hour and a half, but they didn't get to appreciate the scenery, as the moonless sky didn't cast any light onto the rolling hills.

The topography changed quickly when they dropped down from the Carrera Mountains and they were soon driving along the wide boulevards of the Italian seaside town. The streets were deserted and a stiff sea breeze blew cold air between the expensive boutiques and cafés, whistling on top of the car as they pulled up outside a mustard-coloured restaurant on the edge of the Lido. It was closed and looked as if it had been for some time.

'Do you have any idea where this *gelateria* might be?' Colin asked.

'No,' Sean said, shaking his head. 'Right on the beach, Liz said.'

They pulled away from the cafe and drove along the expansive promenade. 'It's a long beach,' Colin said, after five minutes of driving.

'Yes, but all of the areas seem to belong to private beach clubs. We're looking for an old-world ice-cream stand. I think it would have to be on a public beach, close to the centre of town,' Sean replied, scanning the beach side of the road.

Nodding in agreement, Colin said, 'Well, at least it's a starting point,' and turned the car around to head back towards the town centre. Directly opposite the central avenue, there was a small garden filled with fountains, occupying the land between the promenade and the beach. Swerving across the empty street, Colin parked the car and they made their way on foot through the garden, then onto a narrow pier that stretched out across the wide beach, to the Mediterranean Sea.

The pier was empty. There was no ice-cream stand to be seen, as Sean spun around and looked down at the beach. Still seeing nothing, he ran to the other side of the pier. 'It could be anywhere,' he shouted, heading back towards the car.

'Wait, there's something under the pier,' Colin shouted, looking down between the old wooden planks.

As Sean sprinted off the pier and down onto the sandy beach, he nearly ran straight into Papa Luigi's *Gelato* stand, its oak structure was built into the pier and looked like it had been there for a hundred years. The area around him was deserted, with no sign of Liz or Praew. Some old sun loungers had been left out on the beach from the season and Sean shouted to Colin. 'I'm going to wait down here. Why don't you go and sleep in the car?'

Colin shouted his agreement and made his way back to their small Fiat, parked on the desolate promenade. It was bitterly cold on the beach and Sean pulled his hood up onto his head, before facing himself away from the wind and trying to make himself comfortable.

Somehow he must have fallen asleep and he woke chilled to the bone, as the sun started to rise over the sea. In the background, he could see the yellow sparkle where it hit the snow-capped peaks of the Carrara Mountains. Banging his feet into the cold sand to bring them back to life, he stood up from the shabby sun lounger and stretched his arms.

Then, suddenly desperate for the loo, he quickly went to the edge of the pier and relieved himself into a bush. As he was returning, zipping up his fly, he saw two figures walking along the shoreline. It was impossible to make them out, as they had the sun behind them, but when they got closer he could tell one was much shorter than the other and they were holding hands, their big coats protecting them from the cold wind.

'Liz!' Sean shouted, as he began sprinting towards them.

Momentarily shocked, the two figures stopped, but then they parted hands. 'Sean!' the voice came back, as Liz jolted towards him.

Sean and Liz met about 100 metres from Papa Luigi's *Gelato* stand and hugged each other tightly, as their lips locked in a passionate kiss, before Praew joined them and wrapped her arms as far as she could around both of them. When they finally parted, Liz spoke. 'I'm so glad you understood my cryptic message,' she said.

'It took a while, but I managed to dig it out from my useless memory somehow. We can't get a *gelato* though, it's closed,' Sean replied laughing happily.

'I think hot soup would be more in order anyway,' she said. 'Why don't we go back to our hotel to get warm?'

'You have a hotel?' Sean frowned.

'Yes, we flew in from Zurich yesterday,' she smiled.

'I slept on the beach last night, freezing to death,' Sean laughed. 'And poor Colin slept in the car.'

'I thought it was Colin's voice on the phone, but we couldn't see anything. How is he?' Liz asked. When Sean told her the quick story of the rescue and told her that Clive was alive, she beamed with joy.

As they climbed up the steps back onto the promenade, Sean looked around for the small white Fiat that they had rented, but it was nowhere to be seen. 'He must have gone to get breakfast,' he concluded.

Then, from nowhere, a solitary figure stepped out of the park opposite and started walking towards them. As Sean went to shout to him, he realised that it wasn't Colin and when he got nearer, the contorted face of David Findlow came into focus.

'Run!' Sean shouted and pushed Liz away. She grabbed Praew by the hand and began to sprint down the promenade. Immediately Findlow moved to run after them, but Sean moved in the opposite direction, forcing Findlow to make a choice. Turning abruptly, he chose to chase Sean instead.

He can't be carrying a gun, or he would have fired, Sean thought, then realised that he wouldn't be able to get one onto the plane, which answered his second question. How did he know they were there? He must have followed Liz to the airport and then just watched her, knowing that she would lead them to him.

Calculating that Findlow had just made his first mistake, Sean sped away. If he had chased Liz, Sean would have no choice but to follow. As it was, he had allowed Liz and Praew to get away. He jumped down the steps onto the soft sand of the beach and sprinted as fast as he could towards the sea, with Findlow about thirty metres behind him. When he reached the water's edge, the sand became firmer and he increased his speed, in the knowledge that he was no slouch and could beat most people in a sprint. But clearly Findlow was no slouch either and he maintained the pace, not gaining ground, but equally not losing any.

Putting everything he had into his sprint, Sean gained a few metres, but then tired quickly and Findlow somehow maintained the same pace, closing the gap again. The tattooed lean torso he had seem on the TV screen, sprang into Sean's mind, as he realised that he wasn't going to be able to outrun him that easily.

Slowing quickly and losing ground, Sean decided on an alternate strategy and ran into the sea up to his waist. The freezing cold water bit into his body like daggers with each step, before he stopped and turned around.

Findlow had stopped on the edge of the water, watching, knowing that Sean couldn't get away from there. Sean's plan had been to swim out a little. He was a strong swimmer, but he hadn't planned on the Mediterranean water being so cold. With this temperature, he wouldn't get more than a few metres before his muscles began to seize up.

Suddenly Sean had nowhere to go. He was trapped and he couldn't stay in the water much longer, or he wouldn't be able to muster the strength to walk out. In an attempt to get away, he moved to his left, but it was no use; Findlow just moved with him and the resistance of the water meant that he couldn't move quickly. The situation left him with no choice; he breathed in deeply, plucked up his courage and started to move slowly towards his psychopathic assailant.

Observing Sean's resignation to a fight, Findlow smiled sadistically and produced a flick knife from his trousers. The last time Sean had had a fight was in the school playground, at the age of thirteen . . . and he'd lost. Knowing that Findlow had probably been fighting his whole life and that he had a knife, Sean knew the odds were stacked against him, but there was no other way out. To try to swim the four kilometres or so around the headland would be certain suicide. To wait in the water any longer would just sap his strength for the inevitable fight. He had to make a stand and fight, and he had to do it now.

When the water was up to his calves and he was only ten metres from his opponent, Sean stopped, assessing his next move.

Without warning, Findlow rushed forward and lunged at his chest with the knife, but the weight of the water slowed him and Sean easily dodged the shiny blade. Pivoting his body, he raised his knee forcefully into Findlow's rib cage and backed away, as Findlow fell into the water.

Seeing a chance, Sean ran out of the water quickly and onto the hard sand, sprinting away from Findlow, but the trained fighter was up quickly and following, about twenty paces behind. The cold water had sapped some of Sean's strength and he began to tire quickly, as Findlow gained ground with every step.

Thinking of a plan, Sean slowed slightly, purposely allowing Findlow to get closer. He was now only three yards behind and slashing at Sean wildly with the outstretched knife. Just as he felt the blade touch his back, Sean dived down to the sand into a crouching position and Findlow came crashing into him, tumbling over his body. The knife fell from Findlow's hand, into the edge of the water and he rolled over, quickly scrambling to reclaim it, but Sean was on top of him before he could reach it.

Crashing his fists into Findlow's face as hard as he could, Sean felt the crack of broken bone as he smashed his nose across his face. Without stopping, he continued to pummel Findlow with every bit of power that he had left, but suddenly, he felt his body twisted sideways, as Findlow deflected a blow with his arm. Sean lost balance and Findlow flung him to one side, into the water.

Findlow jumped back to grab the knife from the water's edge and as he bent down, Sean kicked him with his full force in the rib cage. The force sent Findlow keeling over and into the water, onto his back.

Seizing the opportunity, Sean sprang forward and landed on top of him. The icy cold piercing pain in his left shoulder came as a shock, as he realised that Findlow had retrieved the knife and forced it into his flesh. Pulling it back out of Sean's shoulder, Findlow lunged again, this time at his stomach. Sean saw the lunge coming and managed to pull back slightly, but the blade still embedded itself into his stomach.

The cold water and adrenalin numbed any pain Sean would normally have felt from his injuries, as he backed away. Holding the knife in his bloodstained right hand, Findlow had a twisted grin on his face and moved in for the kill.

He jabbed at Sean playfully with the knife, but Sean moved back each time, dodging the deadly blade. The failed attacks didn't seem to bother the psychopath. He had the advantage and he knew it. Needing to even up the odds, Sean dodged Findlow and ran back into the icy cold water up to his calves. This time Findlow followed and the two men stood two metres away from each other, twitching to see the other's reaction, readying themselves to make a move.

It was Findlow that made the first move. He rushed forward with the knife pointed at Sean's ribs, but Sean was ready and moved to one side, the knife passing harmlessly between his arm and body. Then, taking advantage of Findlow's stance, Sean grabbed his arm and pulled it towards him, pulling Findlow off-balance, sending him headfirst into the shallow water.

Wasting no time, Sean spun around and jumped on Findlow's back, using both hands to pin Findlow's right arm into the sand, until the pressure forced him to release the knife. Reacting quickly, Sean grabbed the knife and raised it to ram it into Findlow's back, but the movement gave the attacker the opportunity to move and he threw Sean to one side, into the water.

Now on his back with his opponent above him, Sean thrust upwards with the knife, but missed the target and got a mouth full of water, as his head fell backwards into the sea. Before he could get up, Findlow climbed on top of him and pinned his arms down with his knees, forcing him to swallow water again, as his head was forced under the shallow waves.

In an attempt to free himself, Sean flailed around with his legs, but it was no use: Findlow had him pinned down firmly. The water level just covered his head and he held his breath, hoping for an opportunity to move, but with each second, he could feel the desire to breathe growing in him. Soon his body would react automatically: he would draw water into his lungs and that would be his final breath.

Fighting for his life, he struggled again, but Findlow didn't budge. Sean could just make out his face through the shallow water covering his eyes. It looked like Findlow was smiling, taking some perverse pleasure from the situation.

As Sean was about to give up all hope, he saw a flash of light behind Findlow. Findlow's grip went limp and he fell off Sean's body. Gasping for breath, Sean shot upright in the water and turned to continue the fight. His attacker was lying face down in the water, blood running from the back of his head. Then Sean saw Liz, standing calf-deep in the water, holding a piece of metal pipe.

Just managing to stand, Sean walked towards her, falling into her arms as she backed out of the water and onto the beach. As he reached her, she let out a terrifying shriek, pointing towards Findlow. He was starting to come around, twitching in the water and raising his head. Before Sean could react, Praew picked up the metal pipe, ran forward and crashed it hard into the back of his head. The cracking sound as his skull broke was stomach-churning. Sean and Liz watched on as Praew repeated the move four times, smashing Findlow's brain to a pulp.

Without speaking, Liz walked forward and took the pipe from Praew, throwing it into the water, where Findlow's body floated face down, with a growing pool of blood colouring the area around it.

Chapter 45

Sean held onto Liz as they left the beach, walking back up to the promenade and Praew did her best to prop his wobbling frame from the other side. The pain from his wounds was growing as the adrenalin wore off, and the exhaustion from the fight left him barely able muster the strength to walk. When they reached the promenade, there was still no sign of the small Fiat, or Colin. A chilling thought crossed Sean's mind: had Findlow disposed of Colin prior to coming for them?

'We need to find Colin,' he said to Liz.

'You need a doctor,' she replied. 'We're going to my hotel.'

He stopped and looked at Liz. 'Liz, I can't see a doctor with stab wounds. There's a dead body on the beach and we are still wanted by the police. The doctor will be obliged to call them. You're going to have to do the best you can to patch me up. I'm fairly sure they're only flesh wounds.'

'Only flesh wounds,' Liz exclaimed. 'You've been watching too much TV. You have to see a doctor.'

Sean stopped again. 'No, Liz, I'm serious. We're wanted for murder in three countries, maybe four when they find Findlow's body on the beach. Two of those countries still have the death penalty. We can't risk being caught.'

'Surely we can explain now,' Liz said. 'Barker-Willet's gone, so that threat is clear. We'll get good lawyers, we'll be fine,' she said confidently.

'David Findlow didn't run the company,' Sean said quietly.

'What?' Liz said frowning.

'The Brigadier, his brother does. David Findlow was just a figurehead. Anthony Findlow is the brains behind BW and he's still on the loose.'

'So, this isn't over?' Liz looked at him, shattered.

'Not yet,' Sean said comforting her.

A bush suddenly rustled in front of them, as Colin was pushed out onto the pavement and a young man, with short cropped hair, stood behind him, holding a knife to his throat. The young attacker looked at the three tatty, soaking and bloodstained figures in front of him, not speaking.

'What the fuck do you want?' Sean said, dismissively.

'Where's Mr Barker-Willet?' the young man replied, edging the knife into Colin's throat.

Unable to find the strength to make up a story, Sean just told the truth. 'Dead! You'll find him with his skull beaten in on the beach, and if you were supposed to be his protection, I'm guessing you'll be dead soon too. I don't think the Brigadier's a very forgiving man, do you?'

Stunned by Sean's comments, the young knifeman obviously didn't know what to do and was caught in two minds. Seeing the opportunity that his confusion presented, Colin pulled back from the knife, grabbed the soldier's arm and threw him to the floor, then swiftly kicked the knife away. Liz helped Colin tie his legs and arms, gag him, and push him back into the bushes. Somebody'll find him later,' Colin said. 'I'm sorry. I fell asleep in the car.'

'You're hurt?' Colin said, noticing Sean's wounds.

Sean moved his hands to show him the two stab wounds.

'Just flesh wounds,' Colin said, to the sound of Liz tutting loudly. Then he ripped his shirt into strips, making makeshift bandages and straps to apply pressure to the wounds. 'We need to get to a chemist to get something to clean those with. If they get infected, you'll know about it,' he said.

'How about a hospital?' Liz said.

'All hell is just about to break loose here. When they find the body of Charles Barker-Willet on the beach, they are going to be looking for you. We need to get in the car and get the hell out of Italy, to somewhere where we can lie low for a few days,' Colin said sighing.

'Okay, let's go. We don't have anything at the hotel, other than a few minor pieces of clothing,' Liz said angrily.

All in agreement, the four of them climbed into the small car. Liz and Sean sat in the back, so that Liz could monitor Sean's wounds and Praew sat in the front with Colin. At 11 a.m. they pulled into the small town of Brennero on the Austrian border, driving around a few back streets before pulling the Fiat over by a driveway. Without warning, Colin jumped out and removed the number plates from the fiat. Within five minutes, he had switched the plates for those on another similar car and they were on their way again. 'They probably won't notice until the next time it's due for a service.' he said.

They drove for five minutes more, before the satnav sounded, 'Welcome to Austria.'

'Any ideas? We're near Innsbruck?' Colin asked.

'Funny you should ask that. We came through a delightful little ski resort called Seefeld on the way to Zurich. It's near Innsbruck. There are lots of tourists, so we won't stand out and if people see Sean stumbling, we can just say he had a skiing accident,' Liz said.

'Makes sense,' Colin said, and started to fumble with the GPS. An hour later, they pulled into the small town of

Seefeld-in-Tirol. Colin found a car park outside a large Eurospar supermarket and stopped. 'Wait here,' he said and hopped out of the car. Half an hour later, he retuned holding a set of keys. 'Okay I've rented a house. It's not far away.'

Not far away was an understatement. They pulled the car from the car park back onto Olympiastrasse, drove fifty metres and took the right fork onto Leutascherstrasse. The house was another fifty metres up on the right. The exterior was of traditional Tyrolean design, with wooden balconies and a sloping roof, but it was obviously recently built, as there were still signs of building materials outside. Colin pulled the car into the concealed car porch and stopped.

Inside, the house was anything but traditional. The top floor was a vast open-plan statement in modernism, with a state-of-the-art kitchen, a glass log fireplace and designer furniture. The two further floors contained four en-suite bedrooms, a gym and a spa, complete with jacuzzi and sauna.

'Wow,' Liz said. 'What did this place cost to rent?'

Colin laughed. 'A lot, but your granddad's paying, right?'

'I guess so,' Liz said smiling.

Once they'd settled in, Colin went out to get food and medical supplies, choosing to walk, in order to keep the car concealed. Thirty minutes later, he returned, carrying six large shopping bags stuffed with food and all kinds of first-aid items. After putting a pizza on, Colin carefully cleaned and dressed Sean's wounds, then administered the strong blend of painkillers he had been able to find. 'Army training,' he said to Liz who was watching in disbelief.

Considering that he had been stabbed twice, Sean felt surprisingly well. The pain was subsiding and he wanted to get some sleep. He and Liz went down to one of the bedrooms and crawled into bed together. Although he had been waiting for this moment for days, Sean couldn't keep his eyes open and he fell asleep while kissing Liz.

Chapter 46

Saturday, 7th March. Seefeld-in-Tirol, Austria

Sean woke with light still streaming through the window, highlighting the majestic snow-covered mountains in the background, that rose above the pretty sloping rooftops of the town. He noticed a new set of clothing laid out for him on a chair and dressed quickly. Upstairs in the main living area Colin, Praew and Liz were lounging around on the various sofas, all eyes glued to the TV.

'How long was I out for?' Sean asked.

Liz looked up. 'About a day,' she said, smiling sweetly.

'A day? I thought it was about two hours. What are you watching?' Sean shook his head and winced with pain.

'The news. You'll want to see this,' she said.

They were tuned into the *BBC News* channel. A heading on a screen behind the news anchor said 'BW CORPORATION SCANDAL'. The anchor spoke excitedly. 'And the latest from BW is that the London Stock Exchange has suspended trading in its shares, following the seventy-five per cent fall yesterday. Nobody from BW Corporation was available for comment.' There was a slight pause.

'Just to recap the events of the last two days regarding BW Corporation: on Thursday evening, Reuters newswire service received an email from the wanted criminal and journalist Sean McManus. That email contained a story about major corruption at BW Corporation. It suggested that the world's most valuable company was nothing more than an elaborate cover for a horrific operation which preyed upon billions of the world's poorest people.

'It also alleged that Charles Barker-Willet, the CEO of BW Corporation, was really the son of the notorious East End gangster Franky Findlow, and that he had brutally raped a twelve-year old girl in Thailand.

'Perhaps one of the biggest shocks was the revelation that decorated war hero, Sir Anthony John Findlow, was the mastermind behind the scenes at BW. Brigadier Sir Anthony John Findlow, the British Military's senior foreign advisor and a man knighted for his services to peace, is the other son of notorious criminal Franky Findlow. Brigadier Findlow has apparently disappeared without trace, according to the Metropolitan Police.'

'News of these allegations created a run on the BW Bank in Zurich this morning. The bank immediately closed down its operations without comment and Swiss banking regulators raided the bank following its closure. Since then, the Swiss police have issued arrest warrants for all of the bank's senior executives.'

'Yesterday morning it was also announced that Charles Barker-Willet had been found dead, brutally beaten on a beach in Tuscany, Italy.'

'Wow! This really is the scandal to end all scandals,' the co-anchor said in a rehearsed manner.

'Yes, and we're already getting rumours about its repercussions around the world. This morning in Niger, a General was executed for corruption after his name appeared on the list of BW Banking's clientele, which following a leak, was published by various news outlets.'

'That list certainly reads like the who's who of despots,' the co-anchor added again.

'Yes, only hours ago, a leading army general was arrested in Thailand for the same reason. We're also hearing rumours of arrests in China and Belarus. According to the Metropolitan Police, at least seventy-five per cent of the people on the BW Banking client list are wanted by the ICC for war crimes, or crimes against humanity.'

'Where will it end?' the co-anchor asked.

'Who knows? I think there's still a long way to go on this one,' the anchor replied.

'Wait a minute. We have more breaking news,' the co-anchor said.

'That's right, Tom. The Metropolitan police have just arrested Franky Findlow at Lydd airfield, boarding a light plane bound for France. As we reported yesterday, Franky Findlow was meant to be in Portland Bill prison serving a life sentence for murder. However, he didn't serve a single day of his sentence. He switched places with another man, who agreed to go along with the ploy, as Findlow had threatened to kill his whole family if he refused. Apparently, the two had no previous connection and this poor man's only crime was that he looked like the notorious gangster. George Morgan was released this morning to jubilant scenes from his family.'

Pictures of Franky Findlow and George Morgan next to each other came onto screen, and they did look very alike.

'And what of the young man who uncovered this corruption? Sean McManus?' the co-anchor prompted. 'You think he'll win an outstanding journalism award?'

Sean held his breath at the mention of his name. Was this all finally over? Had they won?

'Well, if he does, he may need to receive it in prison,' the Anchor scoffed. 'The Hong Kong and Thai police issued statements this morning saying that he is still wanted for murder, despite the BW revelations. Also, the Metropolitan police say that they still want him to help with their enquiries.'

On one hand Sean was elated by the widespread pick up of his piece; on the other, he was terrified that it hadn't deterred the police from thinking he and Liz were murderers. As his back hit the cushion, he felt a searing pain in his stomach and cried out in agony.

Liz immediately turned. 'What's wrong?'

'I think it's bad,' Sean said, opening his shirt to reveal yellow liquid oozing from the dressing on his stomach

'I think it's infected,' Liz said.

'Shit! I think you're right. He needs proper medical help,' Colin said.

'No,' Sean said. 'You heard what they said. I'm still wanted for murder.'

Colin shook his head firmly. 'If you don't get medical help soon there won't be anyone left to arrest. This is serious. We have to get you to a hospital right away.'

'Okay, but I go alone. Liz is still wanted in Thailand and the UK,' he said.

Liz stood up. 'No way, Sean. I'm not leaving you in this state. In fact, I'm not leaving you again, full stop. Whatever they throw at us, we'll face it together.'

'Liz, it's not just the police. Anthony Findlow is still out there somewhere, and I'm sure he's hell-bent on revenge,' Sean pleaded, and then yelped with pain.

'I don't care,' Liz said. 'Colin, can you drive us to the hospital, please. Praew can stay here, and you'll need to come back and look after her.'

'Okay,' Colin said grabbing his things.

Liz explained the situation to Praew, who looked scared and

wanted to go along, but she did as she was told by Liz and stayed on the sofa.

On the twenty-minute drive to Innsbruck hospital, Sean drifted in and out of consciousness, hallucinating badly. When they arrived, Liz helped him into a wheelchair outside the A&E, as Colin sped away in the small Fiat back towards Seefeld. The triage nurse wheeled Sean straight through A&E and into a theatre prep area, where he was canulated, pumped full of antibiotics, painkillers and then anaesthetic. Liz was shaking with fear, desperate for him to pull though as he was quickly moved into the operating theatre.

Forty minutes later he emerged, still anesthetised, but the theatre nurse nodded positively, indicating that the operation was successful.

As he awoke in the recovery room, a smile broke out on Sean's face. 'He'll be like that for a while. It's the morphine,' the recovery nurse said.

Liz sat by his side as he drifted in and out of sleep, declaring his undying love for her. When he finally woke up properly, she told him she loved him and kissed him on the cheek. Then, she nodded to the nurse, who opened the door to let the Austrian police into the room.

The two Austrian policemen informed Sean that he was being arrested for crimes committed in the UK, and that he and Liz would be returned to the UK on the first available flight, to face charges.

Chapter 47

Sean was allowed to recover in the Innsbruck hospital for another day, before being handcuffed unceremoniously to a policeman, as and he and Liz were escorted to the small Innsbruck Kranebitten airport. The flight to Gatwick on EasyJet proved extremely embarrassing, with people stopping to stare at Sean and Liz, who were seated in the front rows, still handcuffed to Austrian policemen.

When the plane touched down at Gatwick, the other passengers were cleared before the Austrian policemen allowed Sean and Liz to stand. A sense of foreboding filled Sean, as they were escorted to the rear of the plane, where a set of steps had been wheeled to the door. Outside, Sean could see the white prisoner transit vehicle waiting for them underneath the tip of the wing.

At the bottom of the steps, the Austrian handcuffs were exchanged for British ones and the prisoner handover completed. Sean and Liz were pushed into the rear of the vehicle, followed by two uniformed and armed policemen, who both wore helmets, obscuring their facial features.

Neither Sean nor Liz spoke as the vehicle started to move. They both knew that this would probably be their last time together for a while, until the mess was cleared up . . . if it ever was. Sean would be taken to a male remand centre and Liz a female one. Sean stared at Liz across the wide van. He could wait for her, however long it took. In a strange way, he felt secure. They were in the custody of the British police, their arrest in Austria had been reported in the news, and he knew that he would eventually be able to prove that he hadn't killed John. He would need to fight extradition to Hong Kong and Thailand, where he had actually killed people, albeit in self-defence, but that was do-able, wasn't it?

When the vehicle left the airport compound and started to accelerate on what Sean assumed was a main road, the two policemen reached for their helmets at the same time and unbuckled them. Liz's mouth almost hit the floor as the familiar face of Terry came into view, with Phil under the other helmet.

'What the . . .?' she whispered.

Terry laughed. 'Surprise!' he said.

The van seemed to slow down and turn sharply onto a rough road. Then it stopped suddenly.

'We're here,' Phil said. 'Let's go.'

The doors to the van were opened from the outside and Sean immediately recognized two of the other bodyguards from Clive's team. They were quickly uncuffed and rushed into a waiting people carrier with blacked-out windows. Without hesitation, the car sped away from the scene.

'They'll soon work out it's missing, so we have to put some distance between us and it,' Terry explained.

In the next hour, they changed vehicle two more times, before they arrived at a small farmhouse just outside Folkestone. They pulled into a barn and closed the doors behind them, before making their way into the brick house.

When Sean entered the building an immediate smile broke out on his face, as Clive wheeled himself into the hallway in an electric wheelchair. When Liz saw Clive, she ran forward and hugged him. 'I'm so glad you're alive,' she said.

'I'm not that easy to kill,' he said, before bowing his head, a serious expression taking over his face. 'Praew's missing.'

'What? How?' Liz exclaimed.

'We're not sure. Colin's dead, killed at the house in Seefeld, but Praew wasn't anywhere to be seen. I *assume* the Brigadier has her, but I don't *know*,' Clive clarified.

'I'm sorry about Colin; he was a good man,' Sean said.

'He was . . . and a close friend,' Clive said.

'How did he find them?' Liz asked.

'I not sure, but once you turned up at the hospital and the TV channels got hold of it, he probably just blanketed the areas surrounding Innsbruck. Or he had a reason to target Seefeld. Who knows?'

Liz closed her eyes. 'Shit! It might have been my fault. I got off the train there, on the way to Zurich. Maybe it gave him a place to start and they just called all the rental agents and hotels until he found the house. I can't believe it! We should never have gone back.' Tears welled in her eyes and Sean moved to console her.

'Liz, you can't blame yourself for this. It's nobody's fault,' Clive responded.

'Why do you think he's got her?' Liz asked.

'Again, I can't be certain. But if he wanted to kill her, he would've left her body in the Seefeld house, as he did with Colin.'

'She could've got away,' Sean said.

'Possibly, but I think she'd have been picked up by the police now if she had. A twelve-year-old Thai girl wandering the streets of Austria, with no money and nowhere to go, would stand out. Also, there's the weather. If she had nowhere to stay, she'd freeze;

it gets down to minus fifteen overnight there, at this time of year.'

'What do you think he wants with her?' Liz asked.

'Well, thankfully, David Findlow is dead, so I don't think it's some something perverted. I think he'll try to exchange her,' Clive suggested.

'For what? We don't have anything he wants; the damage is done,' Liz said.

'I think he'll want Sean, or both of you,' Clive speculated.

'Why? We're no longer a threat to him. We've published everything we know,' Sean said.

'Maybe he wants to kill you for what you've done to him.'

Chapter 48

'What can we do?' Sean asked, after they had moved into the kitchen and absorbed Clive's comments.

'We need to find Praew,' Liz added.

'The good news is that he's now on the run as well, with thousands of police the world over looking for him. His organisation is collapsing around his ears, so he won't be able to command the resources he did previously. That doesn't mean that we'll be able to find him. Our resources are here, in this room, so we need to let him find us.'

'How?' Liz asked.

'We need to monitor every email account that you've used in the past three weeks, especially the ones that you know he accessed. I think that's how he'll make contact.'

'You're not suggesting that Sean exchanges himself for Praew, so that Findlow can kill him?' Liz said.

'I'm not *suggesting* anything. If and when he sees fit to contact us, we'll decide on a plan of action then. But any involvement will be *entirely* up to the people involved.'

Liz and Sean acknowledged their understanding with a quick nod.

'Where do you think he might be?' Sean moved on.

'He could be anywhere. He'll have stashed plenty of cash somewhere for an eventuality like this, and he'll still have a lot of powerful friends around the world. Although, if the news reports are to be believed, they're dropping like flies.'

Sean grabbed the TV remote and tuned into the news. Instantly an image of the abandoned prisoner transport vehicle came on. 'How did you do that?' Sean asked.

'Findlow isn't the only one with people on the inside of the police,' Clive winked. 'I have friends – good people – in high places. They know you're innocent, but can't play their hands until they know who the rotten apples are in their own barrels. They're keeping me informed on the search for Findlow, but they don't know where we are.'

'So our escape was sanctioned by the police?' Liz asked, surprised.

'By a select few, very senior officers, yes. They thought that you'd be sitting ducks in the remand system, and more use on the outside.'

The news sent a shiver of relief through Sean. If they could find a way to catch the Brigadier, it meant that they may be able to return to a normal life. 'What about Bratic?' Sean asked.

'What's he got to do with anything?' Clive said.

The realisation suddenly hit Sean: of course, only he, Colin and Liz knew of Bratic's plans for the former Yugoslavia. He had deliberately not included it in his piece, on advice from Colin. They had concluded that the way to deal with Bratic was a quiet word to MI6, the British international intelligence service. Then events took over and it had never been discussed again.

Sean explained to Clive what the Brigadier had told him, and his subsequent conversation with Colin.

'Now it makes sense,' Clive exclaimed loudly, fitting the final piece to a complex puzzle.

'What does?' Sean was taken aback by his reaction.

'I couldn't reconcile the revenge motive with the Brigadier's psyche. Everything he's done to date has been cold and calculating. People like that don't normally do things out of passion; i.e., revenge. They do things for a reason.'

'I don't follow,' Liz said.

'The Brigadier still needs to shut you up, to give Bratic time to sew his seeds of destruction. That's why he took Praew.'

'Why would he care about Bratic now his empire's collapsed?' Sean commented.

'Because my guess is that he's with Bratic and they're working this thing together. It would make sense: the Brigadier knows the region well, and he'll have contacts there from his previous posting during the war.'

'Why would he do that?' Liz asked.

'Because it will give him back the one thing he can't get without it . . . power. His money and contacts would probably be able to make his life on the run comfortable, but for a man like the Brigadier, that's not enough. With Bratic in charge in the region, the Brigadier could sit behind him pulling the strings, fulfilling his lust for power.'

'God, you're right! He told me in his office that I'd never understand the aphrodisiac of real power and that *that* was his real quest, not money.' Sean said.

'Where does that leave us?' Liz asked.

Clive considered his response before speaking. 'Walking a very dangerous tightrope between MI6 and the bad guys.'

Sean frowned, showing that he didn't understand the inference.

'If we inform MI6, they'll go after Bratic, and if they find him, Findlow will have no more use for Praew, so he'll just kill her and disappear.'

Sean still looked confused: this kind of thing was the stuff of books, not real life. He struggled for a response but couldn't find one.

Picking up on the confusion, Clive continued. 'We just need a couple of days before we tell them.'

'Okay, so what's the tightrope?' Sean said.

'If we fail and we get killed trying to get Praew back, then there's nothing to stop Bratic starting his war. Once the Security Services find out what he's up to, it will be too late.'

'I still don't understand how he can just start a war like that. Surely he can't just buy an army!' Liz said.

'You only need a match to start an explosion in a powder keg,' Clive said. 'Bratic is just the detonator. The region is boiling with unresolved hostility between the various groups. Somebody with vast sums of money and friends in the right places – of which he has both – only needs to orchestrate a few sensitive events, and follow up with the right propaganda, to seize control of the country. Then he would have legitimate control of the biggest army in the region, plus the funds to arm them to the teeth.'

'Sensitive events?' Sean questioned.

'Assassinations, mass shootings, bombings . . . blamed on one ethnic group or nation, in order to get the angry masses baying for blood. From there, Twitter does the rest.'

'What do we do now then?' Sean asked.

'We wait. If I'm right, the Brigadier will be in touch soon.'

Chapter 49

They didn't wait for long. Within two hours a message appeared in Sean's compromised Gmail account and Clive's previously secure account. It was a simple message: *Contact me or she dies*. A photo of Praew with her hands tied behind her back was attached. It didn't give any clue as to the location.

Clive typed a quick reply: *What do you want?*

The reply came equally quickly. *Dubrovnik, the end of the wide pier in the old harbour. You, McManus and Channing. 3 p.m. tomorrow.*

Okay. Clive typed.

'Croatia? I thought they'd be in Serbia,' Liz said.

'No, they won't go into Serbia until they have flared the hostility. Then they'll enter like returning heroes, there to save the day.'

'How are we going to get to Croatia by tomorrow, with half the world looking for us?' Sean asked.

'Liz, we need your grandfather to get us a private jet from London to Dubrovnik. Tonight if possible. Tell him to put it in the name of Donald Caddick.' Clive passed Liz a cell phone. 'Use this. It's secure.'

Liz took the phone and quickly dialled the number for her

grandfather's house, and explained to him that she needed a jet, but didn't say why. Sean watched as Liz listened, nodding her head. The conversation went on for some time without Liz speaking. Then she spoke a few words in Korean and hung up, looking disturbed.

'What is it? Did we get the plane?' Sean asked.

'Yes. We're to call him back in half an hour and he'll give us the details. It's Bill. Even though they arrested the General, they're still planning to try him for murder. He's been moved from the military prison to a normal prison, and he's heard rumour that one of the General's men is trying to kill him. My family are going to try to bust him out tonight.'

Sean instinctively reached out and hugged her.

'I'm scared, Sean. What if he gets killed?'

'It sounds like he's taking that risk either way,' Sean countered, still holding her.

'You're right. The answer would be the same. They have to try.'

After the return phone call to her grandfather, Liz conveyed the information to Clive and they started to pack for Croatia.

At Luton airport's private terminal, Liz and Sean had been loaded into a plywood box as cargo, along with numerous weapons and some other military looking equipment. Luckily, the Dassault Falcon aircraft had a large rear storage cabin and they were placed in there until the plane took off. They were allowed out of the cramped space for the duration of the two-hour flight, but when the plane started to descend, they took their places in the box again. Clive said that the cargo was artwork for his villa and the Customs officials paid it no further attention at either end of the flight.

'Private flights get away with a lot less scrutiny,' he said to Liz, as she was finally released from the tight space.

During the time out of the box, Liz had remained silent, staring out of the window. Sean knew that she was concerned about the jail-break and how it had gone. She had been told to wait until 6 a.m. in Thailand before she could call her grandfather to find out. By then, her uncle should be in the air and out of Thai airspace. She was tempted to call from the phone on the plane, but her grandfather had said not to call early; there would be no point. They landed in Dubrovnik at midnight; 5 a.m. Thai time.

They had reserved rooms in a small pension overlooking the harbour and even though it was night, they still had a good view of tomorrow's rendezvous point. It was brightly lit by an ornate lamppost on the end of the jetty that cast an orange glare onto the water and over to the ancient harbour wall beyond, which cocooned it from the Adriatic Sea.

Clive scoured the area with binoculars, getting the lie of the land from the small balcony, while Liz sat on the edge of the bed watching the clock.

'It's one. Are you going to make the call?' Sean asked, shaking off the chill as he stepped into the room from the balcony.

Liz didn't speak, but picked up the phone and dialled. After a short pause, the call was answered. She exchanged some brief pleasantries and then listened. Even though Sean couldn't understand what was being said, he could tell that the news wasn't good. Liz hung up the phone and began to cry.

'What's happened?' Sean asked quietly.

'He's missing. Something went wrong and he was separated from the mercenaries Grandpa had paid to get him. Now he's on the run somewhere in Bangkok, with no money and half of the Thai police force looking for him. If they see him, they'll shoot on sight.'

Sean thought quickly. 'Call your grandfather back. Tell him that if Bill contacts him, he should make his way to Girl House on Soi Cowboy and ask for Nok, using my name. He should ask her to get Bank to take him into Burma. Your family can then pick him up in Yangon.'

Liz stared at Sean briefly, then dialled and relayed the same message to her grandfather.

'Well?' Sean asked.

'He says if he calls, he'll tell him and he thanks you for trying to help.' Liz wiped a tear from her eye and made a weak attempt at a smile.

'We need to talk about tomorrow,' Clive said, closing the balcony door behind him and struggling forward painfully on his walking stick.

Chapter 50

As the sunlight broke over the hills behind them and hit the shimmering Adriatic Sea, Sean stood and took in the sight. He hadn't slept at all, spending the night writing a new piece about Bratic and the Brigadier, and putting it in a Cloud account. He had also been deliberating throughout the night about the choice between Praew's life and his own, should it come to a point where he might have to make that call.

They had received a further email saying that the Brigadier would exchange Praew for Sean, but the others needed to be there, where he could see them.

'It doesn't make sense,' Clive said. 'I think they plan to kill us all. I think the swap thing is just a ploy to get us there. He'll know that we all know about his plans.'

'Why would he think that we haven't told anybody else, in which case killing us would be pointless?' Sean suggested.

'Well, we haven't, so he's right there. I assume he's just gambling that we would want to secure Praew before we risked the info getting out. Which brings me back to . . . why just you?'

Sean thought for a moment. 'Because I have the voice. Getting a story like this out isn't easy, unless you're a very reliable source. There are all sorts of crank conspiracy theories running around at any given time. Before a credible news publisher could check this one out, Bratic could have already set his unstoppable ball rolling.'

'So, you don't think we could get this story out without you?' Clive asked.

'Not quickly, no. Anything I say at the moment is hot, so nobody will wait to publish it. In the current competitive news environment, everybody wants to be first with breaking news. Before they publish what *you* say, they'd spend days fact-checking.'

'Which means that whatever Bratic is planning to do, it must be imminent.' Clive added.

'They must still know that you could tell MI6, or another agency though,' Sean said.

'Yes, but they're probably prepared for that, and by the time any other, more official Government involvement came, it'd be too late. Once the bloodlust of the people is fed, it won't be quenched by anything but war.'

'So why would a simple piece from me stop it?'

'Because it would tell the people that they were being manipulated by Bratic and, as much as they might be yearning for another bite at the cherry, they won't let themselves be dragged in by deception.'

Clive stopped and shook his head briefly. 'Something's still not right. It's too complicated: too many ifs, buts and maybes for a man like Findlow. We're missing something. I think you're right, that you're his main threat, but that wouldn't stop you giving *us* the story to release as soon as we had Praew.'

'I typed it up last night, specifically for that purpose. Here's the detail of the Cloud account it's in and email info for newswire services. I'll give Liz a copy as well.'

'Send a copy to Liz's mother too. Tell her only to release it if we've not contacted her by 6 p. m.' Clive returned to the window and started to survey the area again through his powerful binoculars. 'That's odd,' he said to himself.

'What is?' Sean said, overhearing the mumbled remark.

'Take a look at that boat out there, a couple of miles from the harbour.'

Sean pulled the binoculars to his face and looked at the enormous white superyacht, which was anchored a little offshore. He could just make out its name: the *Princess II*. He couldn't see anybody on board. 'What's odd about it?' Sean asked.

'It's flying Bermudan colours, so why is it here in winter? This area is full of boats from everywhere in the summer, but in winter it's only local boats. Why is it here?'

Sean looked at the boat again. 'Do you think it's them?'

'It could be. They've certainly got the money for it. There's not much we can do, as long as it stays where it is. It's out of sniper range so poses no threat in itself, and we certainly can't get to it to check it out. I'll tell the guys to let me know if it moves closer to the harbour. They should be in position now, and have pretty well checked out the best sniper positions.'

A brief conversation on the concealed radio followed and Clive confirmed that they were ready and keeping an eye on the yacht as well as the jetty. Each of them carried a high-calibre military rifle with telescopic sights, and all were excellent marksmen. If Findlow tried anything on the pier, they would be prepared.

Clive woke Liz. 'We need to discuss the plan,' he said, shaking her gently.

'They'll come in by boat. It's the only thing that makes sense. I think we can rule out sniper shots. We've got four men posted around and they can deal with that.'

'So, you think they'll try to make the exchange?' Sean said.

'No, I don't, but we have to be prepared in case they do. I think they'll come in quickly on a boat and shoot at us when they get close enough to make sure they hit the target.'

'What about Praew?' Liz asked.

'In that scenario, I think she'll be on the boat, somewhere we can see her, so we think the deal's going down and don't take cover. Then they'll kill her, along with us.'

'What's the other scenario?' Sean asked.

'That they make the exchange to make sure they get you, then turn their guns on us from close range, to make sure they get us all.'

'God, aren't you the bringer of glad tidings today! One way we're dead; the other way we're . . . dead!' Liz commented. 'Tell me again why we're doing this?'

'Look, we're up against it and the risks are extreme, but please hear me out. Then, if you want to back out, I won't think any worse of you.'

Liz agreed.

'If it's scenario one, Terry's men will take out anybody they see with a weapon in the shooting position on the deck. This will provide us with good protection, as shooting from a moving boat isn't easy and they'll be picked off well before they can get a decent shot away. Plus, we'll have warning and we'll be able to hit the deck, making a long shot almost impossible from a moving boat.'

'What about Praew?' Liz asked.

'In that scenario, it's almost certain that she'll be killed,' Clive said.

'And the alternate scenario?' Liz asked.

'They make the exchange and as soon as I give the signal, we hit the deck. Terry's men will shoot anything standing up in the area. It's much more risky, but I think it's our only chance to get Praew back alive.' Clive said.

'Do you think the Brigadier will come?' Sean asked.

'No. I don't think he'd be that stupid. He'll know that we have our own trap and he'll be setting counter-traps, but he won't come himself.'

'When will you give the signal?' Sean asked.

'As soon as Praew reaches Liz, before you get on the boat. But don't drop too early, or you'll risk somebody getting shot. We all need to drop together.'

'Got it,' Sean said.

'Okay, are we in?' Clive asked.

'Yes,' Sean responded immediately.

'I don't know,' Liz said. 'You're taking the biggest risk, Sean, and I don't know if I can let you do that for Praew. Even though I love her, we've only just met her.'

'I hear you, Liz, but after everything that girl's been through, somebody needs to stand up for her and take a risk. I'll understand if you don't come, but I'm going.'

Liz looked at Sean thoughtfully. 'Okay, I'm in,' she said.

Chapter 51

At 2:30 p.m. they attached their earpiece microphones and made their way out of the small pension. Progress down the hill to the jetty was slow, as Clive was still really not well enough to be out of his bed, let alone out of a wheelchair.

'I've got movement on the yacht,' Terry's voice came over the mic.

'What's happening,' Clive replied instantly.

'Two men in the aft deck. It's a long way, but I'm fairly sure one of them is Findlow: the other is older and a lot taller,' Terry answered.

'Prominent jaw?' Sean asked.

'Massive,' the quick reply came.

'Bratic,' Sean said.

'Any tenders in the water?' Clive asked.

'Not that I can see, but could be round the other side.'

'Okay, keep your eyes on it,' Clive said. 'That's where they'll come from. They'll use one of the tenders,' Clive said to Sean and Liz, referring to the smaller boats superyachts carried on-board as playthings, or as a means to get to shore.

At 2:45 p.m. they arrived on the short stone jetty and walked carefully to the end. Sean looked out to where the superyacht was moored, but it was obscured by the old city harbour wall and not visible. The ancient harbour was dead, Clive, Liz and Sean the only people on show.

'Any movement yet?' Clive asked.

'Nothing,' Terry said.

Clive shook his head, showing that something didn't compute.

'What is it?' Sean asked.

'This isn't the type of thing that people would normally be late for; it would be timed to the second. That yacht is at least three minutes away, even in a fast boat. I would've expected that they'd be preparing by now.'

'As Terry said, maybe they're on the other side of it,' Sean commented.

'Maybe,' Clive said, obviously not convinced.

Clive's reaction sent a jolt of panic through Sean. He immediately started to scan the surrounding area. The marina was filled with small boats bobbing up and down on the light ripples: most were fishing boats, a few were pleasure boats, but he still couldn't see any people. He moved on to the fortified entrances to the old town, it was quiet. At this time of year Dubrovnik was pretty much closed to tourism, only the local townspeople would be beyond the high walls and they obviously didn't like to come down to the cold harbour. Still seeing nothing out of the ordinary, he spun back around to look into the harbour.

Then he saw it. He didn't know why he hadn't seen it before. It was too new, too fancy . . . and too low in water. He squinted to see the name on the side of the white launch. *Princess II*.

'Run,' he shouted to Liz and Clive, as he started to sprint in the direction of the boat.

'What is it, Sean?' He heard Liz through the mic.

'The tender from the yacht . . . it's here in the harbour and it's sitting very low in the water, meaning it's carrying something very heavy.'

At that moment Sean realised that Clive had been right. The Brigadier had just been buying time: he had no interest in an exchange; he just wanted to stop Sean putting out his piece for at least a day, so that Bratic could start his war. *If I'm right, that war is about to start right here, at 3 p.m.* Sean thought. He sprinted as fast as he could towards the tender. When he looked over his shoulder, Liz was following.

'Stop, Liz, run the other way,' he said. But she kept coming.

When he arrived at the tender he hurdled the back safety rail and looked around: nothing. Beside the driver's position, some steps led down to a door, which would lead into the cabin. He jumped down and pulled at the door, before he saw the small brass padlock sitting in a hasp and staple. Searching around he picked up a fire extinguisher and smashed the lock off with one blow.

When he pulled the door back, terror shot through his body. 'Holy shit!' he exclaimed.

'What is it, Sean?' Clive said on the mic.

'I think it's a bomb,' he replied.

'What does it look like?'

'A mass of cardboard boxes, carefully piled up with wires coming out of them everywhere.'

'Does it say anything in the boxes?'

Sean angled his head to get a better look 'Semtex H,' he said with a shiver. Even he knew that it was an explosive.

'How much is there?' Clive persisted.

'A lot. I'd say at least 200 boxes. It fills the whole cabin.'

'Get out and run. Go to the other side of the harbour wall and get in the water. A bomb that big won't just wreck a few boats, it'll take half of the town with it.'

Sean heard Liz jump on board and he pushed her back up the stairs as she caught sight of the huge device. 'Get the hell out of here, Liz,' he said quickly.

'I'm going nowhere without you.' She stood her ground.

'Go!' he shouted aggressively.

'You've got six minutes. I'm assuming it's timed to go off at three. Get out of there.' Clive said.

'I can't, it'll kill thousands of people in the town and start a war where thousands more will die,' Sean said.

Sean quickly scrambled back into the cabin with the bomb and snatched the spare keys he'd seen hanging from the open key safe. Then he ran up onto the deck, turned to the control panel, inserted the keys and hit the start button; the powerful engines came to life beneath him.

'What the fuck are you doing, Sean? Can you even drive a boat?' Liz screamed.

'Yes, now get off,' he said quickly.

'If you're doing this, I'm doing it with you,' she said.

Sean shook his head in anger. 'Okay, there's no time to argue. Go onto the jetty and untie the ropes at the front and back, then jump back on.'

Liz immediately jumped down and slipped the rear tie out of its hook on the jetty, then sprinted to the front of the boat and untied the front rope. As the knot slid open Sean increased to full revs and pushed forward, leaving Liz stranded on the jetty.

'Bastard!' she shouted.

Sean turned away, unable to look at her.

'Sean, don't do this,' she cried.

'I have to. Publish the story,' he said, before removing his earpiece and tossing it into the sea.

He looked at the clock on his phone: 2:56 p.m. *Four minutes or less.*

As he rounded the ancient harbour wall at full speed, Findlow's yacht came into view. He estimated the distance at 1.5 miles and calculated the time it would take him to get there. *About three minutes*, he concluded, as he pointed the bow of the boat straight at the superyacht, in the knowledge that they would never be able to move out of the way in time.

As he hit open water, the swells increased in size and continually knocked him off-course. *Damn,* He cursed, he'd been planning to line the boat up and jump in, but with seas like this, he would need to get closer . . . much closer. He steered back onto a collision course, wincing each time the boat lifted out of the water and crashed back down heavily, expecting the bomb to go off any second. *I hope it's just on a timer and not a remote detonator* he thought.

With two minutes to go, he was about a mile away and still fighting with the steering wheel to maintain course. Just then, he thought he saw the front panel on the cupboard under the passenger side move. *Probably just the rough ride.* He returned his concentration to steering.

Then it happened again. He left the wheel and reached down to undo the latch and the boat veered wildly off-course, listing severely to one side. As it did, Praew tumbled through the open cabinet doors onto the deck. She was tied up and her mouth covered with thick black tape. Her eyes communicated her absolute fear.

Sean ripped the tape from her mouth and searched around for something to cut her restraints with. He tumbled from side to side as the boat bashed aimlessly through the swells. Finally, he found a knife in one of the bins and cut her free. Passing her a lifejacket, he indicated that she should jump as he regained control of the boat.

In the minute or so that it had taken to free Praew, the boat had moved badly off-course. He looked at his clock: 2:58 *Two minutes or less.*

He quickly assessed the distance between him and the superyacht. 'Shit, it's going to be tight!' he said to himself.

Praew still hadn't jumped and he indicated again that she

should, but she refused and just stood in the centre of the deck, stricken with terror. 'Can't you swim?' Sean asked, aware that she wouldn't be able to understand him, but trying anyway.

He pulled the lifejacket over her head and attached it around her waist, before inflating it, whilst keeping one hand on the wheel. Then he indicated again that she should jump in, but still she didn't move.

He glanced at his watch: 2:59. The yacht was now only a few hundred metres away and the gap was closing fast. Praew still hadn't jumped. *I'm going to have to throw her in.*

Sean focused his efforts on the centre of the vessel's side, gunning the boat towards it. Preparing himself to grab Praew and throw her over the side. Just then a hail of bullets ripped into the boat and he dived to the floor, pulling Praew down with him. *I guess that means we're in range*, he thought.

When the shooting stopped, he quickly looked over the steering wheel. They had moved off-course again, but were only 200 metres from the yacht. The waves were pushing the small boat around so much that Sean knew if it was to hit its target, he would need to drive it right into the side himself, just pointing it and jumping was no longer an option. He was running out of time and the bomb would explode any second, so moving out of harm's way wasn't an option either.

A picture of Liz flashed before his eyes, the realisation that he had seen her face for the last time felt like a knife was being rammed into his heart, as his hatred for the evil Brigadier consumed his whole being and drove him on.

He stood aggressively and swung the boat back on track, just as he righted the course, the next hail of machine gunfire was released from the yacht. Again he went to duck down, instinctively grabbing Praew, but this time he was too slow; he felt two sharp piercing pains, one in his neck and one in his chest.

Clutching at his chest, he staggered backwards and tumbled

over the rear safety rail. The icy cold smack of the water instantly attacked his skin.

Almost immediately, a massive fireball erupted in front of him, followed by a thunderous bang and a shockwave that seemed to suck the remaining oxygen from his lungs. When a wall of water headed towards him, Sean's eyes closed and he felt the life force slipping out of him.

Chapter 52

Beep . . . beep . . . beep. Sean heard the strange sound in his head. *What's happening? Was it all a dream?*

He opened his eyes slowly as the bright lights bit into his retina. When the room came into focus, he saw Liz standing next to Clive at the end of the bed.

'Nurse, he's waking up,' Liz shouted. The noise echoed in Sean's mind as if he wasn't really there.

He tried to speak, but his throat tightened quickly and painfully. Liz instinctively knew what he was trying to do and moved in close to him.

'What's happening?' he whispered, as loudly as he could manage.

'You've been in a coma for two weeks,' she said.

'Findlow?' he asked.

'Dead, along with Bratic. You blew their boat to smithereens, stopped a war and saved a city full of people in the process.'

Sean closed his eyes again, memories flooding back to him. 'I'm sorry about Praew. I couldn't save her,' he whispered.

Liz said some words that he didn't understand. As he opened his eyes again, he saw the tiny figure of Praew coming forward from a small gathering of people that had entered the room.

'You were still holding onto her when you fell into the water, so you did save her. Somehow she managed to keep you afloat until Clive and I got there in a boat from the harbour a few minutes later, so she returned the favour very quickly.'

A tear formed in Sean's eye as the young Thai girl touched his hand gently.

'There are some other people here that would like to say hello too.'

Sean squinted into the light as two further people stepped forward. He could just make out the face of Liz's mother and father smiling appreciatively at him.

'Bank wasn't around, so Nok got Bill out herself. He's in hiding with family in Korea until we can sort it out. Thank you, it really helped him.' Liz's mother said.

Sean wanted to laugh at the thought of Nok and Bill squashed onto Bank's cross country motorbike, but his throat and chest hurt too much.

A wave of tiredness was coming over him quickly.

'I love you, Sean.' Liz's words were the last thing he heard before he fell into a deep sleep.

Friday, 1st May. Minsk, Belarus

Three men lay in a growing pool of blood on the dance floor of the closed Minsk nightclub. None moved, nor breathed, and each had a single bullet wound to the back of the head, made when they had been executed at close range just minutes earlier.

Sitting in a booth next to the bloody scene, an army Colonel blew smoke rings from his mouth and holstered his military issue 9mm pistol. As he stubbed out his cigarette on the table, a door opened in the corner of the room. A young athletic man wearing a motorbike helmet and leathers walked over to the Colonel's table and carefully lifted three bundles of US$ notes into a plastic shopping bag. Without speaking, he turned and left through the same door.